Praise for *Against All Odds*

"Brava! Award-winner Hannon debuts the Heroes of Quantico series with a wonderful array of believable characters, action, and suspense that will keep readers glued to each page. Hannon's extraordinary writing, vivid scenes, and surprise ending come together for a not-to-be-missed reading experience."

RT Book Reviews, 4½ stars, Top Pick

"I found someone who writes romantic suspense better than I do. I highly recommend *Against All Odds* as one of the best books I've had the privilege of reading this year. This is a captivating, fast-paced, well-written romantic suspense destined for my keeper shelf. I loved this book, and highly recommend this author."

Dee Henderson, author, the O'Malley Family series

"Nothing like a great romantic suspense novel to engage and delight, and Irene Hannon does it with ease! Coop is the quintessential emotionally reserved hero who finds his heart breached by the woman he is charged with protecting. Irene has perfected the dialogue between Coop and Monica as the sparks fly. Well-drawn bad guys, a dysfunctional relationship between Monica and her diplomat father, and witty male banter between Coop and his partner Mark add intensity and levity in equal measure in this rapid-paced, well-written romance. Irene has garnered herself another faithful reader with *Against All Odds*."

Relz Reviewz

"Hannon delivers big-time in this novel. The intercontinental suspense plot combines flawlessly with a fantastic romance that sizzles. The realism in her FBI details adds authenticity to the novel and allows the book to branch out to a male audience and women who would not pick up a romantic suspense title. The characters are all well developed and the interplay between partners is wonderful. So if you're looking for a great suspense read, pick up *Against All Odds*. I promise you will be delighted that you did."

The Suspense Zone Book of the Month

Praise for *An Eye for an Eye*

"RITA-award-winner Hannon's latest superbly written addition to her Heroes of Quantico series neatly delivers all the thrills and chills of Suzanne Brockmann's Team Sixteen series with the subtly incorporated faith elements found in Dee Henderson's books."

Booklist

"The long-anticipated sequel in the Heroes of Quantico series does not disappoint. Hannon continues to bring her own special brand of suspense and romance to this genre. This winning recipe provides readers with characters that are engrossing, a plot filled with unexpected twists, and a love story that will melt your heart. The only downside to this terrific novel is that you won't want to put it down."

RT Book Reviews, 4½ stars, Top Pick

"You will be hooked from the first chapter with an explosive start, followed by brilliant pacing through the rest of the story and the perfect balance of suspense, action, and romance."

Relz Reviewz

"A new queen of suspense joins the ranks of Brandilyn Collins, Terri Blackstock, and Dee Henderson . . . her name is Irene Hannon. This is masterful storytelling."

Deenasbooks Blogspot

IN HARM'S WAY

Books by Irene Hannon

HEROES OF QUANTICO SERIES
Against All Odds
An Eye for an Eye
In Harm's Way

IN HARM'S WAY

IRENE HANNON

Revell

a division of Baker Publishing Group
Grand Rapids, Michigan

Published by Revell
a division of Baker Publishing Group
P.O. Box 6287, Grand Rapids, MI 49516-6287
www.revellbooks.com

Printed in the United States of America

Library of Congress Cataloging-in-Publication Data
Hannon, Irene.
    In harm's way / Irene Hannon.
        p.   cm. — (Heroes of Quantico ; bk. 3)
    ISBN 978-0-8007-3312-4 (pbk.)
    1. United States. Federal Bureau of Investigation—Officials and employees—Fiction. I. Title.
PS3558.A4793I5 2010
813'.54—dc22   2009048994

Published in association with MacGregor Literary.

10   11   12   13   14   15   16   8   7   6   5   4   3

To my father, James Hannon,
who always wanted me to write a mystery.

I hope suspense counts, Dad . . .
Because this series is for you!

Prologue

In a matter of minutes, the baby would be hers.

Forever.

Debra flexed her fingers inside the snug latex gloves, tightened her grip on the loop of wire in her hand, and melted deeper into the shadows at the back of the dim, gothic-style church. As the final organ notes reverberated through the deserted sanctuary, their hollow echo fading into the murky alcoves along the perimeter, the woman behind the keyboard tilted a bottle of water against her lips, emptying it in two long swallows.

The hint of a smile touched the corners of Debra's lips. Rebecca O'Neil was nothing if not predictable.

Standing, Rebecca leaned over the pew behind her and rearranged the blanket on the infant in a pumpkin seat. She cooed a few words Debra couldn't distinguish, smiling as the child gurgled gibberish in response.

The mother bent close to press a gentle kiss to the tiny forehead, and Debra's fingers twitched on the wire, itching to pick up the baby, to cuddle her close, to breathe her fresh scent. To experience all the sweet joys of motherhood that had been denied her.

But they would be denied her no more.

Today she would rectify that wrong.

Drawing a deep breath, Debra tried to slow her accelerating pulse. She was close, so close to realizing her dream. If all went according to plan, in less than five minutes she would hold her baby in her arms.

And she never intended to let go.

The organist moved toward the back of the church, and Debra's fingers clenched . . . unclenched . . . clenched in a spasmodic rhythm on the wire. Her eyes narrowed as she watched Rebecca approach, and for one fleeting instant, doubt assailed her. The woman seemed like a caring person, a good mother. One who would miss her baby. But three months ago, back in October, Debra had overheard her admit to a friend at the gym that she was overwhelmed. The words had replayed over and over in Debra's mind.

"It's a handful," Rebecca had said. "The kids are a lot more closely spaced than we planned. I never expected to have two in diapers at once. But Megan is such a good baby. It's only been seven weeks, and already she's starting to sleep through the night. Would you like to see her latest picture?"

While Rebecca pulled a photo from her purse, Debra had strolled past and glanced over the woman's shoulder. It had been no more than idle curiosity . . . until she'd seen the baby's copper-hued curls—the same shade as hers—and the blue eyes that matched her own.

The child looked like the baby she might have given birth to, Debra had realized with a jolt. *Should* have given birth to. She deserved a baby. Far more than did Rebecca, who already had one child.

The sudden flash of insight that followed had stunned her. *That baby should be mine.*

She'd known that as surely as she'd known that the pleasant fall breezes would soon give way to the icy winds of winter.

That's why she was sequestered in a house of God on this cold January day, her visit the culmination of weeks of careful planning. Nothing less monumental than today's task could have compelled her to set foot in a church. She and God had parted company long ago.

A familiar ache in the empty place that had held her womb radiated upward, tightening her throat. Natural birth might no longer be an option. Nor adoption. They didn't give healthy Caucasian infants to single parents. Or women with her history. But there were other ways to get babies.

And it wasn't as if she would leave Rebecca childless. She would never do that to anyone. She knew what it felt like to lose a child. But Rebecca already had one daughter.

Besides, Debra's plan would benefit everyone. Rebecca would be less stressed. Both children would receive undivided attention. And she would have the baby that fate, or nature, or God—or the conspiracy of her doctors and her husband—had deprived her of.

Rebecca passed her, mere inches away, and Debra shrank further into the shadows, readying the sturdy loop of wire in her hands. Except for the day she'd seen the baby's picture, this was the closest she'd ever been to the mother. Yet she knew a lot about her from eavesdropping at the gym. Rebecca worked as an organist. She practiced every Saturday morning in the empty church. Brought her new baby with her while her husband watched their two-year-old. Finding her address had been a simple matter of following her to her car one day and copying down her license number. Debra's work provided easy access to research resources.

The location of the church had also been easy to track down. All Debra had to do was wait at the end of Rebecca's street and follow her one Saturday. The next day, she'd attended services to scope the place out. It had been a little trickier to slip into the practice sessions unobserved, but she'd pulled it off. Rebecca always unlocked the church door and propped it open before retrieving the baby from the car, exposing the infant as briefly as possible to Chicago's frigid January weather. That gave Debra the perfect opportunity to slip in.

It had taken just two trips to find the window of opportunity she needed and to formulate a plan. The young mother always brought an oversize bottle of water with her, and about halfway through her practice session she visited the ladies room.

As she was doing now.

Heart pounding, Debra waited while the woman stepped into the restroom and pulled the door shut behind her. As the click echoed in the empty sanctuary, Debra moved to the door and slipped the small wire loop over the knob, her rubber-soled shoes noiseless on the terrazzo floor. Stretching the remaining length of wire taut, she wrapped it around the adjacent knob to a storage closet, securing it with half a dozen tight twists.

The whole maneuver took less than fifteen seconds.

She was halfway to the baby when the knob on the door to the restroom rattled. Rattled again. And again, with more force.

"Hey! Is anyone out there?"

Rebecca's voice sounded faint through the heavy oak door.

More rattling followed.

Debra rounded the pew and smiled down at the tiny baby. Her blue eyes were wide, her coppery curls bouncing as she kicked her tiny legs. She was clutching a Raggedy Ann doll that lived up to its name, its face patched, the hair sparse and limp. Debra gave the worn doll a gentle tug, but the baby tightened her grip and screwed up her face, signaling her intent to register a loud protest. Debra hesitated. A crying baby would attract attention. Not a good thing. She could dispose of the doll later.

Retrieving a stretchy wool hat from the pocket of her coat, Debra pulled it low over her forehead and lifted the infant from the pumpkin seat, relishing the sense of completeness that washed over her as she held the small bundle against her shoulder. The baby felt good in her arms. Like it belonged there.

"Is anyone there? Please . . . let me out!"

Tuning out Rebecca's desperate plea, Debra strode toward the side door near the sanctuary. As far as she'd been able to determine, the small church in the quiet suburb had no security cameras. And the back parking lot was hidden from the street. Getting away unseen should be a piece of cake.

She cracked the door and surveyed the lot. Empty. Slipping out, she shut the heavy door behind her, the stone walls muffling the faint, panicked cries from within.

As if sensing distress, the baby began to whimper.

"Hush, little one." Debra stroked a soothing finger down the child's satiny cheek as she settled her into the brand new safety seat in the rental car. "Mommy will take good care of you. In a little while we'll stop and have lunch, okay?"

Once more, she tugged on the doll. When the baby let out a howl of protest and clutched it against her chest with both hands, Debra wavered. If the doll kept her baby happy—and quiet—during the drive, why not let her keep it for a few hours? She could dispose of it later.

Snow began to fall as she slid behind the wheel. Soft, downy flakes that kissed her windshield. Perfect, each one. And unique. But so short-lived. God had made a mistake with snowflakes, Debra decided as she watched them melt against the glass. They deserved much more than a brief moment of glory.

In truth, God made a lot of mistakes. Like with her, for example. She'd wanted to be a mother for as long as she could remember. *Deserved* to be a mother. Why else would she have married? Put herself through all those treatments? Kept trying after three miscarriages? She'd still be trying, if she could.

But she'd fooled them all. All the people who'd said she'd never have a baby. Her doctor. Her husband. God.

She had her baby now. The child of her heart. The one person in her life who would love her for always. Unconditionally.

Today, at long last, she'd become a real mother.

Smiling, she put the car into gear and began the long drive home.

1

One Month Later

Fast food.

What a joke.

Rachel Sutton tapped her foot on the tile floor by the pickup counter, sighed, and checked her watch. Again. A ten-minute wait did not qualify as fast. At this rate, she'd have to push the speed limit and inhale her lunch or risk being tardy for her first class of the afternoon.

"Rachel!" A harried clerk plopped her order on the counter as he called her name.

Finally.

Elbowing her way through the crowd, Rachel snagged the large bag of sandwiches and chips and settled it into the cardboard tray between two soft drinks. Juggling her purchases, she plowed through the sea of customers and pushed the glass door open with her shoulder.

Unseasonable spring-like temperatures greeted her, an early February reprieve from the past month's harsh weather. If the throng around her was any indication, the nice weather had brought everyone in St. Louis out of hibernation. And no one appeared to be in a hurry. Didn't any of these people have jobs? Commitments? Schedules to keep?

Dodging a stubborn patch of ice, she trudged toward the last spot in the parking lot, where her older-model Camry was squeezed in next to the mountain of plowed snow piled beside the dumpster. *Chill out, Rachel,* she counseled herself. *The world won't end if you're five minutes late for class.*

But the pep talk didn't do much to calm her tense nerves. And for the dozenth time in the past few weeks, she tried to figure out why she felt so stressed and on edge. It didn't make sense. Her life was good, her career fulfilling. She loved teaching music to grade schoolers. Playing piano during high tea on Sundays at one of St. Louis's most elegant hotels was a highlight of her week. Her young piano students were a joy. And she'd found a way to indulge her artistic leanings by starting a very successful mural-painting business on the side. There was no reason for her recent unease.

Yet she couldn't shake it. She hadn't had a good night's sleep in more than a month, and her patience was at an all-time low. Ten days ago, she'd nitpicked one of her piano student's technique until the poor child was almost in tears. Last week, she'd refused to kitsch up a mural with Victorian curlicues, much to the annoyance of a well-paying client. Yesterday she'd snapped at Marta when her co-worker tried to tease a smile out of her.

That display of bad temper was the very reason she was battling the noontime crowd at this popular outlet. Today's lunch was a peace offering—even if she'd never felt less peaceful in her life.

Sidestepping a puddle, Rachel shifted the tray, balancing it in one hand while she dug in her shoulder purse for her keys. Marta had meant well yesterday, she conceded as she edged between her car and the mound of melting snow on the passenger side. She did need to lighten up. The frown imbedded in her forehead was fast becoming a permanent addition. And it was out of character. In general, Rachel was upbeat, patient, and calm. She had no idea why her usual tranquility had evaporated, leaving an unnerving jumpiness in its place.

As if to underscore that point, the horn in the car next to her blared as the owner unlocked it with the remote from across the parking lot. Rachel's hand jerked, and she watched in dismay as the drinks tottered. Somehow she managed to juggle them back to stability, but her luck ran out with the bag of sandwiches. It took a nosedive into the melting pile of snow.

Disgusted, she set the tray on her trunk and bent to retrieve the bag. This whole lunch thing was turning out to be a disaster.

As she snagged the top of the white sack and rescued it from the pile of dirty, melting snow, a tuft of bright orange yarn peeked out at her from beneath the mound. A knit cap perhaps. Or the end of a scarf. No doubt lost in the parking lot on a snowy, windy night and later swept aside as the plows barreled through.

After depositing the food on the front passenger seat, she poked at the orange clump with the toe of her boot. If she wanted to be a good Samaritan, she could dig it out and add it to the shop's lost and found collection. But it didn't seem worth the effort. It may have been buried for a month. The person who'd lost it would have given up all hope of finding it by now.

Suddenly her toe dislodged a large chunk of ice, and a button eye blinked back at her.

So much for her cap and scarf theory. Judging by the patched face that was emerging as she nicked away the ice and snow, the object buried under the pile of frozen slush was a well-loved Raggedy Ann doll. One that would be missed.

That put a whole different light on the situation.

She knew it was foolish, but for some reason Rachel couldn't bring herself to abandon the doll in the parking lot. On the off chance a mother was desperately searching for her daughter's beloved doll, Rachel decided to dig it out and deposit it in the restaurant's lost and found.

Retrieving the ice scraper from the floor of her front seat, she went to work on the frozen snow caked around the doll. The warm sun had softened the surface, but the deeper she dug, the more ice-like the snow became.

"Excuse me, ma'am . . . is there a problem? Can I help you with something?"

Rachel shifted around. An older man, white sandwich bag in hand, was regarding her from under arched, shaggy gray brows. "No. I'm . . . uh . . . just trying to rescue this doll."

"Is it yours?"

"No." Warmth flooded her cheeks. "But I imagine the little girl who lost it would like to get it back."

The man moved closer and bent down to give the jointed cloth leg an experimental tug. It didn't budge. "I don't know. It's stuck pretty good." He backed up and regarded the filthy, sodden doll. "Besides, I'm not sure the little girl's mother would want it back. It has to be full of germs." He regarded his damp fingers with an expression of distaste.

Rachel surveyed the doll, exposed now except for one black-mitted hand. He had a point. The frayed gingham dress was stained, the threadbare white apron gray with dirt. "You're probably right."

"It was a nice thought, though," the man offered.

"Thanks." Rachel shot him a half smile and rose, tossing the ice scraper into the backseat.

"Well . . . enjoy your lunch." He hefted his bag in salute and continued toward his car.

Rachel started to close the door. Hesitated. Gave the Raggedy Ann one more look. It seemed so forlorn, lying there abandoned in a puddle of muddy water. Yet she doubted the restaurant would appreciate her hauling a dirty, dripping doll across the tile floor to the lost and found.

But she could display it in some prominent place in the parking lot. That way, if the mother frequented this restaurant, she might see it—and could reclaim it if she chose. Scanning the property, she spotted an air-conditioning unit. Perfect.

Armed with a plan, Rachel chipped the remaining snow away from the doll's hand with her boot and bent to pick it up. As her fingers closed around the arm, she was already swiveling toward the air conditioner. If she hurried, she might be able to sit for five minutes with Marta and eat part of her—

Two steps toward her destination, Rachel was blindsided by a sudden rush of adrenaline. Her pulse rocketed, and she leaned against the car, sucking in a sharp breath as the world tilted. Her whole body began to tremble, and the doll slipped from her grasp, falling to the ground.

As quickly as the violent reaction had gripped her, it disappeared. Her pulse slowed, her lungs kicked in again, the world righted itself.

What on earth had just happened?

Aftershocks rippled through her, robbing her legs of strength. She clung to the back of her car, scanning the parking lot for an explanation. Searching for anything out of the ordinary that could have triggered such an intense reaction.

But the scene appeared normal. People were walking in and out of the restaurant, talking on cell phones, laughing together, juggling bags of sandwiches. The sky was blue, the sun was shining. A convertible drove past, top down in honor of the unseasonable warmth, the middle-aged driver in sunglasses and shorts, the radio tuned to an old Beach Boys song.

There was nothing around her to account for what had happened moments ago.

Yet her reaction had been real. And there was only one word to describe the emotion that had rocked her.

Terror.

But what had brought it on?

And why had it gone away with such dizzying speed after she dropped the doll?

Her breath hitched in her throat, and she slowly lowered her gaze to the doll. The innocuous, patched face smiled back up at her, as innocent as childhood. Was it possible that . . . ?

Irritated, she cut off that train of thought. She didn't believe in that kind of creepy stuff. No sane, logical person did. Whatever had prompted her reaction had nothing to do with the doll at her feet.

No way.

And she could prove it. All she had to do was pick up the doll again.

Except she didn't want to.

Annoyed, she wiped her palms on her black slacks. Now how ridiculous was that?

Clamping her lips together, she flexed her fingers and snatched up the doll.

Instantly the terror slammed into her again, gripping her lungs in a vise.

Fighting for air, Rachel held the doll at arm's length and stared at it. Sweat broke out on her brow and she began to tremble. Jarring, disjointed images and sounds crashed over her. She heard the distant cry of a baby. Sensed danger. Pain. Anguish.

This couldn't be happening.

She groped for the latch on her back door, fingers fumbling. Yanked it open. Flung the doll inside.

The panicked sensations abated at once, leaving a residue of anxiety—and urgency—in their wake.

It was almost like a message.

A call to action.

But what kind of action?

Stumped, Rachel regarded the doll beaming back at her from the seat. Odd. From a distance, she sensed no danger. Just the opposite. The doll gave her a warm, happy feeling. Only by touch did it convey a more ominous aura.

Aura.

She cringed. Now she was even beginning to *think* in psychic terms.

Torn, Rachel scrutinized the doll. That man who'd stopped a few minutes ago had touched the doll and hadn't had any adverse reaction. Only she seemed to pick up bad vibes.

Why me? she wanted to ask the smiling face. *Why pick me to dump on?*

She'd have spoken the question aloud, except people would think she'd gone off the deep end. Herself included.

Besides, the real question was what to do with the doll.

Leaving it in the parking lot was no longer an option. She might not understand why it affected her the way it did, but the feelings of danger it evoked were too real—and too strong—to ignore.

She supposed she could offer it to the police. They were the danger experts, weren't they? But she could imagine the reaction she'd get if she showed up at a precinct station and told them her story.

They'd think she was nuts.

And considering how odd she'd been feeling lately, maybe she was.

Unsure how to proceed, she slammed the door, circled the trunk, and slid behind the wheel. As she put the car in gear, she glanced at the forgotten lunch on the seat beside her—and inspiration struck. Marta's husband was a police officer. She could run the whole incident by her friend and see what she recommended. Marta knew she was a serious, stable, intelligent person who wasn't given to flights of fancy. They'd shared lots of lunches and laughs over the past two years as they chatted about the antics of their students.

Marta wouldn't think she was crazy.

At least Rachel hoped not.

⭐

Marta stopped eating mid-chew and gaped at her co-worker. "That's crazy."

The bite she'd taken from the sandwich she no longer wanted stuck in Rachel's throat. "Look, I know it sounds weird. But it's true. I feel danger whenever I touch that doll."

Several beats of silence passed while Marta resumed chewing, her attention riveted on her friend. "You're serious about this, aren't you?"

"Yes."

"Okay. Let me get this straight. You found a doll, and when you picked it up it freaked you out."

"Twice."

"And where is this doll now?"

"In the backseat of my car."

"Get rid of it."

Rising, Rachel began to pace in the cluttered lounge, grateful now that she'd been running late. All the other teachers had returned to their classrooms, and she and Marta had the place to themselves. "I considered that. But I can't. I feel this sense of urgency to get it to the right person."

"And who would that be?"

22

"I don't know."

"You know, this is creeping me out." Marta took a long swallow of soda and drummed her fingers on the table. "It's like one of those late-night sci-fi movies you watched as a kid that gave you nightmares for weeks. I think I'll be sleeping with the light on tonight."

Folding her arms across her chest, Rachel shook her head. "I'm sorry. I didn't mean to freak you out too. To be honest, I hoped you might ask Joe's opinion. I thought the police might be interested."

Marta grimaced. "I'll ask if you want me to. But I've heard a few stories from him through the years about people who show up at the station claiming to be psychics and offering to help the police solve a crime."

"I'm not claiming to be a psychic. I don't even *believe* in psychics. In fact, I can't believe we're having this conversation." Rachel shoved her shoulder-length hair behind her ear and re-settled her glasses on her nose.

Marta tipped her head. "This really got to you, didn't it?"

"Yeah." Rachel massaged her forehead and returned to the table. As she rewrapped her almost untouched sandwich, she realized her fingers were trembling. Marta, she noted with a quick shift in focus, was watching them too. She stopped fiddling with her sandwich and shoved her hands in the pockets of her slacks.

"Okay, Rachel." Marta wadded her sandwich wrapper into a tight ball. "Let me run it by Joe. I can vouch for your sanity—or I could until the past few weeks. I've never seen you this stressed. Are you sure everything's okay?"

"Yes. Everything's fine. I have no idea why I've been on edge." Rachel heard the irritation nipping at her voice and softened her tone. "But I appreciate your concern."

"Hey." Marta laid a hand on her arm. "We'll get this sorted out, okay?"

23

Rachel felt the pressure of tears behind her eyes. That, too, was a new—and too frequent—phenomenon in recent weeks. "Yeah."

"Maybe it's some kind of hormone thing."

"I almost wish there was a medical explanation for it."

"There might be. Set up an appointment with your doctor. In the meantime, I'll get Joe's take. Tonight's our once-a-month dinner date without the kids, meaning I'll have his undivided attention. I'll let you know what he says tomorrow, okay?"

"Yeah. Thanks. And listen . . . you guys won't tell anyone about this, will you?"

"Of course not. I know how to keep my mouth shut when I have to. And Joe's the soul of discretion. Just one thing . . . until I get back to you with Joe's input, stay away from that doll, okay?"

Claudia Barnes liked the soup at Le Bistro. The chef had a way with mushrooms, no question about it. And the desserts were to die for, despite the dent they put in her reporter's salary. But tonight, the conversation between the couple in the booth behind her was even better than the food.

Pulling out her notebook, Claudia opened it to a blank page and tuned in, her pen poised.

"Tell her to forget it." A man's voice.

"But Joe, she's really spooked by this." A woman speaking now. "And Rachel isn't the type to go for any of that supernatural stuff. We've worked together for two years, and she's very levelheaded. She thinks it's weird too."

"That's understandable. I mean, come on, Marta. She finds a Raggedy Ann doll buried under a pile of snow in a Bread Company parking lot and says it's sending her a message?"

"I know. If it wasn't Rachel telling me this, I'd dismiss it. But I told her I'd check with you and see if the police would be interested."

"Nope." The sound of ice tinkling in a glass.

"You're sure?"

"Honey, if she shows up at the station, no one will take her seriously. They'll listen to her story with a straight face, but once she's gone, everyone will have a good laugh. Trust me on this. Save your friend the embarrassment."

A heavy sigh. "That's what I thought." The sound of cutlery against china. "What do you think she should do with the doll?"

"Pitch it."

"That's what I told her. But I might have to do it for her. I don't think she wants to touch it again."

More ice clinking. "Listen, don't get involved, okay? Stay away from the doll."

"I thought you said her story was a bunch of nonsense?"

"It is. But weird things happen sometimes."

"What's that supposed to mean?"

"I don't know. Nothing."

"Hey, I'm not letting you off the hook that easily." The woman's tone was half teasing, half serious. "'Fess up. I sense a story here."

"Not much of one."

"Come on, Joe. Out with it. We always said there'd be no secrets in our marriage, remember?"

"This isn't a secret."

"Then tell me."

"Okay. Fine. I had this friend in high school. Nice guy, on the quiet side, very straight-laced. Anyway, a couple of days after I got my first used car, I tossed him the keys and asked if he wanted to drive it. He stood there, jingling the keys, and out of the blue he said, 'I'd lay off the booze and smoking if I were you. It could cause you a lot of trouble.' That blew my mind."

"Why?"

"Because the night before, I'd met up with some friends who were a little more on the wild side, and we shared a twelve-pack and some cigarettes at a picnic table in one guy's backyard. No one was around—but I was scared to death we'd be caught. That was the first time I'd ever done anything like that. The thing is, my keys were on the table the entire evening."

"Are you saying the keys . . . transmitted . . . your secret to him?"

"I have no idea. I never asked. I wasn't about to admit my guilt, so I passed it off as a joke. But I knew he knew. I told myself he must have seen us, but I never did quite buy that. He lived on the other side of town. And he didn't socialize with the fast crowd."

A few seconds of silence followed. The woman sounded more serious when she responded. "Maybe the police *should* check into Rachel's story."

"It's not going to happen, Marta. Trust me."

"Can you offer her some other options?"

"Pitch the doll."

"Besides that one."

"She could always try the FBI."

"Would they be more receptive?"

"Probably not. But it's the only alternative I can think of. Hey, do you want to split this chocolate decadence thing for dessert? I won't feel as guilty if we share it."

As the conversation shifted to mundane matters, Claudia set her pen down and dipped her spoon into the cooling soup, considering her own options. The features editor at the St. Louis tabloid where she worked was always on the hunt for unusual stories. A local woman with some sort of telepathic power ought to qualify. Her tale would be a great lead for a story on ESP or clairvoyance. If she dug around, Claudia was pretty certain she could find some interesting material connecting ESP and crime-fighting. Better yet, if she dug deep enough she might be able to put a local slant on the piece.

If nothing else, a story like that should help circulation. Readers might claim they didn't like sensational stuff, but it sold papers. Look at the *National Enquirer*. And anything that boosted circulation boosted advertising revenue. Her editor would love that.

Too bad she hadn't tuned into the conversation earlier. Claudia propped her chin in her hand and toyed with her spoon. All she had was the ESP woman's first name. Rachel.

There was a way to fix that, though. The woman in the next booth was the psychic's friend. Claudia figured she could trace Rachel through the cop's wife. All she had to do was check the last name on their credit card.

Unless they paid in cash.

Nursing her soup, Claudia listened to the exchange as the waiter presented the couple's bill. Smiled when it was clear the twosome was paying by credit card. Followed the waiter and positioned herself behind a pillar. Ran into him as he passed on his way back to the table from running the card. Beat him to the ground picking it up as he apologized. Scanned the information she needed.

You didn't get to be an ace reporter by being meek, she congratulated herself with a smirk as she slid back into her booth. And that was her goal. Working at the tabloid didn't thrill her, but she was only twenty-four and two years out of J-school. Everyone had to start somewhere. If she could write some unique stuff that got noticed, she could move on to bigger things sooner rather than later.

Claudia jotted down the cop's name in her notebook and smiled. Not bad for a night's work.

Signaling for the waiter, she ordered dessert. And considered charging her meal to the paper.

She figured it qualified as research.

2

I shouldn't have come.

The knot in Rachel's stomach tightened, and she squeezed her laced fingers, whitening the knuckles. She'd never been claustrophobic, but the walls of the small, sterile interview room off the lobby in the glass and concrete FBI office building in downtown St. Louis seemed to be closing in on her. With each minute that passed—ten and a half so far—she grew more uncomfortable. The temptation to flee before she made a total fool of herself was strong.

But the vibes from the doll were stronger.

Strong enough to counter the dubious glance the woman behind the bullet-proof glass in the reception area had given her. And strong enough to convince her that she needed to pass the Raggedy Ann on to someone who was in a position to investigate—whether they chose to or not.

Based on her conversation earlier today with Marta, she knew that "not" was the likely outcome. While her co-worker had been diplomatic in relaying her husband's comments from their dinner last night, Rachel had read "fruitcake" between the lines. And if a local police officer thought her story lacked credibility, she had little hope the FBI would take it seriously.

But she felt a compelling need to try. And if she failed to convince anyone to pay attention to the odd vibes emanating from the doll stashed in a small paper shopping bag at her feet—well, at least she could walk away knowing she'd done her best.

✫

"Nick? Sharon. I've got a hot one for you."

Special Agent Nick Bradley shifted the phone on his ear and checked his watch. Twenty minutes to quitting time. "What's up?"

"A woman showed up in the lobby a few minutes ago. She wants to talk to an agent."

"About what?"

"She wouldn't say."

Stifling a sigh, Nick raked this fingers through his hair. He had an important dinner date, and he didn't want to be late. "I'm working on a 302. Can someone else handle it?" He doubted his excuse of completing a routine evidentiary interview form would carry much weight with the seasoned receptionist in the St. Louis FBI field office, but he decided it was worth a shot.

"I tried. But it *is* Friday. The place cleared out early. I guess everyone has plans."

"Including me."

"Sorry. You're it. Her name's Rachel Sutton."

"Thanks a lot." Sarcasm gave way to resignation. "Okay. I'll be out in a few minutes."

Dropping the phone back in its cradle, Nick surveyed the 302 on his desk. He could let it sit until Monday, but he preferred to fill these forms out while the information was fresh in his mind. Besides, he was almost done. The woman in the lobby could cool her heels until he finished.

Eight minutes later, he slipped his arms into the sleeves of his dark gray suit jacket and picked up a notebook and pen. If he was lucky, this Rachel Sutton would have some innocuous

30

tip he could dispense with quickly. Most off-the-street visitors offered little information of value. No reason this one would be any different.

As he approached the security door to the lobby, Sharon was shutting down her computer. He queried her without breaking stride. "Which room?"

"Two. Maybe it won't take long."

"We can hope."

"Hot date tonight?" She shot him a saucy grin.

With an enigmatic smile, Nick pushed through to the lobby in silence and strode toward the interview room. Being single, he was used to such ribbing. But in truth, his hot dates were few and far between. By choice. There were plenty of women who thought dating an FBI agent was exciting and glamorous. He could pick up half a dozen at most bars.

Thrill-seeking women, however, were not his definition of a hot date. He wasn't in the market for one-night stands or casual romance. A hot date for him would be spending an evening with a woman of substance who had more to offer than her body and whose values matched his.

As he'd discovered, however, that kind of woman wasn't easy to find. And at thirty-eight, after twelve years of serious looking, he was on the verge of giving up the search.

No, his Friday night didn't involve a one-on-one encounter with a special woman. Yet he was looking forward to it nonetheless. He might be the odd man out, but fellow agents Mark and Coop never made him feel that way. Nor did their wives, Emily and Monica. It would be a good evening with good friends, a rare chance for the five of them to get together, since Coop and Monica didn't get in from Virginia very often. And it was far preferable to a solitary evening spent rehabbing his house—his usual Friday-night agenda.

Pausing outside the door to the interview room, Nick adjusted his jacket and grasped the knob. Professional, polite, fast. That was his plan.

He pushed open the door, and a slim woman who appeared to be in her early thirties rose from her seat at a small table.

"Sorry to keep you waiting." He shut the door behind him, closed the distance between them, and held out his hand.

As she returned his firm grip, her slender fingers cold and not quite steady, he did a rapid assessment. Height about five-six. Weight one-fifteen, one-twenty, tops. Shoulder-length brown hair with auburn highlights, parted on the left side. Velvet brown eyes fringed by long lashes her copper-rimmed glasses couldn't camouflage. Classic oval face, pert nose, long, slender neck. Minimal makeup. Her black slacks hugged trim hips, and a gold filigree cross on a slender chain rested against her plum-colored turtleneck.

A pretty woman.

Who didn't want to be here.

It took mere seconds for Nick to reach that conclusion. The uncertainty in her eyes was easy to read, as was the tremor in her fingers when she tucked her hair behind her ear with her free hand.

Trained to pick up such nuances, Nick had learned to use that skill to his advantage. Depending on the situation, he could turn up the heat—or turn on the charm. Whatever best served his purpose.

In this case, he chose the latter tactic.

"I'm Special Agent Nick Bradley, Ms. Sutton." He gave her a relaxed smile. "Why don't we sit down while you tell me how I can help you?"

For a moment, he thought she was going to bolt. He could sense it in the subtle tensing of her muscles, in the way her throat worked when she swallowed, in the quick glance she aimed at the closed door.

He maintained a relaxed stance, his smile steady. "Ms. Sutton? Please, have a seat. I'd like to hear what you have to say." He indicated the chair, reaching over to pull it out—and effectively blocking her escape.

Folding her arms across her chest, she examined the crisp white cuff extending below his jacket. A tiny smile quirked one corner of her mouth. "Interesting technique for corralling nervous subjects. Very smooth." She tilted her head up toward him. "But not necessary. I've come this far. I don't intend to leave without telling you my story."

She retook her seat and perched on the edge of the chair, her posture taut as she intertwined her fingers on the table in front of her.

Sharp woman, Nick concluded. Not to mention insightful and determined. Plus, she had a sense of humor. He admired her ability to dredge it up despite her obvious unease. A lot of people couldn't pull that off.

This might turn out to be interesting after all.

He took the chair at a right angle to her and opened his notebook. Extracting a card from his pocket, he laid it on the table. "So how can I help you, Ms. Sutton?"

She moistened her lips with the tip of her tongue. She had nice lips, he noted. Soft and full and well-shaped.

"I'm not sure where to begin."

Clearing his throat, he picked up his pen and forced himself to raise his gaze and redirect his train of thought. "All right. Let me ask a few questions. What specifically brought you here today?"

She did that distracting lip-moistening thing again, then leaned away from him and lifted a small shopping bag off the floor, holding it gingerly by the handle as she transferred it to the table in front of him. "This."

His expression impassive, Nick considered the bag. It had

passed through the magnetometer and X-ray machine at the entrance to the building, meaning it didn't contain anything overtly dangerous. Yet she was handling it as if it were about to explode. Curious.

"What is it?"

"A Raggedy Ann doll."

Startled, he bought himself a few seconds by tipping the bag toward him. A battered cloth doll was folded inside, the face sporting a large patch above the right eye, the orange hair matted with dirt, the clothing stained. He felt as if he should put on latex gloves before touching it.

Letting the bag resettle on the table, he shot her a cautious look. "Why did you bring this to us, Ms. Sutton?"

She blinked, and her throat worked again as she swallowed, the tension in the room almost palpable. His curiosity was now thoroughly piqued.

"I found it in a Bread Company parking lot." She named the location.

He waited, but when she didn't continue, he tilted his head and leaned back, his posture informal and at ease as he rephrased his previous question. "Why did you think we'd be interested in it?"

She closed her eyes, sucked in a deep breath, opened them. Her gaze met his, and he sensed she was bracing herself. "Okay. This is going to sound crazy. I know that. But it's the truth, whether you choose to believe me or not. I found this doll yesterday at lunchtime, buried in a drift from a snowplow. Except for the orange yarn sticking out. That's how I spotted it. I thought maybe some little girl was missing it, so I dug it out. I planned to set it on the air conditioner next to the building in case her mother was a regular customer."

She gripped the edge of the table, and her knuckles whitened. "This is where it gets . . . weird. When I picked up the doll, I had a . . . reaction."

34

An alarm sounded in Nick's mind, warning him to proceed with caution. Keeping his expression neutral, he studied her. "Could you define 'reaction'?"

"I felt terror. Danger." Her volume dropped. "And I think I . . . could hear a baby crying."

Oh, brother.

In his fifteen years with the Bureau, Nick had seen his share of kooks, from the guy who insisted he'd been abducted by aliens, to the woman who claimed God had told her to assist the FBI by acting as his intermediary on difficult cases, to the guy who believed he was J. Edgar Hoover reincarnated and wanted to be FBI director again.

Now this. At closing time on a Friday, no less.

What a way to end the week.

In the silence that followed Rachel Sutton's revelation, he considered her. She might look normal. No, scratch that. She was well above normal in the looks department. Lovely, even. But nutcases came in all sorts of packages. And her story put her in that category, no question about it. Now it was a matter of getting rid of her in a diplomatic way.

"You don't believe me, do you?"

Her quiet, resigned words—more comment than question—took him off guard. Lots of people who relayed bizarre tales to the Bureau became indignant, even angry, if they suspected an agent doubted their story. But the pink tinge on Rachel Sutton's cheeks, the slight tremor in her words, spoke more of embarrassment than outrage. Not the typical reaction to skepticism.

"I'm not questioning what you experienced, Ms. Sutton." He chose his words with care.

"But you don't think it's real."

Instead of responding, he countered with a request. "Why don't you tell me exactly what happened when you had this reaction?"

"I couldn't breathe. My heart started pounding. I got dizzy. I could feel my adrenaline pumping. I was terrified."

"Has this ever happened to you before?"

"No."

"You've never had a panic attack?"

"No. And I'm not some psychic nut. I don't even believe in that stuff. That's why this experience was so disturbing."

"But the doll is sitting a couple of feet away from you, and you're fine."

"It only happens when I touch it."

Nick debated his next move. He was already running late for dinner, and prolonging this interview was a waste of time. He needed to get the woman's address and phone number, thank her for coming, and get rid of her. That was the best way to handle this. The way he always handled these cases.

But Rachel Sutton's earnest eyes sucked him in. She believed her story, whether he did or not. And for some reason he found it difficult to dismiss her tale with his usual quick dispatch.

He toyed with his pen, turning it end to end on the table. "Why didn't you share this information with the police?"

"I considered that. But the husband of one of my co-workers is a cop, and she ran it by him for me. She was very diplomatic in passing on his message, but it was pretty clear I'd be the laughingstock of the precinct. No one would take me seriously. I hoped I'd fare better with the FBI." She drew an unsteady breath. "I guess I was wrong."

Lifting her chin in what Nick suspected was a last-ditch effort to hold on to her dignity, she unhooked her shoulder purse from the back of her chair and stood, ignoring the card he'd placed in front of her. Taken aback, he rose too. This interview definitely wasn't following the typical pattern. In general, it was hard to shake the weirdos. Rachel Sutton, on the other hand, seemed intent on disappearing as fast as she could.

"Ms. Sutton, I'd like to get some contact information before you leave."

"In case you have any questions about the notes you took?" She sent a pointed glance toward the blank page of his notebook.

Heat surged up the back of his neck. "I wasn't sure what to write. Your story is very . . . peculiar."

"I know that." All at once her shoulders drooped. "And I don't blame you for being skeptical, Agent Bradley. If I were in your shoes, I'd have had the same reaction. I just felt a need to follow through. I've done that. Now I intend to walk away. Thanks for your time."

She turned to retrieve her coat, and Nick pondered his strategy. The smart thing to do . . . the reasonable thing . . . was let her leave. She'd admitted she would do as much herself. Yet he found himself reaching out, touching her arm.

"Before you go, would you do one favor for me?"

She angled toward him, her expression wary. "What?"

"Pick up the doll."

Her complexion went a shade paler and she took a step back. "I'd rather not."

He pinned her with an intent look. "Ms. Sutton, I'll be honest. I've had my share of tips like this through the years. None amounted to anything. That makes me skeptical. On the other hand, you strike me as an intelligent, rational person. I'm curious to see this reaction you describe. Physical evidence is difficult to refute."

She hesitated. Caught her bottom lip between her teeth. Darted a glance toward the shopping bag. Tightened her grip on the strap of her shoulder purse.

Nick waited her out. If this was an act, she was very good. He'd buy her indecision, her dread—her fear—in a heartbeat.

At last, wiping her palms on her slacks, she let the strap slide from her shoulder. Setting the purse beside her coat, she took a step toward him. "All right."

In silence, he picked up the shopping bag and held it open.

She walked to the bag. Sucked in a lungful of air. Her spine stiffened, and she reached in and withdrew the doll.

What happened next was like nothing Nick had seen in all his years of law enforcement.

The little color remaining in Rachel Sutton's complexion vanished, revealing a faint dusting of freckles across her nose. Moisture broke out on her upper lip. She held the doll away from her, arms rigid, and her whole body began to tremble. Her respiration grew shallow and rapid, and she had to struggle for breath. If he checked her pulse, Nick was sure it would be racing.

A few minutes ago, she'd described her reaction to the doll as terror.

She hadn't been lying.

This was real.

Nick didn't want to accept that. But he doubted even a superlative actress could fake the physiological reaction Rachel was having.

Yet it made no sense.

All at once Rachel's knees gave way, galvanizing him into action. He grabbed her upper arms and backed her into the chair she'd vacated sixty seconds ago, easing her down. Without taking his eyes off her, he tugged the doll from her shaking hands and set it on the table.

The transformation was immediate—and startling. Her trembling subsided, her breathing steadied, her muscles began to relax. Color crept back into her face.

It was the weirdest thing he'd ever seen.

"Let me get you some water." He took a step toward the door.

"No. I'll be okay." She resettled her glasses with fingers that weren't yet steady and aimed a probing look in his direction. "Now do you believe me?"

In all honesty, he didn't have a clue what to believe. He couldn't deny what he'd witnessed, but neither could he explain it. Picking up the doll, he examined it, searching for some explanation. But the smiling face offered no answers. Nor did he experience any reaction when he touched it. Only Rachel seemed attuned to its vibes.

He set the doll back on the table, took his seat again, and picked up his pen. "Why don't you give me some contact information, Ms. Sutton? Let's start with address and phone number."

"Does that mean you're going to check into this?"

He thought about spewing the standard line. That all tips were taken seriously and would be given due consideration. Instead, he decided the clear-eyed woman across from him—who he suspected had come here against her better judgment, knowing she faced ridicule—deserved honesty.

"I don't know what I'm going to do." He tapped his pen on the wood-grained surface of the table. "I saw your reaction to the doll. It was unsettling. But whether it indicates a third-party crime or just some very idiosyncratic response . . . I have no idea. I want to think about it."

After a moment, she gave a slow nod. "I guess that's fair. What do you need from me?"

Once she'd answered all his questions, she picked up his card and stood to retrieve her coat. He beat her to it, holding the sleeves as she slid her arms inside. The unusual teal-blue hue caught his eye.

"Pretty color."

A brief smile toyed at her lips as she shrugged the coat into position on her shoulders. "Winter is dreary enough. This brightens it up a bit."

"Nice thought. I'll walk you out."

Surprise flickered in her velvety brown irises. "That's not necessary."

"Where did you park?"

"Around the corner."

"It's necessary." Without waiting for her to reply, he crossed to the door of the interview room and opened it.

She regarded him without moving. "I'm used to taking care of myself, Agent Bradley."

"And I'm used to protecting people. It's my job." He gave her an engaging grin. "Look at it this way. It's dark, and the muggers are out in full force. FBI agents aren't too happy when crimes are committed in their own backyard."

Buttoning her coat, Rachel capitulated with a fleeting smile and a slight lift of one shoulder. "How can I argue with that?"

"It would be tough."

The hint of a chuckle escaped her soft lips as she passed him, and he caught a whiff of a faint, pleasing scent. Nice.

Exiting the building, he motioned toward some slick patches on the sidewalk as they struck out toward her car. "Watch the ice. Those are puddles during the day, but they have a tendency to freeze at night."

No sooner had the words left his mouth than a slippery spot caught Rachel off guard. His arm shot out to steady her, and she quickly regained her balance. "Are you okay?"

"Yes." Her reply came out a bit breathless as she secured her glasses on her nose. "Thanks for the save. I wouldn't want these to go flying. I'm blind as a bat without them."

As they continued toward her car, he maintained a loose grip on her arm. Had he not done so, he doubted he would have noticed the very slight hitch in her gait. A permanent handicap, or a recent injury?

When they arrived at her car, she withdrew her keys from

her purse and faced him. "Look . . . I'd like to thank you for not laughing at my story."

"The reaction you had wasn't funny."

She acknowledged his comment with a dip of her head, then slid into the driver's seat. "Good night, Agent Bradley."

"Good night." He shut her door, lifted a hand in farewell, and strode back down the sidewalk. A quick glance at his watch confirmed he was already running late for dinner. He needed to shift gears and forget about work for the next few hours.

But thanks to a lovely woman with a doll, he had a feeling that wasn't going to be so easy to do.

⋆

As Nick Bradley disappeared into the night, Rachel drew a long, shaky breath.

The last half hour had been tense. Very tense.

But it could have been worse. At least the FBI agent had given her a fair hearing. If he laughed with his colleagues later, so be it. In person, he'd allowed her to hold on to her dignity despite her bizarre story. He deserved high marks for that.

She'd give him high marks in other areas too. Her first impression of him when he'd walked through the door had been classic all-American boy. At six-foot-one or two, with sandy hair and a lean, athletic build, he fit that description to a T. But as they'd talked, she'd realized the firm jaw and fine lines at the corners of his eyes spoke of maturity and seasoning, hinting at a toughness not immediately apparent under his engaging smile. The man projected a sense of leashed power and control, and Rachel had a feeling he'd seen his share of rough-and-tumble action, despite his appealing boy-next-door looks. A faint scar above his temple suggested as much.

It was an arresting combination.

He had also struck her as a man who weighed evidence and options. Rather than entertain wild speculations, he seemed more the sort who would thoughtfully consider facts and draw sound conclusions.

In other words, he had been the perfect man to share her story with.

As she fitted her key in the ignition, a sudden, odd tingle that felt an awful lot like attraction quivered in the pit of her stomach.

Now where in the world had that come from? They'd met less than half an hour ago. And she'd told him a bizarre story that, despite his professional courtesy, probably relegated her to fruitcake land. Besides, even though the third finger on his left hand was bare, he had to have a wife or a hot date waiting for him. No guy that handsome would be unattached.

Opening her window halfway, Rachel filled her lungs with the chilly night air, hoping to clear her head—and chase away any fanciful notions about Special Agent Nick Bradley. There was no way a man like him would have any interest in a woman who claimed to get messages from dolls. And she didn't blame him.

As for the doll—in spite of his civility, for all she knew he was at this very moment throwing Raggedy Ann in his trash can.

But that was beyond her control. She'd done everything she could by turning the doll over to the authorities.

And as far as she was concerned, that was the end of the story.

3

An hour later, as Nick approached the table for five tucked into a private alcove in the quiet West County restaurant, Mark Sanders raised a glass in welcome. "Finally. We were about to call in the FBI. Wait . . . we are the FBI." He grinned and set the glass back on the table.

"Sorry I'm late." Nick dispensed hugs to Emily and Monica and shook hands with Mark and Coop, pausing beside the pumpkin seat next to Monica on the banquette to run a gentle finger down the cheek of two-month-old Michael David Callahan. "I've been looking forward to meeting the newest member of the Cooper clan. Handsome little guy."

"What else would you expect, with Monica for a mother?" Coop put his arm around his wife of fifteen months and gave her a gentle squeeze.

Soft color suffused Monica's face, and she shook her head with a rueful smile. "Blushing. The bane of redheads."

"Russet. That's the color of your hair," Coop corrected, fingering a strand as he examined it. "Like burnished leaves in autumn."

"Whoa! Former HRT member turns poetic. I ought to tell the guys." Mark helped himself to a stuffed mushroom cap from the appetizer tray in the center of the table as he ribbed his former Hostage Rescue Team partner.

"You could." Coop perused the array of appetizers, lingering over his selection of a toasted ravioli. "But then I'd have to tell them about the rose petals you had the florist sprinkle all over the bed in your honeymoon cottage at Wren Lake."

"Rose petals?" Nick took the empty chair beside Mark and grinned. "Getting in touch with our feminine side, are we?"

"Knock it off," Mark growled, his neck turning ruddy.

"I thought it was very romantic." Emily tucked her arm through Mark's, her golden blonde hair shimmering in the subdued lighting. "But how did you know?" she asked Coop.

"Mark ran the idea by me. I told him it would be overkill and advised against it, but he ignored me."

"Good for you, Mark," Monica chimed in. "I agree with Emily. It was very romantic. In fact, the whole wedding sounded romantic. I'll always be sorry I missed it."

"If this little guy hadn't disrupted our plans by arriving two weeks late you wouldn't have." Coop reached across Monica and folded the blanket more securely around the infant. "Trust me, the best man would have been happier to have his best lady by his side." After aiming a smile at Monica, he refocused on Mark. "You know, the more I think about it, the more I'm convinced that rose petal tale deserves telling."

"Coop."

At Mark's warning tone, Coop chuckled. "Don't worry. I can't imagine any of the HRT guys believing either story, anyway. You, romantic; me, poetic. Nah."

"You guys miss the team at all?" Nick took a sip of the raspberry iced tea Mark must have ordered for him. Everyone at the office knew he was addicted to it.

"Once in a while," Coop admitted. "But I like the teaching gig at Quantico. And I especially like being home at night—now that I have a family to go home to."

"I agree," Mark seconded. "I wasn't sure if going back to field-work would be challenging enough after the HRT, but heading the reactive squad here keeps things interesting. And the hours for agents are a whole lot better than for HRT operators. Although you must have gotten tied up at the office tonight." Mark directed his comment to Nick.

"Yeah. We had a walk-in not long before closing. I drew the short straw."

"Tough break," Mark sympathized. "Was it some hanger-on who wanted to tell you his life story?"

"It wasn't a him. It was a her. And she wasn't a hanger-on. Just the opposite. She couldn't wait to leave."

"That's a switch."

The waiter appeared to take their orders, and the conversation shifted gears as they debated the merits of pork tenderloin with a rosemary glaze versus the asparagus and prosciutto risotto special of the day.

Nick wasn't sorry for the distraction. In general, when someone showed up at the office with a bizarre tip, the story circulated around the bull pen and everyone had a good laugh. But for some reason, he didn't want people laughing at Rachel Sutton.

Instead of letting the subject drop, however, Mark resumed the conversation without missing a beat once they'd placed their orders. "Tell us more about this mystery woman."

"She's not a mystery. I have all her contact information. Besides, I'd rather socialize than talk about work. You're all coming to my house for brunch on Sunday, right?"

"I wouldn't miss it," Monica said. "After all the stories I've heard, I want to see this place."

"How's the drywall dust situation?" Coop asked.

"Much better than when you and Mark stayed with me last summer. The first floor is pretty much finished. And I'm not doing a whole lot of new drywall on the second floor. You should be able to breathe without sneezing."

"I can vouch for that," Mark offered. "Your sinuses are safe."

45

"The house is fabulous," Emily told Monica. "It's a two-story, Federal-style brick from . . . 1850, Nick?"

"1852."

"And it had been abandoned for a decade when he bought it a year ago," Emily continued.

"I can't even imagine tackling a project like that." Monica shook her head. "I think it's awesome."

"We had a few other less complimentary words for it last summer, didn't we, Coop?" Mark smirked at his ex-partner.

"I'll take the Fifth."

"Still the reticent type, I see. Better have him reread that communication book you wrote, Monica," Mark teased.

She snuggled closer to her husband. "He communicates just fine, thank you very much."

Mark eyed the infant in the pumpkin seat and grinned. "Yeah. I guess he does."

"Mark!" Emily gave him a playful jab. "We were talking about the house. I think you've done a great job on it," she told Nick.

"Thanks. It's the most ambitious rehab I've ever taken on. But it's really coming together. I'll give you a tour after brunch on Sunday."

"About that." Coop squinted at Nick. "I have one question. Are you serving tofu?"

Mark chuckled and glanced at Nick. "You're never going to live down that health food phase you went through, you know."

"I still eat healthy. And there's nothing wrong with tofu. But you'll be happy to know the menu for Sunday includes eggs Benedict—with real ham."

"Now that's good news." Coop grinned and confided to Monica. "Actually, Nick's not a bad cook, despite all the grief Mark and I gave him last summer. Some woman will be lucky to get him—if he ever decides to love one as much as he loves that old house."

"Speaking of women . . . I still want to hear about the one who showed up at the office this afternoon," Mark interjected. "How come you're holding back?"

"I'm not holding back. I'm trying to leave my job at the office."

"Since when?"

"Since tonight."

The two dark-haired agents exchanged a speculative glance.

"I sense a story here," Coop remarked.

"I do too." Mark turned toward Nick. "You might as well spill it. Or Coop and I will have to dust off some of those interrogation techniques we learned in the HRT."

Nick stifled a sigh. He'd already made a tactical mistake, raising suspicions by dancing around the subject. In any other circumstance, he'd be the first one to talk about a walk-in with an off-the-wall tip. They'd all share a laugh about the weirdo and move on.

Except he didn't think Rachel was weird. Just her story. But he could imagine what these guys would think of it. Of him too, if he didn't dismiss it as summarily as they would. He'd prefer to avoid the whole subject, but he didn't see any way out of the corner he'd painted himself into.

Shifting in his seat, he took a long, slow sip of his iced tea. And prayed for inspiration.

"Do you know what I think?" Emily interjected.

All heads swiveled in her direction. Her authoritative, noted-psychologist voice always commanded attention.

"What?" Monica asked.

"I think Nick had an unsettling encounter this afternoon."

The heads swiveled back to him.

"Is that right?" Mark asked.

"I don't know how Emily knew that. But . . . yeah."

Mark shook his head. "That's amazing. Sometimes I think my wife is psychic."

"That must make marriage interesting." One side of Coop's mouth hitched up, and he popped a salsa-laden tortilla chip into his mouth.

"This has nothing to do with mind reading." Emily aimed a wry look at Coop. "You can get a lot of insight into a person by observing their behavior. Nick isn't his usual laid-back, open self tonight. He seems a bit distracted—and troubled."

If there was any way out of talking about his late-afternoon encounter, Nick would take it. But he was stuck. At least Emily's perceptive comment, along with Mark's mention of psychics, gave him the perfect opening.

"Kudos to Emily." Nick raised his iced tea glass in salute. "You nailed my mental state dead on."

"I have to say I'm intrigued." Monica leaned forward, her attention fixed on him. "What happened?"

"You know, these two would have come in handy during interrogations in our HRT days," Mark commented to Coop.

"Yeah. A psychologist and a communications expert. What a great tactical team."

"The real question is whether their sympathetic technique will work." Mark regarded Nick. "So are you going to talk? Or do we have to resort to less pleasant means of dragging the information out of you?"

"Very funny." Nick took another swig of iced tea and set the glass precisely back in the ring of water on the polished oak surface of the table. "Okay, here's what happened. A woman showed up near closing time. Asked to speak to an agent. Yours truly got the nod. I met her in one of the interview rooms out front. She was dressed nicely, and she had a shopping bag."

"Oh no." Mark rolled his eyes. "The old evidence-in-a-shopping bag routine."

"Do you want to hear the story or not?" An uncharacteristic note of impatience sharpened Nick's words.

Surprise flickered across Mark's features, and he exchanged another glance with Coop. "Yeah. Sorry."

"Okay. There was a very beat-up Raggedy Ann doll in the bag. She said she found it in a Bread Company parking lot, sticking out from a melting pile of snow. She decided to rescue it and turn it in to the store's lost and found."

"She dug a shabby doll out of a frozen pile of filthy snow?" Mark arched an eyebrow.

"She thought some little girl might be missing it, and that her mother might be looking for it." Nick's defensive comeback only seemed to increase his fellow agent's curiosity.

Emily, on the other hand, smiled. "She has a soft heart. I like that."

"Me too," Monica affirmed. "I had a Raggedy Ann doll as a child. It traveled all over the world with me, from one diplomatic post to the next. I'd have been devastated if it ever got lost."

Sensing two allies in the wives of his friends, Nick focused on them as he continued his story. "When I asked her why she thought the FBI might be interested in the doll, she said . . ."

He stopped. Abruptly.

All at once he knew exactly how Rachel Sutton had felt in the seconds before she'd told him the reason for her visit. And his admiration for her mushroomed. It was bad enough to share this story with friends, with people who were predisposed to give you the benefit of the doubt. He couldn't imagine how much more difficult it had been to march into a law enforcement agency, a place she knew would be inclined to treat her with cynicism—at best—and talk about what had happened.

"What did she say, Nick?" Emily reached out to touch his hand.

He stared at her fingers, drawing courage from the comforting, supportive gesture. "She said when she touched it, she had a reaction."

Silence greeted his statement. He kept his gaze fixed on Emily's fingers, expecting them to be withdrawn at any moment, bracing for the rejection. But when the silence lengthened and her fingers stayed in place, he ventured a scan of the table.

Mark and Coop shared identical expressions, eyes narrowed by a combination of caution, doubt, and suspicion. And he wasn't surprised to find an is-this-for-real-or-are-you-pulling-my-leg quirk to their lips.

The two women, on the other hand, seemed far more receptive to his story. Emily's expression was thoughtful. Faint furrows marred Monica's brow as she leaned closer.

"What did she mean by reaction, Nick?"

He wasn't surprised by her question. She was a word person. Clear communication was her thing. He'd asked the same thing of Rachel himself.

"She said when she held the doll, she felt terrified."

"And you bought this?" Mark's question was laced with incredulity.

"Not at first."

"What changed your mind?" Coop joined the conversation.

"I asked her to hold the doll. And I witnessed her reaction."

Silence again.

"Okay, let me get this straight." Mark folded his hands on the table. "She picked up the doll, and she . . . what? Freaked out?"

"She had all the symptoms of terror. Like a panic attack."

"Adrenaline rush, trembling, muscle tension, rapid and shallow breathing?" Emily clarified.

"Yes. And I don't think those kinds of physical symptoms would be easy to fake."

"They wouldn't," Emily concurred.

"Then how do you account for what happened?" Mark directed the question to Nick.

"You mean besides the explanation she offered?"

"Her explanation isn't logical."

"I saw it," Nick countered.

"Okay." Coop stepped in. "Let's skip the discussion on plausibility for a second and ask the next question. What did she want you to do about it?"

"Look into it. She sensed danger and felt compelled to pass the . . . for want of a better word, message . . . on to someone in a position to investigate."

"Where's the doll now?" Mark asked.

"Sitting on my desk."

"Pitch it."

Nick raked his fingers through his hair. "That was my first inclination. But I couldn't do it. She seemed so . . . sincere."

"They all do."

"The thing is, why would she make this up?" Monica tapped a finger on the table, her expression thoughtful.

"To get attention? Because she's delusional? Why do any of these weirdos show up with bizarre stories?" Mark responded.

"She wasn't a weirdo." Nick gritted his teeth. Took a deep breath. "She's a teacher. And she's very intelligent and articulate."

"A woman shows up at an FBI office claiming she's getting bad vibes from a doll and wants us to investigate. You don't call that weird?"

"In theory, yes. In this case . . . it doesn't fit."

"Are you saying you believe her?" Mark pressed.

Nick shifted in his seat. "I don't want to. It's too bizarre."

"But you do." Mark leaned back and regarded him through narrowed eyes. "How old is this woman?"

"Early thirties, I'd guess."

"Attractive?"

Nick frowned. "What does that have to do with anything?"

"Pretty women are hard to dismiss as kooks."

"I didn't say she was pretty."

"I noticed that. You sidestepped the question."

Cornered, Nick folded his arms across his chest. "Okay. Fine. She was pretty. But her looks have nothing to do with this. I saw her reaction. How do you explain that?"

"I can't. But maybe psychology can. And we happen to have an eminent psychologist in our midst tonight. I think I can work out a suitable consultation fee, since she's my wife." He winked at Emily and draped his arm around her shoulders. "Dr. Lawson, what's your take on this?"

"I'm afraid this is really outside my realm of expertise. It dips more into parapsychology than psychology. But I can tell you these sorts of paranormal phenomena in general are not considered by most psychologists to have much credibility. There's been research done in the field, but a lot of the work is unscientific and much of the data is flawed. So despite decades of effort by proponents to prove these kinds of phenomena are real, there've been no conclusive positive results."

"What about people who claim they can sense emotions from objects? Isn't there a name for that?" Monica asked.

"Psychometry," Emily supplied. "It's considered to be a form of ESP. Practitioners say they can read the history of an object and its owners by holding it. There's a lot of interesting anecdotal material about it, but again, virtually no reliable empirical evidence to support its validity."

"In other words, the woman Nick talked to is a fake." Mark settled back in his seat.

"I didn't say that," Emily clarified.

Frowning, Mark leaned forward again. "What do you mean?"

"It sounds to me like her reaction was very real. We can't discount that. I think there could be a legitimate explanation for it. A memory buried somewhere in her past, perhaps. The doll may have been a trigger of some sort."

"Meaning you don't think she's a kook." Relief coursed through Nick. Emily had offered the first logical explanation for the phenomenon he'd witnessed. One that took the "loony" stigma off Rachel Sutton. And for some reason, he was grateful. Which was odd, since she was a stranger to him and he was unlikely to see her again.

"Not necessarily. The sort of extreme reaction you described is rare, but I've had patients who have strong reactions to objects from their past. Sometimes we can track down the reason and sometimes we can't. In my experience, if you're dealing with someone who otherwise seems like a lucid, normal person, there's almost always a logical explanation for a reaction like that if you dig deep enough. From what you've said, I suspect this woman would fall into that category."

"It only happens when she touches the doll," Nick noted.

"The tactile sensation could be tapping into a traumatic subconscious memory." Emily tilted her head and played with her spoon. "It's an intriguing situation."

Their salads arrived, and much to Nick's relief, Mark and Coop got off his case. The conversation moved on to other subjects, and the rest of the evening was pleasant and relaxing.

After lingering over dessert and coffee, they parted for the night in the parking lot. And as Nick watched the two couples leave arm in arm, their heads close together as they shared quiet, private conversations, he thought again of Rachel Sutton.

Now that Emily had set his mind at ease about the woman's sanity, he found himself wondering what it would be like to share a quiet dinner with her. To tuck her arm in his as they walked to his car afterward. To steal a kiss from those full, soft lips beneath a silver moon.

That wayward notion took him off guard. And made about as much sense as the story Rachel had told him this afternoon.

Turning his back on the two happy couples, he strode toward his car. The best thing to do was forget his brief encounter with the velvet-eyed visitor who wore a delicate gold cross around her slender neck.

But as he drove home in the darkness, he couldn't shake the feeling that had they met under less bizarre circumstances, he would have been interested in getting to know her better.

Very interested.

4

It had taken a ton of research to convince her boss she could come up with enough information to write a compelling story, but almost a week after her eavesdropping episode, Claudia got the green light for a piece on paranormal phenomena. With one caveat: it had to have the local angle she'd promised.

That was her next order of business. And she'd already done her homework. Earlier in the week, her computer search of the St. Louis area phone book had revealed only one listing for a Joseph Birkner—the name on the credit card at the restaurant. He and Marta lived at 7135 Willow Lane.

It had been a piece of cake to pin down where Rachel's friend worked. She'd just followed her one morning to Stafford Elementary School. After practicing her spiel for the past few days, Claudia was confident she could pull off her plan without suspicion and get the information she needed.

Stepping out of her cube in the newsroom, she headed toward the conference room—the only available office space with a door in the whole place. That was her one gripe about the paper—and journalism in general. No privacy. How was a reporter supposed to cultivate confidential sources or develop exclusives when everyone within twenty feet could hear your conversation?

She ran through her script once more, withdrew her cell phone, and keyed in the number for Stafford Elementary. At 4:30 on a Thursday, the place could be shut down for the day.

But she hoped not. Now that she had the go-ahead, she was anxious to get started. Tapping her foot, she listened as the phone rang once, twice, three times. By the fourth ring, as she was beginning to resign herself to voice mail, a live person answered.

"I'm so glad I caught you before the end of the day," Claudia returned the woman's greeting, doing her best to sound frazzled. "I was trying to reach one of your teachers, but I can't read my own scribbling. I always did get bad marks in penmanship." She gave a self-deprecating laugh. "It's Rachel . . ." she left the sentence hanging, crossing her fingers the woman would fill in the blank.

"Sutton?"

Yes! "That could be it. Unless . . . is there another Rachel on staff   ?"

"No, we only have one Rachel."

"Then she must be the one."

"Were you wanting to inquire about piano lessons, by any chance?"

Another piece of background information. Excellent. Claudia filed it away for possible future use. "That's right. For my daughter."

"My daughter is one of her students too," the chatty woman offered. "Rachel is a very good teacher. I'm sure you'll be delighted. I'm afraid we can't give staff information over the phone, but I'll be happy to ask her to call if you'll give me your name and a contact number."

"Perfect. It's Judy Denham." Claudia made up a number.

"Got it. I'll pass this on to Rachel."

"Thank you so much. You've been very, very helpful."

More than you'll ever know.

Smiling, Claudia ended the call.

On to step two.

Rachel shivered and slipped the key into the door of her small bungalow. The cold had returned with a vengeance sometime during the afternoon, and she regretted leaving her gloves on the kitchen counter this morning. The short walk from her detached garage to the door had already numbed her fingers.

A frigid gust whipped past, and another shudder rippled through her. The wind chill had to be in the single digits. So much for St. Louis's short-lived mid-winter thaw. And with ominous clouds turning the sky dark as night at only 4:30, she assumed more snow was on the way. Oh, well. It had been nice while it lasted.

Stepping inside, Rachel shut the door against the bitter cold and drew a slow, deep breath. It had been a long week. She'd doubled up on piano students Tuesday and Wednesday night to carve out time for parent/teacher conferences last night at one of the two schools where she taught music. After the conferences, some of her colleagues had convinced her to go out for pizza. It had been close to eleven when she'd stepped through her door.

Tonight, she wanted to relax. *Needed* to relax, after the oddly stressful past month. And she'd planned her Friday evening with that in mind. First, she was going to savor the full order of shrimp and broccoli linguini in a light olive oil sauce she'd picked up from her favorite Italian restaurant on the way home. That would be followed by the generous slice of chocolate torte she'd cut from the cake in the teachers' lounge today. She intended to cap the evening with a soak in a hot bubble bath, accompanied by a good book. And perhaps she'd allow herself one final indulgence—a few fanciful thoughts about a certain sandy-haired FBI agent with cobalt blue eyes.

Since her visit to the agency's office a week ago today, she hadn't thought a lot about him. Hadn't *let* herself think a lot about him. She was too much of a realist. Growing up in foster care had that effect, she supposed. You learned to appreciate kindness, to accept indifference, and to move on without a backward glance no matter how you were treated. It wasn't as if anyone had ever been unkind to her. But the succession of placements had left her yearning for roots. And it had given her a deep, lasting appreciation for home. Her house might be small and unpretentious, but it was hers. That meant the world to her.

And if she had no one to share it with . . . that was just the way life had worked out. She didn't dwell on it. Except, once in a while, on special days that were meant to be spent with someone you loved.

Like today.

Valentine's Day.

Setting the white sack containing her dinner on a small table near the door, she shrugged off her coat—and tried to do the same with her sudden melancholy. Instead of feeling sorry for herself, she'd focus on all the things she should be grateful for. Including the relaxing evening ahead.

In a dozen strides she crossed the small living room and struck a match from the book she kept handy, and lit the kindling under the logs in her fireplace. She'd always said if she ever bought a house, it had to have a fireplace. The homes she could afford in the areas where she wanted to live didn't offer such features, however, so she'd added this soon after moving in. It had been an extravagance—but one she'd never regretted. On a cold winter night, there was nothing like curling up next to the flickering logs with a cup of hot chocolate. Not a bad addition to her activity list for tonight, either. She might end her evening that way. After the bubble bath.

The first order of business, however, was food. Breakfast had been a long time ago and she was starving. Juggling classes at two schools had its challenges, and lunch was often a casualty. On the bright side, however, skipping her noon meal meant she wouldn't have to feel guilty about tonight's pasta spree.

She snagged the bag off the table and was halfway to the kitchen when the doorbell rang.

Torn, Rachel hesitated. She hated to be rude. But she wasn't in the mood for company—or a sales pitch. On the other hand, her caller could be someone who was interested in a mural, or wanting to inquire about piano lessons . . . though most piano customers phoned and the majority of those interested in a mural emailed after viewing the samples on her website. But she'd had a few potential clients show up at her door through the years.

Resigned, she deposited the bag on the table again and returned to the door, checking the peephole.

A young woman stood on the other side, her longish, dark-blonde hair pulled back at her nape with a barrette. A gold choker peeked through the neck of her black wool coat, glinting in the porch light, and a leather shoulder purse was slung over her shoulder. A newer model, sporty red car was parked at the curb behind her. Although she was a stranger to Rachel, her attire and transportation didn't suggest salesperson or survey-taker. That was a good thing. She should be able to dispense with the interruption quickly and get on with her evening.

Pasting a smile on her face, she pulled open the door. "Hi. Can I help you?"

"Rachel Sutton?"

"Yes."

"My name is Claudia Barnes. I'm with *St. Louis Scene.*" She held out a business card. "I was hoping you might give me a few minutes."

Responding by reflex, Rachel took the card. "I'm sorry. I don't think I'm familiar with that publication."

"Not enough people are, I'm afraid. It's only been around for two years. But the circulation is growing. *Scene* is a free, weekly news magazine. It's distributed at restaurants, grocery stores, and various other places of business. I'm a reporter."

The logo on the card was vaguely familiar to Rachel. "I think I've seen it. At the coffee shop I go to, maybe. It's a tabloid, isn't it?"

"Yes."

Puzzled by the visit, Rachel tipped her head and gave the woman a quizzical look. "How can I help you, Ms. Barnes?"

"I'm hoping you'll let me interview you for a story I'm working on about paranormal phenomena."

The request caught Rachel like a left hook—and left her reeling. Several seconds ticked by before she could find her voice. "Excuse me?"

The woman's poise wavered for an instant, her smile flickering the tiniest bit. Clearing her throat, she hitched her shoulder purse a bit higher. Her smile steadied. "I'm working on a feature on the paranormal. A story like that is always more interesting when it has a local angle, and I understand you had an experience recently that falls into this category. With a Raggedy Ann doll?"

Stunned, Rachel stared at her. "Where did you hear that?" The question came out strained and hoarse.

"I'm afraid I can't reveal my sources. That goes against press protocol. It's true, then? You have psychic abilities?"

"No."

"What about the doll?"

"That's the only time I . . ." Rachel stopped. Clamped her lips shut. But it was too late. For all intents and purposes, she'd confirmed her experience with the doll.

"It's a fascinating story, Ms. Sutton. I know our readers would be interested in it. Even if the FBI wasn't."

The woman's eyes narrowed, and Rachel suspected she was fishing now. That she didn't know what the FBI's reaction had been. But how did she know about Rachel's visit to the field office in the first place?

Only one answer came to mind. Someone at the FBI had leaked her story to the press. Perhaps not with deliberate intent, though that didn't matter at this point. It was out there.

But who could it have been? She'd told her story to no one at that office except Nick Bradley, and somehow she couldn't imagine him being that indiscreet. He could have shared the story with other agents, though, and one of them might have commented on it to someone with connections to the media. How else could this woman have gotten the information?

"You know, Ms. Sutton, whether they admit it or not, law enforcement agencies do use psychics in crime solving. I've been researching the subject, and back in the 1970s there was a woman in St. Louis who—"

"Ms. Barnes." Gripping the edge of the door, Rachel cut her off. "I don't know where you got your tip about me, but I'm not interested in your article or in participating in any way." She started to close the door.

"That's your choice, of course." The woman raised her volume slightly. "It's just that I wanted to give you a chance to tell your story in your own words rather than have me paraphrase it with a 'no comment' from you."

Rachel's hopes for a quiet, peaceful evening—make that a quiet, peaceful life—disintegrated. The reporter might be bluffing, hoping that last comment would spur her to cooperate, but if she wasn't, Rachel would face public humiliation. It had been bad enough talking to one person at the FBI. If this was splashed across the pages of a tabloid and read by tens of thousands of people, she'd never shake the loony label.

A wave of panic swept over her.

Clutching at straws, Rachel left the door half open and tried a threat of her own. "You might want to think about libel issues before you use my name without my permission."

"Are you denying that you found a doll, sensed terror or danger when you held it, and that you shared your story with law enforcement?"

Much as she was tempted to say yes, Rachel didn't believe in lying. Instead, she remained silent and did her best to maintain a neutral expression.

"That's what I thought." The woman pulled her keys out of her purse, a satisfied smile tugging at her lips. "It's not libel if it's true, if it's newsworthy, and if there's no malicious intent. If you change your mind about talking with me, you have my card."

With that, the reporter swiveled on her three-inch heels and strode down the walk, the outline of her form blurring in the dim glow from the streetlights. As she slid into her car and started the engine, large flakes of snow began to fall, clinging to the frozen ground as if to erase any evidence of the woman's visit. Seconds later, the sporty red vehicle disappeared down the dark street.

Closing the door, Rachel stumbled to the couch in front of the fireplace and sank down. What was she supposed to do now? What *could* she do? *St. Louis Scene* might not be the *Post-Dispatch*, but a lot of people probably read it. Some of them would know her. Students. Clients. Co-workers. And once they saw her story, they'd either avoid her, pepper her with questions, or laugh behind her back.

None of those scenarios were good.

Too agitated to remain seated, Rachel rose and began to

pace, her initial shock giving way to anger. Because of a careless mistake—or indiscretion—her reputation was about to be ruined. Thanks to the FBI.

When Rachel had walked out of the downtown field office a week ago, she'd never expected to initiate further contact with the Bureau. Her one dealing with the agency had been more than enough to last a lifetime.

But she couldn't let this leak go unreported. The situation needed to be addressed. Someone should be held accountable.

Rachel had just one contact at the FBI. And she had a feeling he wouldn't be happy about this turn of events, either. That he'd do his best to track down the guilty party.

Unless he was the culprit.

A possibility she didn't even want to consider.

"Big plans tonight?" Mark propped his shoulder against the edge of Nick's cube in the bull pen and stuck his hands in his pockets.

"Nope. How about you and Emily?" Nick swiveled around in his chair to face the other agent.

"A nice, quiet dinner for two by the fire. I'm picking up a four-course meal from Gourmet to Go on my way home. Add some candlelight and a little soft background music . . . we'll be set for the evening."

"Sounds like a plan."

"You aren't working on the house tonight, are you?"

"I might."

"It's Valentine's Day."

"I'm aware of that."

Folding his arms across his chest, Mark gave him a speculative look. "What gives with you, anyway? You were quite the man around town in our Academy days. At least by reputation. When did you become a hermit?"

"First of all, my reputation was greatly exaggerated. I've always led a pretty quiet life. But I'm not a hermit."

"You are when it comes to dating."

"Let's just say I'm selective."

"Or hard to please."

"Who are you to talk? You didn't exactly rush to the altar. How old were you when you married Emily two months ago?"

"Thirty-eight. Same as you. But I had a very active social life before that."

"You know, you're falling into that stereotypical newlywed trap." Nick leaned back in his chair and laced his fingers behind his head.

Twin furrows dented Mark's brow. "What trap?"

"The I'm-deliriously-happy-and-I-want-all-my-friends-to-be-this-happy-too trap."

"Well, I am and I do."

"I appreciate your concern. But leave my love life to me, okay?"

"I would if you had one."

"The subject's closed, Mark." Nick swung back to his desk.

"Fine. I'll let it rest. For today." He peeked around a file cabinet into the corner of Nick's cube, where the patched Raggedy Ann smiled back at him from under the work space where it had been shoved, only its head visible above the small shopping bag. "Still have the doll, I see. I thought you were going to pitch it."

"I am."

"When?"

"Soon."

"Is that subject off limits too?"

"Go home to Emily, Mark."

"Okay, okay. I can take a hint." At Nick's dubious look, Mark flashed him a grin. "Have a good weekend. And don't inhale too much drywall dust."

"I'll try not to. By the way, if you and Emily get bored, I can always use a couple extra pair of hands."

"I did my time at your place. And Emily and I can find other ways to entertain ourselves."

Chuckling, Nick waved him off. "See you Monday."

As Mark exited, Nick checked his watch. It was almost quitting time. If the place had cleared out a little early last Friday, today the exodus was even more noticeable. Everyone must have Valentine's Day plans.

One of these years, maybe he would too. But at this point it was in God's hands. He'd bent the Lord's ear about it often, praying that a special woman would grace his life. All he could do now was trust—and be open to opportunities that came his way.

As he shut down his computer, Nick put thoughts of his solitary Valentine's evening aside. What good did it do to wish for the impossible? This year was a wash. Standing, he stretched and reached for his coat. Time to call it a day.

He had one arm in his topcoat when the phone rang. Leaning over, he checked the caller ID. The number was local but unfamiliar. And it was two minutes to five. The day was a breath away from being officially over. Meaning he could ignore this call in good conscience. There was an emergency number if someone needed urgent assistance. He slid his other arm into the sleeve and draped a muffler around his neck.

"You gonna get that?"

At the question from Steve Preston, the reactive squad supervisor in the St. Louis office, Nick stifled a rueful sigh. It was just his luck that one of the bosses would be passing by at the wrong time.

Switching gears, he snagged the phone and gave Steve a mock salute as he spoke. "Special Agent Nick Bradley."

"Agent Bradley, this is Rachel Sutton."

The woman with the velvet brown eyes and soft lips.

Nick forgot all about Steve as he tried to regroup. Rachel Sutton was the last person he'd expected to hear from again. He did his best not to sound too surprised—or too pleased. "Ms. Sutton. How can I help you?"

"You can find out who leaked my story to the press."

He'd missed the anger in her tone when she'd greeted him. It came through loud and clear now. As did her distress. And her message.

"Let's back up a minute." Frowning, he shoved one edge of his coat aside and planted a fist on his hip. "Tell me what happened."

"I just had a visit from a reporter with *St. Louis Scene*. Claudia Barnes. She knew all about my experience with the doll and my visit to the FBI. She's doing a story on paranormal phenomena and wanted to interview me for the local angle. And she says she's going to tell my story whether I cooperate or not. I want to know who tipped her off."

Nick's brain went into high gear. He'd told no one about Rachel's story except his four best friends on Friday night. And he had absolute confidence in their discretion. Besides, he was pretty certain he'd never mentioned her name during that conversation. On top of that, they'd had the secluded corner of the restaurant to themselves. There wasn't much chance anyone would have overheard the conversation. The FD-71 and 302 forms he'd filled out after her visit had gone straight into the file. He'd shared them with no one.

66

"It wasn't the FBI, Ms. Sutton."

"It had to be. I'm not saying it was deliberate. But the whole place was probably laughing about my visit all week. Someone may have let it slip in a casual conversation that was overheard by the wrong person."

"No one was laughing about your story, I can promise you that."

"Maybe not that you observed. But you can't be sure about that—or about how it might have leaked."

"As a matter of fact, I can. Because no one knows about your visit except a couple of trusted friends."

Several beats of silence ticked by. "You didn't tell everyone at your office?"

"No."

A soft sigh came over the line. "I appreciate that. Thank you. But . . . if that's true, how did this reporter get her information?"

It was a good question. And he didn't have an answer. "I don't know. But there has to be a logical explanation." Out of the blue, an idea popped into his mind. One that he wasn't convinced he should pursue. Yet the words came out before he could stop them. "I'm getting ready to leave the office, and I'd be happy to stop by and talk this through. I'm sure we can nail this down."

Silence greeted his offer, and he suddenly remembered what day it was. He'd noted her ringless left hand when they'd met; surely she had plans for Valentine's Day. No woman that good looking would be spending this evening alone.

"Sorry," he amended, feeling like an idiot. "The significance of the day escaped me for a moment. I'm sure you have better things to do tonight. But I'll be happy to help you try and get to the bottom of this another time."

There was a brief hesitation before she responded. "To be

honest, my plans for tonight involved a nice dinner, a good book, and some quiet time by the fire. In light of what's happened, that's a bust anyway. I wouldn't mind some assistance trying to figure out how the press got hold of my story . . . and how I'm supposed to deal with the fallout when this hits the papers."

She didn't have a date.

That surprised Nick as much as the leak. But in a much more pleasant way. "I can be there in half an hour, if that's okay."

"That sounds good. I'll see you then."

As the line went dead, Nick adjusted his muffler and buttoned his coat, the whisper of a smile tugging at his lips. He was sorry about the leak and all the grief it would cause Rachel. It seemed the fates had not been smiling on her the day she'd stumbled across a little girl's lost toy in the parking lot. The grinning, orange-haired doll had caused her nothing but trouble.

But it had brought some good luck too. To him, anyway. And perhaps the very opportunity he'd been praying for. Because thanks to a very shabby Raggedy Ann, he was going to spend part of his Valentine's Day with a beautiful woman after all.

5

She shouldn't have agreed to let him come.

Annoyed with herself, Rachel paced the length of her small living room, her dinner forgotten. A man like Nick Bradley surely had places to go any Friday night, let alone this Friday night. But his surprising offer had thrown her, and she hadn't stopped to consider how an impromptu visit might mess up *his* Valentine's Day plans.

When the imposition occurred to her five minutes after they hung up, she'd tried to call him back. The recorded message that greeted her told her he'd already left. The best she could do now was apologize for her lack of consideration and send him on to whatever lucky woman was waiting for him.

Her doorbell chimed, and she jerked to a stop mid-pace. At least her body did. Her pulse, on the other hand, bounded forward at double speed.

Good grief, Rachel. Get a grip! The man is here on business.

One look through the peephole, however, and what little remained of her composure evaporated as fast as Nick's frosty breath. It ought to be illegal to be that good-looking. Those cobalt blue eyes were to die for, and while tall, dark, and handsome had its merits, she'd always preferred the clean-cut, fair-haired, all-American look Nick Bradley had in spades. Add in a strong jaw, firm lips, and an endearing, slight crook in his nose that suggested he may have broken it once, and the total package was way too appealing.

Too bad they hadn't met under more normal circumstances.

Except it wouldn't have mattered. A man like Nick would never be interested in her. Four-eyes, the kids used to tease. They'd made fun of her limp too, which had been far more pronounced when she was a child. Mousy hair, unremarkable brown eyes, and average looks didn't help, either. It was no wonder she was spending Valentine's Day alone.

The doorbell chimed again, and Rachel jumped. Good grief! How long had she been ogling the tall agent outside her door? Too long, she concluded, watching as parallel grooves appeared on his brow.

Pasting on a fake smile, she stepped back from the peep-hole and pulled open the door. "Thanks for dropping by, Agent Bradley."

The genuine smile he gave her in return dented his left cheek with a dimple—and turned her insides to mush.

"No problem. I'm just sorry this happened." Large, downy flakes of snow continued to fall, their icy facets sparkling in the porch light as they dusted the shoulders of his dark wool coat and settled on his sandy hair. One snagged an eyelash, and she watched, mesmerized, as he smiled and brushed it away with long, lean fingers. "Looks like we're in for another round of dismal weather."

Weather. He was talking about the weather. Somehow she managed to shift gears. "That's what the meteorologists are saying. I'm glad it's the weekend and I don't have to go anywhere until Sunday. Come in, please." She moved aside.

He stepped over the threshold, his tall frame and broad shoulders immediately dwarfing her small living room. As she shut the door behind him, he gave the room a quick sweep. She did the same, certain his astute gaze missed none of the untidiness—the teal blue and violet throw carelessly tossed over the off-white couch; the books of music piled in one of the matching pair of blue upholstered chairs that flanked the fireplace; the art book that lay open on top of the old brass-trimmed trunk that served as a coffee table.

Nor would he fail to notice the fuzzy, hot-pink slippers she'd discarded by the fireplace a couple of nights ago. They were blinking up at him like a neon light from the polished hardwood floor. And two days' worth of mail was piled on one end of the mantel, beside a small framed photo.

"Have a seat while I get rid of these." She snatched up a bud vase of wilting daisies from the end table next to the couch. If she couldn't clean up the rest of the room, at least she could dispense with the pathetic flowers. "I usually replace these on Friday, but the floral counter at the grocery store would be a zoo tonight. I'll be back in a sec."

Leaving him in the living room, she fled to the kitchen. After disposing of the limp daisies, she took a moment to draw a deep, calming breath. If Nick Bradley had struck her as powerful and imposing at the FBI office, his commanding presence in her tiny house was overwhelming. He seemed to fill the room with strength. And muscle. And masculinity. It was a heady combination.

But letting it *go* to her head was foolish. She knew that. She was a sensible person who recognized romantic fantasies for what they were—fantasy. Her reaction tonight was an aberration. Attributable to Valentine's Day, she was sure. And that reminded her of her plan to send Nick on his way with dispatch so he could get started on his own celebration.

He was still standing when she returned. Good. No use getting comfortable. He wouldn't be here long.

She moved behind the couch, keeping it between them as she rested her hands on the damask fabric. "I tried to call you back, but you'd already left. We can talk about the leak another time, Agent Bradley. I'm sure you have plans for this evening."

71

Silence greeted her comment. As it lengthened, the slight narrowing of his eyes, the tiny twitch of his lips, the merest tilt of his head told her he was debating his response.

"Unless working on my house rehab project counts as plans, no, I don't." The words came out slow and measured as he fixed her with a steady, candid gaze.

Rachel tried not to look too astonished at his disarming honesty. "Oh. Well . . . in any case, I hate to infringe on your free time."

One corner of his mouth quirked up. "I'm used to unusual hours. The bad guys never take a day off."

Her own lips twitched in response. "I guess that's true. Okay . . . if you're positive you don't mind, why don't I take your coat?"

He shrugged it off and handed it to her, waiting until she took a seat on one end of the couch before claiming the other end.

"I thought about the situation on the drive over." He shifted toward her and draped one arm across the upholstered back. "I had dinner with two couples last Friday night after you and I talked. They're the ones I told about your situation. Both of the men are agents. One of the couples lives in Virginia and was only here for the weekend. There was no opportunity for him or his wife to tell anyone in St. Louis. The other agent and his wife live here. I called him from my car. They haven't said anything to anyone, either. I'm thinking the leak had to be from your end. You mentioned you'd told a friend about the incident and asked her to check with her husband. Could anyone have overheard the two of you talking?"

"No. We were alone in the teachers' lounge."

"What about your friend or her husband? Could they have told someone else?"

"I asked Marta not to, and she promised me neither of them would say a word. I trust her."

72

Nick raked his fingers through his hair and shook his head. "This doesn't make sense."

"Kind of like the story I told you last week." Rachel flashed him a quick smile devoid of humor.

"Actually, that story seems more plausible to me now."

Rachel leaned forward intently. "What do you mean? Did you discover some information about the doll?"

"No. But the wife of one of the agents I had dinner with last week is a psychologist. She suggested the doll may be a trigger for some memory buried deep in your subconscious. And since the reaction only happens when you touch it, she thought the tactile sensation could be tapping into that memory."

Rachel's brow puckered. "I suppose that's possible. Looking at the doll doesn't bother me in the least. In fact, it gives me kind of a warm feeling. Only touching it is bad. I don't remember having a Raggedy Ann doll, but I spent my childhood in foster care and very little went with me from house to house. So I may have had one at some point."

His eyebrows arched. "You were a foster child?"

"Yes. My mother was killed in a car accident when I was nine months old. From what little I've been able to glean about her, she was a single mom with no family except a father who disowned her after she became pregnant. That's her, on the mantel. It's the only picture I have."

Nick examined the photo of the young auburn-haired mother. The highlights in Rachel's hair bore the same hue, but beyond that, he saw little resemblance. Yet she did remind him of someone, though he couldn't put his finger on who. And this wasn't the time to try and solve that riddle. At the moment, he was more interested in the woman beside him—and her surprising revelation.

Shifting his attention back to Rachel, Nick tipped his head. "No one adopted you?"

73

She gave him a rueful smile. "No one wanted me. I was in the accident too, and sustained serious injuries. You might have noticed my limp. This ankle has lots of bolts and screws." She wiggled her right foot. "I can't blame potential adoptive parents for backing off. Who would want to take on a kid with lots of injuries requiring multiple surgeries? So when I wasn't in the hospital or rehab, I was in foster care. A Raggedy Ann may have been part of my life, but if it was, the memory is buried very deep." She pulled her left leg under her. "Getting back to the reason for your visit—how do you think my story leaked to the press?"

Nick didn't want to talk about the leak. He wanted to find out more about the intriguing woman an arm's length away. Although she'd spoken about her background in a conversational, straightforward manner, the kind of trauma she'd endured must have taken a toll. Yet it didn't show. Rachel Sutton radiated a quiet, steady strength, suggesting she'd weathered the storms in her life admirably. Far better, he suspected, than he had. A dozen questions clamored to be asked. But a personal discussion wasn't the purpose of his visit tonight.

Leaning forward, he clasped his hands between his knees and concentrated on the matter at hand. "If you didn't tell anyone else, I think your friend is the key."

Rachel shook her head. "I don't buy that. The only time she and Joe talked about it was when they went to dinner last Thursday, and she said he agreed to keep it confidential."

"They were in a restaurant?"

"Yes."

"It's not difficult to eavesdrop in a public place."

"I suppose that's true, but the odds of someone in the media just happening to sit close enough to hear their conversation seem very low."

"Stranger things have happened. A lot of the tips we get are the result of people being in the right place at the right time. What restaurant did they go to?"

"I'm not sure. I could find out from her on Monday."

"How about tonight? I can ask the restaurant to check the credit card receipts from last Thursday and see if any of them belonged to Claudia Barnes. That could tell us how the leak happened. I'd rather nail this sooner than later."

"Sure. I can give her a call. With two kids under six, they're spending Valentine's Day watching an animated video." Flashing him a quick grin, Rachel rose. "Give me a couple of minutes."

True to her word, she was back in less than ninety seconds and relayed the information. "If there is a match, is there anything I can do to stop the story?"

Nick wished there was. From the little she'd told him about her past, it sounded like Rachel had endured far more than her share of difficulties. "I'd like to say yes, but the answer is not much. Freedom of the press and all that. Unfortunately, *St. Louis Scene* leans toward the more sensational stuff. They've called our media relations office in the past, trying to dig up information for crime-related stories, and despite our 'no comment' response, they tend to do the pieces anyway. A lot of what they write is speculation and conjecture, but they're careful to couch their coverage in those terms rather than present it as fact. Or they get quotes from pseudo experts or friends of victims. That buys them a lot of wiggle room."

Distress tightened Rachel's features. "In other words, I'm out of luck."

"Unless they decide not to run the story based on your un-willingness to cooperate."

"The reporter seemed very determined. I got the feeling she's not going to back down." Her shoulders slumped.

Nick tried to think of some way to console her. "Look at it this way, Ms. Sutton. Most people who know about or read

St. Louis Scene are aware of its reputation. I think readers take the coverage with a grain of salt. And the publication doesn't have a huge circulation. It's pretty much under the radar screen for the average St. Louisan. I suspect most of the people you associate with aren't the type who waste their time on that sort of tabloid. The coverage is also very fleeting. A week after it comes out, it will be old news."

Rachel's tense posture eased slightly, and the hint of a smile touched those soft lips. "Thanks for trying to put a better spin on this."

"Everything I said is true. But just to satisfy our curiosity, I'll check with the restaurant tomorrow morning and let you know what I find."

"I appreciate that."

His business was finished. It was time to leave. But Nick didn't move. Nor did Rachel.

In the sudden stillness, she ran the tip of her tongue over her lips in a gesture he'd come to recognize as nothing more than a nervous habit. Yet it managed to launch his pulse into overdrive. Her appeal was compounded by the flickering flames in the fireplace, which burnished the auburn highlights in her hair and brought a slight flush to her cheeks. He couldn't recall when he'd last met such a lovely, intelligent woman.

All at once, an idea began to percolate in his mind. Or perhaps inspiration was a better word. Both he and Rachel had unexciting plans for the evening. How would she react if he suggested they spend a couple of hours together? Not talking about dolls and vibes and media, but getting to know each other?

He tried to gauge her mood, but all he could pick up was nervousness. Not unlike what he'd sensed at the office a week ago. Except that day her eyes hadn't grown soft or held the yearning he thought he detected tonight in their depths. Unless he was seeing things he wanted to see rather than reality.

The only way to find out was to test the water.

"I guess that wraps things up for now." He remained seated, hoping for some signal that would suggest she might be open to an offer to extend the evening.

"I guess it does." She fumbled for one of the cushions in the corner of the couch and hugged it against her midsection. "I'm sorry I delayed your dinner. You must be hungry."

Yeah. He was. But food wasn't going to satisfy the sudden hunger inside him.

He cleared his throat. "It won't take me long to throw an omelet together."

She blinked. "You're making an omelet for dinner?"

One side of his mouth hitched up. "Believe it or not, I'm a decent cook."

"I didn't mean to imply you weren't. But an omelet doesn't seem like enough for . . ." The rosy hue of her cheeks deepened, and she lifted one shoulder in apology. "I mean, I'd sort of pegged you as the inch-thick-steak kind of guy."

"See how deceiving looks can be? I rarely eat beef—and have even been known to experiment with tofu, much to the disgust of my friends. But I must admit I made the same mistake about you. When we met, I sort of pegged you as . . ." He let the sentence trail off and gave her a half smile.

"A loony, I'm sure." She smiled in return. "I hope you've changed your opinion."

"Totally. And speaking of dinner . . . I bet you haven't eaten yet, either."

"No. I was getting ready to when the press came calling."

He removed his arm from the back of the couch and rose, his manner unhurried. "I'll let you get to it, then. I'm sure it's a far more exciting menu than mine."

Tossing the pillow aside, she stood too. He prayed her uncertain expression meant what he hoped it meant.

77

"It's not bad. I got a carryout of shrimp and broccoli linguini from one of my favorite restaurants on the way home."

"Definitely a better menu." He gave her an encouraging smile.

She did the lip-licking thing again. Rubbed her palms on her slacks. Adjusted her glasses. Tucked her hair behind her ear. All good signs, he hoped.

"Listen . . . I know this is rather impromptu, but . . . the pasta is in a very light sauce, so it's pretty healthy. I can't claim the same for the bread that came with it, or the chocolate torte I pilfered from the teachers' lounge. I do have the fixings for a salad in the fridge, though. Anyway, I appreciate your coming over, and I'd like to thank you in some way. If you'd care to stay for dinner, I have plenty."

Thank you, Lord.

Nick gave her a slow, warm smile. He couldn't care less about the food. All he wanted was a couple more hours in this woman's company. The gourmet menu was a bonus. "If you're sure, I'd love to join you. Tell me what I can do to help."

Her flush of pleasure at his acceptance kicked his pulse up a notch.

"Everything's made except the salad. And the bread will heat up in ten minutes. There's not much to do other than set the table."

"I can handle that if you point me in the right direction."

She gave a soft, nervous chuckle. "It's pretty hard to get lost in this house." She led the way through a doorway formed by a spindle-topped half wall that separated the living and dining rooms. As she flipped on the wall switch, the rich patina of a walnut table for four was bathed in warm light from a brass chandelier. Nick admired the contemporary glass candleholder in the center, where three large candles were displayed on staggered levels, and ran a swift glance over a small credenza on one side that held a unique raku pottery bowl, its distinctive iridescent glaze shimmering in the light.

But it was the far wall that held him spellbound.

Though the room was very small, a striking illusion of space had been created by a carefully lit mural. Coral-toned stucco arches framed a three-dimensional view of a large expanse of azure sea on the horizon. A few red-tile roofs were visible in the distance on the lush, green hillside, suggesting a Mediterranean setting. Sprays of bougainvillea dipped below the arches, and the fronds of a palm tree peeked into the scene from one side. An ornate white railing, with spindles that matched those above the half wall on the opposite side of the room, was topped with pots of colorful, exotic flowers he couldn't identify.

"Wow." Nick didn't know what else to say.

"I often get that reaction." Rachel grinned and folded her arms across her chest. "The effect is most dramatic from this angle."

Shoving back the edges of his jacket, Nick planted his hands on his hips and studied the rendering. "If I didn't know I was in St. Louis in the middle of winter, I'd try to walk out on that terrace to smell the flowers and take in the view."

"That's the magic of trompe l'oeil painting. It's designed to trick the eye and make you believe what you're seeing is real."

"It sure worked for me." He squinted, searching his memory. "I think I've heard that term somewhere. This technique goes back to the Middle Ages, doesn't it?"

"Very good." She gave him an approving smile. "Most people aren't familiar with the name, let alone the history. Actually, it goes back further than that. There are examples of it in Pompeii. But it was very popular during the Renaissance. A lot of wealthy people used it on the walls and ceilings of their palaces and villas to add drama or to open the rooms up and give them a grander scale. I decided that if it was good enough for them,

79

it was good enough for me. This room needed all the illusion of size it could get."

He shook his head. "It's amazing. Who did it?"

"A company called Painted Illusions."

"How did you find them?"

"It wasn't hard. You're looking at the founder, president, and sole employee."

Nick stared at her. "You did this?"

"Yes."

"I thought you were a teacher."

"I am. Music. This is a hobby that happens to make me a little money."

He examined the mural again. "Some hobby. How did you learn to do this?"

"I didn't have to learn. The talent was a gift." She smiled and leaned a shoulder against the wall beside her. "You know, if we keep getting sidetracked, we're never going to have dinner."

"True. I'll join you in the kitchen in a minute. I want to take a closer look at this."

"Not a good idea."

"Why not?"

"It loses its magic up close."

That was true of a lot of things, Nick mused as he regarded Rachel. Including the women he'd dated. But somehow he had a feeling this woman wouldn't lose her luster at close range.

"I'll take my chances."

At the husky timbre of his words and the sudden sizzle of electricity between them, her eyes widened and she took an involuntary step back. Turning, she pushed through the split, swinging louvered doors to the kitchen. "Take your time," she called over her shoulder.

There was a hint of panic in her voice. He felt a touch of it himself. It was obvious neither had anticipated that powerful jolt of electricity. He decided to follow her suggestion and take his time while he assessed this unexpected situation.

Okay. He'd come here tonight to follow up on her phone call. He'd had nothing better to do, and the thought of seeing the woman with the velvet brown eyes and lush lips had appealed to him. He'd expected to spend a pleasant few minutes with her, then head home to work on his house. That much was clear to him.

After that, things got murky.

He had no idea how his plans for a solitary evening rehabbing his house had evolved to sharing dinner with that lovely woman on the most romantic night of the year.

But he did know two things.

His Valentine's Day was turning out to be a lot better than he'd expected.

And Mark would be pleased.

6

As the doors from the dining room swung into place behind her, Rachel gripped the edge of the kitchen counter and tried to process the radical revision in her Valentine plans. Instead of a quiet, solitary evening she was going to have dinner in the company of a handsome man.

It was surreal.

Putting the bread in the oven, she moved to the fridge on autopilot to pull out salad fixings. Marta would be ecstatic, though. Her friend was always telling her to be more assertive, that if she met a man who interested her she should take the initiative. But that had never been her style. She'd always deemed it too risky.

Yet she'd taken the risk of inviting Nick Bradley for an impromptu dinner.

Why?

She could tell herself she'd issued the invitation out of gratitude. And it was true she was grateful for both his considerate treatment of her last week and his offer to stop by tonight and help her sort out the leak.

But that wasn't the whole truth. Gratitude alone couldn't account for the flutter in her stomach when she was with him. That was attraction, pure and simple. She'd been drawn to him at their first meeting, and his appeal had grown during tonight's visit. Bottom line, she'd taken the chance of inviting him for one simple reason: he seemed worth the risk.

Best of all, it had paid off. He'd accepted.

She tempered her sudden euphoria with realism, however. It was very possible he was just angling for a good meal. He might be a great cook, but most bachelors welcomed hassle-free, gratis meals. She doubted Nick was an exception.

Or he could have accepted because he enjoyed her company and wanted to spend a couple of hours with her. She liked that theory better . . . until it suddenly occurred to her that perhaps he'd read too much into her spontaneous invitation. It was Valentine's Day, after all. And a man like Nick probably received lots of similar overtures from women whose offer of dinner might include more than chocolate torte for dessert.

If that was the case, the evening would end in embarrassment for her and disappointment for him. Rachel had never believed in moving too fast in relationships. And she'd never regretted her caution. The appeal of the two men she'd dated for longer than a month had faded as she'd learned more about them. Even someone as handsome and charming as Nick wouldn't persuade her to change her modus operandi.

The doors from the dining room swung open, and she jumped as his broad shoulders filled the space.

"Reporting for duty." His smile faded as he scrutinized her. "Are you okay?"

She managed a half laugh as she tried to wrestle her nerves into submission. "A bit startled, but otherwise fine. I'm not used to company in my kitchen."

"In that case, I'm honored to be invited in." After one more probing look, he smiled and gave the compact but well-equipped galley a quick scan. "Point me to the cutlery."

"Top drawer next to the stove." She gestured toward the back of the house. "And there are placemats and napkins in the overhead cabinet. Salt and pepper is up there too. Butter's in the door of the fridge."

He rummaged around, withdrawing all the items she'd ticked off as she tossed the salad and filled water glasses. He shouldered his way through the swinging doors several times as he set the table, chatting about inconsequential things and moving with an unhurried efficiency that helped calm Rachel's nerves.

Ten minutes later, as they carried their plates into the dining room, she discovered Nick had lit the candles and put on a CD. His choice of music also eased her apprehension—classical violin versus one of the more romantic selections in her collection.

"This smells delicious." He held her chair as she took her seat. "Far better than any omelet I could have concocted." He sat and shook out his napkin, surveying the appetizing plate of pasta in front of him. "Would you mind if I said a brief blessing first?"

The request took Rachel off guard. A macho guy who not only prayed but wasn't afraid to admit it. Remarkable. And comforting. That request did more to put her at ease about his intentions than anything else he could have said or done. "No. That's fine."

To her surprise, he took her hand in a warm clasp as he bowed his head. "Lord, we thank you for this food and for the opportunity to share a meal. Please keep us in your care, and help us to always appreciate the unexpected pleasures that grace our days. Amen."

He released her hand to pick up his fork, and she immediately missed the touch of his firm, lean fingers.

"I noticed your necklace last week, and again tonight." He gestured to the cross that lay against her forest green angora sweater, suspended from a slender gold chain. "That's why I felt comfortable asking about the blessing. It's lovely, by the way."

"It was my mother's." She fingered the delicate filigreed pendant. "It's the only thing of hers I have, aside from the photo. I wear it a lot. It helps me feel connected to her somehow. And gives me some sense of family."

"Is that the only reason you wear it?" Nick took a piece of the crusty bread from the basket.

"If you're asking me whether it's a statement of faith, the answer is no. I suppose I believe in what it symbolizes . . . in theory, anyway. But during my years in foster care I was exposed to all sorts of denominations, and that smorgasbord of beliefs confused me more than converted me."

"That's understandable. Giving a child too many choices can bewilder instead of enlighten. I was in my mid-teens before the message took root in me, thanks to the intervention of a very caring cop."

"Intervention. An interesting word choice. Is there a story there?"

Uh-oh.

Nick lifted his water glass and took a long, slow sip. He'd walked right into that one. Rachel's question might be innocent, but his past wasn't. And it had been an off-limits subject for years. He could count on one hand the trusted friends who were privy to his checkered youth. Although he'd straightened himself out, he wasn't proud of some of the things he'd done in his younger days. And he saw no reason to dredge up all that ugliness.

Setting the glass back on the table, he forced his lips into a smile. "Not anything worth repeating."

Rachel regarded him for a second, and a faint touch of pink colored her cheeks as she reached for her own water glass. "Sorry. I didn't mean to pry."

As she lifted the goblet, the bottom caught the edge of her plate and tipped toward her. Nick grabbed for it, his hand closing over hers as he steadied the glass. The sloshing water stabilized . . . but he couldn't say the same for his pulse. At the feel of her slender fingers beneath his, his heart began to thud in an odd, erratic rhythm.

"Sorry again." Her color deepening, Rachel tugged her hand out from under his and set the goblet back on the table with exaggerated care. "I don't know why I've been so jittery lately."

"A strange experience with a doll may be one of the reasons." Nick wound some linguini around his fork and speared a shrimp, trying to get his pulse under control.

"My jumpiness predates that incident by weeks. A sense of anxiety just hit me out of the blue one Saturday morning." A sudden frown marred her brow, and a flash of regret echoed in her eyes. "I shouldn't have told you that. It sounds almost as weird as the doll story. And I'd prefer you think of me as a normal person instead of some loony."

"Trust me. I don't think of you as a loony. We all go through stressful periods. Have you been under a lot more pressure than usual?"

"No. That's what makes it so weird."

"Maybe you're too busy. Between teaching and painting murals, you must not have much downtime."

She toyed with her fork, conceding the point with a slight lift of her shoulders. "I do lead a busy life. In addition to work and murals, I also have quite a few private piano students. And I play the piano during high tea every Sunday." She named the upscale hotel.

"Sounds like you're stretched a little thin. I suspect you could use a vacation."

"That would be nice. But it's not likely to happen soon. How about you? I'd be willing to bet no grass grows under your feet. I imagine your job is pretty taxing, yet you mentioned rehabbing a house?"

Rehab was a subject he felt comfortable talking about. Plaster, paint, drywall, flooring . . . all safe topics. "Yes. It's an old Federal-style brick built in 1852. Before I bought it, the bats and cockroaches had called it home for ten years."

"Wow. That's ambitious."

He chuckled. "My friends have less flattering ways to describe it. But despite all the dire warnings, it's coming along great. The only problem is, I doubt I'll have much of a chance to enjoy it. I expect I'll be looking at a transfer about the time it's done."

"Do you move often?"

"Every few years. I don't usually mind heading to a new office, but this house will be tough to leave."

"I can understand that, after all your work." Rachel buttered a piece of bread and sent him a curious look. "May I ask why you took it on, knowing you'd have to leave it behind?"

So much for safe topics. They were moving into "no trespassing" territory again, and he proceeded with caution. "I buy a house wherever I'm assigned. Nothing quite this elaborate, but always a fixer-upper I can rescue and pass on at a reasonable price to a young family that might not otherwise be able to afford a house. For some reason I was blessed with a natural talent for rehab, and I get a kick out of making silk purses out of sows' ears. Although I have to admit plumbing isn't my forte." Nick ended his response on a lighthearted note in the hope Rachel would smile in return and change the subject.

No such luck.

"That's an incredibly generous gesture." Her eyes softened in admiration, and the pleasing, warm glow that radiated through Nick was similar to the feeling he got when he sold a house to a deserving young family. But stronger. Much stronger.

Clearing his throat, he shrugged, unsure how to respond to her praise. "It's a nice hobby. Sawing and hammering are a great way to relieve job stress. I get as much out of it as anyone."

"I suspect the young families who benefit would disagree."

Rachel leaned back in her chair and scrutinized him. He could almost hear the wheels whirring in her brain and braced for whatever she might come up with next. Despite his initial doubts during her visit to the FBI office last week, there was nothing wrong with this woman's mental capacity.

"I'm thinking your childhood was either idyllic and you want to create that same experience for others, or it was far from ideal and you want to support young parents who are trying to make a good life for their children."

Nor was there anything wrong with her insight or deductive reasoning. Plus, she was considerate. She'd commented, not queried, lobbing the conversational ball into his court. He could deflect it—or keep it in play. She'd left the decision up to him.

As Nick debated his strategy, he suddenly thought of the countless prayers he'd uttered asking the Lord to let a special woman grace his life. Maybe Rachel Sutton was destined to be that woman.

If he took the next step.

In his gut, Nick sensed he was at a crossroads. In the past, whenever a woman he was dating started to probe about his past, he'd retreated. His evasive maneuvers had become instinctive, and they were on the verge of kicking in now. But if he chose that route, he sensed he'd be closing the door with Rachel. Because no woman would consider linking her future to a man who shut her out. Whose pride kept him from revealing mistakes as well as triumphs. Who was afraid to trust her with the secrets of his heart.

Not that he was ready to lay out his whole sordid history. It was too soon for that. Yet Rachel had shared much of her past with him tonight, talking openly about her mother, the traumatic accident that had left her with a permanent limp, her rejection by adoptive parents, her foster upbringing. And she'd answered his questions about faith—a very personal subject—with candor.

All he'd offered her in return was a single enigmatic comment about an influential cop and one tiny insight into his rehab projects.

It wasn't enough to sustain an evening, let alone lay the groundwork for future evenings.

As the silence between them lengthened, Rachel flashed him a smile that didn't quite reach her eyes and placed her empty salad plate on top of her dinner plate. "I hope you left room for dessert—unhealthy though it is. But I have to say that's the cleanest plate I've ever seen."

She stood, resting a hand lightly on his shoulder as he started to rise. "It doesn't take two to put on the coffee and cut the cake. Why don't we have dessert in the living room by the fire?" She reached for his plate but froze when he placed his hand on hers.

"My childhood was the latter, Rachel. Far from ideal." He stared at the empty plate in front of him as he spoke.

"I'm sorry, Nick." Empathy softened her words.

"I don't talk about it much."

"I don't talk a lot about my past, either. It brings back memories I'd prefer to forget. Especially the medical stuff. But all the things that happened to me thirty-plus years ago are what made me who I am. To understand me, my friends need to know some of that history. I share on a selective basis."

Her meaning wasn't lost on Nick. Touched, he tipped his head up to search her face. She flushed under his scrutiny; an endearing trait, one he valued for its rarity. And for what it implied.

"If you're still interested in my cop story, I'll tell you some of it over dessert."

Her lips lifted into a smile. Genuine this time. "I'd like that. Make yourself comfortable and I'll be back in a minute."

Nick wandered into the living room to the fireplace. He shoved his hands deep into the pockets of his slacks, trying to decide how much he wanted to share. But Rachel didn't give him a chance to ponder that question, reappearing so fast Nick wondered if she'd rushed the dessert preparations out of fear that if she left him alone too long, he'd change his mind.

89

And she wasn't far off the mark. His feet had already grown cold despite the warm, cheery fire mere steps away.

As she transferred the coffee and cake from the tray to the top of the trunk in silence, the irony of his situation wasn't lost on him. Last summer, when Mark had been using his house as a hotel, he'd given his friend a hard time about not acting on his feelings for Emily. He'd encouraged him to dive into the emotional stuff and be open about how he felt. To count his blessings that someone like Emily had come into his life. He even remembered boasting to Mark that he paid attention to feelings and wasn't afraid to talk about them, and suggesting Mark follow his example.

Now he was learning firsthand how difficult it could be to apply those principles.

"I brought cream and sugar. Do you use either?"

At Rachel's comment, Nick left the fireplace and joined her on the couch, keeping a safe distance between them. "No. Black is fine."

"Strong and straight. How come I knew that?" She smiled at him as she added two teaspoons of sugar to her own mug, plus a generous portion of cream.

"The same way you pegged me as a one-inch-thick-steak kind of guy?"

She wrinkled her nose. "Touché. That faux pas should have taught me never to jump to conclusions or make sweeping generalizations based on stereotypes." She took a sip of her coffee and set the mug on a coaster. Picking up her cake, she sent him a speculative look. "Having second thoughts about sharing the cop story?"

Nick picked up his mug. Nothing got past this woman. She seemed as tuned in to vibes from people as she was from a certain Raggedy Ann doll.

In truth, though, he was way past second thoughts. Third or

fourth would be more accurate. But he'd already promised to share a piece of his history. Taking a fortifying sip of the coffee, he wrapped his fingers around the mug and held on.

"For the cop story to make sense, I have to back up a little. It seems you and I have something in common besides jumping to conclusions based on stereotypes. I was a foster child too."

"This *is* a night for surprises. That's quite a coincidence."

"I agree. Anyway, I entered the system when I was six."

"Why?"

His grip on the mug tightened. "My mother died when I was five, and my father was . . . had issues. The state eventually took me away from him, and I spent the rest of my childhood in a succession of foster homes."

"No one adopted you?"

"No. I didn't have physical problems, like you did, but I wasn't the most loveable kid. I had attitude and behavior issues that turned people off. Those worsened as I got older. During my freshman year in high school, I was picked up for truancy way too often. Plus, I got in with a bad crowd that was into petty theft, minor drugs, vandalism. There's no doubt in my mind that if I'd stayed on that path much longer, I'd have ended up dead down the road. Or behind bars."

"What happened?"

"Dan Foley. A new Detroit truant officer, gung ho and aggressive, who was determined to salvage as many kids as he could. For some reason he took a special interest in me. No one had ever done that before." The last word came out raspy, and he took a swig of his coffee, blindsided by a sudden, choking rush of emotion. He took a second swig as Rachel waited in her corner of the couch, her legs pulled up under her.

"Would you like a refill?"

At her soft question, he nodded. "Yeah. Thanks." He could use a couple of minutes to regain his composure.

By the time she topped off his mug and resettled into her corner, he was ready to continue.

"At first I brushed Dan off. But he kept showing up. Started talking to me. Taking me to ball games or out for a burger. He even gave me his personal phone number and told me to call anytime. Eventually I began to believe his concern was genuine, that I mattered to him."

"He sounds like a remarkable man."

"He was. I met him the September of my sophomore year, a week shy of my sixteenth birthday, and in November he invited me to his home for Thanksgiving dinner. That gesture, more than anything else, convinced me he really cared. And that he trusted me—which blew my mind. The only condition placed on the invitation was that I had to go to morning services with him, his wife, and his two college-age kids who were home for the holiday. But I figured it was a small price to pay for a home-cooked turkey dinner. Anyway, at the risk of sounding overly dramatic, that day changed my life. I found a surrogate family, and I found God."

Rachel drew a deep breath, her forgotten cake resting on her lap. "That's an amazing story."

Yes, it was. And she didn't know the half of it. He'd left out a lot of the more disturbing details, sure that getting just the bare bones out would be hard enough.

But much to his surprise, it hadn't been as difficult as he'd expected, except for that one brief moment when his self-control faltered. Under Rachel's warm, sympathetic gaze, the words had come without great effort. Instead of feeling as if he were taking a risk by sharing his past, he'd felt safe. It was a new—and oddly freeing—experience.

When the silence lengthened, Rachel leaned forward. "How did you end up in the FBI, Nick?"

That part of his story was easy. "I dumped my so-called friends, buckled down in my studies, and ended up winning a scholarship to college. After I got a degree in law enforcement and criminology, I went straight to the police academy. After seven years as a beat officer, I was accepted at the FBI academy."

"Wow. I bet Dan Foley was proud."

"He would have been." A melancholy smile whispered at the corners of his mouth. "He died ten years ago, a few months before I joined the FBI. But I have a feeling he knows." Clearing his throat, he gestured toward her untouched cake and picked up his fork. "You haven't eaten your dessert."

She considered the torte in her lap. "That proves how amazing your story was. There isn't much that can distract me from chocolate."

As they dug into their cake, Nick turned the focus of the conversation back on Rachel, querying her about her music, and laughing over some of her kids-do-the-darnedest-things tales. He insisted on helping with the cleanup, ditching his jacket, loosening his tie, and rolling up his sleeves as he rinsed and stacked the plates, mugs, and silverware in her dishwasher.

"Thanks for pitching in with the dishes, Nick." Rachel wiped down the counter and dried her hands on a towel.

Somewhere along the way they'd slipped into first names. Nick couldn't pinpoint when it had happened. But it felt natural—and comfortable.

"It was the least I could do after the great meal you provided." He rolled his sleeves back down and checked his watch. He wouldn't mind hanging around for a while, but the invitation had been for dinner—and dinner was over. He didn't want to overstay his welcome. "I better be going. The snow's piling up." He indicated the kitchen window, where flakes continued to swirl against the glass. "Besides, I've infringed enough on your plans for reading that good book."

Her momentary blank look suggested the book Rachel had

mentioned had lost its allure. Her next words confirmed that. "It will keep." She leaned back against the counter, gripping it with both hands. "I had a good time tonight, Nick."

He gave her a slow smile. "I did too. Maybe we can do it again."

"I'd like that."

Their gazes locked, and Nick had to fight down the temptation to steal a kiss from those tantalizing lips. Although it seemed like a fitting end to their unexpected Valentine dinner, he was uncertain how Rachel would react. And he wasn't about to shoot himself in the foot by coming on too strong to a woman he hoped to see a whole lot more of.

"Let me get my jacket." With a triumph of will over desire, he returned to the dining room and snagged his suit coat off the back of the chair where he'd draped it. As he slipped his arms into the sleeves, Rachel retrieved his overcoat from the closet by the front door. She handed it to him in silence when he joined her, and he shrugged it on.

"I hope the roads are okay." A slight tremor ran through her words, and her fingers weren't quite steady as she flipped the lock on the door and cracked it open.

It didn't take a psychic to detect her nervousness. And while he saw yearning in her eyes, it was tempered with worry. And uncertainty.

Definitely no kiss tonight.

Instead, he stroked a gentle finger along the elegant curve of her cheekbone—and heard the breath catch in her throat. "Thank you for a memorable Valentine's Day, Rachel. I'll be in touch."

"I'd like that." She pulled the door open, admitting a gusty flurry of snowflakes. "Drive safe."

With a wave of acknowledgment, he bent his head into the wind and strode toward his car. Stalks of dead foliage poked above the accumulating snow along the walk, bringing to mind the wilting daisies Rachel had pitched soon after he'd arrived.

Why wasn't there a man in her life who cared enough to send flowers on this special day? She was smart, pretty, well-read. She had a good sense of humor, great instincts, fabulous listening skills. It blew his mind that some guy hadn't snatched her up by now.

How she'd managed to remain single into her thirties was a puzzle he couldn't solve. But he did know one thing.

A woman like Rachel deserved roses on Valentine's Day.

7

The long-stemmed beauties came on Saturday afternoon, accompanied by a simple "Thank you for a wonderful dinner" note. There was a small postscript at the bottom. "I found a match at the restaurant. I wish all my cases were that easy to solve."

As Rachel tore off the green tissue and inhaled the pleasing fragrance of the crimson blooms, a smile played at her lips. She hadn't expected Nick to send flowers, but she wasn't surprised he had. He struck her as that kind of guy. A man who paid his debts and always tried to do the right thing. A man of integrity, who was strong enough to admit he didn't have all the answers and wasn't afraid to acknowledge his reliance on God. A man who believed in giving back and helping others. A man who could dominate her thoughts—and dreams.

Her other impressions might be perception, but the last was fact. He'd been doing it since he left her at the door last night, keeping her sleepless into the wee hours of the morning.

Good thing she didn't have any urgent tasks on her agenda today.

Rachel set the vase on the trunk in the living room and fingered a velvet petal, rearranged a spray of baby's breath, adjusted the red satin ribbon.

No one had ever sent her roses.

She tried to temper her rush of pleasure with a dose of reality, cautioning herself that it might be standard procedure for Nick to reciprocate with flowers for favors. But even that caution didn't diminish her pleasure in the gesture. Nor lessen her yearning to know more about him. What he'd told her had merely whetted her appetite. Dozens of questions had sprung to mind last night as he'd given her a condensed version of his history.

What had happened to his mother?

Why had the state taken him away from his father?

What sort of behavior and attitude issues had he grappled with as a child?

How had he found his way to God?

Why wasn't he married?

And those were just the tip of the iceberg.

But Rachel suspected Nick wouldn't be comfortable with most of those topics. She'd watched him struggle with his brief disclosures last night. While she was touched—and grateful— he'd made the effort, she knew there was much he'd left unsaid. That he'd wrestled with difficult challenges, and that many of his lessons had been learned in the school of hard knocks. Yet he'd turned into a man who chose to fight crime rather than commit it. A man who rescued houses and prayed and sent roses.

She was intrigued. And she wanted details.

Considering his reticence last night, however, in the light of day he might decide to stay far away from the woman who had nudged him beyond his comfort level. Perhaps the roses were his way of fulfilling his "I'll be in touch" promise.

If she were the praying kind, Rachel would ask God to let the flowers be the beginning, not the end.

But whatever fate held in store, she'd never forget her im-promptu Valentine date. It would always serve as a reminder that life can be graced by unexpected pleasures, as Nick had noted in his blessing before the meal. And that it can be changed by seemingly chance events.

Like meeting a caring cop.

Or finding a battered Raggedy Ann doll.

Claudia drummed her manicured nails on the steering wheel and huffed out a frustrated breath as she stared at the building across the street, behind the black iron fence. Her Monday-morning mission to the FBI office had been a bust. Showing up in person had done zip for her cause. Ellen Levine, the media relations manager, had been cordial but close-mouthed.

Why her editor had suddenly gotten scruples about this article was beyond her. Stacy had approved Mitch's stupid fluff piece on dueling chefs at two rival restaurants. Like that was really going to sell papers. Who cared which guy's toasted ravioli tasted better?

Her article, on the other hand, was both meaty and compelling. She'd done hours of research, unearthing some pretty interesting stuff in the process—including a legendary local psychic from forty years ago who had actually provided assistance to law enforcement. That was her claim in interviews, anyway. And the cops hadn't denied it. But that local angle hadn't been good enough for Stacy. No, her editor wanted a *current* psychic with *proven* law enforcement connections to lead off the piece.

And Rachel Sutton was the only one Claudia had been able to find.

Unfortunately, the woman had refused to confirm she'd talked to the FBI.

Too bad she couldn't corral an agent or two, Claudia mused, watching as two tall men in suits exited the building, perhaps heading for lunch. But neither the dark-haired man or the all-American guy was likely to talk. FBI agents were well-schooled in how to deal with the media. They'd send her back to Levine.

The two men headed in the opposite direction, and she turned the key in the ignition, disgusted.

What a way to start the work week.

But she wasn't giving up yet. An idea would come to her. It always did.

★

"I'll have a small house salad with low-fat dressing." Mark closed his menu and handed it to the waitress.

"What happened to your usual burger?" Nick arched an eyebrow.

"I overdid the calories Friday night. I need to cut back this week."

"Hmm. Turkey club for me," Nick told the waitress, passing over the laminated menu. "Was it worth it?"

"Oh yeah." Mark leaned back in the booth and grinned. "The food was great. But the company was even better. A perfect Valentine's Day. What did you end up doing? Wait . . . let me guess." He pretended to give it serious consideration. "You worked on the house."

"For a while." Nick selected a pack of crackers he didn't want from the small basket on the Formica table in the diner, tore it open, and popped one in his mouth. He'd been too keyed up to sleep when he arrived home Friday night and had spent a couple of hours installing crown molding in the master bedroom. Meaning his response wasn't a lie. "Speaking of houses, did you and Emily do any hunting this weekend? I thought your goal was to be out of her condo by spring."

"It is and no, we didn't. The snow gave us a good excuse to stay home and . . . veg." He winked and his grin broadened.

One side of Nick's mouth quirked up. "Still in the honeymoon phase, I see. Anyway, there's a nice fixer-upper in my neighborhood."

"Forget it. I've already inhaled my lifetime allotment of drywall dust, thanks to you."

99

"I warned you about that before you came last summer."

"I assumed your reference to the house as a construction site was an exaggeration, not a literal description."

"I'm always honest."

"So I learned. By the way, did you ever figure out how the press heard about the doll lady?"

"Yeah. She'd asked a friend whose husband is a cop to see what he recommended, and they talked about it when they went out to dinner. I called the restaurant, and the manager ran the credit card receipts from that night. The reporter was there."

"How did you find out the woman talked to her friend about it?"

"She told me."

"You didn't mention that when you called me Friday night to check if Emily or I had mentioned the story to anyone."

This was starting to get sticky.

"I asked her after that."

"You called this woman back on your night off?"

"No." Nick popped the other cracker in his mouth.

Mark narrowed his eyes. "What's with the crackers?"

"What do you mean?"

"You never eat crackers. You always say they're wasted calories and too high in fat."

"I'm making an exception today."

"Why?"

"What is this, the third degree?" Nick complained.

Several beats of silence ensued. Mark hadn't been selected for the FBI's elite Hostage Rescue Team because he was a slouch, and Nick knew he was rapidly putting two and two together. Nick's vague answer and irritation, plus his admission that Rachel was good-looking, plus his uncharacteristic eating behavior added up to an obvious conclusion.

"You went to see her, didn't you?"

Mark had figured it out even faster than Nick expected.

"Yeah, I did. She was very upset about the leak. I wanted to verify that it didn't come from our end and help her get to the bottom of it."

Folding his arms across his chest, Mark leaned back and smirked. "Whatever you say. Did you have a nice visit?"

"She was very pleasant."

Mark laughed outright. "Give me a break. You said a week ago she was pretty. And I seem to recall you using words like sincere, intelligent, articulate. What's wrong with admitting you like a woman? And now that Emily has offered a reasonable explanation for the doll phenomenon, you don't have to worry about her being a nutcase. The door's wide open—if the lady's interested. What kind of vibes did you pick up when you stopped by?"

"Pretty good." Nick shifted on the seat and wiped up some condensation from his iced tea glass with a paper napkin.

"That's a start. How long did you stay?"

There were few people Nick trusted implicitly. Mark was one of them. Though their paths had taken different directions after their Academy days, converging again on a daily basis only in the past six months, they'd never lost touch. If Nick was going to begin sharing personal information with anyone, the man across from him would be a safe choice.

"Three hours."

Choking on his soda, Mark groped for a napkin from the metal holder and wiped his mouth. "You stayed three hours?"

"Yeah."

"I hope you bought the lady dinner."

"No. She offered to feed me."

Mark chuckled and shook his head. "You're full of surprises today. And here I was worried about your love life."

"It was only a dinner, Mark."

101

"True." He took another, more cautious, sip of soda. "You plan to make it anything more? If the lady didn't have plans on Valentine's Day, she must be available."

"I'm considering it."

"Don't consider too long, my friend. As you advised me last summer when I was trying to decide what to do about Emily, don't let a great opportunity slip through your fingers. I recall you saying that women like Emily don't come along every day. You were right. And the doll lady might fall into the same category."

"Your situation was different. You guys had known each other years before. You had a history together."

"So start creating one with . . . what's her name, by the way?"

"Rachel."

"With Rachel. Maybe you could send her flowers to thank her for dinner."

It was Nick's turn to smile. "I already did."

"Good for you." Mark grinned. "And a smart move. Women melt when they get flowers."

"I'll keep that in mind." Nick stirred his iced tea and sent his friend a wry glance.

"Hey, I'm just trying to help. You wouldn't want to let the right woman slip away."

Nick stopped stirring. "Aren't you rushing things a little? I've known Rachel all of ten days."

"It doesn't take long to sense if a relationship has potential. And this one sounds promising."

"You're jumping to way too many conclusions."

"Nope. I've been there. I know the smitten signs."

"Oh, please. Spare me."

"Look at the evidence." Mark leaned forward and ticked it off on his fingers. "A, you gave Rachel the benefit of the doubt last week despite her implausible story. B, when we all met for dinner that night, you defended her sanity even before Emily proposed her theory. C, you admitted Rachel was pretty and noted her other sterling qualities. D, you went out of your way to visit her on Valentine's night. E, you stayed when she invited you to dinner. And F, you sent her roses." Mark sat back. "Verdict? Smitten."

As an FBI agent, Nick knew how to evaluate evidence. And it was hard to refute Mark's conclusion. He did like Rachel. A lot. And while he had no intention of rushing into a relationship, he did plan to give it a chance and see where things led.

"Well?" Mark prodded when he didn't respond.

"No comment."

Mark chuckled and speared a forkful of lettuce. "I rest my case."

✦

Well, wasn't that interesting.

Claudia slouched in her car and watched the tall, sandy-haired guy she'd seen at FBI headquarters on Monday step out of a car and greet Rachel in the parking lot of Madeleine's restaurant. She smiled as he took the woman's arm, nodded toward the entrance, and escorted her to the door.

Yes!

Claudia now had her connection! Rachel was talking to the FBI. She'd seen it with her own eyes.

And a good thing too. She'd given herself until Wednesday noon to get the psychic story approved, and this was a photo finish. For most of the past two days she'd spent every spare minute trailing Rachel, hoping to find some link to local law enforcement. It had been a long shot, and she honestly hadn't expected it to pay off. This new development was almost too good to believe.

It would be better, though, if she could get Rachel to comment on her contact with the agency. As a plan formed in her mind, Claudia put the car in gear and headed toward the school where Rachel taught in the afternoon. There wasn't much chance the woman would bend, considering her adamant refusal to participate last week. Still, now that Claudia had established a definite connection to the FBI, it was worth a try.

But while her input would be great, Claudia was pretty sure Stacy would give her the green light to proceed with or without Rachel's comment. How could she not? Claudia had observed a meeting between the woman and an FBI agent.

And where there was smoke, there was usually fire.

☆

The only empty parking space Rachel could find at Stafford Elementary was at the far end of the icy lot, requiring a long walk in wind chills near zero. But considering the warm glow left over from her hour with Nick, she doubted she'd notice the frigid cold.

His call last night suggesting they meet for lunch had left her with a tingle of anticipation that had played havoc with her sleep and brightened her morning despite the heavy gray clouds suggesting the imminent arrival of yet another storm. And their too-brief interlude had lived up to all her expectations. In deference to her limited time, he'd chosen a restaurant on the route that linked the two schools where she taught—yet more evidence of his consideration and thoughtfulness. And the small tea room had been charming, with French décor, excellent food, and a quiet ambiance conducive to conversation.

He'd taken charge of the latter from the outset, skillfully guiding the discussion from movies and books to travel and hobbies. It had been more like a typical first date than their unexpected

Valentine dinner had been. Nothing heavy, just a pleasant exchange that put them both at ease. And that was okay with her. If things developed between them, if their comfort level with each other grew, there would be opportunities for heavier discussions later.

Best of all, he'd left her in the parking lot with a promise to call again.

Rachel was so focused on reliving their lunch—and avoiding the icy patches on the asphalt—that she didn't notice Claudia Barnes until the woman fell into step beside her.

"Hello, Ms. Sutton."

Taken aback by the reporter's unexpected appearance, Rachel jolted to a stop.

"Sorry to startle you." The woman smiled. "I wanted to let you know my story will be running in Friday's edition. And that there's still time for me to incorporate a couple of quotes from you. I wouldn't want you to give away anything that might compromise an investigation, of course, but a general comment or two about your discussion with the FBI agent at lunch today would be great."

Tension coiled in Rachel's stomach. "Have you been following me?"

"Doing research," the woman corrected.

"I told you I don't want anything to do with your story. And I also don't appreciate you eavesdropping on my friends during private dinners at restaurants." Rachel resumed her trek toward the school, sorry now she hadn't found a parking place closer to the entrance.

Her comment seemed to take the reporter off guard, but the woman recovered with alacrity and fell into step beside her. "I commend your friendly FBI agent for his investigative skills."

"It wasn't difficult to figure out where you got your lead. I only told the story to a couple of people." Rachel picked up her pace.

"Ms. Sutton, be reasonable." The reporter matched her stride for stride. "The story will run with or without your participation. If questioned on the facts, I'm willing to stand in front of a judge and say I heard the doll story myself from your friend and that I witnessed you conversing with an FBI agent. You might as well make a comment."

Rachel came to an abrupt halt and faced the woman, anger nipping at her words. "For your information, Ms. Barnes, my lunch with Nick had nothing to do with that doll. Furthermore, it's been suggested to me that the doll simply triggered some memory from my childhood. I believe that's a reasonable explanation. Implying I'm a psychic, let alone that there's a crime connection to my experience, is not only a stretch, it's very misleading. Please don't bother me again."

Turning on her heel, Rachel covered the remaining distance to the double glass doors at a half-run. She was afraid the woman would follow her into the school, but to her relief the reporter halted a few steps from the entrance. As the door swung shut, Rachel peeked over her shoulder. Claudia Barnes smiled, waved, and walked away.

Once the woman disappeared, Rachel sagged against the wall, giving her unsteady legs a second to recover. She wanted to ring Nick, but a quick glance at her watch confirmed she was running late for her first class of the afternoon. The call would have to wait. Besides, it wasn't urgent. There was nothing he could do about the situation. Yet the mere sound of his voice would reassure her.

And the pleasant implications of that fact helped dispel the anxiety Claudia Barnes had left in her wake.

★

"I hear you're collecting dolls."

His topcoat half shrugged off, Nick pivoted toward the opening of his cube. Ellen Levine regarded him, her expression difficult to read. A former reporter, the svelte, fiftysomething media relations manager was a savvy spokesperson who knew all the tricks of the trade. She could court—or divert—the media, depending on which tactic best suited the FBI's purpose.

Thoughts of his lunch with Rachel had distracted him all afternoon as he drove around following up on leads for a case, but Nick's focus sharpened at the woman's comment. "Where did you hear that?"

"A certain reporter by the name of Claudia Barnes. *St. Louis Scene.*"

"How did she connect me to this?"

"You'd have to ask her that yourself. She wouldn't answer that question for me."

"When did she call?"

"Two-thirty. That was her second attempt to get information, by the way. She showed up in person on Monday. Claims a psychic by the name of Rachel Sutton brought a doll here ten days ago, saying it gave her bad vibes. Is that true?"

Hanging his coat on a hook in the corner of his cube, Nick perched on the edge of his desk. "Yes. All except the psychic part. Rachel Sutton is not, and did not claim to be, a psychic. I filed a 302 and an FD-71 and considered it closed until Ms. Sutton called to inform me the press had contacted her. This Claudia Barnes overheard a friend of Ms. Sutton's talking about the situation to her husband in a restaurant and decided it was newsworthy."

"I doubt the reporter had your name Monday when she stopped by, or she would have used it. Any idea how she got it?"

"No." Nick knew Rachel wouldn't have given it to her.

"What did you do with this doll?"

He tipped his head toward the small shopping bag shoved in the corner of his office, under the workspace.

Leaning into his cube, Ellen surveyed the disreputable-looking Raggedy Ann smiling back at her from the shadows. "Why did you hold onto it?"

"I'm not sure. It's probably full of germs."

"That would be a safe bet." She straightened. "Barnes claims *St. Louis Scene* is going to run a story on paranormal phenomena and that both you and Ms. Sutton will be mentioned. She wanted a statement from us."

"I assume you said no comment."

"Yes. This is more a heads-up that your name will soon be in print."

"I've had worse things happen. But I'm sorry if this is causing problems for you or the Bureau."

Her lips twitched. "I've dealt with tougher issues. So has the FBI." She gestured toward the doll. "If you want my advice, wear gloves when you pitch it."

As Ellen exited, Nick noticed the blinking light on his phone. Preoccupied, he punched in the code, half listening to his messages. Until he got to the one from Rachel.

"Nick, I wanted to let you know that Claudia Barnes was waiting for me in the parking lot at school after our lunch. She saw us at the restaurant. I think she's been following me. I brushed her off, but I realized later I might have said your first name. I'm afraid, with her tenacity, she might find out your last name and try to contact you. I wanted to warn you." There was a slight pause, and when she continued the worry in her voice had been replaced with warmth. "I also wanted to thank you again for lunch. It was lovely. The best part of my day. Take care." The line went dead.

Another mystery solved. If Rachel had told the determined reporter his first name, it would have been an easy matter for her to track him down. He was the only Nick at the office. A simple phone call to the receptionist asking to be transferred to his line would have supplied the information she was after.

But Rachel's slip revealed her inexperience with the press. And also suggested she was ill-equipped to deal with the fallout the article could produce. While he'd reassured her that most people took the coverage in *St. Louis Scene* with a grain of salt, and that readership wasn't that high, the story would bring a few weirdos out of the woodwork. She needed some preparation for that. And a little moral support wouldn't hurt, either.

He could supply both.

Besides, it gave him a good excuse to hang around with her over the weekend. A smile tugged at his lips as he dropped the receiver back into the cradle.

And that was one piece of fallout he didn't mind in the least.

8

Debra swung into a parking spot near the front door of Little Folks Academy, lamenting as always the need for child care. If things had gone as planned, she'd be a stay-at-home mom. But at least her salary as a paralegal allowed her to be selective in her daycare choice. She tried to take some consolation in that.

As she stepped inside the building, the other harried parents who'd come to claim their children gave her no more than a passing glance or a brief, distracted nod. That was fine with her. She didn't want to get chummy with anyone. Danielle was all she needed.

"Oh, hi, Ms. Kraus." Marsha, one of the college-age girls who helped with the afternoon rush, gave her a frazzled smile. "I'll get Danielle for you in a minute, okay? We're kind of swamped."

"That's fine, Marsha. Thanks."

Debra didn't see why she couldn't go back and get her daughter herself, but they had their rules. Everyplace did. As far as she was concerned, there were too many rules, period. But she shouldn't fault Little Folks for being cautious with the children in their care. The world was a crazy place.

Picking up a copy of a tabloid from the stack on the reception desk, Debra turned her back on the rush-hour melee and paged through the sheets of newsprint, hoping to discourage conversation should any of the other parents be so inclined.

She skimmed the headlines without interest, thinking instead about the weekend ahead. Two whole days with her baby. Perhaps Danielle would begin to crawl. At almost seven months, she was on the verge of it. Debra hoped the big event would happen when she could witness it rather than at daycare, where no one would give it a second look.

She turned the page to read the next headline. Couldn't Marsha move a little . . .

PSYCHIC DETECTIVES: USING ESP TO SOLVE CRIMES
What do a Raggedy Ann doll and a powder puff have in common?

The world tilted. Darkened. Debra clutched the back of a chair for support as she read the first paragraph of the article.

"Rachel Sutton claims she's not a psychic. But when a Raggedy Ann doll the local music teacher found in a Bread Company parking lot gave her bad vibes, she went straight to the FBI."

Raggedy Ann.

Bread Company.

FBI.

The words screamed off the page.

Debra's lungs shut down.

Sinking into a chair, she stared at the photo of a thirtyish woman seated behind a piano in some swanky setting.

The woman who'd found the Raggedy Ann.

But that couldn't be! She'd thrown the doll into a dumpster.

The container had been full, though. She'd had difficulty wedging the doll in once she'd hefted the heavy lid up a few inches. Plus, it had been very dark in that back corner of the parking lot, and the driving snow had blinded her. When headlights had swung across her she'd panicked. Afraid of drawing attention to herself, she'd given the doll one final shove and let the lid drop back into place. It must have fallen out while the trash bin was being emptied.

"Isn't that an interesting article? I read it on my lunch hour."

Debra's hands jerked, snapping the paper, and she swung toward Marsha.

"Sorry, Ms. Kraus. I didn't mean to startle you." The young woman bounced Danielle on her hip. "That kind of stuff can give you the creeps, though, can't it?" She nodded toward the paper. "I've never believed in all that psychic voodoo, but there's some pretty convincing information in there. And that teacher looks normal." She gestured toward the photo of Rachel Sutton. "Who knows?" With a shrug, she smiled at Danielle. "Mommy's here now, sweetie. Time to go home."

As Marsha handed her over, the baby babbled happily and snuggled against Debra's chest. The warm little body felt so good in her arms. So perfect. Debra hugged her close and rubbed her cheek against the child's soft skin. It seemed like Christmas each time she held her. Not that she'd ever gotten anything to rival the little bundle in her arms on that holiday. Her father hadn't believed in spoiling children. Presents had been meager at best, and always practical. But Danielle made up for all she'd missed.

And no one was going to take her away.

"Drive safe, Ms. Kraus. The roads are still tricky. How long does it take to get to Defiance from here?"

With an effort, Debra focused on the girl's question. *Act normal. Don't do anything to arouse suspicion.* "About twenty minutes."

"Really? I thought it was farther than that. It's like a different world from Chesterfield. I mean, are there even any stores out there?"

"I do most of my shopping here before I go home."

"Yeah. I guess you'd have to. Living in the boonies has disadvantages."

But it had advantages too. Debra ticked them off in her mind as she exited the facility and strapped Danielle in her car seat. No nosy neighbors. No one to observe her comings and goings. No questions. During her first few weeks on her new job, as she'd finalized her plans for motherhood, she'd searched long and hard to find a home that offered both easy access to the city and lots of privacy. The little bungalow tucked away on five acres of woods and fields suited her perfectly. From the night she'd brought Danielle home, she'd felt insulated there. And safe.

Until now.

But maybe she was overreacting. Who believed in that psychic stuff, anyway? No one she knew of in law enforcement or the legal community, that was for sure. And she'd seen plenty of case files from the criminal lawyers she'd worked for through the years. She couldn't remember one instance where evidence produced by a psychic was mentioned.

As for *St. Louis Scene* . . . she'd seen it at the daycare center in the past, paged through it on a couple of occasions. It often featured oddball stories more suited to the *National Enquirer* than a reputable newspaper. She suspected people read it more for entertainment than information. Most rational people would laugh off the doll story as far-fetched.

Except it wasn't.

What sort of power did this Rachel woman have that had allowed her to pick up "vibes" from the Raggedy Ann? And how much more did she know?

Too nervous to wait until she got home to read the entire article, Debra pulled into a fast-food outlet, parked under an overhead light, and opened the paper to the story.

A quick scan reassured her. Most of the article focused on a St. Louis woman from the 1970s who'd practiced psychometry—and claimed she'd helped police solve crimes using items like powder puffs. Rachel Sutton, and an FBI agent named Nick Bradley, were only mentioned in the lead and the conclusion. The teacher had refused to comment, except to deny she had any psychic powers, and the FBI had responded to queries with a "no comment."

Okay, so what did they really know?

Forcing her mind into the analytical mode she used when helping prepare a brief, Debra extracted the few factual nuggets pertaining to the doll. A teacher had found it. It gave her bad vibes. She'd discussed it with the FBI. Period.

There was no indication the woman had any specific *information*. Just a feeling.

And law enforcement didn't act on feelings.

Besides, even if the cops tried to check into it, there wasn't anything to connect that doll to her.

Feeling more reassured, Debra folded the paper, set it on the seat, and pulled back into traffic. If the woman had any real information, the police would have shown up in Defiance by now. In all likelihood, the doll had been pitched already and the FBI had written this woman off as a nut.

She was safe as long as she kept a low profile. And made sure her baby didn't look anything like the one who had been abducted in Chicago.

It was time to get out the hair dye again.

★

"Let it roll to the answering machine, Rachel."

Snatching her hand back from the phone, Rachel followed Nick's advice.

"Hi, Rachel. My name is Mildred Watson. I read the article in *St. Louis Scene* yesterday, and I found your phone number in the book. I hope I'm not disturbing you, dear, but my cat is missing and I wondered if your ability works with animals too. I have her toys here at the house and I'd be happy to bring them to you if you think you could get some sort of reading that might tell me where she went." The woman recited her phone number, said a polite thank-you, and hung up.

Rachel shook her head in dismay. "That's the seventh call since the paper hit the stands at noon yesterday. At least this woman sounds rational."

"If you call believing that cats can send messages through toys rational." Nick gave her a dubious look.

"Trust me. Compared to some of the people I've heard from, this woman is rational."

Nick picked up her coat from the back of the couch and held it as she slipped her arms into the sleeves. "Anything scary?"

The question was casual, but Rachel sensed an undercurrent of seriousness. "No. Unless you count the woman who claimed I was doing the devil's work and wanted to perform an exorcism on me." She tried for a light tone but didn't quite pull it off. That one had been a little freaky.

"I expected you to get a few of those. Do me a favor, okay? Double-check all your locks for the next few weeks."

"Do you think I should be concerned?" Rachel stopped buttoning her coat. Moistening her lips, she tucked her hair behind her ear.

"Careful more than concerned. It always pays to be cautious. You never know what an article like that will pry out of the woodwork. How have your friends and co-workers reacted?"

"I warned them ahead of time. Played up the magazine's reputation for sensationalism. Explained the theory your friend's wife proposed. When it came out, I got sympathy rather than weird looks. And a few compliments on the photo." She shook her head and picked up her purse. "I can't believe the paper sent someone to the hotel to take a photo during tea. People often celebrate special occasions there and take lots of pictures, so I didn't even notice. That was pretty sneaky."

"We're talking about *St. Louis Scene*, remember?"

"Good point."

"And the photo *was* nice." He winked, but as the phone began to ring again he grabbed her hand and tugged her toward the door. "We're out of here."

"No argument from me."

As they stepped outside, he pulled the door shut behind them with a firm tug.

"Saved from the bell." Rachel fitted her key in the lock and smiled up at him. "This was such a nice idea, Nick. I haven't been out to breakfast on a Saturday in ages. Where are we going?"

He took her arm and guided her down the walk toward his car. "A place called Nick's."

She shot him a surprised glance. "Your house?"

"You said at lunch the other day you'd like to see it. And my claim last Friday wasn't idle. I *can* cook."

"Are we having omelets?" she teased.

"Nope. Eggs Benedict."

"Seriously?"

"Would an FBI agent lie?"

He gave her that engaging grin, the one that dented his cheek and sent her pulses fluttering. "I hope not."

"You can trust me, Rachel." There was more behind the words than a mere promise of a decent breakfast. The sudden darkening of his eyes told her that. But he didn't give her a chance to dwell on it, switching from intense to teasing in a heartbeat. "Besides, I have a business proposition for you."

"A business proposition. Hmm. That sounds intriguing. Let's see . . . are you considering piano lessons?"

Chuckling, he waited while she slid into the passenger seat. "I don't have a musical bone in my body." Shutting her door, he circled the car, took his place behind the wheel, and picked up the conversation. "I appreciate music, but as for making music—the Lord shorted me on that talent, I'm afraid."

"A lot of people say that without ever giving it a try."

"Not me. I tried. In grade school, one of the foster families I stayed with enrolled me in the band. I guess they thought it might be a good outlet for . . . lots of things. Didn't take. After giving me a chance on the violin, clarinet, and percussion, the teacher suggested I switch to choir. That lasted about a month. I had no ear for harmony."

"Maybe you just never found your musical niche."

"No. The sad truth is I'm not gifted in that way, like you are. But how did you manage to develop your talent, moving among foster families and schools?"

She lifted one shoulder. "Some of the families had pianos. Some of the schools offered lessons. But I didn't have the opportunity to focus on it until college."

"I bet you sing too."

"Some. But you know what I really wanted to do? Dance. I love ballet."

"Why didn't you?" The instant the words left his mouth, he gave her a stricken look. "I'm sorry, Rachel. I keep forgetting about your leg."

She smiled, wanting to reassure him. She'd made her peace with her limitations long ago. "Don't apologize. I consider that validation for all my years of physical therapy. Besides, I may not be able to *do* ballet, but nothing prevents me from watching it. That gives me a lot of pleasure, too. Now what's this business proposition you mentioned?"

"If you can be patient, it might be easier for me to show you rather than tell you."

"Patience isn't my strongest virtue. But I'll try."

Fifteen minutes later, when Nick turned into a long drive, Rachel stopped mid-sentence at her first glimpse of the house he called home. The stately brick two story had all the classic Federal-style features: windows arranged symmetrically around a central doorway; front door topped by a fanlight and flanked by narrow side windows; dental molding in the cornice; black shutters. A wide set of brick steps curved out at the bottom in gracious welcome. The roof looked new, the tuck-pointing recent, the paint fresh. Gigantic oak trees and towering maples dotted the immense, manicured lawn.

"Wow." It was all she could manage.

"You wouldn't have said that a couple of years ago." Nick grinned and set the brake. "The place was falling apart. There was a hole in the roof the size of a large beach ball, a lot of the windows were broken, none of the plumbing worked . . . it was a mess."

"Why didn't some developer buy the place, knock it down, and build three houses on this lot? That's what they're doing in every other hot area of town. And Chesterfield definitely falls into the hot category."

"They tried. But the historic preservation folks raised a ruckus. The house was granted a reprieve while they scrambled to find funding to restore it, but their deadline was approaching when I appeared on the scene. With their help, I got the place for a song, considering the prime location. Some of them still show up now and then to check on my progress."

"How will they feel when you pack up and move on?"

"Saving the house was their main interest. As long as I pick the buyer for this one very carefully, they'll be happy."

While they ascended the brick steps, Nick pulled out his keys. "The back door is my usual style, but you don't get the full effect that way. For your first visit, I thought we'd do it right."

First visit. Rachel liked the sound of that.

Fitting his key in the lock, Nick ushered her in to the sound of a rhythmic beeping. "Security alarm," he explained, entering behind her.

As he opened a small door constructed of decorative molding and punched a code into the box hidden behind it, Rachel surveyed the spacious foyer. She didn't know a lot about architecture, but even her untrained eye could appreciate the careful restoration and decorative details.

Hardwood floors gleamed; white spindles glistened on the stairway that rose, turned, and hugged the wall as it ascended; graceful arches led to what she supposed was a living room on one side and a dining room on the other, though both were unfurnished. Carved marble mantels graced both rooms, and light spilled in from the large Palladian windows. Twelve-foot ceilings enhanced the sense of space and gave the house an airy, open feeling.

No detail had been spared, from the intricate crown molding capping all the rooms to the elaborate plaster ceiling medallion around the crystal chandelier in the dining room.

Awed, she shook her head as he drew up beside her. "My whole house could fit in your living room."

"They built them bigger a hundred and fifty plus years ago."

"I can see that. Did you do all this yourself?"

"Pretty close to 100 percent of the visible work inside. The plumbing and some of the electrical repairs I left to the experts. Let me take your coat and we'll start our tour on the second floor."

She shrugged it off, watching as he hung his leather jacket beside her wool coat in the hall closet. His eyes seemed especially blue today, thanks to the dark blue pullover he wore over an open-necked white shirt and black slacks.

"My lady." He gestured to the stairs with a flourish.

Rachel started up the wide staircase, Nick beside her. The proportions of this house suited him, she noted. His tall frame and broad shoulders had dwarfed her tiny bungalow, but the scale of this house accommodated his lean, powerful physique and larger-than-life presence.

Upstairs, he showed her how he'd combined two of the five bedrooms to create a master suite. Another bedroom had been transformed into a well-equipped gym. Some finishing touches were still in progress, but the heavy work was done.

Descending a back flight of stairs, he walked her through the kitchen—where modern amenities had been incorporated without losing the historic character of the house—and ducked into the small study/library with built-in bookcases, located behind the living room.

Although the master bedroom had contained a bed and dresser, and there were a table and chairs in the kitchen, the study was the only room Rachel considered fully furnished. It boasted a couch, easy chair, lamps, and TV.

"May I ask you a question?" Rachel ran a finger along the chair rail as they returned to the front of the house via the central hall.

"Sure."

She stopped in the arch to the living room and scanned the room. "How come no furniture?"

"Because I spend all my money on rehabbing?" He grinned and shoved his hands into the pockets of his slacks.

"I could buy that."

"And it's partly true. But the real reason is that I've lived in a variety of houses, all different styles, and what worked in one wouldn't have worked in another. My last rehab was a contemporary sixties ranch. Nothing I'd have bought for that house would have fit in here. So it's easier to travel light."

"Makes sense." She gestured toward the front corner of the living room, beside the fireplace. "But if I was furnishing this room, I'd put a baby grand piano right there. If I could afford it."

"I take it they're pricey?"

"Very. A true extravagance. For my needs, the old upright in my spare bedroom-turned-studio is more than sufficient." She folded her arms across her chest and smiled. "Okay, I've been patient. Now what's your business proposition?"

He led the way across the foyer. "It occurred to me after I saw your dining room that this room might benefit from a mural too." He gestured to the blank wall separating the dining room from the butler's pantry that led to the kitchen. "What do you think?"

Hands on hips, Rachel moved to the center of the room and surveyed the blank expanse above the ornate wainscoting. "What would be the purpose? You sure don't need an illusion of space."

"Purely decorative. Before I started this rehab, I researched period Federal-style houses and I noticed some of them had murals."

"That's true. They did. A mural would be appropriate to the period. But I've never tackled anything quite this large. It would take weeks."

"That's what I'm counting on."

She turned to find him regarding her with a slow, intimate smile that curled her toes.

Uncertain how to respond, she tried to focus on practical matters. "This wouldn't"—she had to stop to clear her throat—"be cheap."

"I think it will be worth every penny."

That remark left her speechless.

When the silence lengthened, Nick's smile broadened. "I'll tell you what. Why don't you put some ideas and estimates together for me to consider? If you're interested."

Interested? Was he kidding? Doing the mural would be fun, but the big attraction was spending more time with Nick. And he seemed to feel likewise. She'd do the job for free, except she counted on her mural business to supplement her income and this job would cut into the time she could give to other commissions. But she'd lowball the price.

121

"Okay. Give me a few days."

"Sounds fair. Now how about some breakfast?"

"Lead the way. Considering the magic you've worked with this house, I have great expectations for your culinary ability."

"You might want to reserve judgment on that until after breakfast."

She smiled. "I'll take my chances."

As she followed him back down the hall, she considered her last comment.

And realized that when applied to Nick Bradley, it was true for a whole lot more than breakfast.

9

An hour later, Rachel polished off her second serving of eggs Benedict and smiled at Nick across the table. "You weren't kidding. You really can cook."

"I'm glad you enjoyed it." He took a swig of coffee from his oversized mug and returned her smile. It was nice to have company for a meal. Much as he liked this house, it sometimes felt cavernous when he was here alone. More so since Mark and Coop had stayed with him last summer.

"You've also done a great job with this place. I envy the lucky family who will reap the benefits of your labor."

He dismissed her compliment with a shrug. "I enjoy the work. But I have to admit this house has been special. I like that it's survived for more than 150 years. That it has a history, and roots. The instant I stepped inside the door I got a feeling of substance and permanence and stability—even though the walls were literally falling down around me." He grinned and shook his head. "Go figure."

"I sense that too. I wonder if foster kids are more attuned to those qualities?" She treated the question as rhetorical and moved on. "I do know having a home was always one of my goals. My house may be humble, but it means the world to me. And I love knowing I never have to move again if I don't want to."

Nick rested his elbows on the table and lifted his mug with both hands. He wanted to ask her why she lived in her little bungalow alone. A woman like Rachel should have a devoted husband and a couple of kids to come home to each night, not an empty house. Since Valentine's Day he'd kept their conversations light, but perhaps it was time to shift into a more serious gear.

"I'm curious about one thing, Rachel. And tell me to back off if this is too personal. How come there's no man in your life?"

Surprise arched her eyebrows. Fearing he'd made a tactical error, he backtracked. "Sorry. None of my business."

"No. It's okay." Her swift response eased the sudden tension in his shoulders. "I don't mind answering. Except all I can give you is the standard line. I never met the right guy. No surprise there, I guess, considering my lifestyle. I teach at two grade schools. I give piano lessons to children. Painting murals is a solitary occupation. I've never seen a man come alone to afternoon tea at the hotel. And what little free time I have I prefer not to spend in bars." She propped her chin in her hand. "I could ask you the same thing."

Nick had known when he'd broached the question that she might turn the tables on him. Had almost hoped she would. Unlike his off-limits past, this was a subject he was willing to talk about. With this woman, anyway.

"My job can require long hours. It also carries a certain risk many women find glamorous in dating partners, but not so appealing when it comes to more serious commitments. As for the bar scene, it's not my style, either. In general, the women I've met in that venue don't live by the values that guide my life."

"Did this make you think I do?" She fingered the cross around her neck, watching him.

"My faith is very important to me, Rachel." His gaze held hers. "I'd like to find a woman who shares it. Or at least who hasn't ruled out that possibility."

He'd phrased his reply as a comment, but he could tell by the sudden conflict in Rachel's eyes that she heard the question underneath.

"I admire your faith, Nick." She said the words carefully. "And I would call myself a Christian if asked to name my religious preference. But I don't pray. I don't feel connected to God like you do. I never attend services." She shook her head. "I doubt I could ever get to the place you are."

"Would you like to?"

Rachel touched the cross again, and faint creases etched her brow. "I don't know. I do think about God. Every Sunday I pass several churches on my way to tea, and in nice weather I always see groups of people standing around outside, mingling, laughing, conversing. In the summer, one of the churches has a picnic on the lawn the first Sunday of each month. I've considered asking about membership because I'm drawn by the sense of fellowship . . . of family, almost. But I don't think you should join a church for social reasons."

"Maybe deep inside your reasons are more than social."

She shook her head, and he could see the regret pooling in her eyes. "I'm sorry, Nick. I know what you want me to say. I know what I wish I *could* say. But the truth is, I don't feel a compelling need to establish a closer relationship with God. I believe in him, but I've seen little evidence of his presence. I tend to think of him as an uninvolved deity who watches from afar as we humans make a mess of our world. I don't feel any sense of connection or kinship. I don't know how anyone can if they watch the evening news."

Nick did his best to quell the disappointment that welled up inside him. He'd hoped for more. An openness to the possibility of a relationship with the Almighty, at the very least. He liked Rachel and had begun to believe she might be the one God had sent in answer to his prayers. But perhaps their chance encounter had been just that—chance, and nothing more.

"I appreciate your honesty. And I admire it." Nick tacked on the last as he looked at Rachel across the table and realized how much her admission had cost her. The attraction went both ways; he could read it in her eyes. He doubted she wanted to do anything to jeopardize the tenuous connection they were establishing, but he suspected she'd sensed her lack of faith could be a deal breaker. Yet she hadn't lied to him. That bumped her up another notch in his estimation. And had him scrambling to think of some way to convince her to give Christianity a serious try.

"When was the last time you went to Sunday services, Rachel?"

With one finger she traced the grain pattern in the wooden table. "I can't remember. But it has to be at least twenty years ago."

"Would you consider giving it one more try? I go to the ten o'clock service, and I'd be happy to pick you up. You'll be finished in plenty of time to get to your tea commitment."

She shifted in her seat. "I'd feel like a fraud sitting among a congregation of believers."

"You wouldn't be the only doubter in our midst, Rachel. Even people of faith struggle with their beliefs at times. Besides, it's just one service. Not a lifetime commitment." He kept his tone conversational, bordering on teasing.

Her lips curved into a slight smile. "Are you trying to strong-arm me, Nick?"

"I'm not into strong-arming. I prefer persuading with charm." One side of his mouth hitched into an answering smile and he lifted the mug toward his lips.

"No strong-arming, hmm?" She tipped her head and studied him, mimicking his teasing inflection. "Then where'd you get that scar on your temple?"

Nick's hand froze halfway to his mouth and his smile evaporated.

Her smile faded too, and she reached out to rest her fingers on his. "Nick, I'm sorry."

126

He tugged his hand from beneath hers and shoved his chair back with more force than necessary. Standing, he crossed the room in a few strides and busied himself at the coffeepot as an awkward silence settled in the room.

Outside, a sudden gust of wind rattled the windows. Rachel rose and picked up her plate.

"You wouldn't let me help with the cooking, but I'm not going to leave all this cleanup in your hands." There was a false lightness to her tone.

From his vantage point across the room, Nick watched as she carried her plate and glass to the sink and set them on the granite countertop, rinsing them one by one, each action deliberate. The stiffness in her shoulders, the tautness of her profile, the tremble in her hand when she reached for the glass beside her were telling.

Way to go, Bradley. Ask her personal questions and then act miffed when she reciprocates. That's a great example of kindness and charity. And a surefire way to convince her to accept your invitation to attend services, where she can learn more about how to be a good Christian.

Clenching his teeth, Nick tried to regroup. The scar comment had blindsided him, and his withdrawal had been automatic. He'd avoided talking about his past for so long that retreat was second nature to him. That was true about his youth in general, and the scar in particular. He'd shared the origins of it with no one in the thirty-two years since he'd acquired it. They were too painful to dredge up.

Yet he felt an obligation to offer some explanation to Rachel.

As he grappled with his dilemma, he saw the glass slip from Rachel's hand. Heard her utter a soft exclamation of dismay as it fell against the unforgiving granite. Took a step toward her as she grabbed for it. Watched as it shattered in her hand and her fingers turned red.

He was beside her in three strides, reaching for her hand. "I'm sorry, Nick. It s-slipped."

The quaver in her apology, and the blood on her hand, had the effect of a punch in the gut. "I'm the one who's sorry." His words came out hoarse as he cradled her hand and eased it under the stream of water. The cut on her index finger was long but not too deep, he noted in relief. "Keep this under the water while I go get some antiseptic and a bandage."

"It'll be okay. Don't bother."

"It's no bother, Rachel." Her eyes were inches from his, the gold-flecked irises wide as she stared up at him. With an effort he swallowed past the sudden lump in his throat. "I'll be back in a minute."

Leaving her at the sink, he strode to the foyer and took the stairs two at a time. His fingers were clumsy as he rummaged around in the master bath closet for his first-aid supplies, the streaks of blood on his hand distracting him.

Nick had seen plenty of blood in his line of work. Through the years, he'd built up a pretty thick skin. Spilled blood no longer made him squeamish, nor did images of it keep him awake at night. Yet these smears of red on his palm and fingers coiled his stomach into a knot.

Because they were Rachel's blood.

The significance of his reaction wasn't lost on him. It didn't matter that the cut was minor. He didn't want her hurt, period. And if he got the shakes over a scratch, how would he feel if she sustained a more serious injury?

The answer was simple.

Not good.

The reason for that was also simple. He was beginning to care for her a whole lot. Faith or no faith.

That acknowledgment brought him back to the dilemma that had led to this little incident. Uncomfortable with his invitation to church, she'd tried to lighten things up with an innocent tease about the thin white scar at his hairline. He should have laughed it off.

Instead, he'd overreacted. And his withdrawal hadn't been fair. Rachel had no way of knowing about the less visible scars it represented.

Perhaps if she did, though—if she understood what he'd gone through, if he explained how finding his way to the Lord had been his salvation—she might be willing to give faith a try. To take that first, all-important step toward the Lord.

But close on the heels of that hope came fear.

Sharing secrets was dangerous. It made you vulnerable. And you didn't take that kind of chance unless you had absolute trust in the other person.

Logic told Nick it was premature to take that leap with Rachel. Their acquaintance was too new.

Yet his heart told him otherwise.

Heading back to the kitchen, he paused halfway down the stairs to survey the empty foyer, the bare living room, the vacant dining room. This was a house made for a family. It should be filled with children and laughter and love. As should his life. There was a chance Rachel held the key to those things—unless he shut her out.

Rays of sun streamed in the fanlight above the front door, enfolding him. The warmth seeped into his pores like a calming balm, and he closed his eyes for a brief prayer.

Lord, please guide me—and give me courage.

Rachel was still standing at the sink when he returned, looking a bit too pale for his taste. Forcing his lips into a smile, he turned off the tap, took her arm, and led her to the table.

"I can't claim a great deal of medical training, but I do have experience with minor bruises and abrasions, thanks to my rehab work." He positioned her hand palm up on the oak surface and treated her cut as he spoke. "I've also dealt with burns, pulled muscles, and electric shocks. Fixing up houses is not for the fainthearted, let me tell you." He secured the bandage and picked up her hand to examine it. "There you go. Good as new. Almost. This won't impede your piano playing, will it?"

She flexed her index finger in his palm. "No. I once played with a broken pinkie. I'll manage with this."

"Good." He lowered her hand to the table, but when she started to retract it he tightened his grip. At her questioning look, he took a fortifying breath. "You mentioned this scar earlier." He traced the thin white line on his forehead with his free hand, his tone now serious. "It wasn't a rehab injury."

She went still. "I didn't mean to touch a nerve."

"I realize that. And I'm sorry I upset you enough to cause this." He stroked her bandaged finger.

"My clumsiness wasn't your fault. Not entirely, anyway. I've been tense and unsettled for weeks. I've broken four glasses of my own since the first of the year."

"You're still feeling that way?"

"Yes. I can't shake it."

He weighed her hand in his. "My reaction today didn't help, I'm sure. I'm sorry I pulled back. That was inappropriate."

"I have a feeling it was more like self-defense."

"It was prompted by that," he acknowledged, struck again by her intuitive ability. "I've avoided discussing that scar for thirty-two years. Evasion has become a reflex by now. But self-defense implies a suspicion of danger, and that doesn't fit in this case. I don't feel threatened with you."

Soft color suffused her cheeks, and the hint of a smile softened her lips. "I'm glad."

He played with her fingers, examining their delicate grace as he summoned up the courage to continue. "Would you like to know the story behind it, Rachel?"

His question was met with a moment of silence, followed by a gentle squeeze of his hand that pulled his gaze back to hers. Her eyes were warm, inviting, empathetic, and her voice was husky and not quite steady as she responded. "Very much."

She waited in the silence that followed, giving him space to gather his thoughts—and his nerve. That was another thing he liked about her. She didn't push. And she was tuned in to nuances. He sensed she understood how difficult this was for him and would give him as much support and encouragement as she could. Still, this wasn't going to be easy.

"I should warn you that my story isn't pretty, Rachel."

"I didn't think it was going to be."

He nodded and swallowed. "Okay. I'll give you the abridged version. Straight up. My father was an out-of-work drunk who thought the world owed him a living and who vented his anger and frustration on my mother and me. In an effort to shield me, she took the brunt of his wrath. I went to sleep most nights curled into a ball and trying not to cry while I listened to my father yell at her. Then the abuse would switch from verbal to physical. I could hear the punches and slaps through the thin walls, and my mother's sobs as she pleaded with him to stop."

Nick lifted an unsteady hand and wiped it down his face. "Mom died when I was five. She fell down the basement steps. An accident, my father told everyone. But I knew different. I saw him grab her as she started down with a load of laundry. She tried to pull away, to tell him she had chores to do, and he said, 'Fine. You want to go down the steps? Let me help you.' And then he pushed her." His voice grew raspy, and he sucked in a harsh breath.

"It's okay, Nick." Rachel cocooned his hand between hers, stroking his fingers in a steady, comforting rhythm at odds with the shakiness in her voice. "Take your time."

He downed a swig of his cold coffee, trying to wash the bitter taste from his mouth. It didn't work. It never did. "He knew I saw what had happened. He grabbed me and said if I ever told anyone, he'd take me out some night and drop me off the bridge into the Detroit River."

At Rachel's gasp, he tightened his grip on her hand and searched her eyes. "I told you this wasn't pretty."

"I know. It's just hard for me to imagine a father doing such a thing to his son." Tears laced her words.

"Maybe I should stop."

"No. Please . . . tell me the rest."

Her sincerity was impossible to question. She might be disturbed by his story, might *prefer* not to know any more, but she had realized that to really understand him, she had to hear it.

The lady had guts. And determination.

More sterling qualities to add to her growing list.

"Okay." He gave a curt nod. "With my mother gone, I became the target of my father's wrath and bad temper. I tried to stay out of his way, to do everything he told me to. But I could never satisfy him. He kept raising the bar until there was no way I could succeed. I think he got some kind of perverse pleasure from tormenting me. One of my jobs was to clean the bathroom, and I remember one night it wasn't good enough. As punishment, he forced me to scrub the toilet with my toothbrush—and then brush my teeth."

"Oh, Nick." Distress contorted Rachel's features, and her voice choked.

He tightened his grip on her hand. "I'll spare you all the other similar episodes. And the details of the physical abuse, except to say he put his belt to good use on the parts of my anatomy that were always covered in public. Until one night, in a fit of drunken rage over some minor infraction, he began yelling and pushing me around. The next thing I knew he was chasing me around the house with a carving knife. I dove under his bed, knowing he couldn't follow. It was too low to the ground. But he had a long arm. He reached under and started to swing the knife back and forth. It clipped me before I could get out of the way. If the neighbors hadn't heard a ruckus and called the police, I doubt I would have survived the night."

"Is that when you went into foster care?"

"Yes. The authorities took me away from him that night. My head healed, but the scar remained—along with all of the invisible scars. For months I struggled with fear and insecurity and a feeling of unworthiness. I stopped talking and withdrew into myself. The experts began to think I might have autistic tendencies.

"But gradually the fear gave way to anger. I became rebellious and belligerent and obnoxious. One foster family after another gave up and sent me back into the system. I became a kid without a country. No home base, no one who cared. That's why I was such an easy mark for the group of misfits that recruited me. I would have ended up on the wrong side of the law forever if Dan Foley hadn't saved me."

"How did he manage to get through to you?"

"Persistence. Sincerity. Consideration. He was the first person other than my mother who took a genuine interest in me and my future. He's also the one who tapped into my talent for carpentry. He used to invite me to his house on Saturdays to help with chores, on the pretense of letting me earn a few bucks but in reality to keep an eye on me. The fall we connected, he was expanding his one-car garage. I discovered I had a natural ability for that kind of work, and after we finished the project, he got me involved in building sets for a play at his church. Before I knew it, I was in the youth group.

"Dan is also the reason I ended up finding God. He was a devout Christian, and he lived the values of his faith every day. He went after the kids who needed the most help, and even when they rejected him, he kept trying. I asked him once why he didn't just give up on the really tough cases, and I never forgot his answer. He said that if God never gives up on us, if he's always willing to offer another chance, how could he do any less?"

There was silence for a moment before Rachel spoke.

"What happened to your father, Nick?"

"He went to jail for a while. I didn't keep up with him as a kid. I was just glad he was out of my life. But I checked as an adult and found out he died years ago. He fell down a set of stairs in a drunken stupor. Ironic, isn't it?" His mouth twisted into a brief, mirthless smile. "I'm ashamed to say I felt a sense of vindication at the news. Despite my faith, I'm still working on forgiveness. One of these days I'll get there, with God's help."

"I'm beginning to understand how important your faith is to you."

He locked gazes with her. "It's the center of my life, Rachel. My relationship with the Lord is the most incredible gift I've ever received. The absolute certainty that I'm never truly alone has gotten me through some very tough spots." He gave her hand one final squeeze and released it. "Thank you for listening."

"Thank *you* for sharing."

He didn't miss her slight wince as she flexed the fingers he'd been gripping. "What's wrong?"

"Nothing." She started to pull her hand toward her lap.

"Let me see." He snagged her hand, appalled by the white ridges crisscrossing the angry red skin. Swallowing past the lump in his throat, he began to carefully massage away the evidence of his tight grip as he'd clung to her hand while he spoke of his ugly past. "I'm sorry, Rachel. You should have told me I was hurting you."

"I didn't even notice."

"My story was that compelling, huh?" He tried to smile. Failed.

134

"In a word . . . yes. And I'm intrigued by the power of faith in your life. Plus, the notion of never being alone is very appealing. I'll tell you what . . . if the invitation to attend services is still open, I'd like to go with you tomorrow."

This time his attempt to smile succeeded. "I'll pick you up at nine-thirty. And I promise you won't regret it."

Nor would he. A surge of hope lightened his heart as they both rose to finish clearing the table. Best case, she'd come to some understanding of the appeal of Christianity. Worst case, he'd simply bought himself another couple of hours in her company.

As far as he was concerned, it was a win/win situation all around.

10

Do something productive.

Nick had been repeating that mantra since he'd arrived at his office Monday morning, but it wasn't having much effect. His thoughts kept wandering to his weekend with Rachel. They'd ended up spending all of Saturday together. Breakfast had led to a trip to the Missouri Botanical Garden, where they'd wandered through the tropical Climatron in defiance of the frigid cold on the other side of the glass sphere. From there they'd gone to a movie. A cozy pasta dinner on The Hill, St. Louis's traditional Italian settlement, had concluded their day.

Leaning back in his chair, he smiled. Sunday had been as good, if not better. The morning service had been uplifting, and afterward Rachel had peppered him with questions that suggested she had a sincere interest in learning more. He'd driven her to the hotel for her piano gig and hung around for scones and finger sandwiches. Rachel could no longer say she'd never seen a man come alone to afternoon tea.

He'd gotten nothing done on his house. By his usual measure, that would mean the weekend was a dismal failure. But his yardstick had changed.

"I see you spent time this weekend with Rachel."

At Mark's comment, Nick swung toward the door of his cube. "Have you been doing surveillance on me?"

"No need. That sappy smile on your face says it all."

Stretching his legs in front of him, Nick clasped his hands behind his head. No sense denying the obvious. "It was a good weekend."

"Get much done on the house?"

"Nope. I had better things to do."

Mark grinned. "It's about time. One word of advice, though." He shot a glance over his shoulder and lowered his voice. "Look busy. Steve's on the prowl for someone to follow up on some leads for a Houston case."

"Thanks for the heads-up." Nick sat up straighter and rotated back toward his desk. The last thing he wanted to do was get stuck conducting dead-end interviews or checking bogus leads for another office.

Determined to focus, he zipped through his email, printing out those that were case-related and required follow-up phone calls to gather additional information. He quickly skimmed through the Sentinel system and the bureau-wide teletypes, emails, and intelligence bulletins on high-profile cases; the information from all those databases seldom had much relevance to his day-to-day work.

The bulletin on the O'Neil kidnapping, however, caught his eye, and he scanned the update. Still no breaks. After being snatched seven weeks ago, the five-month-old infant had vanished without a trace. There had been no contact from the kidnapper and few leads. The Chicago office continued to ask agents around the country to keep the case top-of-mind, but after all these weeks Nick knew there was little hope of a happy outcome. In general, if a kidnapped baby wasn't found in the first few days, it wasn't found at all.

To delay starting his real work, Nick clicked on the attached head shot of the infant. Cute baby. Curly reddish hair, big blue eyes, a happy smile. He couldn't begin to imagine what the parents were going through.

His finger was poised on the mouse to close the file when the orange tufts peeking into the bottom of the picture snagged his attention. They looked like yarn.

The kind used for hair on a Raggedy Ann doll.

Nick leaned closer for a better look, then swiveled in his chair to check out the doll smiling back at him from the corner of his cube. Before it had been dragged through dirty slush, this doll's hair could have been the same color as the yarn in the photo.

A sudden jolt of adrenaline nudged up his pulse, but he tamped it down. Millions of kids had Raggedy Ann dolls. Even if the material he saw in the photo was yarn, and even if it was attached to a Raggedy Ann doll, there was nothing to connect the doll in his office with the one in this photo.

Except, perhaps, Rachel's bad vibes.

Another surge of adrenaline shot through him. This one more difficult to contain.

Yet Emily had offered a perfectly rational explanation for Rachel's response to the doll. One everyone had accepted, including Rachel. To think her reaction had been triggered by anything more than a buried memory was nuts.

So how come he wasn't moving on to his *real* cases?

The answer came to him as he examined the cherubic face of the infant on his screen. His own childhood had been shattered. If there was even one chance in a million the doll in his office had some connection to this baby, a remote possibility it could provide the heartbroken parents with answers and a resolution, he had to check it out.

Punching in the numbers for the direct line to the case agent in Chicago, Nick drummed his fingers on his desk and stared at the doll.

"Matt Carson."

"Matt, Nick Bradley from the St. Louis office. I was looking through the intelligence bulletins and saw the photo of the O'Neil baby. Is there more to that image?"

"Yeah. We cropped for the face. Why? You have a lead?"

"I wouldn't go that far. I just want to check out a hunch."

"I'll email you the full shot. We could use a break on that case. It's as cold as a Chicago winter. Give me a few minutes."

"Thanks. I'll be back in touch if this pans out, but it's a long shot."

"I'll take whatever I can get at this point."

Five minutes later, when the *ping* of his email sounded, Nick clicked on the message from Matt Carson and opened the photo.

Megan O'Neil smiled back at him. Clutched in her hands was a tattered Raggedy Ann doll—with a patch above the right eye.

He stopped breathing.

"The coast is clear. Steve gave the Houston leads to . . ." Mark's voice trailed off. "Hey . . . what's up?"

It took a moment for Mark's question to register. Motioning him in, Nick pointed to his computer screen. "Get a load of this."

Mark leaned over his shoulder. "That's the O'Neil baby, isn't it? Why are you . . . "

In the stunned silence that followed, Nick felt Mark turn toward the corner.

"Good God." Mark's soft, shocked comment was half exclamation, half prayer.

"That's my reaction too." Nick swiveled around. They both stared at the doll.

"This doesn't make sense." Mark frowned and shook his head. "Unless your Rachel knows more than she's telling."

The hint of suspicion in Mark's tone raised Nick's hackles.

But it was also a wake-up call. If Mark suspected Rachel might be involved in the crime, others would too. No one would buy her "vibes" story. Yet Nick's gut told him she had nothing to do with the O'Neil kidnapping.

"If she knew anything more, she would have told me on her first visit. Besides, if she was involved in the crime, she wouldn't have come to the office in the first place."

"Then how do you explain the connection between her and the doll?"

"Emily already did that."

"This casts a whole new light on the situation."

"It might be coincidence. Emily's theory could still be accurate."

"I don't know, Nick." Mark rubbed the back of his neck, his expression troubled. "This seems too weird to be coincidence."

Nick rose and folded his arms across his chest. "Rachel doesn't know anything about the kidnapping, Mark."

"Are you sure?"

"Yes."

Mark pursed his lips. "It's gone that far already, hmm?"

"It hasn't gone anywhere. But it might. And I've learned enough about her to be confident she has no connection to that crime." He jerked his head toward the image on his screen.

"You might be right. But we need to talk to her about it."

"We?"

"It would be safer if both of us go, don't you think? In case anyone finds out about the two of you and wonders if your objectivity has been compromised."

He couldn't argue with Mark's reasoning. The fact that he hadn't considered that issue himself suggested his thinking was already muddled. "Yeah. You're right. But I need to talk to Steve and Marty first." Both the reactive squad supervisor and the Special Agent in Charge of the St. Louis office would expect to be notified immediately of a lead in such a high-profile case, and Nick intended to follow protocol on this one to the letter.

"Good plan. I'll clear my calendar for the morning and get the doll to the lab."

As Mark started to exit, Nick restrained him with a hand on his arm. "Listen . . . you take the lead on the questions, okay?"

"Sure. I recall you doing a similar favor for me last summer."

"Yeah." The arrest of the man who had tried to kill Emily wasn't an event either would forget.

As Mark disappeared into the bull pen maze, Nick thought back to that incident—and how close Mark had come to losing the woman who was now his wife. It didn't leave him feeling warm and fuzzy. Neither did this latest twist in the doll story.

There was no doubt in his mind that Rachel was innocent of any criminal connection to the O'Neil kidnapping. But she did have *some* kind of connection. Emily's assessment of Rachel's reaction had been logical, but in his gut Nick was beginning to believe there was more to it than that.

He could only hope that the person, or persons, responsible for the crime hadn't seen the article in *St. Louis Scene* and come to the same conclusion.

Because if they had, things could get very, very dangerous.

★

Thirty minutes later, when Rachel was pulled out of her fourth-grade music appreciation class to speak with the FBI, she half expected Nick to greet her with a smile and suggest she cut out early for lunch.

But when she stepped into the empty office, the somber faces on the two men waiting for her dashed that hope. Bewildered, she looked from Nick to the tall, dark-haired man with him, then focused on Nick again. "Is something wrong?"

"Ms. Sutton, I'm Special Agent Mark Sanders." The dark-haired man smiled and extended his hand as he spoke. "I know you and Nick are already acquainted. We just have a few questions."

"About what?"

Mark gestured to a chair. "Please, have a seat and we'll fill you in."

With another searching look at Nick, she took the chair Mark had indicated and waited while the two men sat opposite her.

"This is about the Raggedy Ann doll, Rachel," Nick said.

"I thought that was over."

"Not quite. Ms. Sutton, do you recognize this child?" The dark-haired man handed her a photo.

Rachel looked at the smiling infant and shook her head. "No."

"Her name is Megan O'Neil. She was kidnapped seven weeks ago in Chicago."

"I remember reading about it in the paper." Rachel's expression softened. "They never found her, did they?"

"No." Mark handed her another shot. "This is an uncropped version of the same photo."

In the blink of an eye, Rachel understood why the FBI had sought her out. The doll she'd found belonged to the kidnapped infant. Her breath hitched, and she looked at Nick. "Does this mean the feeling I had wasn't related to some incident in my past after all?"

142

"I have no idea what it means." Nick leaned forward and clasped his hands between his knees, his gaze never leaving hers. "Do you have any connection to the O'Neil family, Rachel? Or a Pearson family? That's the mother's maiden name."

"No. I don't have any relatives at all. And I have no friends in Chicago." She looked again at the photo. "Do you think my uneasiness these past few weeks is somehow related to this too?"

"What uneasiness?" Mark cast a questioning glance at Nick.

"Rachel says she's felt a little off balance and anxious since the first of the year." His eyes narrowed and he regarded her. "Do you remember when these feelings began?"

"Yes. I can tell you the exact moment because it happened so abruptly. One minute I was fine, working on a mural for a customer, and the next I was overcome by a feeling of panic. It was Saturday, January 4. About ten o'clock in the morning."

Mark riffled through the folder in his lap, scanned a sheet, and handed it to Nick, his mouth grim.

"What it is?" Rachel asked.

After reviewing the sheet, Nick expelled a long breath. "That's the day and time the O'Neil baby disappeared."

For an instant, Rachel's world tilted. This couldn't be happening. She was no psychic. She didn't believe in such things. And she doubted the men across from her did, either. Which would lead them to an obvious conclusion: she had some kind of connection to the crime.

She searched their faces. Mark's was impassive. Nick's was troubled. Neither expression was comforting. Panic clutched at her throat—and this time she could pinpoint the exact cause.

"I didn't have anything to do with this kidnapping." Her words came out taut and choked. "You can't believe that I did." She looked at Nick, but the reserved stranger bore no resemblance to the warm, engaging man with whom she'd spent a good part of her weekend.

"We're not making any accusations, Ms. Sutton," Mark told her. "We're just trying to understand why you're having these . . . feelings."

"I don't understand it, either." She heard the touch of hysteria in her voice, and she sensed a subtle shift in Nick's posture, as if he wanted to reach out and take her hand. She wished he would. Instead, he asked a question.

"Rachel, is there anything else you can tell us about this crime based on the feelings you've been having?"

"I don't know anything about the crime, period. I had no idea the doll or my feelings were connected to it."

With a glance at Nick, Mark closed the file in his lap. "I think that's all we need today, Ms. Sutton. Sorry to interrupt your day. We'd appreciate it if you'd keep the reason for our visit confidential."

The two men rose. Rachel stood too.

"Give me a minute." Nick spoke to Mark but kept his gaze fixed on Rachel.

With a nod, the dark-haired man exited.

As the door shut behind him, Nick started to take a step toward her. Stopped. "I'm sorry about this, Rachel."

She wrapped her arms around herself, wishing they were Nick's arms. "Do you believe me?"

"Yes."

At his immediate response, and the honesty in his eyes, she slowly exhaled. "I don't understand what's going on, Nick."

"We don't, either."

"I don't believe in ESP."

"Neither do we."

"But I can't think of any other explanation. My feelings of anxiety began when the baby was taken. And I had a very strong reaction to the doll." She felt the pressure of tears in her throat and tried to swallow past it. "What happens next?"

"I'm flying to Chicago to meet with the case agent this afternoon and get up to speed on all of the details. While I'm gone, our local agents will interview the staff at the Bread Company."

"That's a long shot, isn't it? The doll could have been dropped anytime that first month after the baby disappeared. I didn't find it until early February."

"It's more likely the abductor ditched it soon after the baby was taken. Maybe even the same night. Our agents will be focusing on staff working those first few days."

"Do you think the baby's still in town?"

"It's possible. The fact that you found the doll at a neighborhood mall suggests the abductor wasn't just making a quick exit from the highway for food while en route somewhere else." He took a step closer and dropped his voice. "I want you to be careful, Rachel."

The intensity in his eyes put her on alert. "Why?"

"Your name's already been connected to this crime publicly."

"You mean *St. Louis Scene*? But the story never mentioned the kidnapping."

"The abductor will make the connection—if he or she read it."

A shock wave rippled through her, and she groped for the back of her chair. Nick's fingers closed around her upper arm, steadying her.

"I never thought of that."

"Don't obsess about this. I doubt the kidnapper saw it. I just want you to be aware—and cautious."

145

She tucked her hair behind her ear with fingers that weren't quite steady. "This isn't the way I expected to start my week."

"That makes two of us."

She took off her glasses to massage the bridge of her nose, and a tremor ran through her words. "I've felt alone before, but never quite like I do now."

Reaching over, Nick lifted the slender gold cross that hung around her neck and weighed it in his hand. "You're never alone, Rachel. Hold on to this when you need a friend. If you talk, he'll listen."

Somehow she managed a half smile. "But he doesn't talk back. Not that I can hear, anyway."

"It takes a little practice to hear his voice." He released the cross. For a second, as his fingers brushed the silk of her blouse, his eyes deepened in color and she thought he was going to step forward and give her a hug. Instead, he shoved his hands in his pockets. "Call me if you need anything."

"Does that mean you aren't going to call me?" She'd intended the question to sound teasing, but it came out wistful.

"I think it would be wise to suspend our . . . social . . . relationship for the duration."

"Because you have doubts about me?"

"No." His response was immediate—and convincing. "But I want to work this case. And if my boss thinks we're involved in any way I'll get yanked."

His response made sense. That didn't mean she had to like this latest turn of events, however.

"Okay. Will you . . . or someone . . . let me know what's going on?"

"Yes. That's a promise." He took her hand and linked his fingers with hers. "And here's another one. When this is all over, you and I will make up for lost time."

146

With a gentle squeeze, he released her and slipped through the door.

Quiet descended in the office, and Rachel sank back into her chair. She needed to get back to her music class—but she also needed a couple of minutes to let her nerves settle. Fingering the cross, she tried to take comfort in Nick's assurance that she was never alone. A passage from the Scripture reading in yesterday's service echoed in her mind: "I am with you always, even unto the end of the world." It was a nice promise. And one day, if her faith grew, perhaps it would console her as it did Nick.

But at this moment, she preferred to take comfort in Nick's parting promise that he intended this unexpected glitch to be merely a brief detour on the road to a relationship.

And she was determined to let that hope sustain her through whatever lay ahead.

11

"I'm happy to go over the case with you in person, but we could probably have done this by phone and saved you a trip." Matt Carson directed his comment to Nick as he set two disposable cups of coffee on the conference room table in the multi-story Chicago field office.

Nick turned away from the wall of glass that offered a panoramic view of the darkening skyline. The shadows under his fellow agent's eyes and fine lines radiating from their corners suggested he'd been putting in long hours on the O'Neil kidnapping. The frustration of being the lead agent on a high-profile case that was stagnating had no doubt added more flecks of white to his liberally salted dark hair.

"There are some rather odd twists to this scenario that I thought would be better discussed in person." Nick took a seat at the conference table, where Matt had stacked multiple files in anticipation of their meeting. Nick added several of his own to the pile.

"I don't care how odd they are if they help us get a better handle on this case."

"You might want to reserve judgment on that until you hear what I've got. But first I'd appreciate a briefing."

The man took a swig of his coffee, pulled one of the files toward him, and opened it. "On January 4, about ten in the morning, Megan O'Neil was snatched while her mother, an organist, was at church practicing for the Sunday service. Rebecca O'Neil went to the ladies room, someone locked her in, and by the time the pastor discovered her an hour later after receiving a worried phone call from her husband when Mrs. O'Neil didn't answer her cell phone, the abductor and baby were long gone. The church has no security cameras, and no one in the neighborhood saw anything suspicious. We canvassed the whole area."

"What about trace evidence?"

"Nothing inside or out. No suspicious prints, no tire marks, no fibers. Nada."

"Did the parents check out?"

"Clean as a whistle. The father is a well-respected architect. In addition to playing the organ at church, the mother teaches at a dance studio. They've been married five years and have one other child, Bridget, who's two. No known enemies."

"And no contact from the abductor?"

"Not a word."

"What did the profilers at Quantico have to say?"

"That our abductor is a woman in her thirties or forties who simply wanted a baby. Her clean escape suggests she's intelligent—but perhaps psychotic. The profiler mentioned delusional disorder as a possibility. She said people suffering from that form of psychosis can be very functional in other areas of their life and often don't exhibit any bizarre or odd behavior except in relation to their delusion."

Nick tapped the end of his pen on the table, his expression thoughtful. "Does that mean you're operating on the assumption the baby is alive and well?"

"Until we prove otherwise. But the behavior of people with mental illness is very unpredictable. If the baby began to annoy her, she could have gotten rid of it. Dumped it in a garbage bin. Stuck it in a freezer. Thrown it in a lake. You know as well as I do the countless creative ways people can be eliminated."

"Yeah." Nick had seen plenty in his years with the Bureau and on his beat as a street cop. Man's inhumanity to man no longer had the power to turn his stomach, but he hoped he never got so immune to cruelty that he took it in stride.

"You're welcome to review all the files." Matt gestured to the table.

"I'd like to make a quick pass through them, at least. Today, if that's okay."

"Sure. Stay as late as you like. But first tell me about the doll."

Nick opened one of the files he'd brought and slid a printout of the Raggedy Ann doll across the table to Matt. "It's the same one that's in the photo of Megan O'Neil. The patch on the face is an exact match. We sent the doll to the lab, but I'm not sure it will yield any useful information. A woman found it in a Bread Company parking lot three weeks ago. We don't know how long it was exposed to the elements."

"Where has it been since she found it?"

Heat crept up Nick's neck. "In the corner of my office."

"You didn't do anything with it?"

"I had no reason to. After we made the connection with the O'Neil baby, I double-checked the descriptions of her the day she was abducted to see if I'd missed anything. There was only a brief mention of a Raggedy Ann doll. Nothing to indicate its condition or the patch above the eye."

"The mother didn't give us too many details about the doll. We didn't press her. We assumed it would be discarded immediately. That was our mistake. How did you get it?"

"This is the odd part of the story." Nick braced for the agent's response, the cardboard cup flexing beneath his fingers as his grip tightened. "It was brought in by a Rachel Sutton, who found it buried in a pile of melting slush. She said it gave her bad vibes."

The skepticism on the agent's face didn't surprise Nick. But it rankled him. Nevertheless, he kept his mouth shut.

"That's pretty off the wall."

"I thought the same thing, until a psychologist offered a reasonable explanation." Nick filled him in on Emily's theory. "After that, I shoved the doll in a corner and forgot about it until I saw the picture of Megan this morning." He took a sip of coffee. "The other odd part of this is that Ms. Sutton has been feeling unsettled and anxious for several weeks. When we pinned her down this afternoon about the onset of that feeling, it coincides almost to the minute with the kidnapping."

The other agent's eyes narrowed. "What do you know about this Rachel Sutton?"

Nick consulted his file, giving Matt the highlights.

"Busy lady," the other agent noted. "Married?"

"No. And no family. She grew up an orphan, in foster care."

"Stable?"

"Yes. There's no history of any psychological problems."

"How does she explain these feelings she gets?"

"She can't. She's as puzzled as we are." Nick closed the file. "I don't believe in ESP, but something strange is going on here. I keep thinking there's some sort of connection we're missing. Some piece of the puzzle that's fallen under the table. That's why I want to review these files."

"Could be a late night." Matt withdrew a business card from his pocket, scribbled on the back, and handed it to Nick. "If you stumble onto anything, call me. Anytime. That's my home number, for insurance." He rose, stretched, and took Nick's hand in a firm clasp. "You know, I'm tempted to tell you not to waste your time. But I've seen more than a few bizarre twists in my career. And I've learned to follow my gut on hunches. If you think there might be a clue in all this stuff"—he waved his hand over the table—"I say go for it. If nothing pans out, the only thing lost will be a night's sleep. Good luck."

Four hours and five cups of coffee later, Nick wished Matt's parting wish had paid off. But luck had been elusive. He'd been through most of the files and was no closer to understanding Rachel's vibes than he had been before.

Pulling the last file toward him, he flipped through it. More photos of Megan, and he'd already seen plenty of those. They weren't going to help.

He was about to close the file and call it a night when a studio shot caught his eye. It showed the smiling family of four in holiday attire, meaning it was pretty recent. Perhaps it had graced their Christmas cards. The mother—Rebecca O'Neil— was holding the newest addition, her features soft with tenderness as she cuddled the infant close.

Nick scrutinized the woman. There was something familiar about her. Although he'd seen her black and white photo in the newspaper after the kidnapping, he sensed there was more to his reaction than that.

Selecting a background file from the stacks on the table, he checked her stats. Born Rebecca Michelle Pearson in Columbia, Missouri. Age thirty-five. Mother, homemaker. Father, university professor. Dual degree in music and education. She'd taught until the birth of her first child. After that, she'd taken a part-time job as organist at her church. She also taught a couple of classes at a local dance studio.

Nothing there to help him.

Nick stifled a yawn and checked his watch. No wonder his brain wasn't clicking on all cylinders. He'd put in an eventful fourteen-hour day. It was time to get some food and a good night's sleep. Tomorrow, when he was fresher, he'd tackle this puzzle again.

Sooner or later, he'd pin down why Rebecca Pearson O'Neil seemed familiar. It might turn out to be irrelevant to this case. But he didn't intend to leave a single stone unturned.

✦

By five-thirty Tuesday morning, after six hours of sleep, Nick was wide awake. The image of the young mother had haunted his slumber, but he was no closer to figuring out why she looked familiar than he had been last night. He had, however, decided on a next step.

Rummaging through his suit coat, he extracted the card Matt Carson had given him and punched the man's cell number into his BlackBerry. The agent answered on the second ring.

"Matt, Nick Bradley. Sorry for the early call, but I'd like to talk with the O'Neils this morning before I fly back to St. Louis."

"Did you find something last night?"

"Nothing specific. I'm following another hunch. Rebecca O'Neil reminds me of someone, and I can't put my finger on who it is. I'm hoping if I see her in person it will click. Any problem arranging a meeting?"

"No. It would be a good opportunity for me to tell them about the doll. They've been through hell these past few weeks, and I hate to raise false hopes. But they need to know about it sooner or later. I'll set things up with them and pick you up in an hour."

Fifty-nine minutes later, Nick was waiting in the foyer of the hotel when Matt pulled up. He stowed his overnight bag in the backseat and slid in beside the agent.

"The good news is we're early enough to miss rush hour." Matt pulled away from the hotel and nosed into the already-heavy traffic. "The bad news is that even though I told Mrs. O'Neil we've made no significant progress on the case, she assumes our visit means there's been a new development that could help us find her daughter. Parents cling to hope in these situations long after there's any reason to."

Twenty-five minutes later, as Matt pulled up in front of the

153

white-clapboard Colonial the couple called home, the door opened to reveal a man with his arm around a woman's shoulders. The distraught parents, who had obviously been watching for them, radiated an almost palpable anticipation.

"See what I mean?" Matt said under his breath as they traversed the brick walkway.

The man pushed the storm door open as they approached and ushered them inside. About five-ten, he looked to be close to forty, with a haggard face and premature flecks of silver in his dark hair. "Agent Carson, it's good to see you." He nodded to the man and extended his hand to Nick. "Colin O'Neil. This is my wife, Rebecca."

"Nick Bradley." Nick shook hands with each of them. The man's grip was firm, but he could feel a quiver in the woman's delicate fingers. She was about five-four, with the high cheekbones of a classic beauty and the turned-up nose of a pixie. An interesting combination. Her short brown hair, soft and fluffed around her face, was touched with auburn highlights. The dark smudges under her eyes offered a stark contrast to her pale complexion, and she was painfully thin.

When Matt had said they'd been through hell, he hadn't been exaggerating. It was obvious the trauma of the kidnapping had taken a heavy toll on both parents.

"Please, come in. Make yourself comfortable." Colin swept a hand toward the living room, where upholstered couches flanked a fireplace mantel topped with long tapers in brass candlesticks.

The two agents took one couch as the parents perched across from them. Colin clasped Rebecca's hand and leaned forward. "You have new information?"

Matt tipped his head toward Nick, giving him the floor.

Withdrawing a file from his portfolio, Nick flipped it open. "This was found in St. Louis three weeks ago and turned over to the FBI. Yesterday, we realized the significance." He laid the computer-generated print of the Raggedy Ann doll on the coffee table between them. "I happened to notice what appeared to be orange yarn at the very bottom of a picture of Megan in the FBI file. I asked for the full shot and discovered we had a match."

Rebecca leaned close to examine the printout. "You found Megan's doll!" She gasped and snatched up the paper, clutching it against her chest. "Where? How?"

While Nick explained, he observed the young mother. In person, the sense of familiarity was even stronger. Yet he was certain they'd never met.

"You mean some woman turned the doll in because she got a bad feeling from it?"

At the cautious question from Colin, Nick transferred his attention to the baby's father. "Yes. We discounted it—until we made the connection to the kidnapping. This woman has also been uneasy since the day and hour your child was abducted."

"Are we talking ESP here?" Skepticism edged out some of the hope in Colin's eyes.

"We don't know how to explain it," Nick replied.

"I don't care what the explanation is, as long as it helps us find Megan." Rebecca leaned forward, her features taut. "What does this discovery mean in terms of the case? Do you think this woman might be involved?"

"No. We checked her out," Nick said.

"And I'm afraid the discovery doesn't mean much." Matt gentled his tone. "The St. Louis office is questioning employees at the restaurant where the doll was found, but it's unlikely anyone will remember anything significant. That's why I told you earlier that we're no closer to finding Megan than we were before."

"Of course we are!" Bright spots of color burned in Rebecca's cheeks. "We have her doll. We know she was in St. Louis. She

155

may still be there. And maybe this woman can help us some more."

"I'm afraid not." Nick hated to dampen her enthusiasm, but he had to be honest. "This is a new experience for her too, and she couldn't offer us anything else."

Rebecca's shoulders drooped. "At least we have the doll." She examined the photo once more, again holding it close to her face.

"Did you forget to put your contacts in, Rebecca?" Colin brushed a wispy strand of hair off her forehead.

"Yes. But I can see well enough to recognize Megan's Raggedy Ann." She stroked the photo of the patched face with the lopsided smile, her features softening. "May I get the doll back at some point?"

"Of course," Nick assured her.

"It was mine as a child. That's why it's in such bad shape. I practically loved it to death, or so my mother tells me." A smile of remembrance whispered at her lips. "Megan loves it as much as I did. She won't go to sleep without it. I gave it to Bridget, our two-year-old, when she was born, but she was never interested in dolls. She's more into finger painting."

"That's because she's artistic, like you." Colin gave his wife a squeeze. "Rebecca did the watercolor over the mantel," he told the two agents.

As Nick turned to give the pastoral scene a polite perusal, he saw Rebecca moisten her lips with the tip of her tongue and tuck her hair behind her ear.

Jolted by the familiar gesture, he froze.

Rachel did the exact same thing when she was nervous or embarrassed.

Refocusing on the woman seated opposite him, Nick took a closer look. Rebecca O'Neil and Rachel Sutton did share some physical characteristics. They were about the same height, had

156

the same body build and eye color, and both had brown hair with glints of auburn. However, the two women didn't look anything alike. Different noses, bone structure, chins. Even the shape of their faces was dissimilar.

But Rebecca O'Neil did remind him of someone . . . and suddenly the connection clicked into place.

She bore a marked resemblance to the woman in the photo on Rachel's mantel.

To Rachel's mother.

In fact, she looked more like Rachel's mother than Rachel did.

And though the two younger women didn't resemble each other, they were similar in other ways. They shared the same gestures. They both had vision issues. Both were involved in music. Rebecca danced; Rachel had always wanted to. Both had artistic talent. Rebecca had once taught music; Rachel still did.

It couldn't all be coincidence.

Yet Rachel had said she had no relatives.

"Mrs. O'Neil." The room went silent, and Nick realized he'd interrupted a conversation. "Sorry. I wanted to ask if, by any chance, the name of the woman who found the doll might be familiar to you. Rachel Sutton."

Rebecca frowned and shook her head. "No. It doesn't ring any bells. Why?"

"You remind me of her in many ways. Do you have any relatives in the St. Louis area?"

"Not that I know of. My dad was an economics professor at the University of Missouri in Columbia, but he took a position at Northwestern soon after I was born. My mother's family was from Boston, and she only had one unmarried sister who died a few years ago. My dad was an only child, like me. He grew up in Wisconsin. I don't have any relatives at all, other than my mom. She lives here in town. My dad passed away three years ago."

157

Dead end.

"Anything else, Nick?" Matt asked.

"No." Nick closed his portfolio.

"Do you need this back?" Rebecca indicated the photo of the doll.

"No. We can print off some more."

"Will you be concentrating your efforts in the St. Louis vicinity now?" Colin asked.

"We'll be working the case in multiple areas."

Matt's evasive answer didn't get past Colin. "Does that mean you don't think she's in St. Louis?"

"She may be," Nick stepped in. "The restaurant was in a neighborhood. Not the kind of place you'd patronize if you were passing through on the highway. That may or may not be significant. But I can assure you the FBI will do everything it can to check out any leads related to this case." He handed him his card. "Call me anytime if you have questions."

He didn't tell the parents about the plans being made even as they spoke to dredge the waste center where the dumpster from the restaurant was always emptied . . . in case the abductor had tossed in more than the doll. They didn't need to start envisioning that possibility.

"We're going to find her, you know." Rebecca took her husband's hand and directed a steady, confident gaze at the two agents. "And she's going to be okay. I'm her mother. I'd know if she was—" she faltered, took a deep breath—"if there wasn't any hope. God is going to bring her home to us, safe and healthy. I have absolute confidence in that."

"We'll do our best to make that happen, Mrs. O'Neil." Matt rose and motioned to Nick. "We'll be in touch with any news."

As the two agents shook hands with the parents and headed back to the car, Matt turned up his collar against the biting wind and shoved his hands in the pockets of his coat. "She's never given up. Prayer has been her coping mechanism. You have to admire her faith."

Nick agreed. But his thoughts were more on coincidence than creed. Wasn't it logical that two women who shared so many characteristics would somehow be related? What was the explanation for the onset of Rachel's persistent uneasiness on the exact day and hour Megan had been snatched? Why did Rebecca O'Neil bear such a strong resemblance to Rachel's mother?

It seemed he now had another mystery to unravel in addition to the kidnapping.

And he didn't intend to rest until both were solved.

12

"Mom? Did I wake you?"

"No, honey. I was up." Jeannette Pearson switched the phone to her better ear, trying to disguise the weariness in her voice. She didn't want Rebecca worrying about her too.

Tightening her flannel robe against the morning chill in the brick bungalow she'd called home for thirty-three years, she slid a cup of decaf instant coffee into the microwave. Warmth had been as elusive as sleep during the past few nightmare weeks. She couldn't seem to chase away the coldness in her house—or her heart. Steadying herself with a hand against the Formica countertop, she blinked back the tears that had been only a breath away since the day her precious grandbaby had disappeared.

"We had some news this morning, Mom. A new lead. The FBI has Megan's doll."

Hope surged in Jeannette's heart. Maintaining her grip on the counter, she worked her way over to the table in her eat-in kitchen and sank onto a chair. "Where?"

"In St. Louis."

"Do they think Megan is there?"

"It's possible. The agents warned us not to get our hopes up, but I have a feeling this is a breakthrough."

"Where did they find the doll?"

"They didn't. A woman dug it out of a snowbank in a restaurant parking lot and brought it to their office. Here's the weird part. She told them it gave her bad vibes."

"And they believed her?" Jeannette would have expected the FBI to write the woman off as a nut, though she was grateful they hadn't.

"I don't think so. Not at first. They've had the doll for three weeks. They didn't realize it was Megan's until an agent in St. Louis noticed it in one of the photos we gave the FBI."

"Do they think this woman might be connected to the kidnapping?"

"No. Colin wondered the same thing, but they've checked her out and she's okay. Here's another strange thing, though. She told them she's been feeling uneasy since the day Megan was taken."

A tiny flutter of alarm quivered at the base of Jeannette's spine. "How odd."

"There's more. The agent from St. Louis said I reminded him of her, and asked if I had any relatives in St. Louis. We don't, do we, Mom?"

"None that I know of." Jeanette's response was automatic—and truthful. A lot of years had passed. People moved all the time, especially in today's world.

"That's what I told him. But he kept watching me. It was rather disconcerting."

The tingle moved higher on Jeannette's spine. Was it possible? No. The odds against such a coincidence would be astronomical. Yet a small flicker of uncertainty, a prod of intuition, compelled her to ask the logical follow-up question. "Did they tell you the woman's name?"

"Yes. Rachel Sutton."

Jeannette's lungs froze. As she struggled for breath, the familiar blue morning glories on her kitchen wallpaper faded in and out of focus.

"Mom? Mom, are you there? Are you all right?"

Rebecca's anxious voice reached into the darkness that was sucking her down and tugged her back to the light. "Yes. I'm fine, honey." The words came out shaky and faint.

161

"You don't sound fine. Listen, I'm going to run over, okay?"

"No. I just need my morning cup of coffee, that's all."

"Are you sure? You're taking your medicine, aren't you?"

"Every day." Since her heart attack two years ago, Rebecca had fussed over her like a mother hen, reversing their roles. Not that Jeannette was complaining. She'd heard plenty of horror stories from friends whose children only gave them a perfunctory check-in call every few weeks. Rebecca, on the other hand, called or visited daily—sometimes twice a day.

Now Megan's disappearance had added to the worry that weighed down Rebecca's slender shoulders. Jeannette wished there was something she could do to smooth the furrows from her only child's brow, to wipe away the shadows under her eyes as she'd once wiped away her daughter's childhood tears.

"I don't mind coming over, Mom."

At Rebecca's comment, Jeannette forced herself to refocus. "I know, honey. But there's no need. I'll call you a little later, after I'm more awake. Okay?"

"Okay."

Rebecca didn't sound convinced, but Jeannette was glad she'd relented. She needed some time alone to recover from her shock and think things through. "I love you, honey."

"I love you back."

Pressing the off button on her portable phone, Jeanette set it on the table. They always ended their calls the same way. With an expression of love. Her friends had often remarked on Rebecca's kind, caring nature, crediting it to her and Stan's parenting skills. And there was some truth to that. She and Stan had lavished love on their only child, who had come into their lives after both had given up hope of having the family they'd always wanted. From the instant they'd held her in their arms, Rebecca had added joy and light to their days. They'd always considered her a precious gift.

162

The microwave pinged, alerting Jeannette that her coffee was ready. Gripping the edge of the table, she pulled herself to her feet and crossed the faded linoleum. For years, Rebecca had been after her to update the house. In recent months, however, her daughter had changed tactics, urging her instead to sell the place and move to a condo.

But Jeannette hated change. Always had. She had a good life, for the most part, except for the increasing reminders from her seventy-four-year-old body that time was passing. Why upset the applecart? If life was good, why change it? You could end up making things worse instead of better.

She retrieved her coffee, pausing to finger the gaudy potholders Rebecca had woven in a craft class the summer before she entered third grade. They'd hung in a place of honor beside the stove for more than twenty-five years. Continuing toward the table, she lingered in front of the refrigerator, where a dozen magnets held photos of happy times, some so old the color had faded.

Taking her seat again, she ran her hand gently over the worn pine surface where she and Rebecca and Stan had shared thousands of meals. Where laughter and conversation had flowed. Where homework had been done and after-school snacks devoured. Where she and Stan had shared end-of-day chats over a cup of coffee after Rebecca went to bed. Fresh-brewed in those days. Not instant.

Jeannette stared into the dark depths of her mug. Things changed, that was the truth of it. No matter how hard you tried to hold on to a perfect moment, it passed. People grew up. Got married. Died. Change happened. Period.

And not all of it was bad, like Stan's death had been. While the black hole that it had left in her life would never be filled, Rebecca's marriage had brought many blessings. Instead of losing a daughter, she truly had gained a son. Colin treated her with the same respect and consideration he showed his own mother. And out of that marriage had come the incredible gift of grandchildren. Bridget and Megan not only helped fill the empty place in her heart left by Stan's death, they added sunshine to her days. Once again, she had begun to taste the sweetness life could offer.

Until Megan disappeared.

And that brought her back to Rebecca's bombshell.

Rachel Sutton.

What a bizarre twist of fate. Never could she have imagined that a choice she'd made decades ago would come back to haunt her, bringing with it new decisions and the daunting specter of change. And her feelings about it were the same as they'd been for thirty-five years. The notion of sharing her secret still scared her to death.

Lifting her mug with unsteady hands, Jeannette took a sip of her coffee. Stan had never understood her fear. Especially once Rebecca reached adulthood. He'd often encouraged her to reconsider her decision. Yet he'd respected her wish to maintain the status quo.

In truth, Jeannette didn't quite understand the fear herself. She supposed, if a psychiatrist dug deep into her background, a cause would be lurking there somewhere. Maybe it was connected to her studious, introverted best friend, who'd told her once that she always felt like an outsider in her boisterous family. Or perhaps the memory of her aunt and uncle's distress when her cousin had run away from home at eighteen to "find herself" was somehow to blame for her anxiety. But the cause didn't matter. The fear was there, no matter the source.

If Stan were here, Jeannette knew what he'd say. And he'd be right. Holding on to her secret when the life of her granddaughter might hang in the balance was unforgivably selfish. From the instant Rebecca had mentioned Rachel's name, Jeannette had known what she had to do.

But first she'd spend an hour seeking strength and courage from the Lord.

"Are you still getting calls about that article in *St. Louis Scene*?" Marta took a bite of her hamburger and slid the bag of fries across the table toward Rachel.

"They've tapered off." Rachel slid the bag back without succumbing to temptation and speared some lettuce and a chunk of meat out of her chicken Caesar salad. "Nick said it would be old news pretty fast, and it's been four days."

"Speaking of Nick . . . I was afraid he'd invite you to some little French café again and you'd stand me up."

Rachel played with her fork. "Not for a while."

Marta looked around the crowded fast-food outlet and lowered her voice. "His impromptu official visit yesterday didn't put an end to your relationship, did it?"

"No. But it's on hold for a bit." Everyone at both schools where she taught had known within hours that the FBI had come calling. A wry smile twisted Rachel's lips. The grapevine was alive and well in the world of elementary education.

"Can you talk about it?"

"Sorry. They asked me not to."

"That's okay. I'm married to a cop, remember? I know all about discretion and confidentiality and not compromising cases. I'm just glad their visit didn't dampen the romance."

"I'm not sure I'd call it a romance at this stage."

"Trust me, it's a romance. The man invites you out to a cozy café for lunch, sends you roses, makes you glow—romance, no question about it. And that reminds me . . . I want to hear all about the weekend you described to me yesterday as amazing. We only had five minutes, and I've been dying to hear the details."

Smiling, Rachel toyed with her lettuce. "It was perfect. We went to the Botanical Garden. Took in a movie. Ate dinner on

165

The Hill. And that was just Saturday. Oh, and did I mention he cooks a mean eggs Benedict?"

Marta swallowed and stared at her. "He cooked for you? Wow." She shook her head. "I've been married ten years, and the one time Joe tried to fix dinner we had to call the fire department."

"Very funny."

"No. Very true. The neighbors still talk about it. What did you do on Sunday?"

"We went to church, and then he drove me to the hotel and stayed for tea while I played."

"You went to church. And he went to tea." Marta mulled that over as she munched on a French fry. "This is serious, Rachel."

"It's too soon to be serious."

"It might be too soon to buy a marriage license, but it's not too soon to know it could be serious. I knew Joe was the one on our first date. Sparks flew from the beginning. They still do. How are you and Nick doing in the sparks department?"

A flush warmed her cheeks. "I'd call it more like an electrical storm. On my end, anyway."

Marta wadded up the wrapper from her burger and dropped it in the bag, grinning. "Yep. Romance with a capital R. And all thanks to a bedraggled Raggedy Ann doll. What a story to tell your grandchildren."

As Rachel followed Marta out, she considered her friend's final comment. Although the foster system had taught her to be cautious about jumping to conclusions or expecting too much, deep in her heart she had a feeling Marta might be right.

And as soon as Nick was finished with the O'Neil case, she intended to find out.

13

"Mrs. O'Neil . . . Sorry to delay you, but do you have a minute?"

Balancing a foil-wrapped muffin on top of a covered dinner plate, Rebecca secured the magazines tucked under her arm and shifted toward the voice.

Dismayed, she watched as Doug Montesi, the reporter from the *Tribune* who'd been covering the kidnapping case, unfolded his long, lanky frame from an older-model car in front of her house. He was nice enough, and he seemed to have integrity, but she was anxious to be on her way. She hadn't liked how her mom had sounded this morning, and she'd picked up a strong undertone of tension when her mother had called back and asked her to stop by. Besides, she'd been diligent about following the FBI's advice to limit her contact with the press to official public statements.

Doug loped across her lawn. "You have quite a handful there. Can I help with anything?"

"No thanks."

"At least let me get the door."

Before she could protest, he pulled it open. Too bad she hadn't loaded up in the garage instead of pulling out first. But with full arms, it was easier to maneuver in the driveway than in a confined space.

"She sure is a cutie." Doug leaned down and smiled at

Bridget, who observed him, finger in mouth, from her car seat.

"What can I do for you, Mr. Montesi?" Rebecca leaned past Bridget to set the plate of food on the seat.

"I thought I'd stop by and see if there was any news. We haven't run any updates on the case for a while, and all I get from the FBI is the standard line."

"I don't have anything to add, either." Rebecca reached under her arm for the reading material she was taking to her mother. As she pulled the magazines out, a single sheet fluttered to the ground.

Doug stooped to pick it up, and Rebecca bent over to dump the magazines on the floor of the back seat. Bridget grabbed her hair, giggling as Rebecca tried to extricate herself.

"I think I'm going to have to call the tickle monster," Rebecca teased, rubbing noses with Bridget as she tickled her tummy. The flaxen-haired toddler chortled, releasing her.

Smiling, Rebecca swung around to find Doug staring at the printout of the Raggedy Ann doll the FBI had given her this morning. Her smile vanished and she snatched the photo from his hands, slammed Bridget's door, and backed toward the driver's seat.

"That's the doll Megan had when she was abducted, isn't it, Mrs. O'Neil?"

"No comment." She groped for the door handle behind her.

"But you mentioned it in a press conference, remember?" He stuck his hands in his pockets, his stance casual, his eyes probing. "It's public knowledge. The doll is awfully dirty, though. I'm surprised you let an infant play with it."

"It wasn't dirty before . . ." Her voice trailed off.

"So the FBI found the doll."

Rebecca opened the door and slid behind the wheel without responding. She'd said too much already. But the picture alone would probably have tipped off the reporter. The journalist might have a friendly, aw-shucks demeanor, but you didn't get to be the lead crime reporter on a paper like the *Tribune* without a lot of smarts. Plus some sense of integrity.

And as she shut the door, put the car in gear, and backed out of the driveway, she prayed he would use both when dealing with this new information.

★

At the chime of the doorbell, Jeannette's heart began to thump. She'd prayed for fortitude to get her through the coming ordeal, and she hoped the Lord had been listening.

Pulling open the front door, she held out her arms for Bridget as a distracted Rebecca handed her over.

"I have some magazines and food in the car. Can you take off her snowsuit?" Without waiting for a reply, Rebecca headed back to her car at a jog.

Five minutes later, after boots had been removed, coats hung, and food stowed in the fridge, Rebecca pulled out her cell phone. "Do you mind if I make a quick call before we visit, Mom? A reporter cornered me at home, and I want to let Agent Carson know about it."

"Was there a problem?"

"No. But he saw this." She pulled the photo of the Raggedy Ann doll out of the stack of magazines and handed it to Jeannette. "I'm assuming he figured out that it's turned up."

Jeannette studied the image. It was Megan's doll, no question about it. She'd put the original patch on that face three decades ago. It had been replaced several times through the years, and new ones had been added on the arms and legs, but the large one above the right eye had been the first.

The condition of the doll alarmed her, however. And convinced her she'd made the right decision. She wanted her grandbaby back safe and sound—not torn and tattered, like this doll. Putting credence in Rachel Sutton's vibes might be a long shot, but she couldn't ignore any lead, no matter how improbable.

"Don't hurry, honey. I'll put Bridget down for her nap so we can visit."

Ten minutes later, after Bridget had dozed off in the portable crib in the spare bedroom, Jeannette found Rebecca in the kitchen. Her daughter was staring out the window at the frozen, lifeless backyard, the weary droop of her shoulders a silent testimony to the toll these past few weeks had taken on her usual upbeat spirit.

Jeannette set a dusty shoe box on the kitchen table and wiped her fingers on her slacks, leaving smudges on the dark fabric.

Turning, Rebecca eyed the yellowed cardboard container. "What's that?"

"A long story. How about some hot chocolate?" That had always been Rebecca's comfort drink. Whenever she'd faced a crisis—being snubbed by a friend, losing out on a part in the school play, missing the senior prom because of a flu bug—Jeannette had offered hot chocolate and a shoulder to cry on. In the past, the home remedy had worked as a soothing balm.

She hoped it still did.

"That would be nice, Mom. Thanks. Do you want me to make it?"

"No. I could do it in my sleep. Sit down and relax."

As if that were possible for any of them.

"Did you have trouble putting Bridget down?" Rebecca took the spot she'd occupied since the day she'd sat at this table in her high chair.

Jeannette measured instant cocoa powder and filled two mugs with milk.

"No. I sang her a couple of songs and she went right to sleep."

"That worked on me too, as I recall. You had a way of making me feel safe and secure. You were always my protector." Rebecca blinked and looked down at the table. "I didn't do a very good job following in your footsteps, did I?"

"Don't ever think that." Jeannette's tone was fierce as she moved beside Rebecca and put an arm around her shoulders. "You're a wonderful mother. What happened wasn't your fault."

"I shouldn't have left Megan alone."

"You only went to the bathroom. You couldn't have known someone was hiding in an empty church."

"I should have been more careful."

"Look at me, Rebecca." Jeannette waited until her daughter lifted her chin. For the first time she saw a crack in the strong, determined face Rebecca had maintained since the kidnapping, and her throat tightened. "You did nothing wrong. There was no reason for you to think you were a target. Whoever did this planned it well."

"It doesn't matter. I should have taken Megan with me." Rebecca pushed her fingers through her hair, distress pinching her features.

The microwave pinged, and Jeannette removed the mugs of hot chocolate. She put one in front of Rebecca and settled into her place with the other. Pulling the yellowed box toward her, Jeannette prayed for courage. "Mothers always have some regrets, Rebecca. It goes with the territory, I suppose. Hindsight is twenty-twenty, as the old saying reminds us." She traced a design in the dust on the box. A heart appeared as she completed the second curve.

"You shouldn't have any. You were—and are—a wonderful mother."

171

"I hope you still feel that way when you leave here today." A tremor shook Jeannette's voice.

Frowning, Rebecca covered Jeannette's hand with her own. "Of course I will. Why would you worry about that?"

"Because of what's in here." Jeannette rested her fingers lightly on the box.

Rebecca gave the box a look that was both curious and dismissive. "I already know what's in your heart. Whatever is in that box won't change how I feel about you."

As she lifted the lid, Jeannette prayed that was true. Sifting through the meager contents, she withdrew a photo and placed it face down on the table in front of her. "I've had this box for thirty-five years, Rebecca. For a long time, I told myself that I was keeping the secret for your sake. That I wanted you to have a secure childhood unencumbered by uncertainties or angst.

"But as the years went by and you grew into a confident, grounded young woman, that excuse didn't hold up anymore. Your father thought it was a mistake to keep it from you, but I held back. For selfish reasons. I was afraid if you knew the truth, you'd stop loving me. And I couldn't risk that. You meant the world to me, and I was terrified of losing you."

Jeannette turned the photo over and examined it. "After all these years, I thought the secret was safe. That it wasn't important for you to know. You have your own family now, and the past seemed of little consequence. Then the Raggedy Ann doll led to Rachel Sutton. I can't begin to imagine the odds against that happening by chance. I have to believe it's a sign your paths were meant to cross. That you're supposed to know each other."

Sliding the photo toward her daughter, Jeannette folded her hands into a white-knuckled knot on the table as her heart lurched into a staccato rhythm. "Rachel Sutton is on the right."

For several long seconds, Rebecca kept her gaze on her mother's drawn face, fighting the fear sluicing through her. She didn't want to look at the five-by-seven photo on the table in front of her. Some instinct told her it would turn her world upside down. And she'd had enough tumult in the past few weeks to last a lifetime. Two lifetimes.

Yet the fact that her mother had a photo of the woman who'd found Megan's doll and had gone to the FBI with her bizarre story couldn't be mere coincidence, as her mother had noted. She had to face what was in this picture. Whatever the consequences.

Without touching it, Rebecca looked at the photo. The first thing she noticed was the brand-new Raggedy Ann doll. A seated toddler, with curly copper hair and a quarter-sized birthmark on her right temple, was clutching it.

She moved on to the rest of the picture. In the center, a young woman with long auburn hair parted in the middle smiled at the camera. A filigree gold cross hung around her neck. She had one arm around the child holding the doll—and the other around the child's mirror image on her other side.

Identical twins.

Except for the birthmark, it was impossible to tell the two little girls apart.

But everyone in the photo was a stranger to Rebecca.

Puzzled, she looked back at her mother. "I don't understand. How do you know these people?"

"That's your Raggedy Ann doll, Rebecca."

She examined the photo again. "But . . . I don't have a birthmark."

"No. But your sister did."

The world tilted. She had a sister? Rachel Sutton, the woman who'd found the doll, was her *sister*?

173

But that would mean . . . the woman in the photo must be . . .

"That's your birth mother, Rebecca. Your dad and I adopted you a month after that photo was taken."

Shock rippled through Rebecca. "That . . . can't be. I've seen my birth certificate."

"When a child is adopted, the birth certificate is amended by court order so it bears the surname of the adoptive parents. The original certificate is sealed by the court."

Jeannette leaned over and took Rebecca's cold hand in hers. "I'm sorry, honey. I should have told you long ago. But in the beginning, I didn't want you to have to wonder who you were or if you were loved. Your dad and I couldn't have loved you more if we'd been your birth parents. Later, I was afraid if you knew, you wouldn't think of me as your mother anymore. My ego couldn't handle the competition. I'm so sorry, honey."

A barrage of questions clamored for answers as Rebecca tried to process her mother's bombshell. "What was my birth mother's name?"

"Michelle Sutton."

"Who was my father?"

"He wasn't listed on the birth certificate."

"Is Rebecca my original name?"

"Yes."

"What happened to her. To . . . Michelle." Rebecca stared at the young woman in the photo, feeling numb.

"She was killed in a car accident when you were nine months old. We learned that she was an unwed mother who had been disowned by her family. There was no one to take you after she died. Your dad and I had been on a wait list for years for an infant adoption. We wanted a newborn, but the agency called us about you, and after one look we knew you were meant to be our daughter."

"Why didn't you take Rachel too?"

"She was hurt very badly in the accident, Rebecca. Your dad and I were older, and we didn't think we could cope with two toddlers, one of whom would need ongoing medical care—if she survived. Her side of the car took the brunt of the impact. You suffered only minor injuries."

"But . . . if she's my identical twin, why don't we look alike? The agent from St. Louis would have noticed if there was a strong resemblance."

"She had major facial injuries that required reconstructive surgery. I assume that could dramatically alter a person's appearance."

Rebecca touched the photo. "And this is Megan's Raggedy Ann doll."

"Yes."

"Yet Rachel is holding it in the picture. How did I end up with it?"

"It was found in the car after the accident. It must have flown out of Rachel's hands at the time of impact. We didn't know who it belonged to, so the authorities gave it to me. I didn't discover until the pictures were forwarded to us that it belonged to your sister. But you never let it out of your sight. Perhaps it reminded you of her."

"So I have an identical twin." Rebecca spoke the words, hoping that if she gave voice to them the reality would sink in.

"Yes. And identical twins are linked in ways science is still trying to understand. For example, you suffered from headaches when you were young, and the doctor could never find a physiological reason for them. I often wondered if it had something to do with your sister's facial injuries."

"Do you think this . . . link . . . is why Rachel has had a feeling of uneasiness since Megan was taken?"

"I think there could be a connection." Jeannette slid the box toward Rebecca. "This is everything the agency sent to me. Your mother had very little worth keeping. I selected one photo of your mother for Rachel, and gave her the cross in that picture as well. With all of the medical problems she faced, I thought she needed the hope it represented. There's not much in here . . . mostly photos, a few personal items, a couple of pieces of costume jewelry."

Rebecca sifted through the items, dazed.

"Are you okay, honey?" Jeannette placed a tentative hand on her arm.

"I don't know."

"Please don't hold this against me." Jeannette's voice broke. "I've always wanted what's best for you. I'm so sorry I let my own insecurity stop me from sharing information you had a right to know."

"It's okay, Mom." Rebecca squeezed her hand, not certain that was true, yet feeling compelled to offer a reassurance to the only mother she'd ever known. A woman who had earned the title in every way. "I just . . . need to think this through. And I want to meet my sister."

"I understand that. Why don't you ask the FBI agent from St. Louis to set that up for you? And maybe if you see her, she'll have other feelings that could help the authorities locate Megan."

"Do you think that's possible?" The fading ember of hope in Rebecca's heart flared.

"I don't know what to think. But I wouldn't want to leave one stone unturned."

"I agree. I'll give the agent a call." Rebecca wrapped her hands around the mug of hot chocolate, trapping in her palms the residual warmth that remained in the cooling beverage. "You know, I've been praying for a reunion. But I expected it to be with a daughter, not a sister."

"Perhaps it will be with both."

"I think it will. I'm more convinced than ever that Megan is safe, and that I'll hold her in my arms again soon. I don't think God brought Rachel back into my life as a substitute, but as a bonus."

"Hang on to that hope, honey." A tear spilled out of Jeannette's eye, and she wiped it away with shaky fingers. "Now call that FBI man and go meet your sister."

14

Nick's phone was ringing as he strode into his office late Tuesday afternoon after spending three hours on the tarmac at O'Hare thanks to an ice storm. For once he hadn't minded the delay. He'd been too busy sorting through theories that might explain the uncanny resemblance shared by Rachel, Rebecca, and Rachel's mother. The most prominent one was that the three women were related in some way. And he was determined to figure out how.

But the mystery was cleared up without any further effort on his part when he picked up the phone, gave his standard greeting, and found Rebecca O'Neil on the other end. As he listened to her story, he felt relief rather than surprise. His instincts were usually sound, but he'd been starting to think he was off base on his hunches in this case. Instead, he'd been right on the money.

Rebecca concluded with a request. "Since you've already had dealings with Rachel, I wondered if you'd be comfortable breaking the news to her and seeing if she'd be willing to get together with me. I can drive down as early as tomorrow if that works with her schedule. I'm anxious to meet her and to thank her for following up on those vibes she felt about the doll."

"I'll be happy to arrange it. May I call you later tonight?"

"That would be fine. Thank you."

As Nick hung up, Mark stuck his head in the door to the cube. "How was the trip to Chicago?"

Nick turned toward him. "Eventful."

"Yeah? How so?" Mark stifled a yawn and leaned against the doorway.

"Rebecca O'Neil and Rachel Sutton are identical twins."

"What!" Mark straightened up, his posture morphing from relaxed to rapt in a heartbeat.

"Amazing, isn't it? I knew Rebecca's photo in the file last night looked familiar. And when I met her this morning, she shared some of Rachel's gestures. That's when I realized she bore a striking resemblance to a photo Rachel has of her mother."

A frown creased Mark's brow. "But I've seen pictures of Rebecca O'Neil. And I've met Rachel. They don't look alike. How can they be identical twins?"

"According to Rebecca, Rachel was badly injured in the accident that killed their mother. Surgery could have altered her appearance. Rachel may be able to fill in those blanks."

"I wonder if their relationship also explains the vibes she's been getting?"

"That's my guess. Do you think Emily could shed any light on the situation?"

"Let's ring her and find out. The conference room is free. Want to duck in there?"

"Yeah. Give me a minute, though. I just walked in the door and I need to check messages."

"Don't rush. She may be with a patient. I'll buzz you when I get her."

Ten minutes later, Mark summoned him to the conference room. As Nick walked in and closed the door behind him, Mark switched the call to speaker. "Nick's here, Em."

"Hi, Nick. Mark just filled me in. You've been dipping into

some unusual stuff on this case. Parapsychology. Psychometry. Now twin telepathy."

"Is there such a thing?"

"If you're asking whether there's absolute scientific proof for it, no. But there's a lot of anecdotal evidence suggesting some identical twins have it."

"Even ones who don't know of each other's existence and have been separated since they were nine months old?"

"Yes. It's a fascinating subject. There are cases in which one twin is injured and the other feels a physical sensation or pain in that part of the body. Identical twins have also been known to have similar jobs, cars, pets, and favorite foods. There's even a theory that identical twins share a unique language when they're young."

"Rebecca and Rachel do share gestures," Nick offered. "And they're both into music and art. What about the telepathy part you mentioned? Could it account for the feelings Rachel has been having?"

"I still think Rachel's reaction to the doll relates to past experience," Emily said. "Perhaps deep in her subconscious she has a tactile memory of holding it at the time of the accident. As for the uneasy feelings that began the day her sister's daughter was kidnapped, they could be related to twin telepathy—if you accept the theory that it exists. In general, a sense of shared experience would involve some very traumatic, highly emotional incident, and the kidnapping certainly fits that description."

"Rebecca has asked to meet Rachel. Do you think there's any chance, once they meet, that Rachel might be able to offer us any more insights into this case?"

"I wish I could say yes. But her telepathy, if she has it, is related to her sister's experiences, not to her niece's."

"Okay. Thanks, Emily."

"Glad to help, Nick. Mark, are you still planning to pick up pizza for dinner?"

He grinned. "Have I ever forgotten anything food related?"

"Good point."

"See you later, Em." He severed the connection, leaned back, and regarded Nick. "Interesting stuff."

"True. But unless Emily is wrong about the telepathy thing not extending beyond Rachel and Rebecca, it's not going to help us find Megan."

✯

Rachel had just shoved her bare feet into her fuzzy pink slippers and picked up a load of laundry when the doorbell rang.

Pausing at the head of the basement stairs, she checked her watch. Almost nine o'clock. Not a good sign. Maybe it was that pushy reporter from *St. Louis Scene.* Or someone who'd read the article and wanted her to communicate with some long-lost relative.

Neither option was appealing.

She considered ignoring the bell, but when it rang again—twice in a row—she decided to check it out. Dumping the laundry at the head of the stairs, she edged over to the door and quietly put her eye to the peephole.

Nick stood on the other side, collar turned up against the bitter cold, hands shoved deep into the pockets of his topcoat.

A warm rush of pleasure swept over her. After their brief conversation yesterday, she hadn't expected to see or hear from him again until the O'Neil case was solved. But perhaps his trip to Chicago had resulted in a lead that had helped wrap things up. Meaning they could pick up where they'd left off last weekend.

That thought sent a tingle up her spine and put a smile on her face.

Rubbing her palms against the worn denim of her jeans, she pulled open the door. "Hi. This is a nice surprise."

He smiled, and the warmth in his blue eyes told her he was glad to be there. But the crinkles at the corners spoke of weariness.

"Does that mean I can come in?"

Stepping back, Rachel created space for him in the tiny corner of her living room that served as a foyer. "Let me take your coat."

"Thanks." He shrugged it off and handed it to her.

The wool fabric was frosty to the touch, and she held it away from her as she slipped the sleeves onto a hanger and stowed it in her small closet. A shiver rippled through her, and she gave him a rueful shrug as he cocked an eyebrow. "The cold goes right through me. I should live in the tropics. White sand, palm trees, warm breezes . . . and no more cold feet."

"You seem to have found a solution for that problem." One side of his mouth hitched up as he directed his attention to her slippers.

She wiggled her toes and grinned. "They may not be fashionable, but they do the trick."

"I think they're cute."

Flushing, she decided it was time to change the subject. "Tell me about Chicago. Since you're here, can I assume you have good news on the case?" She snuggled into one corner of the couch, her feet tucked under her.

"I do have news. But it's not directly related to the case."

Some nuance in his tone put her on alert. "What kind of news?"

"I may have an explanation for the uneasy feeling you've had since the O'Neil baby was kidnapped."

That snagged her attention. "Tell me, please. I've wracked my brain for answers and come up with zero."

"It has to do with Rebecca O'Neil." He walked over to the mantel and retrieved the photo of her mother, then took a seat beside her. "As she herself just discovered earlier today, the two of you share a very special bond. Rebecca's mother told her this afternoon that she was adopted thirty-five years ago. And that she had an identical twin sister who was badly injured in the car accident that killed their mother. A sister who was put into the care of the foster system." His gaze locked on hers. "You and Rebecca O'Neil are twins, Rachel."

Seconds ticked by as Rachel stared at Nick. The only sounds in the room were the crackle of the fire, the hiss of water vaporizing from the damp wood, and the sudden collapse of spent logs as they disintegrated, sending embers flying.

I have a sister. A twin sister.

The words echoed in Rachel's mind. She understood Nick's message but couldn't quite absorb it. All her life she'd thought she was alone. That there was no one in the world she could call on in time of need, nor anyone to share special occasions with. So many solitary Thanksgivings and Christmases and birthdays had passed. And all along, she'd had a sister—*a sister!*—who could have been part of her life.

Her stomach twisted into a knot at the injustice of it.

"Rachel? Are you okay?"

Nick's gentle question pulled her back to the present. His long, lean fingers rested on her arm, his tender touch reassuring yet strong, offering support if she needed it. When she lifted her head, she found his discerning blue eyes fixed on her, and a slight frown wrinkled his brow.

"Shock doesn't even begin to describe how I feel." Her unsteady reply came out in a whisper. "How could Rebecca's mother keep this a secret all these years?"

183

"I think Rebecca is struggling with the same question." He set the photo on the coffee table. "She bears a strong resemblance to your mother, by the way. But while the two of you share some characteristics, you look nothing alike."

"I've had a lot of facial reconstruction. The accident did a number on my face as well as my leg." She responded automatically, still grappling with the emotional tsunami.

"That's what I heard. Rebecca has a photo of the two of you with your mother, and you were identical back then. That photo revealed another interesting fact. The Raggedy Ann doll belonged to you, Rachel. You had it with you in the car when the accident happened. Emily thinks that's why you had such a strong reaction to it."

Rachel gave a slow nod, forcing herself to focus on the conversation. "I guess I can buy that. I might have a memory of that event on some subliminal level. But what about this uneasiness? Did she have an explanation for that too?"

"Nothing the world of science recognizes. But she said there have been many recorded cases of telepathy between identical twins. Even between those who've been separated since birth. And you and Rebecca had nine months together before you were split. Rebecca's mother told her she often had headaches as a toddler, with no physiological basis. And that she occasionally limped, again for no obvious reason. It could have been related to your surgeries."

"This is bizarre."

"I agree. But the anecdotal evidence does suggest you two share some sort of special link." He leaned closer and laced his fingers with hers. "She'd like to meet you, Rachel. As soon as possible. She's offered to drive down tomorrow if you're willing to see her."

"Of course I am!" She might be confused about a lot of things, but the decision about whether to meet her sister wasn't one of them. "I have a family, Nick! A family." She repeated the words, her voice filled with wonder. "I feel like you probably felt when Dan Foley took you under his wing and gave you a sense of belonging. It's an incredible gift."

"I hoped you'd look at it that way."

"How else could I look at it?"

He stroked the back of her hand with his thumb. "You have every right to be angry. It wasn't fair that you were kept in the dark about your sister."

"I am. But I learned long ago that life isn't always fair, Nick. And being angry doesn't change anything." She fingered the cross at her neck, recalling the minister's comment in Sunday's sermon about leaving judgment in the hands of the Lord. "Instead, I'm going to try to focus on being grateful for this amazing blessing. It's almost big enough to inspire me to pray."

She was only half joking, and Nick seemed to recognize that. "You already made a start on that last Sunday. Maybe we can go together again once this case is settled."

"I might take you up on that."

He squeezed her fingers and released her hand. "What time shall I tell Rebecca to arrive tomorrow? I promised to call her back tonight, after I talked with you."

Rachel tucked her hair behind her ear. "Do you think she'd want to come here for dinner? Or should I meet her somewhere?"

"I suspect she'd prefer the privacy of your house."

"Okay. But . . . could you come too? At least for a while? Join us for dinner, maybe. Stay until the ice is broken?"

"If you want me here, I'll be here. And now"—he glanced at his watch—"it's time for me to head home. And for you to get some sleep."

He rose, and she trailed behind him toward the door. "I doubt I'll sleep a wink tonight."

"Why do I think Rebecca feels the same way?" He smiled as he retrieved his coat from the closet.

"Nick? Is she nice?"

At her soft question, Nick slid his arms into the sleeves and turned toward her. "Very. Just like her sister." He touched her cheek . . . let his fingers linger against her skin . . . then retracted his hand and shoved it into his pocket. "And you'll have a lot to talk about. She's into music and art, like you are."

A sudden cloud robbed some of the joy from Rachel's heart. "Do you think the main reason she wants to meet me is because she hopes I can help with the case?"

Searching her eyes, Nick closed the distance between them and took her upper arms in a light but reassuring grip. "I'll be clear about that with her tonight. But I doubt it will make any difference. I think she's as happy to discover a sister as you are."

"I hope so." A wistful longing crept into Rachel's voice. "I've done okay on my own, but it gets lonely sometimes when you don't have anyone who really cares about you. You know?"

"Yeah. I do."

As Nick looked down at her, Rachel watched his eyes begin to smolder. Felt the spark of electricity zap between them. And knew he wanted to kiss her.

Perhaps as much as she wanted him to.

But he was a professional through and through. A man who didn't believe in mixing business and pleasure. So while he might be tempted to make an exception tonight, she wasn't surprised when he released her and stepped back.

"I'll call you later, as soon as I talk to Rebecca."

"That would be great."

She followed him to the door, waiting as he pulled it open. "Lock up behind me."

Once more he touched her face.

Once more he pulled back.

Then, stepping into the night, he lowered his head against the icy wind and strode toward his car.

A gust of frigid air chilled Rachel's cheeks as she watched him retreat, but she hardly noticed. Because her heart was warm.

15

"Hi, Claudia. Got a minute?"

Claudia tucked her cell phone under her chin and kept typing, trying to block out the noise in the newsroom as she responded to her sister. "That's about it, Keri. I'm on deadline. What's up?"

"There was an article in the *Tribune* this morning I thought you might find interesting."

"Yeah? What about?"

"You know that psychic piece you emailed me last week? I thought it was a hoot. But the *Tribune* ran a follow-up today on the O'Neil kidnapping, and guess what? The baby's doll has been found. A beat-up Raggedy Ann, like the one in your story. Think there's any connection?"

Claudia's fingers froze on the keyboard. "It's a long shot."

"When has that ever stopped you from following a lead?"

"True. Okay, I'll pull up the online version of the *Tribune* story and take a look. How did you happen to notice this, anyway?" Claudia loved her sister, but Keri was a bit of a flake. She was usually more interested in going on auditions for dog food or deodorant commercials than reading her city's daily paper.

"I was at my agent's office and the paper was lying there. It was a front-page story. I noticed the picture of the baby—cute kid—and skimmed the first few lines. The reference to the doll was at the beginning."

"If this pans out, I'll owe you big time."

"Just invite me to the ceremony when you win the Pulitzer Prize."

"Yeah. Right." She had about as much chance of that as Keri had of winning an Oscar. "Any good gigs lately?"

"I'm up for a spot in a toothpaste commercial."

"Break a leg, kid. Talk to you soon."

As Claudia flipped her cell phone closed, she checked her watch. Five o'clock. Stacy would still be around. The editor never left before the end of the official work day, and often stayed late. Good thing. Because Claudia needed her permission to put the people-with-unusual-pets piece she was working on aside and focus on a follow-up to last week's psychic article. With copy due at noon tomorrow, she would need every single waking minute to glean enough new information to write an intriguing story.

Rachel smoothed a tiny crease out of the linen tablecloth, adjusted a spray of the baby's breath she'd salvaged from Nick's roses and worked into a fresh bunch of carnations, and refolded a napkin at the table set for three. A pork tenderloin was roasting, homemade biscuits were sitting on a baking sheet on the kitchen counter ready to be popped into the oven at the last minute, an apple pie was cooling on a rack. From the second she'd left school she'd been in a frenzy of preparation for tonight's momentous meeting.

But that was okay. Activity helped dispel some of her nervous energy. Sitting around waiting would have stretched her taut nerves to the breaking point.

The bell chimed, and Rachel's hand flew to the cross around her neck—a gesture that was becoming instinctive at times of stress. Where once she'd looked upon it as no more than a lovely piece of jewelry and a link to the mother she'd never known, more and more she was beginning to recognize it as a symbol of a far greater truth. One she didn't yet fully understand but which drew her in a compelling way. And, thanks to Nick, she intended to explore it further, as soon as her life quieted down a bit.

Taking a deep breath, Rachel crossed the living room. Nick had said he would arrive first, at six, and a quick peek through the peephole confirmed he'd kept that promise.

When she opened the door, he smiled and gave her green silk blouse, slim black skirt, and classic black pumps a quick but thorough inspection. "Nice."

Her pulse quickened at his appreciative perusal. "It's not too dressy?"

"It's perfect." A gust of wind buffeted him from behind, and he took a step inside, chuckling. "I think that's my cue to come in."

As he shrugged out of his coat, she opened the closet door. Fumbled with a hanger. Dropped it.

He bent to retrieve it, his eyes inches from hers as he rose. "Nervous?"

"Is it that obvious?"

"It's normal." He hung the coat himself and closed the closet door. "I'm sure Rebecca feels the same way. Is there anything I can do to help you get ready?"

"Pray?" Her tone was half teasing, half serious.

"I've already done that." There was no humor in his response, and she was touched by his concern. "Anything else?"

I could use a hug.

In the silence that followed his question, Nick's eyes darkened, and an ember flared in their depths. Had she actually spoken the words? No, of course she hadn't. But she began to suspect Nick might have some psychic abilities himself. She had the distinct feeling he'd read her mind.

Thrown, she took a step back and tried for a conversational tone. But the slight catch in her voice gave her away. "I j-just need to put the salad together."

She watched, mesmerized, as he slowly tamped out the ember, admiring his self-discipline even as she had an irrational wish that he had a little less self-control.

"I'm good with salads. Let me take care of that for you."

His mild reply was a stark contrast to the electricity zipping between them. But she did her best to follow his lead as she led the way to the kitchen. She had enough emotions to deal with tonight. Adding a romantic encounter would *not* be a good idea.

But it sure was appealing.

Interesting.

Very interesting.

As Claudia slowed to a stop several houses away from Rachel's bungalow, she scrutinized the dark sedan parked in front, her lips tipping up into a smug grin. Pulling out her notebook, she flipped through the pages. Yep. It was the FBI agent's car, the one she'd seen in the restaurant parking lot when the man had met Rachel for lunch. The description and license plate number she'd jotted down that day matched. It always paid to be thorough. You never knew when those kinds of details would come in handy.

Before driving to Rachel's house, she'd also done some research on the O'Neil case. Scanned back issues of the *Tribune*, studied the photos of the infant and parents. It was a sad situation. The baby had been gone for eight weeks. A long time in the world of law enforcement. Claudia doubted there was much chance the FBI would find her unless they got some kind of big break.

Like a psychic who picked up vibes from a Raggedy Ann doll.

Not that she put much credence in such things herself. Who did? But neither did she have a closed mind. Perhaps once in a great while there was a person who had special abilities. She'd learned a lot while writing the original article, and there were definitely things in the psychic world that logic couldn't explain. Maybe this was one of them. If the FBI was still in touch with Rachel Sutton, *they* must think so.

Neither the Bureau nor Rachel had been willing to talk to her before, but Claudia intended to give it one more try. Even one quote would enhance the article.

Retrieving her purse from the seat beside her, Claudia was about to open her door when a second car pulled to a stop across the street from Rachel's house.

Fingers poised on the handle, she watched—and waited.

One minute passed. Two. Three. There was no movement from the car, and it was too dark for Claudia to see who was inside.

Five minutes went by. Her car began to chill in the sub-freezing temperature, and she tapped one gloved finger on the steering wheel. Who was in the car? What were they waiting for? Did they have any connection to Rachel Sutton, or was it just a teenage couple that, by chance, had chosen this spot to do a little making out?

After six minutes, Claudia decided she'd waited long enough. Her fingers were getting numb, and whoever was in that car didn't seem inclined to move.

Slinging her purse strap over her shoulder, she settled her notebook in the crook of her arm and slid out of her car.

She'd gone no more than a dozen feet when the door opened on the other vehicle and a slender woman stepped out. Claudia slowed her pace, watching. The woman adjusted her coat, smoothed her hair, tucked a clutch bag under her arm. Crossing the street, she headed for Rachel's house.

She seemed familiar, though the ornate streetlights were more decorative than practical, leaving her face in shadows. Wanting a closer look, Claudia picked up her pace.

Not until the woman stepped from the street onto the sidewalk in front of Rachel's house did she notice Claudia. She stopped, twisted away, fiddled with her handbag. Claudia, on the other hand, didn't falter. She kept on walking, directing an innocuous smile at the woman as she drew close.

"Cold night, isn't it?"

The woman lifted her chin, offering a return smile that seemed forced as the dim glow from the streetlight illuminated her face. "Yes. Very."

Claudia almost had apoplexy.

It was Rebecca O'Neil.

The kidnapped baby's mother.

She recognized her from the newspaper photos she'd seen less than an hour ago.

Somehow, Claudia managed to rein in her shock and keep walking. She couldn't turn around until Rebecca O'Neil entered the house. That might raise suspicions.

But in three minutes, she planned to run, not walk, back to her car.

Because this was the scoop of a lifetime! Rachel Sutton and the FBI could say they didn't believe in psychics, but as far as Claudia was concerned, actions spoke louder than words.

St. Louis Scene readers would eat this up.

★

Rebecca checked her watch. Six-thirty on the dot. It was time to meet her sister.

She lifted her hand, preparing to knock. Hesitated. Tried to regulate her breathing. Failed.

What if they didn't like each other? What if this reunion disrupted both their lives? What if . . .

The door was pulled open, interrupting her panicked musings. Special Agent Nick Bradley stood on the other side, as if he'd been watching for her. As if he'd suspected she'd get cold feet. As if he'd guessed she might need a final nudge to walk over the threshold and into a different future.

"Hello, Mrs. O'Neil. We've been waiting for you." He smiled and leaned closer, dropping his voice as he winked. "And Rachel is just as nervous about this as you are."

Some of Rebecca's tension melted away. It was going to be okay. She'd prayed about this, and in her heart she knew she was doing the right thing. Meeting Rachel might not restore Megan to her arms—the FBI agent had already explained that there was little chance the link Rachel felt toward her would extend to her daughter—but sisters should know each other.

Taking a fortifying breath, she stepped inside.

★

From her spot next to the fireplace, beside their mother's picture, Rachel watched Rebecca O'Neil—her twin sister—enter her home. She'd searched out her picture on the internet after Nick dropped his bombshell, so she'd known what Rebecca looked like. But a photo couldn't compare to seeing the living, breathing person.

As Nick slipped the coat off Rebecca's shoulders and took her purse, the sisters locked gazes. In unison, they moistened their lips with the tips of their tongues and tucked their hair behind their ear. Startled by the mirror-image gesture, Rachel stared at Rebecca. Rebecca stared back.

Unsure if her unsteady legs would support her, Rachel managed a tremulous smile. She walked toward her sister and held out her hand. "Welcome."

Instead of taking her hand, Rebecca enfolded her in a hug. "I think sisters can do better than a handshake, don't you?"

The tears in Rebecca's voice paralleled the ones welling in Rachel's eyes as she returned the embrace. "Absolutely. I'm just sorry our meeting was under these circumstances."

"Me too." Rebecca stepped out of the hug but took both of Rachel's hands in her own. "But I haven't given up hope. I know everyone is doing everything they can to find Megan. Just like you did, by going to the FBI with the doll. That took a lot of courage. I can imagine the reaction you got."

Rachel flicked a glance at Nick over Rebecca's shoulder. "To be honest, I was shown a lot more consideration than I expected."

"I'm glad for that, anyway." She blinked again and swiped the moisture out of her eyes, managing a shaky laugh. "You know, even if we didn't have the paperwork to prove we were identical twins, this is pretty powerful evidence." She gestured toward their attire.

Now that Rebecca had pointed it out, the striking similarity in their choice of clothing for the evening registered. Like Rachel, Rebecca wore black pumps, a slim black skirt, and a silk blouse in the very same jacquard pattern and style. Hers, however, was teal blue instead of teal green.

Rachel shook her head. "Wow. This is weird."

"Here's something else weird." Rebecca walked over to the couch and fingered the wool throw. "Is this from Pottery Barn?"

"Yes."

"I have the exact same one in our family room."

Perching on the arm of the couch, Rachel folded her arms. "Nick told me you're into music too. What's your favorite musical?"

"Camelot." At Rachel's grin, Rebecca smiled. "Let me guess. Yours too?"

"Yep. Do you like chocolate?"

"Love it."

"Dark or milk?"

"Milk. Is there any other kind worth eating?"

"I agree." Rachel tipped her head, beginning to enjoy this. "But I hate coconut."

"Me too. I can also live without peas. Unless we're having them tonight . . ."

"Not a chance. I put peas in the same category as castor oil. Now broccoli . . . that's another story."

"I love broccoli."

"Good. Because it's on the menu. And speaking of food, dinner is served. I thought you might be hungry after your long drive."

"Starved. May I freshen up first?"

"Of course. First door on your right, down the hall."

As Rebecca disappeared, Rachel turned toward the kitchen— and caught sight of Nick by the front door. He stood with one shoulder propped against the wall, arms folded, one leg crossed over the other, toe planted in her carpet. With a smile, he pushed off and ambled toward her. "Looks like you don't need me to run interference after all. The ice has not only been broken, it's melted. How about I make a quiet exit and leave you two to catch up?"

"No way. I promised you dinner." She took his arm and drew him toward the dining room. "Besides, there might be a lag in the conversation and we'll need you to step in."

"Okay. You don't have to twist my arm. The food smells great."

But in the end, Rachel had to admit his presence was super-fluous. She and Rebecca gabbed nonstop during dinner, as if they'd known each other for all of their thirty-five years, often finishing each other's sentences. Periodically they remembered Nick's presence and tried to include him in the lively exchange, but she wasn't surprised when he set his napkin on the table after dessert and rose.

"I think I'm ready to call it a night, ladies."

Both women checked their traditional-style gold watches.

"I can't believe it's nine o'clock already." Rebecca shook her head.

"You're sure you can't stay a little longer?" Rachel asked Nick.

"Not tonight."

"I'll walk you out, then. Excuse me for a minute, Rebecca?"

"Don't hurry. I'm loving this Irish cream coffee. Nick, thank you for setting this up." She extended her hand.

"It was my pleasure." After taking her fingers in a firm grip, he followed Rachel to the living room. She already had his coat out, and he grinned. "Anxious to get rid of me, I see."

"Not at all." She lowered his coat. "Would you like to stay longer?"

He touched her cheek, his eyes softening. "I was kidding. I'm happy you two hit it off."

She leaned into his touch, and at the pressure against his fingers he cupped her chin and smoothed the hair back from her forehead. When he spoke, the husky cadence in his voice told her she wasn't the only one affected by the simple contact. "Enjoy the moment, okay? These kinds of special nights don't happen often."

"Rachel, is there any more cream in . . . oops, sorry." Rebecca took a step back and gave them a rueful smile as Nick dropped his hand. "I'll find some in the kitchen. Don't rush your good-byes on my account."

"I have a feeling I'm going to get teased about this later. Siblings are like that, from everything I've heard." Rachel smiled, liking the sound of that word. "But you know what? I don't mind in the least."

"What will you tell her?" Nick took the coat and slipped his arms into the sleeves.

She gave him an assessing look. "What *should* I tell her?"

"How about the truth? That we're dating."

"Are we?"

"Count on it. As soon as this case is over."

A delicious tingle zipped through her. "Too bad I can't speed the process along. I wish this telepathy thing extended beyond Rebecca." Some of her happiness dimmed. "She's put up a good front tonight, Nick, but losing a child to kidnapping . . . it has to be awful. When I hugged her, I could feel her bones. She's way too thin. And even makeup can't camouflage the dark circles under eyes."

"I noticed. But we don't have a lot to work with. The leads have pretty much dried up."

"Rebecca hasn't given up."

"I know."

"Has the FBI? Please, Nick . . . tell me the truth."

He searched her face, and she could tell he was weighing his response.

"It's been eight weeks, Rachel. The kidnapper could be any-where by now. Megan may not . . ." He stopped for a moment. "Let me put it this way. We don't often see happy reunions after such a long time."

She appreciated his honesty. But she wasn't going to give up. Not yet.

"Rebecca and I had one after thirty-five years, Nick. That was a long shot too. I'm on Rebecca's side. I have a feeling the kidnapping will end well also. And soon."

"I agree it's an outcome worth praying for. Good night, Rachel."

As Nick strode down the walk toward his car, Rachel eased the door shut, her spirits dipping. While she was deeply grateful she and Rebecca had found each other, perhaps a reunion of mother and baby as well might be too much to hope for.

Yet she had the oddest feeling that something big was about to break on this case.

16

"Debra? Is that you?"

Heart pounding, Debra clicked Danielle into the safety seat, shut the door, and turned, blocking the view into her car. What in the world was Warren Peterson doing in St. Louis? She'd chosen the city because no one here knew her. To avoid encounters like this one.

As her ex-husband's co-worker strode across the strip-mall parking lot toward her, Debra tried to curb her escalating panic. She had a story prepared for such an emergency. *Stay calm. Act normal. Get rid of him as fast as you can.*

"Hello, Warren."

"I thought it was you. I didn't know you were in St. Louis."

"I moved here a few months ago. After the divorce."

"Yeah." He shoved his hands into the pockets of his oversized coat. "I was sorry to hear about the split."

"It happens." She managed to keep her tone neutral while fighting down the urge to scream, *"Go away. Leave me alone!"*

"So how've you been?"

Small talk. The man wanted to make small talk when all she wanted him to do was disappear. She'd never liked Warren. He was such a nerd. No social skills—or fashion sense. Today he wore gold corduroy pants that were too short, scuffed hiking boots, and a putrid green coat missing a button. But a lot of her ex-husband's fellow academicians were like that. Typical absentminded-professor types. At least Allen had managed to find matching socks each morning.

"I'm fine, Warren. What are you doing here?"

"Attending a chemistry conference."

"Is Allen here?" Her panic surged again.

"No. I came by myself. I could have driven back tonight, but I thought I'd wander around, take in the sights. After I got lost three times, though, I decided a movie was safer." With a sheepish smile, he gestured toward the cinema across the mall parking lot. "Never did have a sense of direction. Anyway, I'll be heading home in the morning. I've got an easy Friday this semester. Just one class in the afternoon, and I'll be back in plenty of time for that. I'm always up with the chickens, anyway."

Debra jingled her keys. Of all days to decide to stop for Chinese on the way home. Warren had cornered her once at a faculty Christmas party and talked her arm off until she'd ditched him. He seemed poised to do the same tonight. Too bad he wasn't more like Allen. Her ex-husband's introverted quietness might have bothered some wives, but it had never been a problem for her. She hadn't married him for conversation.

She turned up the collar of her coat and affected a shiver. "I've got to get in out of the cold."

"It is pretty chilly here." He didn't move.

So much for dropping subtle hints. Turning, Debra opened her door and started to slide behind the wheel.

"Cute baby."

She jerked upright again. Warren was smiling at the infant in the backseat, doing the kind of idiotic facial gyrations adults always inflicted on babies. Or perhaps they were an indication of his real personality. Debra aimed a dark frown at him as she fought off the urge to push him away from the car and burn rubber getting away.

"I'm watching her for a friend. Good-bye, Warren." Congratulating herself on her calm tone despite the churning in her stomach, Debra slid into the driver's seat and shut the door.

Warren didn't move away until she started the engine, put the car in gear, and began to back out of the parking spot.

He was still waving, a stupid grin plastered on his face, as she drove off.

Watching him recede in her rearview mirror, Debra tried not to let fear muddle her brain. She had to think rationally, like she did on the job.

Don't let panic confuse you. Confusion could lead to mistakes. And mistakes could destroy your dream.

She repeated that over and over until a cheery gurgle from the backseat drew her attention to the rearview mirror again. Danielle was pumping her fists and bouncing in her car seat. Such a happy little camper. At her antics, Debra's lips relaxed into a smile, and contentment eased the tension in her shoulders. The little cherub was the light of her life. If that light ever went away . . .

Her trembling fingers tightened on the wheel. That wasn't going to happen. She wouldn't *let* it happen. She was ready to do whatever it took to keep her little girl with her. For always.

As for Warren . . . it had been dark in the parking lot, and the backseat had been shadowed. He couldn't have gotten a clear look at Danielle. And even if he had, it wouldn't matter. Her hair had grown, and the brown hue was unremarkable. Not that Warren was likely to notice, anyway. A guy who regularly forgot where he parked, as he'd admitted to her once at a faculty party, wouldn't be inclined to pay attention to details.

Still, Debra had no doubt he'd mention their meeting to Allen. The man had a chronic case of flapping gums. But Allen would have little interest in details about his ex-wife. He'd made it clear when they split that he wanted no further contact with her.

The feeling had been mutual.

There could be other threats down the road, however. Ones more dangerous than Warren. She'd realized that after reading the *St. Louis Scene* article last week, which hadn't amounted to anything, either. But it had prompted her to action. She'd spent Saturday playing with Danielle—and drawing up a contingency plan. On Sunday, she'd scouted around the rural area within a few-mile radius of her house and found the perfect place to dispose of any . . . problem. Earlier this week she'd purchased the necessary equipment.

She didn't need to implement her plan for Warren. Running into him had been more annoying than menacing.

But she was ready to deal with anyone who did become a threat.

✫

"You're in the news again."

Nick turned from the coffeemaker in the FBI lunch room to find Ellen Levine in the doorway. His stomach clenched as she waved the latest edition of *St. Louis Scene* at him.

"What are they up to now?"

"Top of page three." She thumbed through, folded back the tabloid, and handed it over. "Hot off the press. I picked it up when I went out for lunch."

Taking the paper, Nick read the headline.

**LOCAL PSYCHIC HAS LINK
TO O'NEIL KIDNAPPING CASE**

The subhead was even more specific.

**Doll found by Rachel Sutton
belonged to Megan O'Neil;
Kidnapped child's mother meets with Sutton and FBI**

The tabloid had rerun the photo of Rachel it had used the previous week, and picked up photos of Rebecca and Megan O'Neil from AP and official press releases.

Nick's lips settled into a grim line. "That reporter must be stalking Rachel again." The speculative item in the *Tribune* on Wednesday about the discovery of the doll had been marginal journalism, as far as he was concerned. But this was worse.

"I've already had a call from the *Post*. Also the local Fox affiliate. I expect I'll get more."

Nick bit back a word that wasn't pretty. If the kidnapper was still in town, the odds were decent she wouldn't be a *St. Louis Scene* reader, given the paper's limited circulation. But if major papers and TV stations began to pick up on this, the news would spread. And if the kidnapper bought into the telepathic mumbo jumbo, she wouldn't be too happy about a psychic sleuth on her trail. Things could get dicey.

"What's the plan?" His question came out terse.

"I'm on my way to see Marty. Want to come along?"

"Yeah." Nick set his untouched coffee on the counter. A lot of SACs were political figureheads who spent their days attending meetings. Not Marty. In this kind of high-profile case, he'd make the final call on press dealings—after conferring with the Chicago office. But Nick had a vested interest in the decision and he wanted in on the discussion.

Trailing Ellen down the hall, he speed-read the article. For the most part it was a recap of the case, culled from previous stories in other papers and press releases. Very little new information had been added, other than the connection between Rebecca, Rachel, and the doll. But that complicated things.

A lot.

At best, Ellen and her cohorts would find a way to make the disclosure work to the FBI's advantage.

At worst, it could put an innocent woman in jeopardy.

And the latter possibility made his blood run cold.

✫

Ten minutes later, after listening to Ellen's update, Marty Holtzman pushed back from his orderly, uncluttered desk, moved to the window, and stared through the glass. Nick knew he'd been a top field agent in his heyday, and he remained lean and wiry, still moving with the panther-like grace of a born athlete. When he swung toward them, a beam of afternoon sun silvered his short gray hair. "What's your recommendation, Ellen?"

"We could hold our 'no comment' position, but it might be to our advantage to provide some additional information. I talked with Shaun Watson, the media rep for the Chicago office, and since the *Tribune* piece ran Wednesday, they've been getting queries too."

Nick understood the rationale for Ellen's suggestion. The strategic release of information to the media often resulted in tips. Most were useless. But sometimes all it took was one good lead to crack a case. The problem was, they had little new data to share.

"What would we say?" Nick interjected. "We don't have any news. Our questioning of Bread Company staff didn't turn up anything helpful. All we have is a doll."

"On the contrary," Ellen disagreed. "We have a great human interest angle. Rebecca and Rachel are identical twins. They were separated at birth, and the doll Rachel found belonged to her as an infant. That's pretty powerful stuff. The media will love it."

"I doubt Rebecca and Rachel will." Nick tapped a finger on

204

the arm of his chair. "And that connection isn't relevant to the case. It hasn't contributed anything to our investigation."

"True," Ellen conceded. "But my main goal is to get the story back in the headlines. Flush out some new leads."

"It could also spook the kidnapper." Marty sat back in his chair and folded his arms on his desk. "If Megan O'Neil is still alive and we turn up the heat publicly, our kidnapper could decide the baby is no longer worth the risk."

"But if this is positioned correctly, it could have the opposite effect." Nick mentally worked through an approach that would reduce the risk to Megan—and Rachel. "Let's assume our kidnapper has heard about the psychic angle. If she's gullible, she may have bought into it. We could use the press conference to shift the focus from psychic abilities to twin telepathy—and make it clear the latter doesn't extend to nieces. That should relieve our kidnapper's mind on that score. And an implication that the active investigation is waning should calm her down too. But it wouldn't stop tips, which is what we're after."

"I agree." Marty looked at Ellen. "You okay with that approach?"

"It was more or less what Shaun and I had in mind."

"Okay. Let me run this by the SAC in Chicago and headquarters. Nick, get in touch with Rebecca O'Neil and Rachel Sutton. Alert them to the *Scene* article and make sure we have contact numbers for them 24/7 for the weekend. I'll call you both later."

As Marty picked up his phone, Nick stood, stepping aside to let Ellen precede him into the hall.

"Considering the calls I've already had, you might want to give the two sisters a heads-up ASAP," Ellen suggested.

"Any advice you want me to pass on?"

"Tell them to stick with 'no comment' until we have a firm game plan. Hopefully by end of day." With a wave, she headed back to her office.

Returning to his cube, Nick checked his watch. Rachel was still in class, so he left a message on her cell and rang Rebecca. After briefing her on the latest news story, he relayed Ellen's advice and promised to call as soon as they had a firm plan.

By the time that conversation ended, his message light was blinking. Rachel, he assumed. After tapping in her number, he wasn't surprised when she answered on the first ring.

"Nick? Is everything okay?"

The anxiety in her voice tugged at his gut. He hated to be the bearer of bad news. But she'd find out about the article anyway, and he'd rather she heard about it from him. "I wanted to warn you that we've caught the attention of *St. Louis Scene* again."

"Tell me you're kidding." Dismay flattened her words.

"I wish I was. I'm speculating your friendly reporter saw the *Tribune* article, made the connection to the doll, and decided you were still newsworthy. I don't know if she's been following you or just decided to pay you a visit and got lucky on her timing, but she's aware that you, me, and Rebecca met at your house on Wednesday night. She implied in her piece that the FBI is pursuing a psychic lead on the O'Neil kidnapping."

"But that's a lie!"

"We're talking about *St. Louis Scene* here, Rachel."

She gave a frustrated sigh. "What happens now?"

"We're working on a game plan. Until it's implemented, I'd suggest you lay low. Stick with 'no comment' if the press contacts you."

"What about the people who want me to communicate with their dead uncle? Or find their missing dog? This will bring a whole new batch of them out of the woodwork."

"Let your phone roll to the answering machine."

"Trust me, I will." She huffed out another breath. "You know, I'm beginning to think this *Scene* reporter Claudia has psychic abilities of her own. Or is very, very lucky."

"I agree. But we should have a plan later today to counter her claim. Will you be home tonight? I could stop by and put Rebecca on speaker so we can all discuss it."

"I'll be here. But I can think of better ways to spend a Friday night."

He chuckled. "Me too. And we'll get to those once this is over. In the meantime, how about I bring over a pizza?"

"That sounds nice and normal. You're on. You know, I'm very quickly learning that I don't have the temperament for cloak-and-dagger stuff. My taste runs to safer things—like art and teaching and playing the piano. Oh—speaking of taste . . . no olives on the pizza, okay?"

"No olives. Check. I'll call you before I leave the office to let you know I'm on my way. It could be a little later than usual. And Rachel . . . go straight home, okay?" He reread the headline in the *Scene* article, fighting down a feeling of unease.

"Why? Do you think some nut might try to corner me in the grocery store for a séance?"

"I'd prefer not to take any chances. Just be a little careful until we implement the plan. You have my cell number . . . call me if you spot anything suspicious."

"Now I *know* I'm not cut out for cloak-and-dagger stuff." She tried for a joking tone but didn't pull it off.

"Everything will be fine, Rachel. We've got it under control."

"Okay." She still sounded shook up. "See you soon."

As the line went dead, Nick wished he felt as confident as he'd sounded when he'd reassured her. But he'd been in the business a long time. And he knew even the best-laid plans sometimes went awry. While he was certain the strategy Ellen and her cohorts devised would be sound, there were never any guarantees.

If he thought it would do any good to request protection for Rachel, he'd ask. But the FBI didn't have sufficient staff for that. No law enforcement agency did. Only VIPs and witnesses merited security, and the U.S. Marshals Service usually handled that.

All he could do was try his best to keep Rachel safe until the risk went away.

And until Ellen and her cohorts came up with a plan that would put to rest the psychic drivel perpetuated by *St. Louis Scene* and reassure the kidnapper that Rachel wasn't a threat, he intended to stick close.

"Hi, Ms. Kraus." Marsha flipped her long blonde hair over her shoulder, set aside the newspaper she was reading, and gave Debra a bright smile. "You're early today. Getting a head start on the weekend?"

"Yes." In truth, Debra had left work at three on the premise of a dental appointment. Since her run-in with Warren yesterday, she'd been feeling jittery. And her nightmare-plagued slumber hadn't helped. In her dreams, she'd kept waking up to find her baby's crib empty. She'd finally risen before dawn to sit in the rocking chair beside her daughter's bed and watch her sleep. Only that gave her some semblance of peace.

This morning, she'd been tempted to call in sick. But she was loathe to change her routine or do anything that would attract attention. She'd worked with enough legal briefs to know that out-of-pattern behavior was a red flag. So she'd left Danielle at daycare as usual, even though it had been agony dropping her off, and gone into work. By mid-afternoon, however, the need to hold her daughter in her arms had overpowered the need to maintain a normal schedule.

"Good for you. I wish I could cut out early once in a while on Friday." Marsha slid off her stool at the front desk. "I'll go get Danielle. Have a seat for a minute. Oh, and take a look at this while you wait." She handed over the paper she'd been reading. "Remember that article we talked about last week? The one about the psychic? Looks like there was something to it, after all. Pretty weird, if you ask me."

As Marsha punched numbers into the security keypad on the wall behind the desk and disappeared through the door, Debra read the headline. And almost threw up.

All her conclusions about last week's article had been wrong.

The FBI *hadn't* written Rachel Sutton off as a nut. The woman *had* had specific information. And she'd led them to Rebecca O'Neil.

Megan's mother.

Hands trembling, Debra scanned the article. It didn't say much more than the headline. But those few facts were plenty.

Except the reporter had left out one important piece of data.

Megan O'Neil had ceased to exist two months ago, the day Danielle—*her* daughter—had taken the other infant's place.

It was too bad for the mother that Megan was gone. Debra could empathize with her, could understand her sense of loss. But she had another daughter. Bridget. Why couldn't she be satisfied with that?

She probably would have been, if it hadn't been for Rachel Sutton. Debra scowled at the photo of the woman at the piano. If this Rachel had picked up vibes from the doll, if she'd led the police to Rebecca, what other information might she discern now that the women had met and talked? Would she be able to tune into some wavelength that could lead the authorities to her and Danielle?

Debra's first instinct was to grab her daughter, get in her car, and take off. Disappear.

Except . . . maybe it wasn't possible to vanish if a psychic was involved. Maybe this Rachel would be able to pick up vibes no matter where she and Danielle went.

The contingency plan she'd developed after her encounter with Warren flashed through her mind. It was a drastic step, though. Not one she'd expected—or wanted—to take.

But nothing was more important than protecting the life she'd created for herself and Danielle.

Nothing.

"Here she is, Ms. Kraus." Marsha pulled up the hood on Danielle's snowsuit as she stepped through the door. "We want to stay warm, don't we, sweetie? The weatherman says we're going to have a cold, cold weekend. We wouldn't want Jack Frost to get you, would we?" She tapped the baby's nose, and Danielle giggled as Marsha shifted her into Debra's waiting arms. "Here you go, Mommy. Such a cutie. She must be lots of fun."

"Yes, she is."

And that wasn't going to change.

Debra headed toward her car, shielding her baby from the gusty, frigid air. After settling Danielle in her car seat, Debra handed her the teddy bear her daughter had come to love. A replacement for the doll that had caused far too many problems.

She should have listened to her instincts and gotten rid of the Raggedy Ann in Chicago, tears or no tears from her daughter. But she couldn't change the past. All she could do was protect her future.

By getting rid of something else instead.

17

Three hours later, Nick took a seat at a right angle to Rachel and set his BlackBerry on her dining room table. "Rebecca? I'm here with Rachel. You're on speaker."

"Hi, Rachel." Rebecca's voice came over the line. "Did you guys eat your pizza yet?"

Nick arched an eyebrow at Rachel.

"I talked to her after I talked to you," Rachel whispered, then raised her voice. "Not yet, Rebecca. We thought we'd get the business stuff out of the way first."

"Then let's get started. Nick, Colin's here with me, like you asked."

"Good." Nick folded his hands on the table. "The St. Louis and Chicago offices have worked together to come up with a plan we hope will generate some renewed interest in the case. But it all depends on how willing you and Rachel are to share personal information with the media."

"What kind of information?" Rachel asked.

"The discovery that you're identical twins. Your thirty-five year separation. And how the doll led you to each other."

"I'm willing to do anything that will help us find Megan," Rebecca responded. "But I don't see how going public with the twin thing would do that."

"According to our media relations experts, this kind of story has great human interest value and will get wide play. It will remind people of the case, and perhaps encourage anyone who

211

has new information to come forward. As Matt Carson has told you, we've exhausted all our leads. We need to generate some new information. Plus, we feel it's important to publicly counter the psychic claims made by *St. Louis Scene*."

"Do you think anyone believes those?" The skeptical question came from Colin.

"Most people won't. And if the coverage was confined to that tabloid, we wouldn't be too concerned. But today's story generated local media queries, and we expect interest to ripple. We need to quash any speculation on that score." He looked at Rachel. He hated to alarm her, but forewarned was forearmed. "For safety reasons."

She stared back at him as Rebecca spoke. Her sister's words were slow and deliberate. "You're worried the kidnapper might consider Rachel a threat." It was a comment, not a question, and the concern in her voice matched that on Rachel's face.

"It's possible. Kidnappers aren't always the most rational people."

Rachel folded her hands into a tight knot on the table but remained silent.

"Then we need to go public with our story. Set the media straight on why Rachel had the feelings she did. Let them focus on the twin telepathy thing rather than the psychic detective angle," Rebecca declared.

"I agree," Colin added.

"Rachel?" Nick reached over and covered her cold hands with his.

"I'll vote with the majority."

"So what's the plan?" Colin asked.

"A press conference Monday morning, with everyone in attendance. We'd like this to hit the Tuesday papers. That's often a slow news day, and we could get front-page coverage in a lot of cities. We'd prefer to do it here, because this is where the doll

212

was found and that's our most recent lead. Can you manage that, Rebecca?"

"I'll take Monday off and we'll drive down late Sunday afternoon," Colin replied.

"Rachel, can you get the morning off?" Nick asked.

"Yes. I'll work it out."

"Okay. We'll have a briefing at our office at eight-thirty, hold the press conference at ten. Our SAC will handle the formal remarks, then we'll open it to questions. We can go over talking points in our pre-press conference meeting."

"Does this kind of thing usually generate leads that help?"

Nick heard the glimmer of hope in Rebecca's question and tried to be honest without raising false expectations. "It can. Sometimes all it takes to solve a case is one strong lead."

"That's good to know." Rebecca stopped, cleared her throat. "Now go eat your pizza. We've already had dinner. And be careful, Rach."

"I will. See you Monday."

The line went dead, and Nick released Rachel's hands to turn off the speaker. As he moved his suit jacket aside to slip the BlackBerry into its holder, Rachel's gaze dropped to the Glock on his belt.

She swallowed and tucked her hair behind her ear. "I'll get the pizza."

As she started to rise, he caught her cold fingers in his hand again. "It's going to be okay, Rachel. Don't worry."

The whisper of a smile tugged at her lips. "Am I that transparent?"

"No. But you told me yourself you're not into cloak-and-dagger stuff. I know this is stressful for you."

"More so for Rebecca and Colin. We need to find Megan, Nick. If sitting through one press conference and watching my back for a few days will help make that happen, I can deal with it."

"You sit through the press conference. I'll take care of watching your back. And other things." He grinned and winked. "As a matter of fact, I was hoping you'd let me hang around a lot over the weekend."

She gave him an uncertain smile. "I thought you wanted to keep your distance until the case was over, except for official business."

"I think this qualifies. Though I wouldn't call it hardship duty."

A soft flush suffused her cheeks. "I'd welcome the company. Now let's have that pizza."

As Rachel disappeared through the swinging doors to her kitchen, Nick contemplated the appealing Mediterranean scene on her dining room wall. He wished he could transport her to a place like that for the duration, somewhere safe and far away, where no one would *need* to watch her back.

Since that wasn't possible, he would do his best, as he'd promised. And in reality, there was very little chance Rachel faced imminent danger.

Yet Nick was uneasy at some deep, intuitive level.

He tried to attribute his edginess to his growing feelings for the woman who'd walked into his office—and his life—three weeks ago, clutching a tattered Raggedy Ann doll. Given how he felt about her, it was logical that any whiff of danger would put him on red alert.

But he sensed the source of his apprehension was more sinister in nature. That it had less to do with his feelings for Rachel and more to do with some peril lurking close by.

It wasn't a new feeling for Nick. He'd had hunches before. And he'd learned to trust his instincts. Though this one was vague, it was strong. And he didn't intend to ignore it.

Meaning Rachel was about to acquire a shadow.

★

"Hey, Allen. What are you doing at work on Saturday?"

Allen Harris looked up from the academic journal he was reading. Warren Peterson stood in his office door, bulging satchel in hand. "I should ask *you* that question. You never come in on the weekend."

The man shrugged and stuck his free hand in his pocket. "I got behind while I was out of town. I needed to grade some papers, and it's quieter here than at home. Caitlin had a sleepover last night for her tenth birthday, and the house is chaos. Picture this: a dozen pre-pubescent girls, the yapping puppy Joan agreed to watch for her sister, and that high-volume noise the girls call music. Joan took pity on me and shooed me out the door."

One corner of Allen's mouth quirked up, but a touch of melancholy tinged his voice. "She's one in a million, Warren."

"Don't I know it. I'll never understand what she saw in me. And talk about patience. She doesn't even get mad when I forget our anniversary, the way most wives would. Oh, that reminds me." He set the briefcase down with a thump. "I ran into your ex in St. Louis."

That was a surprise. Allen had assumed Debra was still in Chicago. But he didn't really care where she was. Unlike Warren, he hadn't been lucky in love. His marriage had been a disaster from the beginning. He'd give ten years of his life if he could erase the three he'd been Debra's husband.

"She lives there now," Warren offered when Allen didn't respond. "Had a cute little baby in the backseat of her car. Said she was watching her for a friend."

"We don't stay in touch, Warren. How was the conference?"

"Sorry." The man flushed and bent to pick up the briefcase. "Sensitive subject, I guess. Never was good on picking up nuances. The conference was okay. A couple of interesting papers were presented. Want me to pass along the material I picked up?"

"Yes. Thanks."

With a nod, the other man ambled off.

Swiveling toward the window, Allen stared at the lifeless winter scene. The trees were bare, the sky gray, the grass dead. It was pretty much how he'd felt after Debra entered his life and sent it spiraling out of control.

He'd called himself every kind of fool over the past few years. Told himself he should have seen through her from the beginning. But she'd been good. Very good. And very focused. She'd gone after what she'd wanted with single-minded determination, and despite his PhD, his academic honors, and his high IQ, he'd fallen for her subterfuge hook, line, and sinker.

Yet he'd had no reason to suspect her feelings for him were less than genuine. She'd flattered him with her attention from the day they'd vied for the single table remaining at a popular lunch spot and ended up agreeing to share it. He hadn't called her afterward; she'd called him. And for a thirty-eight-year-old introverted chemistry professor, that kind of attention from a lovely woman was heady. While he'd always wanted a wife and family, shyness had hindered his pursuit of that dream. Debra had made it easy. She'd charmed and teased him into marriage.

But her focus had shifted once they'd wed. In her relentless pursuit of pregnancy, he'd begun to feel more like a means to an end than a husband and partner. Their relationship went from romantic to utilitarian with a swiftness that left him reeling.

He'd tried to talk to Debra about it. Words, however, had never been his strong suit. As time passed, as she miscarried once, then twice, she'd grown frantic. He'd done his best to convince her to seek help for her emotional issues. He'd believed in the for-better/for-worse vows they'd taken. Believed he should stick by his wife despite her problems.

Except her problems hadn't exactly been run-of-the-mill.

And they'd overwhelmed him, especially after the third failed pregnancy had left her barren. He'd found himself sinking with her, unable to cope, stressed to the point that his doctor prescribed Valium. His professional life had begun to suffer. He hadn't been able to sleep at night. He'd even begun to worry about his physical safety.

That was when he'd known he had to get out.

It had been a matter of survival.

In the end, much as he'd dreaded the added turmoil a breakup would cause, he'd felt as if a great burden had been lifted from his shoulders the day the divorce decree arrived in the mail. He'd walked out of Debra's life and never looked back. Nor did he think about her, unless prompted.

Like a few minutes ago.

And even that brief discussion had elevated his pulse.

Leaning his head against the back of his leather chair, Allen did some of the breathing exercises he'd learned in the meditation class he'd taken last fall. They were better at restoring calm than any of the tranquilizing medication he'd weaned himself off of. As was the reminder that Debra was gone. Her problems, whatever they might be these days, were no longer his.

Thank God.

★

With a flourish, Rachel finished the rendition of her final signature piece, "Our Love Is Here to Stay," acknowledged the smattering of applause from the patrons who'd lingered over their tea and pastries, and closed her music. She was eager to get home and call Nick, as she'd promised. That conversation would be a lovely end to a lovely weekend.

True to his word, he'd stuck close for the past two days. They'd had lunch together on Saturday, lingering in the café well into the afternoon as they discussed the dining room mural sketches she'd prepared for his consideration. From there they'd taken in a movie, followed by a late dinner of Chinese takeout, shared at her house.

This morning she'd gone to services with him. Again, she'd found the experience uplifting, and the minister's sermon on the sixty-first psalm had offered unexpected comfort.

Nick had planned to drop her off at tea, run a few errands, and come by for her afterward, but at the last minute Mark had paged him. The SWAT team was being called out to assist with the arrest of a high-risk suspect—and he was on it, as she'd discovered this morning. Apparently it was an ancillary duty for a select group of agents on the reactive squad. That news hadn't left her feeling warm and fuzzy. Nor had the term "high risk." Risk to whom—the suspect or the SWAT team?

He'd been evasive when she'd asked that question, his concern more for the risk to her than to himself. But she'd assured him she'd be extra careful. She'd promised to park close to the hotel entrance, go straight home, and call him on his BlackBerry as soon as she arrived.

In truth, she wasn't very worried as she retrieved her coat from the employee lounge and slipped it on. The newest *Scene* article hadn't incited any more contact from crazies. They must all have called after the first story. The media had been pretty quiet too. A couple of calls from local outlets, including a radio talk show, but she'd let them roll to her answering machine and hadn't returned them. Nick's concern was touching, but she was beginning to think it was the proverbial tempest in a teapot.

Tucking her music in the crook of her arm, she pulled on her gloves and headed toward the lobby.

"Bundle up, Rachel." The tall, portly doorman smiled and pulled the door open for her. "Last check, the temperature was fifteen. You don't want to know the wind chill."

"Thanks for the warning, Henry." She turned up the collar of her coat. "What's the forecast?"

"Temperature is supposed to drop into the single digits after midnight."

"Then I think I'll head home and snuggle up by the fire with a good book."

"Sounds like a plan. See you next week."

A gust of icy wind whipped past as Rachel stepped outside, and she burrowed deeper into the collar of her coat. As far as she was concerned, spring couldn't come too soon. She picked up her pace, anxious to crank up the heater and get home.

She was mere steps away from her car when a voice stopped her.

"Rachel Sutton?"

Turning, Rachel glanced at the person who had addressed her. From the vocal quality and build, she was sure it was a woman. But it was impossible to confirm that visually. The figure was dressed in a long, shapeless gray coat. A wool hat, pulled low, hid the hair. Oversized sunglasses obscured the upper half of the face, and a purple tweed muffler concealed the bottom half.

It was the sunglasses that set off alarm bells in Rachel's brain. The day was overcast, and what little light remained was waning. No protection from the sun's glare was needed.

She edged toward her car. "Can I help you with something?"

"I recognized you from the picture in *St. Louis Scene.*"

Oh, great. Another psychic groupie. The woman was probably harmless, but Rachel gave the parking lot a surreptitious sweep. Just in case. Unfortunately, the cold seemed to have driven everyone indoors. Where she wanted to be. The sooner the better.

"I'm sorry, I need to go."

As she started to back away, the woman moved close.

Too close.

In-your-face close.

Before Rachel could jerk back, the woman grabbed her arm. Rachel gasped and lost her grip on her folder. It fell to the pavement, spewing music in all directions.

The woman cursed in her ear, and Rachel felt a jab in her side. Even through the layers of wool, she could tell the object was hard. And blunt.

"This is a gun. I'll use it unless you do exactly what I say. Pick up the music. And trust me . . . one false move and you'll die on this parking lot."

This can't be happening.

As that thought ripped through Rachel's mind, a prod in her side refuted it.

"Pick up the music." A sharper jab.

Moving on autopilot, Rachel bent. Tried to grab the loose sheets. But her gloved hands fumbled the task. Nor did the trembling in her fingers help.

"Hurry!"

The woman sounded more agitated now. Rachel snatched up the music as fast as she could, fearing her assailant would become frustrated by her clumsy efforts and pull the trigger.

When she grabbed the last sheet, the woman moved beside her, her hands in her pockets. "Stand up."

Rising, Rachel hoped her shaky legs would support her. "What do you want?"

"Start walking. Over there." The woman nodded toward a side street, as if she hadn't heard Rachel's question.

Rachel tried to assess the situation, to come up with a plan of action, but the woman didn't give her a chance to unscramble her panicked thoughts.

"Move. Now." She closed the distance between them and shoved Rachel.

Stumbling, Rachel managed to put one foot in front of the

other. Was the woman a psychic freak, looking for a private entrée to the third dimension? A religious nut who thought psychic phenomena were an affront to the Almighty? Or had Nick's concerns been realized after all?

Was this woman Megan's kidnapper?

It didn't much matter at this point, though. What mattered was that she wasn't rational. And she was wielding a gun. Rachel didn't doubt for a minute she would use it.

But the gun was in her pocket. And a quick glance over her shoulder as they approached the end of the parking lot told Rachel the woman was distracted. Nervous. Her head was twisting back and forth as she checked out the surroundings.

Rachel scanned the area too, hoping to spot someone who might be able to come to her assistance if she called for help. No one, however, had ventured out on this bitter day. Every sensible person on the quiet residential street adjacent to the hotel was hibernating.

"Head for the black car." The woman gestured toward a late-model sedan parked at the end of the dead-end street, backed close to a wall of shrubbery that shielded the high-end neighborhood from curious eyes.

As they drew alongside the car, Rachel heard a jingle of keys, followed by the click of the trunk release.

"Move to the back."

A sick feeling of dread swept over her, and her step faltered. In the few seconds since she'd spotted the car, she'd decided that if the woman was going to force her to drive somewhere, she'd wait until they got into traffic and ram another car. It wasn't much of a plan, but at least other people would be around. And in the shock of acceleration and impact, she might be able to wrestle the gun away from the woman.

But her assailant had other ideas.

She was going to put her in the trunk.

No way, Rachel decided. Once she was in there, she wouldn't have a chance. If she was going to die, she'd prefer to do it here. In the daylight. Putting up a fight.

As if reading her mind, the woman grabbed her free arm and twisted it behind her back, ignoring Rachel's gasp of pain. "Don't think about trying anything."

Once more, Rachel felt the blunt jab in her back. Propelled by a shove, she stumbled forward. They passed the back door. The trunk appeared. A tarp covered the bottom.

The spot where she was supposed to lie.

Rachel didn't care if the woman shot her on the spot. She wasn't getting into that trunk.

Wrenching her arm free, she spun around.

And lost her balance in the dress heels she always wore for her tea gig.

That brief moment of instability was her downfall. As the woman shoved her back against the car, Rachel groped for a handhold. Anything that would help steady her.

But as she struggled to regain her balance, she was powerless to do anything but watch the woman lift her hand. Twist. Swing toward her.

The barrel of the gun smashed against her temple.

Once.

Twice.

She staggered back.

And the world went black.

18

Nick checked his watch. Again.

Five o'clock.

Rachel should have called by now.

Resting one shoulder against the peeling wallpaper in the vacant first floor apartment, Nick turned his back on the other nine black-clothed men in the room. There wasn't much privacy in the SWAT team staging area, but it would have to do. He pulled out his BlackBerry and dialed her home number.

After four rings, the answering machine kicked in.

He tried her cell phone.

Same result.

Sliding the device back onto his belt, he considered his options. No way was he getting out of this duty. The guy holed up in the tenement across the street had murdered three women in as many states, and the FBI had been trying to find him for weeks. A full crew was on hand. The local police had formed an outer perimeter, while FBI agents had taken close-in positions. Snipers were in place. A negotiator was standing by. The SWAT team was suiting up. This thing was going down tonight.

Unfortunately, Nick didn't expect the arrest to happen anytime soon. They knew the guy was in the building, thanks to a tip from a reputable source, but no one had emerged from the apartment in four hours. Clearing out the adjacent units without alerting the suspect to the presence of law enforcement had taken time. Now they were using technical investigative means, including mikes, to find out if there was anyone else in the apartment who could become a hostage. If so, they'd try to make contact with the subject and perhaps negotiate. The whole operation was being directed from the tactical operations center that had been set up nearby.

It was going to be a long night.

"Okay, listen up."

At Mark's command, the SWAT team members closed in on him. Nick joined the circle.

"I just talked to Steve at the TOC. It's been confirmed that there's a woman in the apartment with the subject. Blueprints of the building have been secured and are on their way over. As soon as we have them we'll put together an ops plan before the negotiator places a call and tries to talk the guy out. Any questions?" When no one responded, he continued. "Okay. Be sure you're all in full body armor and use your earpieces. Nick, I need to talk to you." He motioned the other man to join him.

The summons surprised Nick, and he followed Mark to an adjacent empty room.

Propping his fists on his hips, Mark pinned him with an intent look. "What's up?"

Nick frowned. "What do you mean?"

"You're not with us 100 percent. This is a dangerous operation. I need full focus."

At Mark's comment, Nick's neck grew warm. He should have known Mark would pick up on his distraction. Since the former HRT member had joined the reactive squad in St. Louis and taken over leadership of the SWAT team, he'd beefed up the already rigorous training, cutting no one any slack. And his easygoing manner vanished on call-outs. As he'd told them, in the HRT he'd faced many situations where a life could be snuffed out because of a moment's lapse in concentration. As a result, he demanded focus and discipline from his team. Nick respected that—and his perceptiveness.

"I'm worried about Rachel."

"Why?"

In a few brief sentences, Nick explained the situation. When he finished, twin furrows creased Mark's brow.

"Any chance she could have forgotten to call?"

"No."

"Okay. I'll ask Steve to have the local police run by her place, see if she's home. I'll also ask him to have one of our people contact the hotel. Find out if anyone saw her leave. Anything else you can think of?"

"No. That's where I'd start."

"Consider it done." Mark folded his arms across his chest and assessed Nick. "I'll need you if this gets dicey. But I'm not willing to put you or any member of this team in danger. If you can't give me total focus, tell me now."

Not once in his years of law enforcement had Nick let personal feelings compromise his ability to do his job. And he didn't want to start now. Mark was implementing the appropriate steps to track down Rachel. Until they had some answers from the police and the hotel, there was no role for him to play. And he owed his team his support. They'd trained together, and they relied on each other. This was where he belonged. For now.

"As long as I know the situation is being checked out, focus won't be an issue." He returned Mark's gaze steadily.

For a few seconds, Mark continued to appraise him. Then he gave a brief nod. "Okay. I'll let you know when I have any information."

Pulling his BlackBerry out of its holder, Mark punched in some numbers and strode away.

As Nick watched him leave, the rest of the team members began to quietly converse or check equipment. He didn't do either. His equipment was ready, and the only conversation he wanted to have could be held in the quiet of his heart.

Lord, please keep Rachel safe.

✫

Something was prodding her in the side. Hard.

With a moan, Rachel pried open her eyes. Blinked. Tried without success to focus. She reached up to adjust her glasses, only to discover she wasn't wearing them.

"Get up."

The order was faint and reverberated like an echo, as if it had come from far away. Rachel blinked again and peered up. Beyond the dim glow surrounding her was darkness. Only the vaguest outline of a shadowy figure suggested the source of the command.

"I said, get up."

An arm gripped her shoulder. Shook it.

Her head exploded.

Moaning again, Rachel curled into a ball. A shiver convulsed her, and her teeth began to chatter.

Why was her head pounding?

Why was she so cold?

All at once, a face appeared in her field of vision, inches away. The mouth was concealed behind a tweed muffler, but the eyes were visible. Slightly glazed, they looked through her rather than at her.

The muffler jump-started Rachel's memory. She'd been abducted from the hotel parking lot. And when she'd balked at getting into the trunk of a car, this woman had hit her. With a gun.

No wonder her head was throbbing.

"If you don't get out, I'll close the trunk again and drive this car

226

to a bluff by the river." The woman spoke in a singsong voice, as if she were talking to a very young child. "There's a nice high one not far from here. It's a long way down. I doubt you'd survive the fall. Even if you did, the water's very cold. And swift. You'd drown before you got to shore. That's not what you want, is it?"

Another shiver raced up Rachel's spine. And this one had nothing to do with the cold.

"Are you coming or not?"

The woman asked the question as if she were inquiring whether Rachel wanted to go to with her to a movie.

As suffocating panic clawed at her throat, Rachel tried to coax her sluggish brain into operation. She could stay in the trunk and hope that by the time the woman got to the river she'd feel stronger—and better able to defend herself. But what if the woman decided to let the car roll over the bluff without ever opening the trunk again?

Not a good option.

She had to take her stand here.

Wherever here was.

Propelled by fear and adrenaline, she managed to sit up despite the spinning in her head. The woman backed into the darkness, waiting and watching, as Rachel struggled to swing her legs over the edge of the trunk, shredding her hose in the process. She scooted forward. Gripped the metal. Fought back a wave of nausea as her feet touched the ground.

Don't get sick! The woman might get angry and finish you off right here.

"Stand up."

Bracing herself, Rachel stood on her shaky legs. Swayed. Grabbed the end of the car. Fell. Her shoulder took the brunt of the impact.

She gasped in pain. And gasped again as the woman moved behind her, grabbed her hair, and yanked.

"I said stand up." She was still using that eerie, singsong, other-worldly voice—a bizarre counterpoint to her violent behavior.

Choking back a sob, Rachel gripped the back of the car and pulled herself to her feet. Before she grasped what was happening, the woman jerked her arms forward and snapped on a pair of handcuffs.

Bile once again rose in Rachel's throat as she stared at her restrained wrists.

Without the use of her hands, she had little hope of defending herself.

"Move. That way." The woman gestured with the gun, slammed the lid of the trunk down, and picked up a tote bag at her feet.

Rachel peered into the night, attempting to focus. Without her glasses, everything was fuzzy. And the bump on her temple wasn't helping. No artificial light broke the darkness, but the three-quarter moon in the clear winter sky illuminated what appeared to be dense woods on either side of a narrow road that was delineated by two gravel tire tracks.

This isolated place was as bad as the river bluff. Rachel's panic escalated.

"I'm not planning to kill you, if you cooperate." The woman waved the gun in her face, and Rachel recoiled. "That way." She gestured again toward the woods.

God, what should I do?

The silent, desperate cry came from deep in Rachel's heart. Lifting her hands toward her chin, she folded them and bowed her head.

"What are you doing?" A note of suspicion changed the tenor of the woman's voice. "Are you praying?"

"Yes."

"That's a waste of time. God doesn't listen."

"How do you know?" Rachel raised her head.

"I used to pray. A long time ago. It never made any difference."

She sounded more lucid now. And she spoke as if she believed in God. Maybe that was a good sign.

"I have a friend who thinks it does. He says it helps him make decisions."

"I make my own decisions. I don't need God."

"Maybe he could help you make better decisions. You know God doesn't want us to hurt each other."

The woman's expression grew distant again. "I never hurt people. I wouldn't do that. Now move. Down that path." She gestured with the gun toward the woods.

Rachel didn't see that she had much choice. Whatever brief, rational moment the woman had conjured up was gone. The best she could do was follow her abductor's instructions, buy herself as much time as possible, and try to figure out some way to escape.

Once they left the rutted road, the terrain became more uneven. The heels of her pumps found every hole in the rough ground, and brambles and bare tree limbs snagged at her coat on the overgrown path.

Leave a clue behind.

The words flashed through her mind, like a message. Yes. Good idea. Someone would come looking for her eventually. Lots of someones, if Nick had anything to say about it. She had to leave them some kind of clue to work with.

Tugging off her gloves, she wadded them into a ball and lurched to one side of the trail. Falling to her hands and knees, she shoved them under some leaves.

"What's wrong? Get up."

She felt the gun in her back. Heart pounding, she grabbed a tree trunk and pulled herself to her feet. "I slipped." She started walking again.

229

"It's those shoes. Take them off."

She kept walking. Away from the spot she'd dropped the gloves. "But the ground is rocky."

"We don't have far to go. Take them off."

Bending, Rachel slipped them from her feet.

"Leave them on the ground."

Rachel dropped them.

"Move forward a few feet."

Once she complied, the woman bent, retrieved the shoes, and stuffed them into the tote. "Go on."

Sharp rocks and the stubble of dead, ice-encrusted foliage cut into the soles of her feet as she stumbled forward on the frozen ground.

"Stop."

At the sharp command a couple of dozen yards later, Rachel halted and peered ahead. She thought she detected a small structure in a clearing ahead, but without her glasses, it was impossible to tell for sure.

For a full thirty seconds, they stood in silence. A gust of frigid wind cut through Rachel, and she began to shake even harder. She wasn't dressed for the cold. Her tea attire of slim black skirt and long-sleeved white silk blouse was designed for indoor wear, not winter nighttime hiking. Nor was her dress coat warm enough to provide much protection from sustained cold. And her shredded hose left her bare legs exposed. Rachel could never remember being so cold.

Or so afraid.

"Okay. Go ahead. Toward the shed."

Rachel took a few tentative steps into the clearing. They'd arrived at their destination. Her time was running out. She had to take some kind of action.

"Stand over—"

Before the woman could finish her sentence, there was a

sudden crashing in the brush. They turned in unison. A deer emerged from the woods, as startled by their presence as they were by his.

This was her chance, Rachel realized, her adrenaline surging. Probably her only one.

Lifting her arms, she lunged toward her abductor and shoved as hard as she could. The woman fell. The gun flew out of her hand. Rachel dived for it.

Just as her hands closed around the barrel, the woman rolled toward her. Flipped her over. Gripped her neck. Squeezed.

Rachel tried to shake her off, tried to suck in air, but the earlier blow to her head and the intense cold had robbed her of strength. As she thrashed, the woman's fingers tightened on her neck. Waves of blackness began to wash over her, and her struggle grew more feeble.

Her final thought before she lost consciousness was of Nick . . . and the promising future they would never have a chance to explore.

☆

Allen Harris settled into the easy chair by the fireplace in his small bungalow and opened the front section of the *Tribune*. The leisurely perusal of the paper was one of the weekend rituals he most enjoyed. It capped a Sunday that always included church, brunch at his favorite restaurant, and a few hours of woodworking in his basement workshop. After he finished the paper, he would prepare a simple dinner. A turkey or ham and cheese sandwich with chips.

Some might call his routine boring. He found it soothing. These days, he took comfort in—and appreciated—predictability.

The O'Neil kidnapping was in the headlines again, he noted, scanning the front page. Sad case. And the FBI didn't seem to be making much progress, according to the article. The only real piece of news was that the child's Raggedy Ann doll had been discovered in St. Louis, leading to speculation the baby might be in that area. According to an article in a St. Louis paper, quoted in the *Tribune*, a psychic was involved. The baby's mother had even visited her.

Allen shook his head. When people were desperate, they'd try anything.

The notion of desperate people brought Debra to mind. She'd wanted a baby more than anything in the world. Far more than she'd wanted a husband, as he'd soon discovered.

But he didn't want to think about his ex-wife. It was too painful. That was why he'd cut off the conversation yesterday with Warren and blocked out all thoughts of her once his colleague left.

Yet something in their exchange had struck him as odd. He frowned, replaying Warren's comments. A remark about a baby, that was it. His colleague had said Debra had a baby with her. That his ex-wife had said she was watching the child for a friend.

Except Debra had never had any friends in Chicago. Not one, though she'd lived in the city her whole life. Only later had he understood that was the reason she'd insisted they forego a formal wedding and elope. She'd had no one to invite besides her father, and she'd been estranged from him for years.

He had no idea how long she'd been in St. Louis, but it couldn't have been more than a few months. They'd only divorced a little over a year ago. Given her history, it seemed improbable she'd have formed a friendship already. Especially one strong enough that a mother would trust Debra to take her infant somewhere in the car. Alone.

As Allen stared at the O'Neil story in the *Tribune*, a single word suddenly flashed through his mind.

Desperation.

Dear God . . . was it possible she'd . . . ?

No. He cut off that train of thought. What a ridiculous notion. Debra wouldn't resort to kidnapping.

Yet desperate people did desperate things. The use of the psychic in this case by otherwise rational people was clear evidence of that.

And Debra had been desperate. He thought of her wild-eyed hysterics after her final pregnancy had ended in disaster. Recalled the way she'd pummeled him with her fists in the hospital room after he broke the news. The nurses had had to restrain and sedate her.

When he'd taken her home, it had gotten worse. Hour after hour she'd cuddled a doll in the empty nursery, crooning to it. He'd forced her to get psychiatric help, almost physically dragging her to the appointments, and medication had helped—when she took it. But their already fragile marriage had shattered.

More than anything, her indifferent response to his announcement that he wanted a divorce had hurt. She couldn't have cared less that he was leaving. He was dispensable now that he couldn't help her get what she most wanted.

A baby.

He remembered her parting comment the day he'd moved out. She'd glared at him across the room, her eyes flashing, defiant.

"I *will* get my baby, Allen. With or without you."

But kidnapping—was she even capable of pulling off such a thing?

Maybe, he conceded. She might be a loner, but she functioned fine in her career. And she was smart. She could plan. Only when it came to the issue of children was she obsessive. And delusional.

Still, it was a real leap to connect her to the O'Neil kidnapping based simply on what Warren had seen.

Yet something didn't feel right.

Stymied, Allen shoved his fingers through his hair and sighed. He couldn't very well go to the authorities with a feeling. Although that psychic woman had, after she'd found the child's doll. And they'd listened to her.

But there was a very good chance his suspicions were groundless. He'd trusted his instincts about Debra once, and look where that had led him. He had no confidence this "feeling" about a connection between her and the kidnapping had any merit. He was probably getting himself worked up for no reason.

Better to let this rest. Debra had enough problems already. The last thing she needed was the FBI showing up at her door.

Setting aside the front page, Allen picked up the sports section. And pushed thoughts of his ex-wife and all her issues back into a remote corner of his mind.

Where they belonged.

19

At six o'clock, after a brief conversation, Mark slid his Black-Berry back onto his belt and moved to the center of the dingy apartment. "Okay, guys. It's a wrap. The negotiator talked the subject out. Let's pack up and head home."

There was an almost palpable release of tension in the room. Taut postures relaxed and serious demeanors eased. Most SWAT team call-outs ended this way. But there were always exceptions, and the team approached every deployment with the assumption it would be one of those exceptions. Adrenaline pumped until the situation ended with either a negotiated or tactical resolution.

As the team members began loading up gear, Mark motioned to Nick and moved into the adjacent room again.

The SWAT team leader's grim expression sent Nick's pulse off the scale as he joined him.

"Steve just gave me an update on Rachel. The police checked out the house. No one was home, and the garage was empty. Our guys talked to the people at the hotel. The doorman saw her leave at four-fifteen. They ran her plates and checked the lot. Her car's still there. We've issued a BOLO alert."

Nick's gut twisted and a muscle in his jaw clenched. "What about security video from the parking lot?"

"It's being retrieved as we speak. Kurt's on it. I told him to call you with updates."

"I'm out of here." Turning away, he began stripping off his

gear as he headed back to the front room. A hand on his arm stopped him, and he looked over his shoulder.

"Want some company?"

"Yeah. If you're up for it after all this." He gestured around the apartment.

"I'm up for it. Consider it a return favor for a late-night hospital vigil last summer."

Neither man would forget the night Emily had come within minutes of losing her life. Nor the fact that Nick had stuck with Mark through the long, dark hours.

"Thanks." Nick took a deep breath. "We need to get the county K-9 unit on standby too."

With a nod, Mark pulled out his BlackBerry. "Give me five minutes to wrap things up here and talk to Steve. Is your car at the TOC?"

"Yes."

"We'll take yours, then. I bummed a ride to the call-out."

Fifteen minutes later, after huddling with Steve at the tactical operations center to discuss next steps and exchanging their black SWAT team fatigues for jeans, Nick and Mark headed toward Nick's car.

As they approached it, Nick's BlackBerry began to vibrate. He pulled it off his belt and tossed the car keys to Mark. "You drive, okay?"

"We've got some interesting video," Kurt said in response to Nick's clipped greeting. "The victim was approached on the parking lot near her car. It appears the assailant had a weapon, but the clip is too grainy for us to verify that without enhancement. We also can't tell whether it was a man or a woman. A couple of minutes later they walked off the parking lot and out of range of the security cameras."

Never in his professional career had Nick panicked. Yet he was close to it now.

236

"You there, Nick?"

Kurt's question helped him regain his balance. He slid into the car. Closed the door. "Yeah. I'm here."

"We need to pull in K-9."

"They're on standby."

"Okay. I'll put in a call. Can we get our hands on some clothing from the victim?"

"I'll take care of that and meet you at the hotel. Give us half an hour." He jabbed the end button.

As Mark pointed the car toward the highway, he shot Nick a look. "News?"

"Yeah." Nick tried to swallow past his fear. Failed. "Someone abducted Rachel in the hotel parking lot. We need to swing by her house and pick up some items for the K-9 unit."

"You have a key?"

"No. But she mentioned once that she keeps one under the birdbath in her backyard."

They were treading on tricky legal ground by entering Rachel's house. Nick knew that, and was glad Mark didn't make an issue of it. The paperwork and red tape to "legalize" their entry would take time they might not have. Besides, Rachel had told him once that the key was for emergencies.

He figured this qualified.

At her house, Nick didn't waste a second as he went about his task in a methodical, efficient manner. He tried not to picture her warm, intelligent eyes and the auburn highlights in her hair as he stripped the case off her pillow. Tried to ignore the faint floral scent that was all Rachel as he grabbed a few pieces of clothing from drawers and closets. Tried not to remember their impromptu Valentine's dinner as he stowed the items in a plastic bag he found in her kitchen from the Italian restaurant that had supplied their entrée that night.

Most of all, he tried to stop the parade of grisly scenarios parading through his brain.

But he couldn't stop the tremors that shook his hands.

And as he rejoined Mark in the car and they sped toward the hotel, Nick sent another silent plea heavenward.

Please, Lord, keep Rachel safe until we find her.

✯

The darkness was absolute.

The cold was brutal.

The throbbing pain in her head was excruciating.

But she was alive.

For now.

Fighting her way back to consciousness, Rachel tried to take inventory and get her bearings.

She was lying on what felt like a hard-packed dirt floor. Her shaking fingers confirmed that with a quick exploration of the uneven, textured surface. She must be in the small shed she'd noticed in the clearing.

And the handcuffs were gone. That was good news. But her coat was missing too.

Relief gave way to renewed panic.

With temperatures in the teens and slated to fall into the single digits before a new day dawned, she doubted she would survive the night without her coat. She had to find a way out.

On her hands and knees, Rachel explored the small space. Eight-by-ten, she estimated. Empty except for a small, sharp rock in one corner. Her coat and shoes had vanished.

Using the wall for support, Rachel pulled herself to her feet, trying to maintain her balance. Even without the blow to her head, her equilibrium would be off in the disorienting, silent darkness. Nevertheless, she worked her way around the walls, every inch of her body aching, her throat raw as she swallowed. The structure seemed to be constructed of concrete blocks. No

238

windows. One heavy wooden door that gave slightly but was obviously locked.

A wave of despair swept over her, but she wrestled it into submission. She should be grateful. The woman could have killed her. This was a reprieve. Another chance to escape.

If she didn't panic.

If she didn't die of hypothermia first.

She had to find a way to stay warm until Nick found her. And he would. She knew that with absolute conviction.

What she didn't know was if he would arrive in time.

But she would do her part. She would buy herself every possible minute.

Shivers convulsed her, and she wrapped her arms around her body, trying to conserve warmth. Shivering was good, though. Hadn't she read somewhere once that shivering increased heat production? For a while, anyway.

The important thing was to keep moving. Stay active. Not enough to break a sweat, however. She seemed to recall that there was a connection between dehydration and hypothermia. But active enough to generate some heat.

And while she was generating heat, she might as well do it in some activity that would also help her get out of this icebox. So . . . okay . . . maybe she could work on the door hinges with the sharp rock she'd felt on the floor. Perhaps dig out the wood around the plates, loosen them. Yes, that was good. It was a plan. And plans kept you focused.

As Rachel eased down again to her hands and knees to search for the rock, the cross around her neck swung forward. Sitting back on her heels, she gripped it in her cold fingers and tried to recall the Bible verse the minister had preached on—was it only this morning? It seemed days ago. It had been a message about God being a person's rock and salvation. About how he was the soul's source of rest and hope. And that if you believed in him, you wouldn't be disturbed.

Nick believed. And it showed in his demeanor. He projected a quiet, inner peace, a confidence about his place in the world. It was clear he was comfortable with himself and his relationship with God.

Another shiver convulsed her. Perhaps she should follow his example. Put her trust in God. She would do her best to find a way out of this. That was her nature. Besides, wasn't there an old adage about God helping those who help themselves? But if she tried and failed, she needed to accept that as God's will.

And be grateful he'd graced her life with a wonderful man and a newfound sister, if only for a short time.

"Is that a shiver, honey? Want me to crank up the heater?"

Rebecca turned up the collar of her coat and stuck her hands in the pockets, twisting around to check on Bridget, who was asleep in her car seat. Despite the toasty air, she felt chilled to the bone.

"No, that's okay. How much longer to St. Louis?"

"About an hour. Want to stop and get some food?"

"No. I'm too nervous to eat."

"I'm sure the FBI will walk us through what to expect at the press conference tomorrow."

"I'm not worried about that."

"Then what's wrong?"

Rebecca stared out the car window into the darkness. "I don't know."

"Maybe it's stress. And lack of sleep. These past few weeks have been rough."

"No. This just started. About the time we left home." Another shiver rippled through her and she fidgeted in her seat. "I think I'll call Rachel."

Silence fell as Rebecca dug her cell phone out of her purse and tapped in Rachel's number. Already, she knew it by heart.

After four rings, the answering machine kicked in.

Another shiver swept over her.

Followed by another surge of uneasiness.

And then she knew.

"Colin . . ." Panic tightened her voice. "Rachel's in trouble. I have to call Nick."

She could feel Colin's scrutiny in the dark as she fumbled for her purse and groped inside for Nick's card.

"Honey . . . are you sure? It's Sunday night."

"Yes. I told you what Rachel and I talked about the night we met. I had headaches and limped as a child when she was going through surgery for injuries from the accident. Rachel, who never gets sick, had to take off work with what she thought was an intestinal bug both days I was in labor with the girls. She's been unsettled since the day Megan was kidnapped. We have some kind of connection, Colin. I can't explain it, but it's real. I know she's in danger."

"Okay. Then go ahead and call Nick."

Rebecca lifted the phone to her ear. "I already did."

★

The dead-end street where Rachel had disappeared lived up to that description. Nick raked his fingers through his hair in disgust and surveyed the upscale lane of stately brick homes. The FBI's investigation had yielded nothing. The K-9 unit had picked up Rachel's scent and led them to the end of the street, but the trail ended there. More agents had shown up, and they'd canvassed the neighborhood, assisted by the local police. They'd drawn a zero too. None of the residents had seen or heard a thing. The Evidence Response Team was on-site, but to the naked eye there was little to recover. And if any trace evidence was discovered, the analysis wouldn't happen fast enough to help them find Rachel.

Alive, anyway.

The knot in his gut tightened.

Lord, please give us a break here.

"Ellen's here." Mark passed on the news as he joined them.

"Is the press already on this?"

"Yeah. And one of them talked to the doorman, who mentioned Rachel's name. Now that there's a link to the kidnapping, they're all over this. Ellen's polishing the formal comments that were supposed to be given tomorrow. Marty talked to Chicago, and they agreed we should move on this tonight, in light of the new development. The SAC up there is going to hold a press conference at the same time and read the same statement. My guess is Rachel's photo will be all over the ten o'clock news."

Good. Now that Rachel had been snatched, there was no point in waiting to reveal the connection between Rachel and Rebecca. They needed leads. Fast. If Rachel's picture was circulated, maybe someone who'd seen her would call.

"We need to keep the K-9 unit on . . ." His BlackBerry began to vibrate, and he pulled it out. "Bradley."

"Nick, it's Rebecca O'Neil."

"Rebecca." He exchanged a look with Mark. He'd been putting off this call, hoping to have better news to pass on. "I knew you were on your way down. I was going to call you at the hotel in about an hour. I have some—"

"Nick." At her abrupt interruption, he frowned. "Look, I know this is going to sound weird, but I'm convinced Rachel is in trouble. I can feel it."

His antennas went up and he motioned for Mark to stick close. "Tell me about it." He wanted to hear what Rebecca had to say before her impressions were adulterated by his news.

"For the past four hours or so, I've been very uneasy. Colin thought I might be nervous about the press conference tomorrow, but it's more than that, Nick. And the other thing is, I'm freezing. I can't stop shivering, and Colin has the heater cranked all the way up. Wherever Rachel is, she's really cold." Her words came out shaky, and she took a deep breath. "Now I know how Rachel must have felt when she brought you the doll. It sounds crazy, doesn't it?"

A few weeks ago he would have said yes. He'd always based his investigative work on facts, not feelings. But he'd learned a thing or two since then.

"Not anymore. I now have a healthy respect for twin telepathy." He swallowed, and his grip on the BlackBerry tightened. "Your feelings are valid, Rebecca. I knew you were already en route or I would have called sooner. Rachel has been abducted."

He heard her gasp. "I was afraid it was something like that." Her words grew muffled as she relayed the news to Colin. "What happened?"

Nick filled her in. "When will you be here?"

"In less than an hour. Who did this, Nick? Is it Megan's kidnapper?"

"We don't know. And the abductor was too bundled up for us to make a visual ID. Is there anything else you can tell me that might help us pinpoint Rachel's location? Like whether she's inside or outside?"

"No. Just the coldness. Wherever she is, there's no heat. Nick, it's supposed to get down to single digits tonight!"

He heard the panic in her voice. Felt it in his gut. Did his best to respond in a calm tone. "I know. We're working as fast as we can. We hope the press coverage after our statement will generate some leads. I'll call you with any developments, okay?"

"Okay. But Nick . . . please find her. I don't want to lose the sister I just discovered." She choked on the last word.

243

"I don't want to lose her either, Rebecca." His own voice hoarsened, and he cleared his throat.

"Is there anything I can do to help?"

"Prayer would be good. And call me if you have any other feelings, okay?"

"Okay."

"I'll be in touch." He pushed the end button and slipped the BlackBerry into its holder on his belt.

"What's up?" Mark asked.

"Twin telepathy again. Rebecca knew something had happened to Rachel. And that she's somewhere very cold."

"Anything more specific?"

"No. But if she's exposed to the cold, we need to work fast." *And hope for a miracle.*

✯

Pulling into the driveway of the house Marsha shared with three other college students, Debra shut off the engine and checked her watch. Seven-forty-five. She'd told the daycare worker she'd pick up Danielle by eight, and she was early, thanks to a heavy foot on the gas pedal. She wanted her baby back in her arms as soon as possible.

Still, her hours apart from her daughter had been well spent. Rachel Sutton wouldn't be a threat to her anymore. She'd disappeared off the face of the earth, just as Megan O'Neil had. And Debra was confident she hadn't made any mistakes this time with items that could turn up later and cause problems. The psychic's coat and purse, along with the tarp and the tools, were in a place no one would ever think to look.

After checking her hair and makeup in the rearview mirror to confirm nothing was amiss, Debra forced the car door open against the frigid, blustery wind. She'd have to wrap Danielle up extra well to protect her against the foul weather. Mother Nature was a fickle thing, wreaking her fury on humans with detached abandon. Hurricanes, floods, earthquakes . . . cold. All of them could kill. And the blame rested solely on the forces of nature. On an act of God, as the courts and insurance companies often referred to it.

Debra quickly traversed the short walkway to the front door and pressed the bell. She'd hated to ask Marsha to watch Danielle, but she'd had no one else to call on. And she'd needed total concentration for this afternoon's task.

But now it was time to take her baby home.

"Hi, Ms. Kraus." Marsha was juggling Danielle on her hip as she pulled the door open. "We've been waiting for you, haven't we, sugar?" She touched the baby's nose, eliciting a giggle from the infant. "Come on in while I put her snowsuit on. It's a cold one, isn't it?"

Debra took one step in. Two other young women were lounging in a living room filled with eclectic furnishings. Debra stayed just inside the door. "I can do that."

"I don't mind." Marsha carried the little girl into the room, forcing Debra to follow. She set Danielle on the couch and guided her arms and legs into the one-piece outfit. "Did you finish your project?"

The question puzzled Debra—until she remembered the excuse she'd given Marsha for needing her babysitting services on Sunday. An urgent project for a hot case at work that had to be completed by tomorrow morning.

"Yes. All done."

"Good. It's the pits to have to work on the weekend, isn't it? But I suppose that will be my lot too, once I get my nursing degree." She grinned, zipped up the suit, and passed Danielle to Debra. "I'll see you both tomorrow."

"Thanks for watching Danielle." Debra handed over some folded bills.

"No problem. I can always use a few extra bucks. Drive safe, okay?"

With a wave, Debra exited.

"Time to go home, sweetie," she whispered as she curved her body around the baby to protect her as much as possible from the wind. "Just me and you. Isn't that nice?"

In response, Danielle gave a soft sigh and snuggled closer.

Debra's heart melted. Anyone could see the two of them belonged together. That this was how it was supposed to be. She'd known from the day she'd seen Megan's photo and overheard Rebecca O'Neil talking about the challenges of dealing with two young children that Danielle was meant to be hers.

For a brief second today, when Rachel Sutton had talked about God, she'd had a fleeting doubt about her plan to dispose of the psychic. But it had passed quickly. She'd built a new life for herself and her baby, and she was entitled to defend that from threats. It was a mother's prerogative. Rachel shouldn't have stuck her nose in where it didn't belong. Her decision to take that doll to the FBI had prompted what followed. She had no one to blame but herself.

But that was all over now. Debra drew in a slow, calming breath as she strapped the baby into the car seat. There were no more dolls to be found. Rachel was out of the picture. There wasn't anything or anyone who could jeopardize the life she'd created.

She and her baby were safe.

✯

"We have some breaking news on the O'Neil kidnapping." The anchorman for the nine o'clock news picked up a piece of paper while a photo of Megan O'Neil, her mother, and a young woman at a piano flashed on the screen.

As the man began recounting the connection between the

two women and provided details on Rachel's abduction, Allen moved closer to the TV in his bedroom and sat on the edge of the bed.

"According to the FBI profiler's evaluation of Megan O'Neil's kidnapper, the abductor is thought to be a woman in her thirties or forties who simply wanted a baby. She may be intelligent and functional in most areas of her life but could be suffering from delusional disorder. The FBI has asked that anyone with information on tonight's abduction call as soon as possible." The anchorman recited the number as it flashed across the bottom of the screen.

Without thinking, Allen grabbed a pen from the nightstand and jotted the number on a test paper he'd been grading, staring at it as the anchorman moved on to other stories.

Since reading the *Tribune* story earlier in the evening, he'd been unable to get thoughts of the O'Neil baby out of his mind. While he'd done his best to talk himself out of a possible connection between Debra and the kidnapping, the FBI profiler's description of the abductor fit his ex-wife. And she was in St. Louis. With a baby of unknown origin.

It was still a long shot. He knew that. And he'd be bringing all kinds of grief down on Debra if there was an innocent explanation for the coincidence.

But what if there wasn't?

What if the life of that abducted woman hung in the balance?

Could he live with himself if he remained silent, only to find out later his hunch had been right and someone had died?

In the end, Allen knew he didn't have a choice.

Praying he wasn't making a huge mistake that would embarrass everyone, he picked up the phone.

20

"Rebecca, why don't you lie down for a while? You could rest, even if you can't sleep. The FBI will call if there's any news."

Pacing the hotel room, Rebecca shook her head at Colin's suggestion. "I'm too restless. And too cold." She had on two sweaters and still felt chilled. Pulling out her cell phone, she dialed Rachel's number, as she'd been doing every fifteen minutes.

"She's not going to answer, honey."

"How do you know?" Rebecca snapped, then immediately regretted her sharp response to his gentle comment. "Sorry." She tucked her hair behind her ear and wrapped her arms around herself. "I keep thinking maybe, if she's unconscious, she might come to and answer. It's the only thing I can do, Colin. I know it's not much, but it's better than sitting around waiting."

"I understand." He flipped off the news program and patted the bed. "Come over here. I can at least try to keep you warm."

Crossing the room, Rebecca paused by the crib the hotel had provided. Bridget was sleeping, her golden ringlets framing her sweet, innocent face. Rebecca stroked her daughter's smooth, perfect cheek, her throat tightening with tenderness. Since Megan's disappearance, Rebecca had hovered and fussed over Bridget far too much. Even her daughter was growing tired of it. When this was over, she'd have to remember not to smother her daughters.

Plural.

Because Megan *was* coming home.

After adjusting the blanket over Bridget, Rebecca continued toward the bed, tapping in Rachel's number as she scooted beside Colin and settled back against the headboard. He put his arm around her, and she snuggled close. The phone rang.

Once.

Twice.

Three times.

After the fourth ring, voicemail kicked in.

Colin was right. Rebecca sighed and tamped down her disappointment as she closed the phone. The exercise was probably a waste of time. Wherever Rachel's cell phone was, there was little chance anyone was going to hear it.

Nevertheless, she intended to keep calling.

Just in case.

✫

Gary Feltrop came to an abrupt stop as he crossed the fallow field adjacent to the two-lane country road, his breath forming frosty clouds in the clear night air. He'd heard the faint buzzing sound a few minutes earlier, as he'd headed out to make sure the nose pump he'd fixed this morning for the cattle in the back pasture hadn't clogged up again, but he'd been unable to identify it.

It was closer this time, however. And though muffled, it was very recognizable.

A phone was ringing.

Puzzled, he looked in the direction of the sound and scanned the deserted field. The moonlight provided enough illumination to verify that he was the sole occupant. Besides, who but a cattle farmer would be out at nine o'clock on such a bitter night?

Yet the intermittent sound continued.

He took a few steps toward it.

The sound stopped.

He halted.

Lifting his arm, he swept the beam of his flashlight over the area. Two theories came to mind. Someone was hiding behind the abandoned well, or a trespasser had dropped the phone while crossing his field.

Trespassers didn't worry him. He'd caught the local high school kids taking a shortcut across his fields on a few occasions, but they never hurt anything.

Someone hiding behind the well on a cold night like this, however—that was a bigger concern.

He circled the well from a distance, keeping his beam fixed on the crumbling stones. Years ago, the shallow, hand-dug well had provided water to a long-gone house that had stood near a country lane. The lane had disappeared too, and the now-dry well had long outlived its usefulness. He ought to tear it down, fill it in. He would, one of these days.

His circuit complete, he moved closer. Nobody there. He could check the field for the lost phone in the morning.

Sweeping the beam of his flashlight over the stones, he noted that a few were missing. That was new. The thing must be falling apart. Pretty soon it would cave in, leaving a dangerous hole in the ground. One more chore to add to his to-do list. He shook his head and tugged his cap lower over his ears. On the positive side, though, it wouldn't take much to demolish this pile of rubble. And there ought to be plenty of room in the pit for all of the stones.

To verify that, he leaned over the opening and flashed his light into the dark void.

Frowned.

Squinted.

What was that gold, shiny thing reflecting in the bottom, half buried by the stones from the surrounding wall that had fallen in?

Digging his glasses out of his pocket, Gary slid them on and looked again.

It was a decorative buckle. On what appeared to be a woman's purse.

What in the world was a purse doing in the well?

He peered in, wishing his light was stronger. The well was only ten or twelve feet deep, but the dark mud walls absorbed the light. Yet he could make out a flap of beige peeking up from among the rocks. It looked like canvas. The kind used for a tarp. And it was clean.

Meaning someone had thrown this stuff into his well recently.

Very recently.

And whoever had done it sure hadn't been up to any good. At the very least, the purse was stolen. At the worst . . . well, he'd watched enough cop shows to know that lots of bad stuff happened in the world. Here in rural Missouri, though, he hadn't seen much of it.

He doubted whether the local police chief had, either. Joe was a good guy, and his laid-back style worked great in farm country. But Gary was pretty certain he wouldn't appreciate being awakened on a Sunday night to come check out what he would assume to be a stolen purse. Better to fish out the purse himself and take it over to Joe in the morning. He had to go into town anyway to pick up a few supplies.

After a quick, cold hike to the barn and back, he dropped a grappling hook into the dry well, snagged the strap of the purse, tugged it out from beneath the stones, and hauled it up.

Just as it reached the top, the phone in the side pocket began to ring again.

No longer constrained by the dirt walls, the sharp jangle reverberated with startling clarity in the still night air. Gary almost lost his grip on the hook but managed to snag the purse before it slipped back into the recesses of the well.

As the phone continued to ring, he stared at it, unsure what to do. This was the third time he'd heard it ring in the past forty-five minutes. It could be someone trying to reach the owner of the purse. Someone who cared. And was worried. A father, perhaps? Or a husband?

Gary was both. He could empathize. So he followed the dictates of compassion.

He answered the phone.

✫

There was no reason to hang around the scene. Nick knew that. The FBI, joined by detectives from the local police force, had questioned every member of the hotel staff who had been on duty at the time of the abduction, but no one had seen anything. They'd also checked the security tapes for the ten minutes before and after Rachel had been forced to walk out of view, identifying anyone they could from the cars they'd driven. They'd managed to contact most of those people, and none of them had noticed any out-of-the-ordinary activity, either. The ERT effort was yielding zilch too.

So what was he supposed to do, go home and sleep?

Right.

A disposable cup of coffee appeared in front of his face.

"I filched some from the hotel." Mark took a sip as Nick accepted the offering.

"Thanks." He took a gulp of the brew. The hot liquid scalded its way down his throat. "Look, you don't need to hang around. You can take my car if you want to and I'll grab a ride with someone later."

"I'm in for the duration."

Nick flashed him a grateful look. "Thanks."

"We'll get this figured out."

"I know."

Neither voiced the obvious worry.

Will we be in time?

Nick's BlackBerry began to vibrate, and he pulled it from his belt. "Bradley."

"Matt Carson." The Chicago agent dispensed with the niceties and moved straight to business. "We may have a break on the kidnapping."

The coffee cup flexed as Nick tightened his grip. "I'm listening."

"A call came in about ten minutes ago from a guy who thinks his ex-wife might be involved. I'm en route to his house, ETA about ten minutes. I'd like to pull you in by conference call when I talk to him. Will that work for you?"

Motioning for Mark to follow, Nick began striding toward the hotel. "Yeah. I'm at Rachel Sutton's abduction site with Agent Mark Sanders. We'll find a place and both sit in on the call. Who is this guy?"

"He's legit. A tenured chemistry professor." The agent named the university. "His record is clean. The ex-wife's name is Debra Kraus, and she's living in the St. Louis area. He didn't have an address. You might want to start tracking her down."

"I'll take care of it. Call me as soon as you're set."

Without breaking stride, Nick filled in Mark, who'd fallen into step beside him. As he finished, his BlackBerry began to vibrate again. He recognized the caller ID.

"Rebecca, we have a—"

"Nick, a man answered Rachel's phone!"

At her semi-hysterical tone, Nick came to a dead stop. "What?"

"I've been calling and calling her number, and he just answered it." The last word came out on a sob.

253

"Rebecca, start over. Are you talking about her home phone or her cell?"

"Here . . . I'll let you talk to Colin."

As the phone changed hands, Nick's heart began to pound.

"What's up?" Mark asked.

"I don't know. I'm hoping Colin will make more sense."

"Nick? Colin here. Rebecca's been calling Rachel's cell phone every fifteen minutes, and a guy just answered. A farmer, I think, by the name of Gary Feltrop. Lives near a place called New Melle. He was out working with his cattle and heard the phone ringing. He fished it out of . . . it was in the bottom of a dry, abandoned well."

The breath whooshed out of Nick's lungs, and he had to force himself to ask the next question. "Was anything else in there?"

"Yes. A piece of fabric he thinks might be a tarp. But there are rocks on top of it. Like the wall of the well caved in—or was pushed in."

"Hold a second, Colin."

Hitting the mute button, Nick tried to breathe.

"What's wrong?" Mark frowned and moved closer.

"Rebecca's been calling Rachel's cell. A farmer in New Melle just answered. He found it in a well."

A muscle twitched in Mark's jaw.

"Colin? Give me the man's name and phone number." Nick signaled for Mark to get out his pen and notebook, then dictated the information as Colin recited it. "Okay. Sit tight. We also have a break in Chicago we're investigating, thanks to the news story. Tell Rebecca we're following up on everything."

As the line went dead, he changed direction, heading for his car instead of the hotel. "Can you make the calls while I drive? We need the ERT and K-9 unit at this guy's farm in New Melle ASAP. And we need our people to see what they can find out

254

about a Debra Kraus. I have to leave my line open for the call from Carson."

Before Nick finished, Mark was punching numbers into his BlackBerry.

Five minutes later, as Nick sped west from the city, the Chicago call came through and he briefed the agent on the situation in St. Louis.

"Anything else in the well?" the man asked.

"We're heading that way to check it out." Nick could hear Mark talking to the farmer, issuing instructions. His fingers clenched on the wheel.

"I'm with Allen Harris. He's okay with the conference call. You want to proceed or wait?"

"Let's proceed. I don't want to waste any time. If we have to pause for a couple of minutes as I get updates, I'll let you know."

"Okay. I'm putting you on speaker." There was a click, then he spoke again. "Professor Harris, Special Agent Nick Bradley is on the line from St. Louis and may ask a few questions as we go along."

"No problem."

"Please tell us what prompted your call tonight."

"The article in the *Tribune* this morning. And tonight's newscast. I'm afraid this may be a red herring, and I apologize in advance if it is, but something doesn't feel right and I'd never be able to live with myself if someone died because I was afraid to be embarrassed."

"We appreciate that, Professor Harris," Matt assured him. "Can you be more specific when you say something didn't feel right?"

"Yes. My ex-wife, Debra Kraus, was desperate to have a baby. It was like an obsession. In fact, to be honest, that's the only reason she married me. But things didn't work out. In our three years of marriage, she had two miscarriages, both of which devastated her, and she had life-threatening complications during her third pregnancy. When that ended badly, well, she lost it."

"Define 'lost it,'" Nick interjected.

"At first she refused to believe she'd miscarried again. She was convinced the baby had been stolen from her. And she'd sit in the nursery for hours, singing to a doll and pretending it was her baby. I dragged her kicking and screaming to counseling, but she didn't respond well. And it was a battle to get her to take her medication. I don't think she ever fully accepted the fact that her final pregnancy didn't produce a child."

"Why do you think she might be involved in the O'Neil kidnapping?" Matt asked.

"A colleague of mine ran into her in St. Louis a few days ago. In an area called Chesterfield—I checked with him on the location before I called you. She had a baby with her, and she told him she was watching it for a friend. But the thing is, she had no friends here. She's a loner. And during her treatment I discovered she's had mental health issues her whole life."

"What kind of issues?" Nick pressed.

"Episodes of depression. Instability. She also had a nervous breakdown in college that forced her to drop out. At least that's what her father told me. I tracked him down when I was desperate to figure out what was going on with her. He wasn't any more specific than that."

"How long have you been divorced?"

"A year."

"Any chance the baby your colleague saw her with could be her own child?"

"No. She had a condition called placenta accreta during her last pregnancy. She lost the baby and had to have a hysterectomy. And she would never be approved for adoption, given her mental health history."

"Do you know where we can find your ex-wife?"

"No. I had no interest in staying in touch. But she's a paralegal, if that helps. That's the odd thing. She's able to function on the job. The psychiatrist who saw her called her problem delusional disorder, just as your profiler did. He said people who suffer from it can often perform well occupationally, that their bizarre behavior is confined to their delusion. I assume she's still working in that field."

Mark, who had been conversing in a low voice, motioned to Nick.

"Matt, I need to put you on mute for a minute." He depressed the button and glanced at Mark.

"Mr. Feltrop pulled out the stones with a grappling hook and lifted up the tarp. He says there appears to be clothing and a few tools underneath."

"That's it?"

"Yeah."

"What kind of clothes?"

"The only thing he can identify for sure is a greenish-blue coat."

Rachel's. But at least there was no body.

"Okay." The word came out hoarse, and he cleared his throat as he turned off the mute button. "Professor Harris, in your opinion is your ex-wife capable of violence?"

"I don't know. Maybe. If she's angry enough, or delusional enough."

"Would her father know where she is?"

"I doubt it. They've been estranged for years."

"We'd like to check in with him anyway. Do you have a contact number?"

"Yes. As of a year ago, he lived in town. That may have changed."

"We'll start there," Matt said. "I'll get the information from you in a minute. Nick, any other questions?"

"Not now. But Professor Harris, we may need to get back in touch."

"I'll help in any way I can."

The line clicked, and when Matt spoke again the conference-call echo was missing. "I'll check out the father."

"And we'll try to track down Debra Kraus. She fits the profile our people developed. Call me if you come up with anything."

"Will do."

Both Mark and Nick finished their calls within seconds of each other.

"What do you think?" Mark asked.

"I think Debra Kraus is a key suspect. According to her ex, she has some very serious mental issues, not to mention delusions about motherhood that could translate to violence if she feels threatened. What have you got?"

"The ERT and K-9 unit should arrive about the same time we do. No record of a Debra Kraus in the phone listing. We're trying utilities now. Both in St. Louis county and outlying areas."

"Her ex says she's a paralegal who is probably employed in that field. That would be one way to find her."

"Considering the number of legal firms in St. Louis, tracking her down that way on a Sunday night would take a long time, Nick."

Too long.

The unspoken message came through loud and clear. In this weather, exposure to the elements would be deadly for a clothed person, let alone one who had little protection from the cold. The classy silk blouse and black skirt Rachel wore for tea provided barely adequate warmth *indoors* in frigid winter weather.

"We need to get a helicopter on standby to do a thermal sweep once we isolate an area, in case she's outside." Nick did his best to maintain a calm, professional tone, but Mark knew him too well.

"Already done." Mark put a hand on his shoulder. "We'll find her, Nick. We've had two good breaks. I think we're close. And I'm praying."

"I am too."

For most of his life, Nick had relied on prayer to guide him, to comfort him, to sustain him.

Tonight he hoped it would do even more.

He hoped it would save the life of the woman who was fast laying claim to his heart.

★

"Hey, Marsha, look at this." Kristal stopped reading her psychology textbook and called over her shoulder to her roommate.

"What?" Marsha picked up her soda and ambled from the kitchen to the living room.

"It's a story about the O'Neil kidnapping." She motioned to the TV as a photo of the baby flashed on the screen. "They think she's in St. Louis."

"I know. That reporter from *St. Louis Scene* suggested she was here a while back."

"But now the psychic from that article has been kidnapped. Turns out she's the sister of the baby's mother. Identical twins, separated at birth."

"No kidding." Marsha sat on the arm of the couch.

"Anyway, don't you think that baby looks an awful lot like the one you watched this afternoon?"

"Danielle?" Marsha tipped her head and studied the photo on the screen. "That one's younger. And the hair color is wrong."

"Yeah, but did you notice that brownish stain behind Danielle's ear? I saw it when you were holding her against your shoulder."

"I caught a glimpse of it when I put her in her snowsuit. Why?"

"It looked like hair dye to me." Kristal ran her hand through her own russet tresses. "Take it from one who knows, that stuff is insidious. It gets everywhere. And that picture on the screen must be from Christmas. Her outfit's red and green. Babies change a lot in a couple of months. Do you know anything about the mother?"

"She doesn't talk much. But I know she moved here recently from Chicago." Marsha frowned and swirled the liquid in her soda can. "You know, when I showed her that first article in *St. Louis Scene* about the psychic, she did seem a little upset."

"According to the FBI, Megan O'Neil has a small strawberry birthmark on her right hip," the anchorman continued. "The baby has blue eyes and . . ."

"Oh my word." Marsha's mouth dropped open and she froze, the can of soda halfway to her mouth.

"What?" Kristal tipped her head back to look at her roommate.

"Danielle has that kind of birthmark on her hip."

"Wow." Kristal pulled out her cell phone and handed it over. "I think you better call the FBI."

⋆

The rock slipped from Rachel's numb fingers. Again.

Tears sprang to her eyes, and she fought them back.

Don't cry! Don't give up! Keep working!

She'd been repeating that mantra for what seemed like hours, but in truth she had no idea how long she'd been nicking away at the wood around the hinge. She'd lost all sense of the passage of time.

She was losing other things too. Her capacity to think clearly.

And her ability to remain upright. There had also been a dramatic drop in her motor coordination. But at least she wasn't as cold as she had been, despite the intense shivers that continued to wrack her body. Nor did she care as much about sticking to her plan. Her motivational chant was beginning to lose its effect.

Lowering herself to the ground, she considered staying there. It would be the easy thing to do. She could let herself drift into oblivion, end the nightmare. Why prolong this agony?

She toyed with that idea. The prospect was tempting. She'd tried her best, hadn't she? What good would it do to get one or two more slivers of wood out of the door? She was still on the first hinge. In the end, her efforts wouldn't matter. There was no way she was going to work one hinge loose, let alone two.

Hang in and keep moving forward.

The voice urging her on came from somewhere deep inside. It was the same voice she'd heard through the years whenever life got rough. Through the emotional upheavals of the foster system, through the pain of multiple surgeries, through the lonely adult years without anyone to come home to, she'd listened to that voice, heeded its directive.

And her stick-to-itiveness had paid off. In self-respect, if not always in results. Giving up would be a terrible way to end her life.

Mustering her waning strength, Rachel groped around the dirt floor until her fingers found the sharp rock.

She willed her uncooperative fingers to close around it.

Lifted it.

And went back to work.

21

The first thing Nick saw when he arrived at the well was the blood.

It was smeared on the tarp the ERT technician was pulling out of the black hole as he and Mark strode across the field toward the circle of light created by the floods that had been set up.

He stumbled.

Mark gripped his arm.

Nick stopped. Fought for composure. Pulled away. "I'm okay. Let's see what they have." He moved forward, leaving Mark to follow.

Clair Ellis, the lead ERT technician, was known for her lead foot on the gas pedal, and she'd obviously put it to good use getting from the hotel crime scene to the farm. As he and Mark stepped into the light, she examined the tarp, her short blonde hair peeking from beneath her wool cap as she pushed her glasses higher on her nose.

Stopping beside her, Nick looked at the dark maroon smears. His only consolation was that there weren't many of them.

"What do you have?" His strained words came out in a puff of frosty breath.

"The purse is over there." She gestured toward a drop cloth that had been spread on the ground. "It doesn't appear as if anything is missing. Wallet's inside, with ID and money. There's more stuff in the well. We're bringing it up now."

As she spoke, another technician pulled Rachel's coat out of the murky depths. Clair set the tarp aside to join him, holding the coat carefully in her latex-gloved hands as she examined the fabric. "No blood. And it's intact."

Meaning a bullet or knife hadn't ripped into it. Nick read between the lines of her comment.

He stepped aside, watching as other items came up. With a video camera rolling, Clair slipped them into evidence bags, sealed the bags, signed them, and recorded the number on the outside of each in the evidence log.

Nick took a mental inventory as he watched. A pair of black pumps. A screwdriver. A bolt cutter. A large, rusted padlock. Each bagged object was laid on the drop cloth, like the pieces of a puzzle.

Except he had no idea how to put them together. Or where to find the missing pieces that would lead them to Rachel.

"That lock sure has seen better days."

Turning, Nick surveyed the stocky, late-fiftyish man who stood just outside the circle of light. His shaggy, gray-streaked brown hair was visible beneath a knit cap, and a few unruly locks had fallen across his forehead. He wore a bulky, well-broken-in work coat, worn jeans, and heavy-duty gloves.

It had to be Gary Feltrop.

Nick walked over and introduced himself. "I understand you discovered the cell phone."

"Yep. Heard it ringing on my way back from the pasture. Strangest thing, how that sound come out of nowhere. Glad I stopped to check it out."

"So are we. You didn't see or hear anyone in this area tonight, did you?"

"Nope. I don't use this pasture much in the winter. But I got a pump on the back forty that's givin' me fits, and this is a shortcut. Didn't see a soul, though. Just heard the phone."

"Any idea where that lock might be from?"

The man stepped into the light and examined the rusted piece of metal at closer range. "No. Lots of people in the area use that kind. Mostly on sheds and such. They're not real secure, so we use 'em more to keep pranksters and kids out. This one wouldn't even do that, though. It's rusted through. Looks like it's been out in the weather for a good long time."

"Nick." Mark spoke in his ear. "One of the K-9 units is here."

Excusing himself, Nick turned toward Mark as the farmer melted back into the shadows. A county police officer with a dog was visible in the background. He tipped his head toward the drop cloth. "Any thoughts?"

Mark inspected the array of items. "My guess is the tools were used to remove the rusted lock. Clair's team should be able to confirm that."

"Our farmer friend pointed out that the lock is useless. It's rusted out. That says abandoned building to me. We could be looking for the kind of storage shed that he indicated is often secured with this type of lock. The abductor might have left Rachel inside and replaced the rusted lock with a new one." He raked his fingers through his hair and shook his head. "But I don't get the coat and shoes."

"Maybe our subject didn't have the stomach for outright murder," Mark theorized. "Cold can be as fatal as a bullet. It kills too. Just not as fast."

"Hey, guys, get a load of this."

At Clair's summons, Nick and Mark joined her. She was holding a Glock, similar to the one they carried. Except . . .

Nick leaned closer to examine it. "That's not a real gun."

"Nope. It's a toy. Pretty authentic looking, though." Clair hefted it in her hand. "And heavy duty. It almost fooled me."

And it would certainly have fooled someone who didn't have much experience with guns.

Like Rachel.

Nick closed his eyes as he came to the obvious conclusion.

Rachel had been abducted with a toy gun.

If the situation wasn't so deadly, it would almost be laughable.

But laughing was the farthest thing from his mind. Especially when the next item retrieved from the well was a tote bag containing Rachel's music. He felt as if someone had kicked him in the stomach when Clair opened the folder and a single sheet fluttered to the ground.

It was the opening page for "Our Love Is Here to Stay."

Dear God, could this get any more difficult?

As Nick's BlackBerry began to vibrate, he took a long, slow breath. *Don't lose it. You're not going to be able to help Rachel if you get emotional. Think of the music as a positive message.*

He noted that Mark was reaching for his belt too. They angled away from each other to take their calls.

"Bradley." His greeting came out hoarse.

"Nick, it's Matt. I talked to Debra Kraus's father. He's a piece of work. I think I can see where her mental problems come from."

"Did he know where she is?"

"No. And he didn't care. According to him, she's been nothing but trouble since the day she was born. He described her as lazy, selfish, less-than-bright, unattractive, unsuccessful in her efforts to attract or keep a husband, and a failure in her attempts at motherhood. Those are just a *few* of the things he said. All he cared about was whether we were offering money for information."

Disgust left a sour taste in Nick's mouth. "Not exactly father-of-the-year material."

"You've got that right. After I listened to his tirade, I did a little more checking into Debra's background. Found out her mother died when she was nine. She was an only child, and her father raised her. I dug up a few police reports from back then indicating he spent an occasional night in jail for disorderly conduct. The pattern would suggest he was into picking fights. Our suspect could have been in an abusive situation as a child, although a cursory check didn't turn that up. Did you have any luck tracking her down?"

"Not yet, but we're on it. I think . . ." He stopped as Mark gestured to him. "Hang on a second, we may have some news." He pressed the mute button.

"The electric company has an account for a Debra Kraus in Defiance," Mark told him. "I have the address."

Nick released the button. "We've got an address. I'll be in touch."

"Steve is on his way." Mark slid his BlackBerry back onto his belt. "He also called in backup. The bad news is, the K-9 unit lost the scent on the road."

"I'm not surprised." Nick assumed the abductor had been in a car and stopped only long enough to drop the items in the well. "But I have a feeling we're close. Why would someone drive around for very long with incriminating evidence in the car?"

"I think we're all on the same page. Steve wants to set up a TOC at the New Melle police station. He's bringing in the local chief to brief us on the area, and our people are contacting the owners of Debra Kraus's rental house to see what they know. The house is about five miles from here, halfway between Defiance and New Melle."

"What's Steve's ETA?"

"About twenty minutes."

"Let's head over to the police station."

As they traversed the uneven ground toward Nick's car, a frigid gust of wind whipped past. Neither spoke. Out loud, anyway.

But Nick had a feeling he and Mark were thinking the same thing: plummeting temperatures were as deadly as a ticking bomb.

✦

The police chief was waiting when they arrived.

"Joe Richter." He introduced himself and shook hands. "I put coffee on. Would you like some? Could be a long night."

Nick's mouth settled into a grim line. Not if he could help it.

"Thanks. That would be good," Mark responded when Nick remained silent.

"What can you tell us about the house our suspect is renting?" Nick asked as the man poured Mark's coffee.

"It's the Schroeder place. Peggy and Harold. Nice folks. Harold used to bowl on our team. Won some championships in our day too. They moved into the city a few months back. Harold has a heart problem and they wanted a hospital nearby. Just in case. You start to worry about that kind of thing when you get older, I guess." He took a sip of his coffee. "They couldn't bring themselves to sell the place, though. Lived there for fifty years. Thought they'd try renting it out for a while."

"About the house," Nick prompted, reining in his impatience.

"Oh yeah, the house. Nice little place. Frame, one story. Been in there many a time. Sits on about five acres of woods and fields. House is about three hundred feet back from the road. Cozy living room, nice kitchen with a big breakfast area. Three small bedrooms."

"Could you draw us a floor plan and site layout?" Nick asked.

"I'm not much of an artist, but I can try."

As the man concentrated on his sketch, Steve arrived, followed in short order by several additional agents.

267

In typical fashion, the reactive squad supervisor got right to business. "We talked to the couple who owns the house, and they confirmed that Debra Kraus is the tenant. She did tell them she had an infant daughter. Harold Schroeder has been out there once since she moved in to check a leak in the roof. He saw the child and said she seemed happy and well cared for, but he had no recollection of what she looked like."

"That would be Harold," Joe interjected. "Never was the most observant guy."

"Bring me up to speed." Steve planted his fists on his hips and aimed his directive at Nick.

As Nick filled him in, recounting what they'd learned about Debra Kraus, the discovery in the well, and Rebecca's unexplained chills, twin furrows appeared on the squad supervisor's brow.

"Our first priority needs to be Rachel Sutton. If she's still alive and out in this cold without a coat, her time is running out. The temperature is continuing to hover at about fifteen degrees, but the wind chill is fierce. And according to the forecast, the temperature's going to dive after midnight. If Ms. Kraus has the O'Neil baby, and if she abducted Ms. Sutton, we need to know. Now."

"Do we have a search warrant?" The question came from Mark.

"No." Steve squinted at him. "Guess you were in the HRT so long you forgot how the real world works. The search warrant is in process. But it's not going to happen as fast as we need it to."

"If we can confirm that Debra Kraus has the O'Neil baby, we don't need a search warrant," Nick pointed out.

"And how do you suggest we do that?" Steve folded his arms across his chest. "It's ten o'clock on a Sunday night. My guess is they're both in bed. If Ms. Sutton's life wasn't in imminent danger, we'd sit this out and confront the woman when she leaves the house with the baby in the morning to go to work. Since that's not an option, we need an ops plan to . . ."

He stopped mid-sentence and reached for his BlackBerry. "Preston."

The conversation was mostly one-sided.

"Get a full statement. But that's all I need for now." He slipped the device back on his belt.

"We have a new development, gentlemen. The daycare worker at the center where Ms. Kraus leaves her baby called a few minutes ago. She heard the newscast tonight and confirmed that the Kraus baby has the distinguishing birthmark Megan O'Neil's parents told us about. She also babysat the child today from two o'clock until almost eight. And she noticed a stain by the baby's ear that could have been hair dye."

A surge of adrenaline shot through Nick. "Everything fits."

"Agreed. We now have both probable cause and exigent circumstances. Let me have some input."

"Considering the toy gun, I doubt she's armed," Mark offered.

"Maybe not. But from everything I've heard, we're not dealing with a rational person. I want vests on everybody if we go in."

"What about danger to the baby?" Mark asked.

"From what the daycare worker said, Ms. Kraus appears to be a caring mother who dotes on the child. The infant is healthy and happy. I doubt she'd hurt the baby, but we do need to factor in that possibility."

"The safest plan would be to create a diversion that gets her outside for the arrest." Nick folded his arms across his chest.

"We could always try the fake utility serviceman or pizza guy ploy," Mark suggested.

"It's late. She could just ignore the bell. Or we could arouse suspicion," Nick countered.

"How about a fire?" The police chief, who had been watching the exchange from the background, moved forward and indicated a square on the diagram he'd drawn. "There's a small, makeshift woodshed not far from the garage. I doubt she'd want to call the fire department and draw attention to herself. She'd probably try to put it out."

"You may be right, but that could be dangerous." Steve frowned and folded his arms across his chest.

"I can have our fire crew stand by in case it gets out of control," Joe offered. "And our fire chief knows everything there is to know about fires. He could get that baby started in a flash. Pardon the pun."

"I still don't like it, but I have to agree there's a good chance it will get her outside and away from the baby." Steve looked at Nick. "You want to call the parents? We need them standing by for a visual ID."

"I'll set it up."

"Okay. Let's talk tactics."

★

Fifteen minutes later, suited up in ballistic vests and the black fatigues they'd worn earlier for the SWAT team call-out, Mark took the wheel while Nick placed the call to Rebecca.

She answered on the first ring.

"Rebecca, it's Nick. We have some good news. Thanks to a tip after the news program, we're pretty certain that a woman named Debra Kraus has Megan. We're en route to her place now, and we'd like you and Colin close by."

He heard her gasp, then her voice grew muffled as she turned away from the phone to inform Colin. "Tell us where you want us," she said to Nick, her voice quavering.

"An agent is on the way to pick you up. Another one will stay with Bridget. Can you be ready in ten minutes?"

"We're ready now. Nick . . . what about Rachel?"

"No news. I'm hoping Debra Kraus is the key to that too."

"Do you think she'll admit to the abduction? And tell you where Rachel is?"

"I hope so. Are you still cold?"

"Yes. And sleepy. Which is odd, considering how keyed up I am."

A muscle in Nick's jaw twitched, and he swallowed past a sudden surge of fear. Sleepy wasn't good. It could mean Rachel was slipping. But he didn't intend to share that with Rebecca. She was stressed enough. "I think we're all tired, Rebecca. I'm planning on twelve uninterrupted hours of sleep myself once this is over. I'll see you in a little while."

As the line went dead, Nick stared out the window into the dark countryside. He'd glossed over Rebecca's questions about Rachel, but she'd homed in on the same ones that had been plaguing him for the past couple of hours.

He knew how to conduct an effective interrogation of a normal subject. But from all indications, Debra didn't fall into that category. Not even close. And he had no idea how to persuade a woman tottering on the edge of sanity to cooperate.

But he knew someone who might.

He shifted in the seat toward Mark. "Our suspect sounds like a loose cannon. I don't have the expertise to get the kind of information we need from her quickly if she balks. Do you?"

"No."

"Do you think Emily might be willing to offer some suggestions if we run into a brick wall?"

"She's already standing by for a possible phone consultation. I called her before we left the New Melle police station."

He should have known Mark would be one step ahead of him on this. Mark lived with Emily. Saw firsthand how she dealt

271

with troubled people every day. Knew tonight's situation was desperate. "Thanks."

As they sped through the night, Nick hoped they wouldn't need Emily's expertise. Hoped Debra would cooperate and, without much prodding, tell them where she'd left Rachel.

But he had a feeling it wasn't going to be easy.

Or fast.

And at this point, every minute mattered.

✯

By eleven o'clock, everyone was in place.

From his crouched position behind a bushy yew at the back corner of Debra's dark house, Nick could see the New Melle fire chief working in the shadow of the small woodshed. Mark was stationed behind a matching yew at the opposite corner of the frame structure. A half dozen other agents had been spaced around the house. Everyone was linked with earpieces to Steve, who was situated beside a small toolshed with a good view of the back of the house and woodpile.

As Nick watched, his earpiece crackled to life.

"I'm set." The fire chief's voice.

"Okay. Proceed," Steve replied.

Five seconds passed. Mark pulled out his Glock. The fire chief scooted for cover. Five seconds later, a small but noisy explosion behind the wood shed sent flames licking up the sides.

A light in the room above Nick's hiding place flicked on. One of the bedrooms, according to the police chief's sketch. A shade was cracked, and Nick melted back into the shadows.

As Steve kept the rest of the team apprised of Debra's movements, the porch light came on. Nick crouched lower behind the bush. He heard her slide the latch on the back door, but he couldn't see her movements and relied on Steve's play-by-play narrative.

"She's at the back door. She's got a coat thrown over the sweat suit she's wearing. She doesn't appear to be armed . . . She's on the back porch . . . Looking at the fire . . . Coming down the steps . . . Heading to the wood pile to investigate . . . Wait for my signal . . . Now!"

Moving with quiet stealth, Nick and Mark closed in on her from behind as Steve stepped out of the shed, his gun pointed at her chest.

"FBI. Raise your arms straight out from your sides, palms back."

At the command, Debra jerked as if she'd been struck. She whirled around. Spotted Nick and Mark. Her gaze darted beyond them, where other agents were emerging from the shadows. It was too dark to see much, but Nick detected the wild look in her eyes before she turned back to Steve.

"Raise your arms straight out from your sides, palms back," Steve repeated.

After a brief hesitation, she followed his instructions.

"Now slowly move both hands behind your back."

As she started to comply, Nick closed in, cuffs ready. But all at once she whipped around and swung her arm. He saw it coming as the coat slipped off her shoulders and fell to the ground, but didn't have a chance to react before she clipped him with her fist above his right eye. His head snapped back. Grunting, he staggered from the power of the unexpected blow.

By the time he regained his footing, Mark had Debra prone on the ground, her hands cuffed behind her back.

"You okay?" Mark shot him a glance.

"Yeah." Not quite true. He could feel his eyelid swelling already.

Holstering his gun, he glared at the frenzy-eyed woman. She

couldn't be more than five-four or five-five, and she'd almost decked him. He'd never live this down.

One more reason to dislike her.

But there were plenty of others.

And Rachel's abduction was top of the list.

The sudden, muffled cry of a baby came through the half-open back door, and Debra reacted at once. Though her hands were cuffed behind her, she thrashed on the ground and tried to stand. It took two agents to restrain her.

"My baby needs me!" Debra's plea came out in a keening wail that echoed through the night.

"She's not your baby, Debra." Steve said the words in a calm, matter-of-fact tone.

"Yes, she is." Debra's chest was heaving. "I'm her mother. I have her birth certificate. It's in the house. In Danielle's room."

The squad supervisor flicked a look at Nick and Mark.

"She's a paralegal," Nick reminded him. "She'd know how to fake legal documents."

Steve motioned Mark and Nick toward the house and addressed the two agents restraining Debra. "Wait here while we retrieve the baby."

As they jogged across the lawn, Steve spoke. "Clair is on her way. She can't wait to get her hands on the car. The O'Neil couple should be at the police station in ten minutes, and a doctor's on-site as well to evaluate the baby. I'll head there with Megan. Another K-9 team is on the way out. You want to talk to Ms. Kraus here about Rachel Sutton's disappearance?"

"Yes. I'd prefer not to waste time on transport," Nick said.

"Agreed."

Pulling on latex gloves, the three men pushed through the back door and followed the sound of the cries to the nursery. Nick flicked on the light.

Froze.

It was every baby's fantasy room. Painted pale pink, the walls were topped with a colorful nursery-rhyme border. A mobile of garden fairies was suspended over the white crib, and framed pictures of Debra with the baby were arrayed around the room. A lamp base in the form of a Cinderella statue was topped with a swagged shade, and a toy box in one corner was overflowing. Gauzy curtains patterned like butterfly wings hung at the windows.

"Wow." Mark summed up the reaction as the three men crowded into the small room.

But they didn't have a chance to focus on the décor. At the appearance of the three large strangers, the baby gripped the edge of the crib where she stood and let out an ear-piercing wail.

Dressed in a warm fleece sleeper with feet, she stared at them with large blue eyes as tears rolled down her chubby cheeks. She didn't look much like the smiling cherub with a rosebud mouth Nick had seen in the file photos in Chicago, perhaps because the hair was a huge disconnect. Megan O'Neil had striking copper-colored hair. This child's was a dingy brown.

"Who wants to check for the birthmark?" he asked.

They studied the howling baby. When neither of the other two men volunteered, he moved forward.

"Okay, we need to get this done." Slowly he reached out a hand to stroke the baby's hair. "Hey, it's okay," he crooned. "We're not going to hurt you." As he talked he eased the zipper down the front of the sleeper. "Mark, check it out while I talk to this little lady, okay?"

He felt Mark move beside him as he continued to murmur to the baby. Heard the sound of the diaper tape being pulled off.

"That daycare worker was right. The birthmark's where it's supposed to be." Mark refastened the diaper and stood.

"I checked out the bathroom," Steve told them. "There's hair dye on the counter. Brown."

"Somebody find a coat for the baby. And an extra blanket." Nick lifted her from the crib and bounced her gently in his arms. "And hurry before I lose my hearing." He raised his voice to be audible above the baby's cries.

A few minutes later, as he watched the squad supervisor disappear out the front door with the bundled baby, Nick thought of the joyous reunion about to take place.

It was a happy day for the O'Neil family.

But they were only halfway home, and he didn't plan to settle for less than two reunions tonight. His jaw hardened.

Debra *would* tell them where Rachel was.

Whatever it took.

22

"All right, Ms. Kraus. Let's talk about Rachel Sutton." He'd read Debra her rights, and now Nick moved in close, his face inches from hers as they stood behind the house. The other two agents backed off a few steps. Mark took a position on the other side of Debra, arms folded across his chest. The fire chief was extinguishing the embers of the blaze in the woodshed.

"I want my baby."

"We're talking about Rachel Sutton."

"I don't know her."

Nick jangled the cars keys he'd grabbed off the kitchen counter. "No? We're about to find out."

Clair moved out of the shadows and he tossed them her way. She took off at a trot for the garage, and a few seconds later they heard the door slide up.

Pinning Debra with a grim look, Nick stripped off his latex gloves and stuffed them in the pocket of his coat. "Where did you take Rachel, Debra?"

"I don't know a Rachel. I want my baby." She looked everywhere but at him, her gaze darting frantically around the shadowy backyard.

"Debra."

No response.

"Debra, look at me." Nick leaned close to her face, his breath a frosty cloud against her skin. Her gaze skittered toward him, not quite focused, but he decided it was the best he was going to get. "Did you kill Rachel?" The harsh words tasted bitter in his mouth.

She blinked, and shock rippled across her face. "No!" Her tone was adamant. "I would never kill anybody."

"Then where is she?"

"I don't know."

Clair approached, stopping a few feet away.

Frustrated, Nick turned to the technician. "What have you got?"

"I found these wedged into a corner of the trunk, under the mat." Still wearing her latex gloves, she held up a pair of glasses. One ear piece was bent at an awkward angle.

Nick recognized the copper hue of the metallic frames. He swallowed. "Those are Rachel's."

"There are some specks of blood in the trunk too. My guess is it will match the blood on the tarp."

"Anything else?" The question was directed at Clair, but Nick's attention had returned to Debra.

"Nothing obvious. We'll give it a thorough workup once we have a warrant."

"Thanks." He folded his arms across his chest and waited until Clair reentered the garage.

"Rachel Sutton was in your trunk, Debra." His words were slow. Deliberate. Deadly.

Panic flitted through her eyes. "I want a lawyer."

"You can make that call after we take you in. But a lawyer can't change the fact that Rachel's blood is in your trunk. We found the things you threw in the well too."

She jerked as if she'd been struck. "You couldn't have . . ." She clamped her lips shut and twisted away from him. "It's cold out here. I want to go inside." She shivered inside the coat someone had re-draped over her shoulders.

Anger bubbled up in Nick, like a pot about to boil over. He reached over and yanked her coat off, tossing it to Mark.

278

"Hey! What are you doing? It's freezing out here!" She glowered at him.

"Rachel doesn't have a coat, either, Debra." Nick ground the words out through clenched teeth. "And she's been out in this weather a lot longer than you have. How cold do you think she is?"

A shiver rippled through the woman beside him. Nick didn't feel one iota of sympathy.

"I don't know Rachel. I don't have to talk to you. I want a lawyer. And I want my coat."

Nick directed his next comment to Mark. "Can you get Emily on the line?"

Motioning to the other agents to take their places, Mark pulled his BlackBerry off his belt. As he moved toward the garage, he called out to the technician working inside. "Can we borrow your van for a minute, Clair?"

"Sure." She waved at him without looking up from the trunk of Debra's car.

They climbed into the front seat and were closing the doors as Emily answered. Mark put her on speaker and set the Black-Berry on the dash.

"Em, Nick's with me. We need your help. Debra had the O'Neil baby, and we found Rachel's glasses in her trunk, but she won't tell us where she left her."

"We're hoping you can suggest an approach that might get her to open up," Nick added. "If Rachel's out in this cold, she's not going to be able to . . ." His voice hoarsened and he stopped.

"I understand, Nick. And I'm glad to help. But without talking to Debra, I can't really make any kind of formal assessment. This is all going to be gut feel."

"This is off the record, Em," Mark assured her. "And we'll take whatever you can offer. We don't have time for any kind of of-

279

ficial psych workup." He gave her the rundown on their brief interrogation session.

"Okay. Here's my take, factoring in what Mark told me about her when he called earlier. It sounds as if this woman has convinced herself the O'Neil baby is hers. That's your bargaining chip, guys. You have to promise her whatever will get you the information you need. If that means you tell her she'll get her baby back, that's what you need to do. Nothing else may work in the short term."

Nick frowned. "I'm not in the habit of lying, Emily. Even to suspects."

"Do you want to see Rachel alive again?" Emily countered.

Her blunt comeback helped him put things in perspective— and sowed the seed of a plan. "I agree we need to take some kind of drastic action. And you've given me an idea, Emily. Thanks."

As Mark slid his BlackBerry onto his belt, Nick took a deep breath. "Okay. Here's what I think we should do."

Cuddling Megan on her lap, Rebecca lifted a trembling finger and touched the familiar faint sprinkling of freckles on the bridge of her daughter's nose. Traced the graceful curve of her perfectly shaped ear. Drank in the sight of the sweeping lashes that rested against her downy cheek. Smiled at the tiny rosebud mouth suckling in sleep.

Her baby was home.

At last.

The solid little body in her arms had done more than anything else to chase away the chill that had plagued her for hours.

"Mr. and Mrs. O'Neil?" After a discreet knock, Steve Preston stuck his head in the tiny office where she and Colin had been reunited with their daughter and left in privacy to savor the moment.

"Come in, Agent Preston." Colin remained seated in the chair beside her, one arm around her shoulders, the other hand resting on the soft, comforting warmth of their baby.

"Is there any news about Rachel?" Rebecca forced herself to look up from Megan.

"No. Nick and Mark have tried to question Debra Kraus, but she's not talking. And the situation is getting desperate. If your sister is still alive, Mrs. O'Neil, she won't be in another couple of hours. The temperature's supposed to plummet after midnight, and we're only half an hour away from that."

"I know she's alive, Agent Preston. I still feel cold."

"Is there anything we can do to help find her?" Colin asked.

The man settled one hip on the desk in the small office and faced them. "We have a plan that may persuade Debra to talk. But we'll need your cooperation."

"We'll do whatever we can," Rebecca assured him.

"Maybe you better wait until you hear our idea before you say that," he cautioned.

As the squad supervisor laid out the proposal, Rebecca understood his warning. It would take every ounce of her courage to go along with the FBI's plan.

When Steve finished, he rose. "I understand that this is a difficult decision. I'll wait outside while you two discuss it."

The door closed behind him, and Rebecca looked at Colin. His eyes reflected the conflict in her heart.

They both wanted to save Rachel.

But could they put the daughter that had just been restored to them at risk to do so?

★

The violent shivering had stopped again.

Rachel was aware of that change in her body on some peripheral level of consciousness as she lay on the dirt floor, curled into a ball. The shakes had been coming in waves for a while now. The pattern had shifted soon after her hands had grown useless and her legs had given way. She was no longer able to do anything except lay on the ground.

And pray during the lucid moments that were becoming less and less frequent.

At least she didn't feel the cold anymore. In fact, she didn't feel much of anything. Including fear.

She groped for the chain around her neck. Her fingers could no longer feel the thin links or the cross they supported, but she knew she'd snagged it when she pulled and felt pressure on the back of her neck. She willed her fingers to close around the cross, hoping she'd succeeded, recalling Nick's suggestion not long ago to hold on to it if she ever felt alone.

God would hear her whether she succeeded in grasping it or not, though. Nick had told her that. And she trusted him. He wouldn't lie to her. If he thought God listened, Rachel was certain he did. She'd expected to have the chance to discover for herself the truths that had laid the foundation for Nick's confidence in the Lord, but it seemed God didn't intend to grant her that time. She hoped he would accept her second-hand pledge of faith. It was the best she could offer at this early stage of her spiritual journey.

As her awareness began to seep away, Rachel managed one last, brief prayer.

Be with me, Lord. Forgive the wrongs I've inflicted on others. Please restore Megan to Rebecca. Bless Nick. And please let him know in some way how much he meant to me.

✯

"The O'Neils are on board with the plan."

At Steve's news, Nick closed his eyes. *Thank God.*

Shifting the BlackBerry on his ear, he waited until Mark looked toward the passenger seat and gave a thumbs-up.

"What's your ETA?" Steve asked.

"Less than ten minutes."

"Okay. Here's how we're set up for your arrival."

As Nick listened, he glanced over his shoulder. Debra was wedged in the back seat between the other two agents, still minus her coat, her face vacant. She'd been less and less responsive as they loaded her into the car and began the drive to the New Melle police station. He prayed their plan would pull her back to reality long enough to produce some usable information.

"Front door," he told Mark as they swung into the station a few minutes later.

They found Steve waiting as they stepped inside. He gave Nick's eye an assessing scan. "You need to put some ice on that."

"Later."

Without pressing the point, he ushered them into the office where Rebecca and Colin had sat earlier with Megan. The child's snowsuit had been left on the desk.

Debra noticed it at once.

Some of the haze lifted from her eyes. As Mark and Nick seated her in a chair, she stared at the pink garment. "My baby . . . Is Danielle here?"

Instead of responding, Nick moved the garment aside and spoke to Steve. "Would you get Ms. Kraus a cup of coffee? It's a little chilly in here. Or do you drink tea?" He kept his tone conversational.

"Coffee."

In silence, Steve left the room. Mark stood behind Debra and folded his arms across his chest. Nick took the chair beside her and leaned back in a relaxed pose. He'd already spotted the mike the FBI had set up. It was between two books on top of the metal filing cabinet. Steve and some of the other agents would be listening in an adjacent room.

"Ms. Kraus, would you like to see your baby again?"

Her head jerked up and she stared at him, her eyes not quite focused but more responsive. "Is she here?"

"Down the hall."

The woman tried to rise, but Mark pressed her back into place with firm hands on her shoulders.

"Would you like to see her?" Nick repeated, maintaining his casual position.

"Yes."

"I can make that happen."

Her eyes narrowed as she studied him. He could see her cognitive processes kicking in again. Good.

The door opened, and Steve entered. He handed a large ceramic mug to Nick and set another one on the desk in front of Debra, depositing packets of creamer and sugar beside it. He left in silence, closing the door behind him.

Lifting his steaming mug, Nick took a sip and addressed Debra. "Do you want cream or sugar?"

"I want my baby." A shiver rippled through her.

"We'll get to that. Cream or sugar?"

"Sugar. One packet."

After stirring in the sugar, Nick pushed the cup toward Debra. "Mark, why don't you take her handcuffs off so she can drink her coffee?"

As Mark complied, Nick continued to sip his own brew.

Once free of the cuffs, she wrapped both hands around the toasty mug and gave him a suspicious look. "Why are you being nice to me now?"

"You have information I want. I figure we can make a deal."

"What kind of deal?" She took a sip of the coffee.

Setting his cup on the desk, Nick leaned forward and clasped

284

his hands between his knees. "Let me tell you how I see this situation. You didn't hurt the baby. On the contrary. As far as I can tell, you took wonderful care of her. That will work in your favor, Debra. The courts like good mothers. Now, a murder charge? That's not so good."

"I didn't kill anyone."

"What about Rachel?"

"I didn't kill her."

"Then she's alive?"

"I don't know. It's cold outside. People can die in the cold. That's not my fault." She took a long gulp of the coffee.

"But you left her somewhere in the cold."

"I didn't kill her."

They were going in circles. Nick dangled the bait again. "If you tell me where you left her, I'll get the baby."

Debra glanced at Mark, who was juggling the handcuffs in his hand.

"I think I should talk to a lawyer."

"Okay." Nick pulled the phone on the desk toward her. "You can make one call. But Debra . . ." He waited until she looked at him. "If you do that before you tell us where Rachel is, this deal's off."

The woman's hands started to shake. "I want to see my baby."

"Then tell me where Rachel is."

Desperation tightened her features. "I want to see my baby first."

Nick leaned back, considering. "Here's the deal. You tell me what I want to know, then I'll get the baby. Yes or no."

"Get Danielle first."

Several beats of silence ticked by before Nick gave a slow nod. "Okay. I'll be back in a couple of minutes."

Exiting the room, he found Steve waiting in the hallway.

"Despite her mental problems, the analytical side of her brain is still functioning," Steve said. "I didn't expect her to bargain."

"I don't care how much she bargains as long as she agrees to the deal. Where are the O'Neils?"

"Conference room at the end of the hall." Steve led the way, pushing open the door and stepping aside for Nick to enter.

Rebecca looked up as he entered. Megan was in her arms, the child's face peaceful in slumber. Colin was sitting beside her but rose as Nick stepped into the room.

"Nick . . . what happened to your eye?" Rebecca inspected the abrasion with concern.

"A little accident." He wasn't about to tell them Debra had slugged him. To reveal her capacity for unexpected violence. Closing the door, he moved beside them. "Thank you both for doing this."

"We prayed for guidance," Rebecca said softly as Colin laid a hand on her shoulder. "And we realized if it hadn't been for Rachel, we might never have found Megan. Her discovery of the doll, and her trip to your office to try and get someone to listen to her, took a lot of courage. Even if she wasn't my sister, I'd feel an obligation to return the favor. Colin and I couldn't live with ourselves if we didn't do everything we could to help you find her. Despite the risk."

"We'll minimize that as much as possible," Nick told her.

"I know. Agent Preston explained the plan. And this woman took excellent care of Megan. The doctor who examined her said she's in perfect condition. I choose to believe she'll continue to nurture her."

"I think that's true," Nick replied.

But all of them knew they were dealing with an unstable personality. With a woman who had taken extreme measures to secure a child and who had abducted the person she considered a threat and left her somewhere in the cold to die.

A woman who was already highly stressed and agitated.

A woman who could flip out with very little provocation.

286

The FBI would do its best to protect the baby.

But there was risk, and they all knew it.

Nick held out his arms, and Rebecca's grip on Megan tightened for a brief instant. After a squeeze on the shoulder from Colin, she lifted the sleeping child toward Nick.

The transfer was made without waking her. Megan simply shifted her position and cuddled into the crook of Nick's arm.

"I'll have her back to you as soon as I can, safe and sound."

With a nod, Rebecca swiped at her eyes and gripped Colin's hand.

And as Nick stepped back into the hall, he prayed he would be able to keep that promise.

23

Steve fell into step beside Nick as he strode down the hall. "We're ready to move as soon as you have an approximate location. The K-9 units are standing by and I also have medevac on alert."

"They need to be prepared to treat severe hypothermia."

"I've already alerted them to the situation. They've called in one of their crew who used to be a search-and-rescue specialist with the Coast Guard. He has extensive experience with hypothermia."

"Okay. Sounds like all the bases are covered." Nick paused at the office door and took a deep breath.

"Good luck." Steve moved out of the line of sight.

Twisting the knob, Nick entered the room.

Debra was on her feet instantly. Another agent had joined Mark, and both men grabbed her arms to restrain her as she tried to surge forward.

Nick took a step away. "Sit down, Debra, or the deal's off."

Her gaze never left the sleeping baby, but she complied.

"Now tell me where Rachel is."

If he didn't have such a heavy personal investment in this case, the acute yearning on Debra's face would be almost enough to rouse his sympathy.

Almost.

Any such inclination evaporated at her next comment, however.

"I don't remember."

288

Panic threatened to choke him, and Nick fought it down. Given her unstable mental state, she might very well be telling the truth. And if she was, they were doomed.

Trying to maintain a calm demeanor, Nick moved his chair out of touching distance and retook his seat. "No information, I take the baby away, Debra."

"I don't remember where Rachel is."

"Okay. I'll try to help you. Did you leave her inside or outside?"

"Inside. I do remember that."

That confirmed their theory. And it was good news. At least Rachel would be protected from the windchill. On the flip side, however, a thermal scan would be useless. They'd need the dogs.

"What kind of building was it?"

"I don't know. Small. Empty. Dark."

"Was Rachel alive when you left her, Debra?"

He didn't like the sudden uncertainty on her face. "I think so. Yes. I saw her breathing."

"Did you hurt her, Debra?" Nick's grip on the infant tightened. Megan wiggled and emitted a soft sound, reminding him to relax his hold.

Debra's eyes glazed over. "She wouldn't do what I asked. And she tried to hurt *me*. It was self-defense. This is all her fault anyway. If she'd left the stupid doll alone instead of going to the FBI with all that psychic stuff, I wouldn't have had to do anything to her. I want to hold Danielle now."

"You haven't told me where Rachel is."

"I'm not sure." Debra's eyes narrowed as she watched him. "But I might remember if I was holding Danielle."

He was running out of options. And time. Nick glanced at the two agents, who moved in even closer as he scooted his chair a few inches toward the woman. Near enough for her to lean forward and touch the sleeping baby's foot.

"Are you remembering, Debra?"

No response as she stroked the tiny toes through the fleece sleeper.

"Debra."

Still no response.

"I'll take the baby back if you don't talk to me."

At the threat, panic gripped her features. "I'm trying. It was off a dirt road. Through the woods. I saw a lake nearby."

"What road was it?"

"I don't know. There wasn't a sign."

"How far off the road was this building?"

"I'm not sure. I could see it through the trees in the daylight. When I was there by myself, I walked to it in a few minutes. It took longer with her. She kept tripping. I made her take off her shoes. Wearing high heels in the woods is silly, anyway."

Stroking the baby's toes, she began to croon in a singsong voice. "You're Mommy's little girl, aren't you, sweetie? If you could talk, you'd tell them that, wouldn't you? You'd tell them you and I are supposed to be together. And how much we love each other."

She was slipping. And they didn't have enough information. Nick's adrenaline surged.

"Debra." It was everything he could do to maintain a normal tone.

When she didn't respond, he leaned over and gave her shoulder a slight shake. She lifted her head. "Is the building where you left Rachel close to your house?"

She seemed to have difficulty processing the question. "My house?"

"The house where you live with Danielle." He spoke slowly, enunciating each word. "Did you have to drive very far to get home after you left Rachel in the building?"

Her face took on a dreamy quality. "I didn't go home. I had

290

to pick up my little girl. She was waiting for her mommy. Weren't you, sweetie?" She transferred her attention back to the baby.

Nick and Mark exchanged a look. The urgency in the room was almost palpable.

"Ms. Kraus, how did you find the building where you left Rachel?" Nick persisted.

She blinked. Once. Twice. "I drove around one day . . . trying to find . . . a place."

"Near your house?"

"Not too far away. I didn't want to drive a long way on country roads with Danielle in case I had car trouble. It wouldn't be good for a baby to be out in the cold, you know."

"What kind of road was the building near?" Mark interjected.

"It was just two tire tracks. It didn't seem like anyone had been down there in a long time. There was an old, rusted plow where I turned in. Someone didn't take very good care of their tools. My father wouldn't have liked that." Her features tightened in distress. "He always got mad when I left my toys out. Like the night I forgot to put my bicycle in the garage. He gave it away the next day. Said I didn't deserve to have it if I couldn't take care of it." Her lower lip quivered. "I loved that bike." She stroked Megan's foot again. "I would never do anything like that to you, sweetie. I wouldn't expect you to always be perfect."

Motioning to Nick, Mark slipped through the door into the hall. He was replaced by another agent a few seconds later.

As Nick rose, panic flashed through Debra's eyes. "I want to hold my baby!"

"She's not your baby, Ms. Kraus."

He joined Mark in the hall, muting her keening wail by pulling the door shut behind him.

"I don't think she knows any more than she told us," Mark said.

"I don't, either."

A door opened down the hall, and Steve emerged, followed by the police chief. "I think we have a possible location. Chief Richter says there's some property a few miles from here that has a rusted plow near the entrance."

"Some city slicker bought it a few years back," Joe added. "Investment property, I guess. Never see him around. There's no house on the land, but there could be a shed of some kind. Haven't been on the place myself."

"Is there a lake?" Nick asked.

"Could be a small pond in there. Like I said, it's on the edge of my jurisdiction, and I've never had any reason to wander around on the land. I could call Floyd Mueller, though. He owns the next spread. Might be able to answer that question."

"Get him on the line," Nick said.

After rousing the farmer from a sound sleep, Joe confirmed the presence of water on the property. "Floyd says there's a couple of small ponds on the land. A few outbuildings scattered around too. Most of them are falling down."

It sounded like the place. Nick's adrenaline kicked into high gear. "We need to get there. Fast."

Five minutes later, after restoring Megan to the arms of her anxious parents, Nick took the wheel as he and Mark followed the police chief's patrol car at speeds far in excess of the posted limit. An ambulance and both K-9 units were on their tail, followed by Steve and a few of the other agents. The medevac helicopter had also been dispatched.

As they raced through the dark night, Nick's gaze kept straying to the digital outdoor temperature reading on his dash. Half an hour ago it had been holding at fifteen. It had now dropped to twelve.

Time was running out.

★

"This is it." Mark gestured ahead as the chief pulled to the side of the road and opened his door.

Easing in behind him, Nick set the brake and stepped out of the car. The other vehicles lined up behind him. One K-9 team drew alongside.

"That's the road." The chief gestured to an overgrown two-track path leading into the woods. "And there's the plow." He pointed out the rusted implement that had been abandoned near the entrance. He also handed Nick a hammer. "I'm assuming there's a new padlock on the shed. Hit it on the latching side."

As Nick took the tool, he prayed he'd have a chance to use it. They were pinning all their hopes on one piece of information in Debra's story. Perhaps she'd just remembered seeing the plow during her scouting expedition. Maybe it had remained in her memory not as a marker for the spot where she'd left Rachel, but because it reminded her of the story about her bicycle. Maybe . . .

"You want to ride or walk?"

At Mark's question, Nick did his best to tamp down his panic. The K-9 vehicle that had pulled up next to them had already headed down the road. The plan was for the dogs to begin at opposite ends and work toward each other as they tried to pick up Rachel's scent. Nick and Mark would follow the one that began at the main road.

"Walk." Despite the bitter wind, Nick wanted to be on the ground, not cocooned in warmth. "You can follow in the car."

In response, Mark tossed him one of the black balaclavas they wore on cold-weather SWAT call-outs. Pulled his own on. Turned up the collar of his coat. Set off down the road.

The measure of friendship was often taken in high-pressure

moments, Nick knew, and his throat tightened with emotion as he tugged on the protective head covering and followed Mark.

The K-9 team beginning its search at the entrance to the road had already started down the two-lane path, and Nick and Mark fell in behind the officer and dog. The sky was clear and the moon bright, rendering the flashlights they'd retrieved from the car almost unnecessary.

They walked in silence, the only sound the crunch of their feet on the frozen ground stubble, the rattle of bare branches as the wind shook the trees, and the panting of the dog who was tackling his task with focus and enthusiasm.

With every minute that ticked by and every yard they covered, Nick's anxiety grew exponentially. According to the farmer on the adjacent property, the overgrown road they were traversing was only about a quarter of a mile long. It wouldn't take the two dogs long to cover that distance.

And if this turned into a wild goose chase, Rachel would die.

Because they were out of time.

Five minutes later, Nick's heart sank when he spotted the other K-9 team a hundred feet ahead.

"Is there a secondary location?" The officer in front of them called the question over his shoulder as the dog continued to nose along the ground and tug on the harness.

"No." Mark answered when Nick remained silent.

"We can retrace our route, but these dogs are good. Rico's never missed—"

All at once, the dog stopped, sniffed, grew excited. He tugged on his harness, urging the officer to the side of the road, straining toward the woods.

"I think we have something."

Yanking his BlackBerry off his belt, Mark punched in Steve's number and relayed the news as the police officer and dog plunged down an indistinct path through the woods.

Please, God, let this be it! Nick's pulse began to pound as he followed close on the team's heels.

They'd gone no more than a hundred feet when Rico stopped, sat, and perked up his ears.

Nick had done enough work with K-9 units to recognize the dog's posture as a passive alert. He'd found something. But it couldn't be Rachel. There was no building of any kind in sight.

The officer bent down and carefully moved aside the dead and decaying leaves with a stick. Nick joined him, watching as his probing uncovered a pair of thin, supple leather gloves. He recognized them at once.

Rachel's.

He recalled teasing her about them the day he'd gone to tea, pointing out their limited practicality in cold weather. She'd laughed, responding that her bulky thermal pair weren't quite appropriate for the chic hotel where she played. And that a woman had to sacrifice warmth for style on occasion.

His spirits soared. They were on the right path!

"Look how these were left. I don't think they were dropped by mistake." Mark crouched to examine them.

Nick took a closer look. He was right. The gloves had been folded together into a small ball and tucked off to one side of the path, under some leaves.

Rachel had left them a clue.

Despite her fear, despite possible injuries, she'd been trying to send searchers a signal.

Amazing.

"Good for her," Mark said softly, echoing Nick's thoughts. "I'll get the local EMTs in here." He pulled out his BlackBerry as he stood.

Once the officer rewarded the dog with a treat, he urged Rico to move ahead. The dog didn't need much encouragement. As if sensing that the object of his search was nearby, the animal surged forward.

Two minutes later, when the small group emerged in a clearing, Nick took cursory note of the small pond off to one side as the dog headed straight for a decrepit outbuilding constructed of cement blocks.

But as he swung his flashlight across the façade, what he noticed most was the shiny new padlock.

"Pay dirt," Mark declared, pulling out his BlackBerry again.

Hammer in hand, Nick sprinted across the uneven ground, his heart pounding. *Please, God, let her be alive!*

While the officer rewarded his canine partner with another treat, Nick went to work on the padlock. It took several blows, but at last the shackle disengaged.

As he unhooked the latch and prepared to enter, Nick knew that as long as he lived he'd never face a moment this terrifying again.

Because what he found on the other side of the door would affect the rest of his life.

For better or for worse.

24

The beam of Nick's flashlight found her at once. She was curled into a fetal position just inside the door, her back to him.

Lying still as death.

His heart lurched, and he tried to swallow past the rancid taste of fear as he stepped over Rachel and knelt beside her. He took a quick inventory, noting the shredded stockings, the abrasions on her feet, the soiled blouse that would never be pristine white again. Her hair had fallen across her face, and he gently lifted it aside. The bloodied bump on her temple quickened his pulse. As did the iciness of her pale skin as his fingers brushed over it.

Worst of all, he saw no indication that she was breathing.

Steeling himself, he leaned forward to press his fingers against the carotid artery in her neck. He thought he detected a very shallow pulse. But he wasn't sure.

"Come on, Rachel, stay with us." The plea came out in a ragged whisper as he stroked her cheek.

A commotion at the door caught his attention, and he looked up. Two EMTs stepped over the threshold, followed by Mark and a couple of other agents, who wedged themselves into the corners of the small building and used their flashlights to provide some illumination for the emergency technicians.

"The helicopter's five minutes away," Mark told him. "We're

setting up flares in the field to guide it in. There's plenty of room to land. How is she?"

"I don't know." Nick choked out the words and moved aside as the EMTs took over.

The silence in the small space was heavy as the two technicians checked Rachel's vitals, then exchanged a look.

"What?" Nick asked, tensing.

"Pulse and respiration are very slow." As the technician spoke, the EMTs spread a thermal pad on the ground. "Lift her slow and easy," he warned his partner. "On three. One. Two. Three."

In one smooth motion, they transferred Rachel to the pad, still curled in the fetal position.

The whump-whump-whump of rotor blades registered in Nick's consciousness. The sound grew rapidly louder as one of the EMTs placed a light blanket over Rachel.

"Didn't you guys bring anything warmer than that?" Nick snapped.

"We're trying to avoid afterdrop."

"What's that?"

"A further decrease in core temperature. If we rewarm the periphery, the vessels in the arms and legs will dilate and send cold blood to the core, causing a further decrease in temperature. You can kill people that way. It's important to rewarm the core first."

Nick swallowed. Hard. If he'd been in charge, he'd already have made a deadly mistake. "How do you do that?"

"With specialized equipment like IV warmers and warm, humidified oxygen. The medevac team will be equipped to measure her core temperature."

As he waited for the paramedics on the helicopter to arrive, Nick moved closer to Rachel. She was curled on her right side, and he reached for her left hand—only to discover that it was

298

clenched around the cross she still wore around her neck. He couldn't pry her white fingers loose, so he closed his own hand around hers. And continued to pray.

Sixty seconds later, the medevac team arrived and took over, led by a man Nick estimated to be in his late forties. He had the tanned, weathered face of a sailor, and his light brown hair—cut in a short, military style—was liberally salted. As the two local EMTs moved aside, he stepped over Rachel, noting Nick's grip on her hand before he nudged him aside.

"You look like FBI."

"Special Agent Nick Bradley."

"Kevin Callahan. You have a personal interest in this case?"

"Yes." At this point, Nick saw no reason to hide his feelings for Rachel. Besides, he wasn't about to budge from her side.

"Okay. You can stick close. Just stay out of my way."

"You must be the Coast Guard hypothermia expert."

The man was already checking Rachel's pupils, but his lips twitched into the glimmer of a smile. "I guess we'll find out how expert I am." He examined her exposed skin as he spoke to the two paramedics who'd accompanied him. "We've got some cyanosis. Let's get a tympanic sensor on her. See if you can find a vein that isn't collapsed and start an IV. Normal saline."

The small space fell silent except for the rustle of movement as the paramedics worked. Kevin eased Rachel onto her back and carefully worked open the buttons on her blouse. He pushed the fabric aside, revealing the delicate lace edging of her camisole—and angry bruises on her neck.

Nick sucked in a sharp breath. He'd seen marks like that before. On strangulation victims.

"Someone was trying very hard to make sure this woman didn't live to see tomorrow," Kevin remarked as he began to hook her up to the cardiac monitor, attaching sticky pads to her chest.

"IV is in," one of the paramedics said.

"Tympanic temperature is thirty-one point six," the other technician reported.

Nick did the math for the conversion to Fahrenheit. About eighty-nine degrees. His gut knotted. She was way too cold.

"Someone tell the pilot to shut down." The directive came from Kevin.

"Aren't you transporting her?" Every muscle in Nick's body stiffened. He could think of only one reason why there'd be no urgent need to get Rachel to a hospital. And he wouldn't even consider that possibility.

"Yes. But I don't want her exposed to rotor wash with the outdoor temperature this low."

"I'll take care of it," Mark offered, disappearing out the door.

"Let's get the stretcher in here," Kevin said.

One of the paramedics rose to retrieve it, and thirty seconds later he passed it through the door of the shed.

"Okay, let's move her very gently," Kevin said. "We don't want to jar her and send any cold blood from the arms and legs into the central circulatory system."

"What about the vibration from the helicopter?" Nick asked.

"We'll cushion the stretcher as best we can. Cover her head too," Kevin directed the technicians as they cocooned Rachel in blankets.

While they eased Rachel through the door, Nick tossed Mark his keys. "Take my car, okay? I'm going on the helicopter."

"No problem." He restrained Nick with a hand on his arm and aimed his flashlight at one of the hinges. "She made a valiant effort. I found this on the floor." He opened his hand. A small, sharp stone rested in his palm.

As Nick looked from the blood-stained rock to the gouged wood beside the hinge, his vision blurred. Working in the cold and dark, by feel alone, Rachel had managed to dig one of the hinges almost out of the wood before she succumbed to hypothermia.

Wiping the back of his hand across his eyes, he stepped out the door, into the dark. "Call Rebecca, okay?" He choked out the hoarse request.

"I'll take care of it. And I'll meet you at the hospital."

With a wave of acknowledgement, Nick sprinted across the field, the flares around the perimeter giving off an eerie glow in the dense blackness of the night. The rotors were already turning when he reached the helicopter. He ducked through the wash and climbed aboard.

"I figured you'd want to ride along," Kevin said, sliding the door shut behind him.

Taking a seat near Rachel, he touched her pale cheek. It was still ice cold. "Is she . . ." He stopped. Cleared his throat. Tried again. "Is she going to be okay?"

"The first half hour after the rescue is critical." Kevin scooted onto the bench seat beside Rachel as the helicopter lifted off. "But we're doing all the right things. Hypothermia protocols are much better than they used to be."

"Are you saying the prognosis is good?"

Kevin checked the cardiac monitor before he replied. "I've seen people in worse condition survive."

The paramedic's cautious response did nothing to quell Nick's anxiety.

And as the helicopter churned through the dark air, the fierce turbulence it left in its wake was like a gentle breeze compared to the roiling in his gut.

301

The noisy ride to the Level 1 trauma center in St. Louis was the longest of Nick's life. And once there Rachel was whisked away, leaving him alone in the waiting room.

During the next forty-five minutes, he visited the intake desk five times. But no one told him anything. He wasn't family.

The only thing they'd done for him was offer an ice pack.

Shifting on the cushioned seat of a wood-framed chair, he tipped his head back against the wall and wedged the compress against his eye. This whole setup reminded him of the vigil he'd held with Mark the prior summer.

They were not good memories.

But Emily had survived. And Rachel would too.

She had to.

"Nick!"

He jerked upright. Rebecca burst through the door, Mark on her heels. He was on his feet instantly.

"How is she?" Rebecca asked.

"I don't know. They won't tell me anything. You have to be family to get any information." He cast a dark scowl at the middle-aged nurse seated behind the counter. She ignored him.

"You saved her life. That ought to count for something." Rebecca marched over to the desk. "I'm Rachel Sutton's sister. I'd like an update on her condition."

The nurse peered over her glasses at Rebecca, then at Nick, who had moved behind her. "I'll get one of the doctors."

She rose and disappeared through an inner door.

"Not exactly Miss Warmth," Mark noted, joining them.

"You'd think they'd have someone with a little more empathy in the ER," Rebecca said, irritation nipping at her voice.

"Where's Colin?" The ice pack was numbing his fingers, and Nick shifted it to his other hand.

"One of the agents dropped him and Megan off at the hotel. I bummed a ride with Mark." She rubbed her eyes, calling his attention to the smudges underneath. She was dead on her feet. "How was she when you arrived, Nick?"

"No change that I could see."

A door to one side of the desk opened, and a woman of about fifty wearing a white coat stepped through. "Are you the family of Rachel Sutton?"

"Yes," Rebecca answered for all of them.

"I'm Dr. Kent." She shook hands with each of them. "Let's sit for a minute." Surveying the deserted waiting room, she gestured toward a grouping of chairs and led the way. "Slow night. I guess no one felt sick enough to venture out at two in the morning on one of the coldest nights of the year. Except Ms. Sutton."

"How is she, doctor?" Rebecca leaned forward, twisting her hands in her lap.

Nick's fingers clenched around the arms of his chair as he braced himself.

"Holding her own. Her core temperature has risen two degrees, to ninety-one. We're rewarming as aggressively as we can without putting her at further risk. We've done a chest X-ray, an electrocardiogram, and we're running blood work now. We've seen no evidence of arrhythmias, meaning her heart doesn't appear to have been overly stressed by her exposure, but we'll be keeping a close watch on that for a while. She also suffered a concussion, has various contusions and bruises—including some nasty ones on her neck that appear to be the result of an attempted strangulation—and a few fingers and toes have second-degree frostbite."

"What's the prognosis?" Nick asked.

"If all goes well with the rewarming, she'll regain consciousness soon and begin talking not long after that. The concussion shouldn't cause any major problems. We've already rewarmed her fingers and toes in warm water. That can be quite painful, so in a way it's a blessing she's not conscious. I expect to see some blisters and edema—swelling, in lay terms—on them in the next twelve hours, and she'll have some discomfort for a while, but we can treat that with pain medication. She could also have some longer-term tingling or loss of sensitivity in the affected fingers and toes, though. Other than that, by tomorrow there should be little physical evidence of her traumatic experience beyond her bruises. Hypothermia puts the body into a safe mode that protects the vital organs. It's really quite amazing."

For the first time in almost ten hours, the tension in Nick's shoulders eased a fraction. "Can we see her?"

"Two of you can come back. Don't be alarmed by all the equipment. She's doing well."

As they rose, Mark spoke in a low tone to Nick. "I'll wait. And I'll take Rebecca back to the hotel whenever she's ready to go. She's about to fold. What are your plans?"

"I'm staying."

"That's what I thought. I'll have Emily follow me into work in the morning and I'll drop your car off."

"Thanks."

"No problem."

The doctor and Rebecca were waiting at the door to the ER, and Nick hurried to catch up, following them to a curtained alcove.

As the doctor swept aside the draping to allow them to enter, he was glad she'd already given them a positive report on Rachel and warned them about the equipment. Because if he'd stepped in here unprepared, he'd have panicked. An oxygen mask covered her face, IVs were positioned on either side of the bed, a cardiac monitor was displaying continuous data, and there were several other pieces of equipment he couldn't identify. She was also covered with an odd blanket.

"That's a warming blanket. It contains heated air," the doctor explained as Nick placed a tentative hand on top of it. "We're also giving her heated, humidified oxygen to speed the core rewarming."

As she spoke, he moved closer to the head of the bed. "What's the tape on her cheek?"

"It's securing the tube for the esophageal probe. That's the most accurate way to monitor her core temperature."

"May we stay with her?" Rebecca asked, moving to the other side of the bed.

"Yes. It will be good for her to see a familiar face when she begins to regain consciousness. But it's obvious you've both had a tough night too. One of you might want to try and get some sleep. Nothing much will happen here for at least an hour."

"There's an empty couch in the waiting room," Nick said to Rebecca. "Why don't you stretch out for a little while? I'll call you as soon as she starts to stir."

"I don't know . . . I feel like I should stay here." Rebecca tucked her hair behind her ear and moistened her lips as she cast an uncertain glance at Rachel.

"I second the gentleman's recommendation," the doctor joined in. "No sense everyone losing sleep."

With a sigh, Rebecca capitulated. "Okay. But you'll call the minute she begins to wake up?"

"You have my word," Nick promised.

"I'll walk you out. And round up a pillow for you," the doctor told Rebecca.

With one last lingering look at her sister, Rebecca exited. The doctor pulled the drapes back into place, leaving Nick alone with Rachel.

For several minutes he stood unmoving, watching her, saying a silent prayer of thanks. Then he leaned over and traced a gentle finger around her hairline, over skin that was still too cool, stopping when he came to the bruised bump on her temple. As he thought about how close he'd come to losing her, his throat tightened and his eyes misted.

Blinking to clear his vision, he slid his hand under the warming blanket until he found hers. Covering her fingers with his, he eased a hip onto the edge of her bed and settled in.

Because he intended to stay put until she opened those velvet brown eyes and he knew she was back. For good.

25

Someone was holding her hand. And it felt good.

Sighing, Rachel burrowed deeper into the warmth surrounding her. That, too, felt good. Yet even enveloped in this balmy cocoon, she felt chilled to the bone. How odd. And why were her fingers throbbing? She tried to flex them. Frowned. That hurt worse.

All at once the hand holding hers disappeared. She immediately missed the comforting pressure—and the warmth.

She tried to lift her heavy eyelids. Once. Twice. When both efforts failed, she let herself drift.

Some time later . . . a minute, an hour, she had no idea . . . the murmur of voices pulled her back. She felt someone take one hand in a gentle grasp. The other hand received the same treatment. She tried again to lift her eyelids. Managed to drag them open.

"Rachel, can you hear me?"

Nick's voice. At least she thought it was his. But he sounded hoarse. As if he'd caught a cold.

She blinked, trying to focus. Realized her glasses were missing. She attempted to ask for them, but could get only a hoarse croak past her aching throat.

"It's okay, Rachel. Don't try to talk." Nick leaned in close and gave her hand a gentle, reassuring squeeze. Though the pressure was slight, she winced. He loosened his grip at once. "Don't squeeze her hand." Nick aimed that remark at someone to her right. "The frostbite must be painful."

Frostbite. She had frostbite?

Another figure leaned in, looming over her. Rebecca.

Rachel looked from one to the other. Now that they were closer, she could make out their features. Sort of. Everything looked fuzzy. But she could see enough to set off alarm bells in her mind. Rebecca's face was way too pale. Nick was sporting a shiner worthy of a bar fight.

She tried to speak again. Couldn't form the words.

"You're okay, Rachel." Despite Rebecca's encouraging message, a tremor ran through her words. "Nick found you in time. Megan too. She's safe. The nightmare is over."

Her sister's words registered, but Rachel began to drift again. It was so hard to concentrate. She wanted to ask questions. But she couldn't muster the energy. Or get the words out.

She knew one thing, though. If Nick and Rebecca were with her, she was safe. She could let herself sink back into oblivion. And maybe the next time she surfaced her mind—and tongue—would be functioning again.

★

Nick took a sip of black coffee as he stood at the foot of Rachel's bed. After she'd awakened forty-five minutes ago, he'd convinced an exhausted Rebecca to go back to the hotel and get some sleep. Now, at 3:45 in the morning, as the tension in his body slowly eased, he, too, was fighting to stay awake. He couldn't remember ever being this tired, not even on his longest stakeout.

The doctor had urged him to go home and get some sleep. But she'd also said Rachel could awaken at any time. Her temperature had risen to ninety-seven, and as far as the medical folks were concerned, she was pretty much out of danger. They'd taken her off the heated oxygen a few minutes ago, and the staff wasn't hovering as much. While the doctor wanted to keep her in the hospital for twenty-four hours because of the concussion, plans were being made to move her to a regular room. It was possible she'd sleep through the night.

He didn't need to stay.

But he couldn't go home, either. Not until he heard her speak. He needed to assure himself she was back—and lucid—before the last knots of tension in his shoulders would ease enough to allow sleep.

"Nick?"

At the whispered summons, his hand jerked and he almost spilled the coffee. Grasping the cup with both hands to steady it, he skirted the foot of the bed and moved beside her in two long strides, noting in relief that her eyes were clear.

"Hey there." He dredged up a shaky smile. "I was beginning to think you were going to sleep around the clock."

"What happened to your eye?" She tried to lift her hand to touch his bruised and swollen skin, but it was buried under a blanket.

He pressed it back into place with a firm but gentle touch. "You're hooked up to industrial-strength IVs. Don't try to move much. Lie still and rest."

"If I promise to be good, will you tell me what happened to your eye?"

Her voice was raw and raspy, but at the teasing light in her gold-flecked irises, his grin came more easily. "You're in no position to bargain, you know. I could always call the nurse if you don't cooperate."

"If you do, see if she can find my glasses, would you? Everything is fuzzy."

"I'm afraid they're in an evidence bag."

"There's a spare pair in a case on my piano." She gave him a hopeful look.

309

"I'll see what I can do."

"Thanks. Back to your eye. Did you put ice on it?"

She'd almost died, and she was worried about his eye. He swallowed past the lump in this throat. "Yes, ma'am, I did."

"What happened to it?"

"I forgot to duck."

"Not a good enough answer."

"I'll expand on it later."

To his relief, she dropped the subject and moved on to more important things.

"Nick . . . when Rebecca was here earlier . . . she did say Megan was okay, didn't she?"

Setting his coffee cup on the bedside stand, he reached under the blanket to take her hand again in a loose, reassuring clasp. This time her fingers curled around his, warm and responsive, though he could feel the blisters and swelling on a couple of them.

"Yes. Megan is fine and sound asleep as we speak in a hotel room with Rebecca, Colin, and Bridget."

"So the woman who abducted me . . . she was Megan's kidnapper?"

"Yes." Nick eased onto the bed beside her and brushed some strands of hair back from her face. "How much do you remember about what happened, Rachel?" he asked gently.

A frown creased her brow, and he detected an immediate change in her respiration. "Pretty much everything, I think. Mostly, though, I remember being cold. And praying you'd find me before it was too late. I'm assuming the kidnapper saw the media coverage about my so-called psychic abilities and got spooked."

"That's our assumption. You were a threat she was determined to eliminate."

Tears welled in Rachel's eyes. One spilled out to trickle down her cheek, and Nick brushed it away with his free hand.

"Sorry." She tried to smile. "I'm not usually the weepy type."

310

"You're entitled today, after all you've been through."

"When I think how close she came to succeeding . . ." A shudder rippled through her, and she tightened her grip on Nick's hand. "The worst part was feeling so helpless."

"You were hurt, and she had a weapon. You did everything you could to help yourself. We found your gloves. And the rock you used to work on the hinge." He stroked her hand with his thumb, then skimmed a finger over the discolored skin on her neck. "You fought back too, if these bruises are any indication."

Rachel closed her eyes and sucked in a deep breath. "Just b-before we got to the shed, a deer ran out of the woods. She was distracted, and I figured that was my last chance to escape. I pushed her. When she fell and dropped the gun, I tried to get to it, but I had handcuffs on and I . . . I couldn't do it." She swallowed and opened her eyes. "She wasn't lucid, Nick. Her mind wasn't . . . normal. Do you know anything about her?"

"Some." He gave her the highlights, keeping his recap as brief as possible.

"How sad," Rachel murmured after he finished. "She's obviously a very disturbed woman. I feel sorry for her, in a way."

Since he was the professed Christian, Nick knew he should be the one offering understanding and forgiveness. But he wasn't there yet. Not even close. The terror he'd felt when he'd thought he might lose the special woman now clinging to his hand was too fresh.

"She'll get professional help, Rachel. I'm more worried about you."

She glanced at the monitors surrounding her bed. "I'm a little afraid to ask about my prognosis, considering half of the hospital's equipment seems to be parked in my room."

"It's a good one. The hypothermia's almost gone, your frostbite shouldn't leave any permanent damage, and your concussion hasn't caused any serious problems. The doctor said you can

311

go home tomorrow." He checked his watch. "Sorry. Make that today."

"What time is it?"

"Getting close to four o'clock."

"In the morning?" Her eyes widened.

"Yes."

"Go home, Nick. Get some sleep."

"I will. Later."

"Now."

One side of his mouth hitched up. "You must be feeling better. You're getting bossy."

"Only because I care about you. A lot." She shifted her hand to entwine her fingers with his.

The soft, candid comment took him off guard. As did the tenderness in her eyes.

"And I can't leave for the very same reason." His words came out husky. Leaning over, he brushed his lips across her forehead. Might as well put all his cards on the table.

At the touch of his lips against her skin, Rachel closed her eyes, smiled, and sighed. "I never thought I'd find anyone like you," she murmured.

"I feel the same way."

"Do you know what one of my biggest regrets was, right before I lost consciousness?" Her gaze locked on his as she whispered the question.

"What?"

"That we'd never have the chance to see where our relationship might lead."

"Well, you can put that fear to rest." He cupped her delicate jaw with his hand and rested his fingers against her cheek. "Because as soon as you're out of this place, I intend to make that investigation my top priority. And I'm a very thorough investigator." He grinned and winked. "Just ask my boss."

Four and a half hours later, after a sound sleep not even a gurney ride could disturb, Rachel awoke in a different room with a new cast of characters clustered around her bed. Of the group, she'd met only Rebecca, but she recognized the others from the photos her sister had shared with her on her first trip to St. Louis. The tall man with the silver-flecked dark hair and pleasant face was Colin; the flaxen-haired toddler on his hip, finger in mouth, was Bridget; and the brown-haired baby nestled in Rebecca's arms had to be the little lady whose kidnapping had started the whole incredible chain of events.

"Welcome back." Rebecca smiled at her. "I thought it was time you met your family."

My family.

The words resonated sweetly in Rachel's heart.

"Hi, Rachel. I've already heard a lot about you." Colin smiled and bounced Bridget on his hip. "Say hi to your aunt Rachel, Bridget."

The child buried her head in Colin's shoulder but peeked out to give Rachel a shy smile.

"And this is Megan." Rebecca said the name softly and moved closer. "Colin, would you crank up the bed so Rachel can hold her?"

As he searched for the correct button, Rachel pulled her arms out from under the blanket, eager to gather the infant close despite the throbbing in her fingers. But she retracted her hands in dismay when she caught sight of them. Clear blisters had appeared on several fingers, the skin around them swollen and red. She had the same throbbing sensation in her toes, and she suspected they looked no better.

"Oh, Rachel . . . do they hurt much?" Rebecca hovered over her, lines of concern etching her features.

"A little. But I'd still like to hold my niece."

The bed settled into position and Colin helped Rachel adjust the pillows with his free hand. Then Rebecca placed the sleeping baby on Rachel's lap, avoiding the IV line that remained in her left arm.

"She's perfect." Awed, Rachel examined the peaceful features of the sleeping infant.

"Wait until you see her real hair color. I'm going to wash that dye out as fast as I can." Rebecca perched on the edge of the bed beside her as she fingered Megan's locks. "Rach . . ." At the sudden uncertainty in her sister's voice, Rachel transferred her attention from the child in her arms to her twin. "Mom and I had a long talk this morning. And I think we'll be having more long talks in the coming days. But I do know she deeply regrets her decision to keep my adoption—and your existence—a secret. She'd like to meet you, when you're feeling better. Would you consider it?"

Rachel thought about the request. It was hard not to resent the woman who'd consigned her to a solitary existence for so many years. Who'd deprived her of the family connections she'd always yearned for. She and Rebecca had missed so much. But forgiveness was part of being a Christian. She'd learned that much already, from the two services she'd attended. If she wanted to embrace that faith—and during her cold, dark entombment she'd decided she did—forgiveness would have to be part of her life. This was as good a time as any to start practicing it. Besides, with God's grace, she and Rebecca would have many more years to make up for the time they'd lost.

"Yes."

Moisture welled in Rebecca's eyes, and she swiped at them with a sheepish smile. "I'm such a sap for happy endings."

Rachel smiled through her own tears. "Me too. Must run in the family."

As Colin lifted Megan back into his arms and Rachel fished a tissue out of the box on the bed beside her, a slight rustle at the door caught her attention. A huge basket of colorful flowers floated in. Once it cleared the narrow entry corridor, Nick leaned around the mini garden and smiled.

The curve of his lips flattened, however, when he saw her tears, and he came to an abrupt halt. "What's wrong?"

"Nothing," Rachel assured him. "These are happy tears."

The sudden stiffness in his shoulders eased.

"Where in the world did you get those at this hour of the morning?" Rebecca gestured toward the basket.

"I have a few connections. Mark picked them up for me on his way here to drop off my car. I happen to know a special lady who likes fresh flowers." He gave Rachel a tender smile and set the basket on a cabinet near the foot of the bed. "He brought these too." He passed Rachel's glasses to Rebecca, who handed them to her sister.

She put them on and gave the flowers an appreciative scan. "Wow! They're beautiful, Nick. Thank you."

"You're welcome." His words were like a caress, and for a long moment his gaze held hers. Then he cleared his throat and shoved his hands into his pockets. "Listen, I didn't know you had visitors. I can come back later. I need to clean up and shave anyway."

"You look fine. And we're not visitors. We're family," Rebecca told him.

He hesitated and glanced at Rachel.

She smiled and held out her hand. "Please stay, Nick."

Rebecca looked back and forth between them. "Colin, I think our two little stinkpots are overdue for a diaper change. Let's duck into the waiting room for a minute."

Without giving either Nick or Rachel a chance to protest, Rachel's newfound family disappeared through the door.

"I feel like I chased them away." An unrepentant Nick drew close and cradled her blistered hand in his.

"They'll be back." She lifted her free hand and touched the swollen, discolored skin above his eye. "We're quite a pair, aren't we? No beauty contests for us anytime soon."

"The good news is, we'll both heal." He sat beside her and brushed his fingers across her cheek. "And we have so much to be grateful for."

"I know."

Smiling, he leaned close, until his face was mere inches from hers. "Remind me to thank Rebecca for her impeccable timing."

And then he lowered his head to claim her lips in a sweet, gentle, exploratory kiss that spoke of hope and promise and new beginnings. A kiss that offered a tantalizing taste of a future filled with love and tenderness and sharing.

As Rachel lost herself in Nick's embrace, her heart overflowed with joy. A few short weeks ago, she'd been alone in the world. Now, thanks to a chance encounter with a tattered Raggedy Ann doll, she had a sister. A family. A man to cherish. And the seeds of a faith she knew would grow and flourish and nurture her through all the days of her life.

Except Rachel chose to believe her rendezvous with the doll hadn't been just a chance encounter. Once, long ago, she'd read a quote that now replayed in her mind: a coincidence is a small miracle in which God chooses to remain anonymous.

Now, cherished and safe in the shelter of Nick's arms, she gave thanks for miracles great and small.

EPILOGUE

Four Months Later

Rachel pulled into Nick's driveway, rolled to a stop near the front door, and set the brake on her car. It was going to be tight, but she was determined to finish the mural in his dining room by her self-imposed deadline of Fourth of July.

Tomorrow.

Reaching for her purse on the seat beside her, she shook her head. Talk about a photo finish While the date hadn't seemed unrealistic when she'd begun, progress had been far slower than she'd expected. Two of the fingers on her right hand continued to give her problems, the tips alternating between tingling and loss of sensation. Though the aftereffects of the frostbite were diminishing, holding a paintbrush—or playing the piano—still proved challenging. It had taken her two months to recover enough dexterity to perform at tea again, and even now she stuck with simpler pieces. She'd gone back to painting a couple of months ago too, but completing a scene took far longer than usual.

Although Nick didn't seem in the least concerned that his dining room had been transformed into an art studio and had urged her not to push herself, she wanted to finish before Coop and Monica came into town with their baby for the long holiday weekend. Tomorrow, when they gathered here for a barbecue along with Mark and a newly expecting Emily, she wanted them to be able to appreciate the tranquility of the scene she'd painted rather than be distracted by the clutter of a work-in-progress.

As she stepped out of the cool car, the stifling air of a typical Missouri July enveloped her in a muggy embrace. On such days in the past, she'd been prone to complain about the oppressive heat of St. Louis summers.

Never again.

She knew all too well that the other extreme was far worse.

Pulling the key Nick had given her out of her purse, she slipped it into the lock of his stately brick home. Now that school was out, she was able to put in a lot of time on the mural during the week while he was at work. All that remained today were a few finishing touches that shouldn't take more than a couple of hours to complete.

She turned the knob and entered the gracious foyer, marveling as always at the sense of homecoming she felt whenever she stepped through Nick's door. She liked it best when he was there to welcome her with a warm hug and kiss. But even alone in the house on workdays like today, she felt happy and content.

Perhaps because she felt happy and content with Nick.

As she deactivated the security system and set her purse on the dining room floor, she inspected her mural. Like the painting, their relationship had grown in the preceding months, taking on depth and dimension. Spurred by the dramatic incidents early in their acquaintance, their initial romance had quickly blossomed into something far deeper. While both believed in the value of prudence and patience, and both wanted to avoid the pitfalls inherent in hasty decisions, it was clear to Rachel they were headed down a serious path. Barring some sort of bizarre twist of fate, she expected that one day in the not-too-distant future Nick would ask her to marry him.

And she already knew what her answer would be. She'd prayed about it at the Sunday services she attended with Nick, and often during the week in between. She knew with absolute certainty the two of them were meant to be together.

Smiling, she took a step back and tipped her head as she examined her work. It was the largest piece she'd ever tackled, but the scale and subject matter fit the room. Two rows of tall poplars receded into the distance, flanking a formal garden of patterned boxwoods, reflecting pools, and fountains. It was the kind of garden common in France or England in days gone by, and it fit the character of the Federal-style house perfectly. Restful shades of green dominated, but Rachel had added spots of color by placing overflowing stone urns of flowers in strategic spots. Today she wanted to add a few more deep pink blooms to two of them and tuck a bench into the poplars on both sides of the pool.

But first . . . she needed to check the kitchen. On mornings Nick knew she was coming, he always left some sort of decadent bakery item for her on the counter, along with a pot of fresh-brewed coffee. On her last visit, she'd found a fabulous caramel pecan roll. What treat awaited her today?

Stepping into the foyer, she pulled out her cell phone. She needed to find out when Rebecca and her family were planning to arrive tomorrow. An emergency at Colin's office had delayed their departure, but Rachel still hoped they'd make it in before the afternoon barbecue at Nick's.

As she headed for the kitchen, tapping in her sister's number en route, she cast an idle glance toward the living room.

And froze.

Tucked into the front corner beside the fireplace, where she'd pictured it the first time she'd seen this room, was a baby grand piano, the patina of the satiny walnut finish gleaming in the morning light.

Stunned, Rachel took a few uncertain steps toward it, afraid it was a mirage that would disappear if she approached too quickly. Paused. Took a few more steps. She was close enough now to read the title on the crisp, new piece of sheet music resting on the stand: "Our Love Is Here to Stay."

Her signature piece.

"Like it?"

At the soft question, Rachel gasped and spun around. Nick stood in the doorway leading to the study, one shoulder resting against the molding, hands in the pockets of his jeans, a tender smile warming his face.

"I didn't know you were home. The security system was on."

"I took the day off. And there aren't any motion sensors in the study."

She gestured behind her, confused. "You bought a piano?"

"Yep. It was delivered yesterday."

"You don't play."

"No. But I know someone who does."

He pushed off from the doorframe and strolled toward her. An undercurrent of excitement zipped through the air as he approached, sending a tingle racing up her spine.

Taking her hand, he led her toward the piano. "Do you like it?"

Flustered, she tried to focus on his question. "It's gorgeous. But Nick . . . it had to cost a fortune."

"It's okay to splurge on special occasions."

"Is this a special occasion?" A tremor ran through her voice as she regarded him.

"I hope so." He guided her to the piano bench and urged her to sit.

She didn't need much persuasion. Her legs were getting more wobbly by the second.

Perching beside her, he tugged the phone from her grasp, laid it beside the music stand, and lifted the piece of sheet music. She noticed that his fingers weren't quite steady. That was okay. Neither were hers. "We found your original copy of this in the well after you were abducted. I remember standing in the cold, looking at it, wanting to believe it was a message. And with every day that's passed, I've become more convinced it was."

Nick set the music back on the stand and turned to her, enfolding her hands in his. "I know we said we'd take our time, Rachel. And I don't want to rush you if you're not ready. But these past few months have been the best in my life. And I don't want them ever to end." His fingers tightened on hers, and his lips flexed into a brief, nervous smile. "You know, I used to rib my buddies about being too reserved. I was always encouraging them to open up, communicate, share their feelings. Now I understand why they held back. This is a very scary place."

"Why?" Rachel tugged one of her hands free and touched his cheek.

He grasped her fingers and pressed a kiss to her palm. "Fear of rejection. That's harder to deal with than any armed fugitive I've ever faced."

She felt the pressure of tears in her throat at his candid reply. "You don't need to be afraid, Nick." Her words were soft, and he leaned close to hear her as she touched the piece of sheet music and stared at the words of the familiar Gershwin song. "The truth is, while music has always been part of my life, it was an external thing. I studied music. I played music. I taught music. But you put the music in my heart." Her voice caught on the last word.

There was a suspicious sheen in his eyes as he slid off the bench and onto one knee, putting them at eye level as he cocooned her hand in his. "You brought music into my life too. And I want the melody to go on forever." He took a steadying breath. "Rachel Sutton, would you do me the honor of becoming my wife?"

The room went silent. Yet Rachel heard soaring notes, a joyous crescendo, a blare of trumpets in her heart as she gazed into the blue eyes of the man she had come to love with a depth and intensity that sometimes overwhelmed her.

"Yes," she whispered.

The tension melted from his features, leaving relief—and elation—in its place. Cupping her face in his hands, he leaned toward her and . . .

The sudden, strident ring of her cell phone shattered the tender moment.

He stopped, his lips hovering inches from hers. "Talk about rotten timing," he murmured.

"We could ignore it. Or shut it off." She draped her arms around his neck and scooted toward him.

"Good idea." He groped for the phone. Checked the caller ID as he searched for the power button. Hesitated. "It's Rebecca."

"I can call her back."

He jabbed the button and set the phone back on the piano. "Now where were we?"

"I think we were about to seal our engagement in a very traditional way."

"Oh yeah." He smiled. "I remember. Let's try this again."

He stroked her cheek, tipped his head, moved closer, and . . .

His home phone began to ring.

Heaving a sigh, he rested his forehead against hers. "This isn't working out quite like I expected."

The answering machine in the adjacent study kicked in, and Rebecca's voice came over the line. "Rachel, are you there? I think you told me you were going to work on the mural today. Listen, sorry to interrupt, but I'm standing here folding clothes and I just had the most incredible feeling of happiness. Since doing laundry doesn't usually engender such positive feelings,

322

I wondered if you might have some . . . news. Anyway, call me. Nick, if you get this message first, well . . . never mind. See you both tomorrow."

The line went dead.

"That's weird." Nick backed up a few inches, raked his fingers through his hair, shook his head. "I think she already knows about this."

"She doesn't know anything for sure." Rachel scooted forward again, closing the gap between them. "We just get vague feelings about each other."

"This is going to take some getting used to."

"We don't know details, if that makes you feel any better. Rebecca might have an inkling that something momentous has happened, but that's it. She'll want all the romantic details later, down to what I'm wearing." Rachel cast a wry glance over her paint-spattered jeans and T-shirt. "Except I'm not sure how I can make this outfit sound romantic."

"You look gorgeous to me. As appealing as if you were wearing a designer gown from the most expensive French couturier. How's that for romantic?"

"Wow. I'm impressed."

"Oh, I have more." He rose and pulled Rachel to her feet, looping his arms around her waist as he smiled down at her. "Tell her I gave you a baby grand piano because I want to make beautiful music with you for the rest of our lives. Tell her that when you accepted my proposal, I felt like the sun had come out after a long, cold winter. Tell her I adore you, and that when you're in my arms, I feel as if I've finally come home."

"Double wow." Rachel breathed the words. "But you know what? She's only going to get a condensed version of that. Much as I love her, she doesn't need to know *all* the details."

"That's good to hear. Because this next detail is just between us."

And as he gathered her close and bent to claim her lips at last, Rachel gave thanks.

For the caring cop in Nick's past who had taken a chance on a wayward kid.

For the sustaining faith that guided their lives today.

And for the extraordinary gift of love that would grace all their tomorrows.

Acknowledgments

As always when I tackle a suspense novel, the research challenge is intimidating. While I rely a great deal on books and the internet, in the end I always ask experts in a variety of fields to supplement my knowledge and review my material for accuracy. For this book, a few people deserve special thanks for taking on that chore.

FBI veteran Tom Becker, now the chief of police in Frontenac, Missouri, read the FBI-related sections and answered my many questions with patience, thoroughness, and incredible promptness. Tom, you are the best!

Christopher Van Tilburg, MD, author of *Mountain Rescue Doctor* and editor-in-chief of *Wilderness Medicine*, the official magazine for Wilderness Medical Society, lent me his expertise on hypothermia. His input was invaluable.

D.P. Lyle, MD—Edgar-nominated fiction novelist, author of *Forensics for Dummies*, and technical consultant for popular TV shows such as *Law & Order*, *Cold Case*, and *Medium*—reviewed the final hypothermia sections and gave them his seal of approval.

The incredible team at Revell—especially Jennifer Leep, Twila Bennett, Deonne Beron, Kristin Kornoelje, Janelle Mahlmann, Claudia Marsh, Michele Misiak, Carmen Pease, and Cheryl Van Andel—went above and beyond with this book . . . as always. It has been a pleasure working with all of you on my Heroes of Quantico series.

Chip MacGregor of MacGregor Literary found the perfect home for this series. Thank you for believing in my stories.

Special thanks go to my husband, Tom, for his endearing enthusiasm and incredible support, and to my mom and dad, who have always believed in me.

Finally, a heartfelt thank-you to you, my readers, for joining me on this incredible ride with the Heroes of Quantico. I am so grateful you embraced this series, and I hope you'll join me for the next one too, which will debut in early 2011!

Irene Hannon is a bestselling, award-winning author who took the publishing world by storm at the tender age of ten with a sparkling piece of fiction that received national attention.

Okay . . . maybe that's a slight exaggeration. But she *was* one of the honorees in a complete-the-story contest conducted by a national children's magazine. And she likes to think of that as her "official" fiction-writing debut!

Since then, she has written more than thirty romance and romantic suspense novels. Her books have been honored with a coveted RITA award from Romance Writers of America (the "Oscar" of romantic fiction), a HOLT Medallion, and a Reviewer's Choice award from *Romantic Times BOOKreviews* magazine.

Irene, who holds a BA in psychology and an MA in journalism, juggled two careers for many years until she gave up her executive corporate communications position with a Fortune 500 company to write full time. She is happy to say she has no regrets! As she points out, leaving behind the rush-hour commute, corporate politics, and a relentless BlackBerry that never slept was no sacrifice.

In her spare time, Irene enjoys hamming it up in community musical theater productions. A trained vocalist, she has sung the leading role in numerous shows and is also a soloist at her church (where she does *not* ham it up!).

When not otherwise occupied, Irene loves to cook and garden. She and her husband also enjoy traveling, Saturday mornings at their favorite coffee shop, and spending time with family. They make their home in Missouri.

To learn more about Irene and her books, visit www.irene hannon.com

DON'T MISS IRENE HANNON'S BESTSELLING
HEROES OF QUANTICO SERIES

WATCH FOR BOOK 1
IN IRENE HANNON'S NEXT
ROMANTIC SUSPENSE SERIES,
COMING IN EARLY 2011

Revell
a division of Baker Publishing Group
www.RevellBooks.com